WEST OF TEXAS LAW

WEST OF TEXAS LAW

WALKER A. TOMPKINS

**WHEELER
CHIVERS**

This Large Print edition is published by Wheeler Publishing, Waterville, Maine USA and by BBC Audiobooks Ltd, Bath, England.
Wheeler Publishing is an imprint of Thomson Gale, a part of The Thomson Corporation.
Thorndike is a trademark and used herein under license.

LIBRARY OF CONGRESS CATALOGING-IN-PUBLICATION DATA

Tompkins, Walker A.
  West of Texas law / by Walker A. Tompkins.
    p. cm.
  ISBN-13: 978-1-59722-447-5 (softcover : alk. paper)
  ISBN-10: 1-59722-447-2 (softcover : alk. paper) 1. Newspaper editors —
Fiction. 2. Washington (State) — Fiction. 3. Texas — Fiction. 4. Large type
books. I. Title.
  PS3539.O3897W47 2007
  813'.54—dc22   2006035237

BRITISH LIBRARY CATALOGUING-IN-PUBLICATION DATA AVAILABLE

Published in 2007 in the U.S. by arrangement with
Golden West Literary Agency.
Published in 2007 in the U.K. by arrangement with Golden West Literary Agency.

U.K. Hardcover: 978 1 405 64028 2 (Chivers Large Print)
U.K. Softcover: 978 1 405 64029 9 (Camden Large Print)

Printed in the United States of America on permanent paper
10 9 8 7 6 5 4 3 2 1

To Reid Edward Tompkins
My Little Buckaroo

DM

LIST OF CHAPTERS —

CHAPTER ONE:
ULTIMATUM

Grass had sprouted early along the Chisholm Trail this spring. Already the sweet air over the greening plains was freighted with dust, as Texas cattle began their annual hegira to the shipping pens at Dodge and Abilene.

Prime beef to feed a young and lusty nation was on the move, and the first pulsings of this lifeblood of the West sent a quickening spirit far abroad through the land.

Men in the slaughterhouses of Omaha and Kansas City and Chicago unracked their poleaxes, whetted skinning knives. And new life stirred in the somnolent trail towns which had attached themselves like parasites along the Chisholm's arteries of commerce, ready to bleed their tribute from the free-spending drovers.

The town of Longhorn was one of these. Like a malevolent and brooding spider, it sprawled beside the Red River where the converging trails funneled out of Texas into the Indian Nations. Longhorn's fleshpots were strategically placed to prey on each outfit which reached the hub of the web-work of trails.

A month earlier than usual, this awakening had made itself manifest in Longhorn.

Painted Jezebels flocked to the honky-tonks. Gamblers cleaned house, readying their halls of chance. Saloons laid in extra stocks of trade whisky for the seasonal boom. Longhorn was waiting and prepared to garner its share of the golden harvest which the spurred and booted breed would scatter with prodigal abandon along the historic highway of hoofs and horns, this year as it had done in the past.

But something was amiss this year.

Longhorn was being shunned by the Chisholm Trail outfits, and the townsmen did not bestir themselves to inquire into the reason therefor. They brooded and chafed in unaccustomed siesta, their eyes studying the trail dust on the far horizons. Day after day, more herds sought less favored fording places up and down the Red.

If the boycott continued into the peak of the beef-drive season, Longhorn would wither on the vine. And alone among its citizens, Cole Kerrigan of the weekly *Cru-*

sader divined the cause of the quarantine and aimed to do something to halt it.

In the back of the *Crusader*'s stuffy print shop, old Dixie Whipple was setting Kerrigan's editorial into type. It was a piece that might well be Longhorn's epitaph — or else the clarion to herald the town's resurrection. The knowledge that Destiny had made him an instrument in such a vital hour put a tremor in the printer's gnarled fingers as he plucked quads out of the cabinet before him and justified the final line in his composing stick.

Dixie Whipple did not look like a man of destiny, even remotely so. He had drifted into Longhorn eight months ago, a tumbleweed journeyman printer, ludicrous in high silk hat and a fustian Prince Albert. In common with his roving breed, his gnomelike body emitted an aroma which advertised that Dixie had no affinity for soap and water over extended periods of time.

Dixie had protruding ears, veiny as autumn leaves. He was onion-bald and toothless as a bantam rooster, which fowl he resembled closely in temperament and stature. He had a capacity for consuming vast quantities of corn whisky without showing it. He slept with a corncob pipe in his mouth. His speech was a reedy, measured drawl peculiar to certain backwoods well south of the Mason-Dixon line. To Dixie Whipple, "Yankee" was invariably prefixed with a "damn." He was a man of uncertain years and positive opinions. And in an alley of type cases he reigned as a master of his craft.

Dixie Whipple carried his tray of type over to the galley proof table as gingerly as if it had been a stick of dynamite. He was unhappily aware that there was literal truth in the parallel that had crossed his mind.

This galley of inanimate type metal would blow the lid off Longhorn when it appeared in print. Kerrigan's editorial would expose the greed and corruption which had given the trail town its evil reputation. It delved to the very taproot of the reasons for north-bound cattlemen avoiding the Longhorn crossing.

Old Dixie was stirred with a vague dread, wondering if the *Crusader* would still be here when the smoke cleared away. Or if, for once, its hard-hitting editor had stuck his horns into something too big, too dangerous.

He picked up a tube of printer's ink and squeezed a fat black worm onto a glass palette. He worked the ink out thin with a roller and transferred it to the stick of type. He covered the tray with a ribbon of newsprint, and then paused.

Old Dixie had a habit of fortifying himself from a bottle in moments of high crisis. This was such a moment, surely. He worried a pint flask from a hip pocket and downed a stiff dram of forty-rod before picking up the hickory block and mallet, ready to strike the proof.

He had a feeling that fate was holding its breath now, waiting for him to pull this first impression of type, to give life and meaning to Kerrigan's words. He discarded a vagrant impulse to pi the type. Kerrigan was reserving a hole on the front page for this editorial.

"Might as well be drivin' the nails in Cole's coffin," Dixie soliloquized, tapping the proof block expertly with the rubber hammer. "Pity he's got more guts than brains —"

The type released the paper with an adhesive crackle as Whipple peeled it off and scanned the results dubiously.

EITHER LONGHORN OR KIOWA MCCORD MUST DIE! the bold-faced heading declared bluntly.

Old Dixie took another shot from the

bottle, wiped his hands on a grimy canvas apron and plodded toward the front office. He waved the wet proofsheet between thumb and forefinger as if he held the guidon banner of a Cause. Again, his mental simile was close to the truth. Today the *Crusader* was running up its colors, in open defiance of Kiowa McCord and the lawless element which was throttling Longhorn's future.

Whipple paused in the doorway of the front office, reluctant to break the preoccupied mood of the man whose six-foot length was stretched in a swivel chair beside the front window.

Cole Kerrigan's rangy legs were propped on his littered roll-top desk, his eyes brooding abstractedly at the flat expanse of Texas prairie, where trail dust was crawling toward a ford fifteen miles down the river. He read in that dust the shadow of approaching oblivion for the trail town where his own future was at stake.

"She's ready, boss," the old printer announced, breaking Kerrigan's reverie. "Reckon you-all realize this here piece is the same as writin' your own death warrant —"

Kerrigan's metallic blue eyes held a glint of humor as he swiveled the chair around and took the proofsheet from old Dixie. His face was lean and young and vital under an unruly shock of leaf-brown hair, skin weathered to the hue of leather in testimony of the fact that he spent more time rustling business on horseback than he did behind his desk.

"Always the optimist, aren't you, Dixie?" he commented dryly. "This time had to come sooner or later. Maybe we're already too late."

Kerrigan scanned the editorial impersonally, proofreading it. The context was already burned deep in his soul. This emphatic black print gave finality to convictions which had been forming in Cole Kerrigan's mind for years.

His words were the embodiment of the *Crusader*'s policy, the verification of its aggressive masthead:

EITHER LONGHORN OR KIOWA MCCORD MUST DIE!

Longhorn owes its existence to the fact that it lies on the crossing of the Red River, the last Texas way station on the historic Chisholm Trail. That prestige is now threatened with extinction.

The coming of railroads to Texas has doomed the Chisholm Trail traffic as we knew it in former times. Never again will traffic reach the half-million mark. Even so, the Trail will continue to be a highway of empire for years to come. Longhorn's future is tied up in the annual beef drives.

Last season saw cattlemen in increasing numbers refuse to pay toll to cross the bridge which Kiowa McCord built across the ford five years ago. The Crusader feels that McCord has sucked at Longhorn's lifeblood long enough. The Crusader can prove that Kiowa McCord is directly responsible for the wave of murder and robbery long rampant here, even if Sheriff Paul Palmquist appears to be blind to that fact.

The Crusader believes:

— that McCord's toll bridge must be opened to free traffic.

— that McCord's saloons and gambling dives should be locked up.

— that Sheriff Palmquist should be replaced by a lawman impervious to bribery.

— that Kiowa McCord can be jailed or even hanged for his flagrant crimes.

These are grave charges. The Crusader is not unaware of libel laws. It would not print these words if it were not sure of its ground.

Elsewhere in this issue will be found sworn affidavits by prominent citizens of this and other Texas counties, which the Crusader publishes in the interest of justice.

Longhorn, the issue is squarely up to you, Either Longhorn or Kiowa McCord must die!

"Give that a two-column box, Dixie," Kerrigan ordered. "Right alongside the story of that Circle Bar drover's murder in McCord's barroom. The two sort of complement each other."

Dixie Whipple opened his mouth to protest. In eight months — the longest period the old tramp printer had ever lingered in one place — he had come to know an almost paternal affection for the lean, reckless young editor. But Kerrigan had swung his chair around to peer again at the bleak Texas landscape which shimmered in the heat waves beyond the town. The ageing printer shrugged and trudged back into the shop.

A few minutes later Kerrigan heard Whipple cussing Pancho and Primotivo, the ragtag Mexican urchins who stoked the steam boilers which powered the rickety flatbed press. He strolled back into the shop to get the first run-off, to satisfy himself that old Dixie hadn't left out his inflammatory editorial. The old gaffer was capable of such shenanigans when he was far gone in his cups.

Pancho and Primotivo folded the copies for the Longhorn subscribers by three o'clock. By three-thirty they had distributed them to every reader in town and had come back to fold the remainder of the run for mailing.

Kerrigan settled back in his chair to await developments. They were not long in coming.

Just as the courthouse clock was chiming the three-quarter hour, the batwing doors of the Jack of Diamonds saloon swung open, across the street. Kiowa McCord and Sheriff Paul Palmquist strode down the porch steps and headed for the newspaper office at a determined stride.

Little knots of men had gathered under the wooden awnings along the main street during the past ten minutes. A copy of the *Crusader* was the focal point of each subdued and thoughtful group. Kerrigan knew that a hundred pairs of eyes followed McCord and Palmquist as they neared the *Crusader* office.

Kerrigan appeared to be engrossed at his bookkeeping when boots thudded to a halt on his threshold. He waited until he had tallied up a column of figures before turning around. Saloonman and sheriff stood in

18

the doorway, crumpled copies of the newspaper clutched in white-knuckled fists, their eyes hostile.

"You're only thirty-two, ain't you, Cole?" Kiowa McCord inquired softly. "Kind of young to be courtin' suicide."

Kerrigan ignored the implied threat of Palmquist's hand, splayed fingers poised over the stock of his six-gun. "If you only came over here to discuss my age, gentlemen," he said evenly, "don't waste my time. This is my busy day."

Palmquist's face twitched spasmodically, a mahogany shade diffusing his neck and cheeks. He shot an uneasy glance toward Kiowa McCord and licked his mouth tentatively.

"Me an' McCord demand a full retraction of these God-damned lies, Kerrigan!" wheezed the sheriff, obviously parroting a rehearsed theme. "And we ain't waitin' a whole week for your next paper. You're publishin' an extry. Before sundown. *Sabe?*"

Kerrigan gestured toward the rear of the shop, from whence came the babble of the Mexican kids at the folding table and the monotonous jangle of Dixie Whipple's press.

"Dixie suffers from alcoholic fatigue — an occupational disease common to all itinerant printers," he commented irrelevantly.

19

"He'll be lucky if he stays sober long enough to finish our regular run. No, gentlemen, I'm afraid an extra edition is out of the question."

The sheriff backed out of the door, not having rehearsed an adequate retort. Kiowa McCord faced Kerrigan's indolent grin alone, the ruthless streak he had inherited from his Indian mother reflecting itself in his cruel, wintry smile.

"You heard what the sheriff told you, Cole," the breed said quietly. "You print that apology today."

Kerrigan's fingers drummed the arms of his chair.

"That sounds," he said, "like an ultimatum."

"If the boot fits, haul it on!" flared McCord. "I don't warn a man twice."

McCord turned on his heel and stalked out of sight. Almost immediately his place in the doorway was taken by the rawboned figure of Ford Fitzharvey, the United States Marshal who was in town investigating the murder of a stock buyer in McCord's place the week before.

Fitzharvey paused to spit a gobbet of tobacco juice at a darting lizard. Then he entered the office and drew up a chair, straddling it. The grin under his sandy waterfall mustache didn't match the gravity in his cold gray eyes.

"It took guts to print that piece," the federal marshal admitted. "But who's going to write your obituary, old Dixie?"

Kerrigan shrugged, aware that Fitzharvey was not jesting. "My broadside wasn't loaded with blanks, Marshal. Those depositions I published will put a hangrope around McCord's neck. And chase Palmquist from hell to breakfast. It's as simple as that, Ford."

Fitzharvey wagged his balding head sympathetically.

"Every decent citizen in Texas is backing you — from the side lines," he mused sadly. "But I got my doubts if you live long enough to see those things come to pass, Cole. I think I'll stick around and be one of your pallbearers."

CHAPTER TWO:
REVENGE

The raw odor of wood smoke roused Cole Kerrigan from sleep around midnight, floating into his bedroom on the second floor of the Trail House.

He kicked back the blankets and crossed to the window, instantly awake.

His ears caught the ominous crackle of flames unleashed on the night air. The sky was smeared scarlet, throwing the hard angles of Longhorn's tar-paper roofs and false fronts into stark relief. Shouts came remotely across the dark, the frenzied excitement of throngs drained from saloons and honkytonks.

Understanding hit Cole Kerrigan like a blow in the belly as he oriented the leaping geyser of pink sparks in relation to Mc-Cord's saloon and near-by landmarks.

"They've fired the Crusader —"

When the shock passed it left a cold, mounting rage in the man's heart. So this was Kiowa McCord's answer, when the sunset deadline for his apology had passed, ignored.

Kerrigan hauled on shirt and Levis and cowboots, trying to crowd out of his mind the memory of years of struggle which had gone into establishing the newspaper, a struggle that had taken the prime energies of his manhood to achieve.

He removed the chair with which he had barricaded the doorknob against the almost certain possibility of attack. But McCord had chosen to destroy the printing plant which had issued the damning challenge to the half-breed's lawless rule.

Kerrigan was clawing at shirt buttons and belt buckle as he left the hotel and cut across the deserted side street. He entered an alley flanking the Jack of Diamonds saloon and halted in the red glare which beat across the main stem in successive waves of heat.

The *Crusader* building was doomed. Smoke vomited through windows and under eaves. The composing room appeared to be a seething inferno, fueled by stocks of paper and inflammable drums of printing ink.

The crowd of spectators was pressing back before the heat. The whole town, it seemed, had turned out to witness the destruction of Cole Kerrigan's dreams, nor was a single hand raised to combat the blaze.

Kerrigan crowded back his anger, remembering that old Dixie slept in the lean-to behind the building where the steam engine which ran the printing press was housed. The oldster had been dead drunk when Kerrigan and the Mexican kids put him to bed at sundown. Dixie faced suffocation if the holocaust sucked the oxygen from his living-quarters —

Kerrigan sprinted unnoticed across the street, heading for the rear of the building. He found the back door latched on the inside. Snatching up a rusty gear wheel from a discarded job press, he smashed it through the tightly shuttered window.

Straddling the sill, Kerrigan groped toward the printer's cot in the far corner opposite the steam boiler. Firelight slotting through cracks in the partition revealed that the disheveled cot was unoccupied.

Dixie's pants still hung from a wall peg where Kerrigan had put them. His boots were under the cot.

The door to the plant was ajar, tendrils of smoke spiraling through the opening to befog the shed, feeling for lung and nostril.

Kerrigan whipped a quilt off the cot,

plunged it in the water barrel which supplied the steam boiler, and draped his head and body in the saturated folds. Then he headed into the print shop, the first suffocating blast of heat drawing steam from the soggy quilt.

He was sure that Dixie Whipple had not escaped through the shed door, which was still bolted on the inside. The evidence of the printer's boots and pants proved that Dixie hadn't roused from his alcoholic binge and ventured forth in quest of liquor earlier in the evening.

Whipple must have been awakened by the flames. The old gaffer's stubborn loyalty would have made him venture into the furnace heat of the print shop in hopes of combating the blaze.

Crawling on all fours, his water-soaked quilt trailing a moist smear behind him, Kerrigan rounded the printing press and scuttled down an alley between the stone-topped composing tables and the type cases.

He gained the partition which fenced off the front office without locating any trace of Dixie Whipple's body. The roar of the flames to his left and behind him were deafening.

Siding was already warping off the south wall, every studding timber a fiery pillar. Overhead, rafters and shingles were caving in, burying the press and paper cutter and barrel stove under a mountain of criss-crossed, blazing wreckage.

His retreat was cut off now. The quilt had dried out, was beginning to smolder.

Low to the floor where the smoke was thinnest, Kerrigan bellied his way across boards which blistered his palms and snaked through the doorway into his editorial office.

The roll-top desk was a bonfire. The side window of the office had been smashed out, feeding a draft to the flames.

Then he caught sight of Dixie Whipple.

Clad in undershirt and drawers, the old man lay crumpled beside the front door, blood seeping from a welt on his bald crown. But a pulse was throbbing on Whipple's skinny neck.

Kerrigan leaped to his feet and flung the smoking quilt over the printer's limp body. Flames from the desk licked off his brows and eyelashes as he hoisted Dixie to his shoulder and lunged toward the window.

He shouldered through the opening and landed in a litter of broken glass outside. The roof of the *Crusader* building collapsed with a roar like thunder as Kerrigan staggered off across a vacant lot, where the ankle-deep grass was beginning to ignite under the pelting sparks. Smoke screened him from the street throng.

The searing temperature of the gutted building pursued Kerrigan half the length of a block before he gained a corral at the outer edge of the dancing fireglow. He deposited old Dixie on the adobe mud alongside a horse trough.

Behind him, the town had finally turned its belated attention to preventing the spread of the conflagration. Relay teams trundled a tank wagon to and fro between the blazing ruins and the river. There was no wind tonight, or Longhorn would have been leveled to ashes before dawn.

Oblivious to his own blistered flesh and singed hair, Kerrigan located a tin can and doused water on Dixie's face and chest.

The crotchety old printer had won a warm place in Cole Kerrigan's heart. He knew little of Dixie's antecedents, tolerated the weekly debauches which were common to his breed, but which had never interfered with the publication of the paper from week to week.

The old man rallied, finally, lisping profanity across his toothless gums. He was sick and dazed and bewildered, but Kerrigan knew he was cold sober.

Finally Whipple sat up, clamping his ink-stained hands against his temples and staring dizzily about him. He drew his rheumy eyes into focus on Cole Kerrigan, recognition dawning slowly as he stared at the young man's face, limned harshly in the undulating firelight.

"Take it easy, pardner," Kerrigan said gently. "We'll get you over to my room and patch that lump on your noggin. You'll be all right."

Whipple rubbed his aching skull and cursed fluently.

"I tried — to fight 'em off," he lamented. "Too damn' drunk to remember where I'd stashed my Colt."

Kerrigan helped the oldster to his feet. Whipple's legs buckled and he thumped down on the edge of the water trough, a thread of crimson leaking down from his gashed scalp and trickling across his face.

"Fight who off, Dixie?"

Whipple snorted. "McCord — who else? Him an' four-five of his hard cases was sloshin' coal oil around the front office when I got there. McCord walloped me with the butt of his gun."

Kerrigan's mouth drew into a hard white line. Confirming his hunch that McCord had been the author of tonight's outrage came as no surprise to the man.

"He slugged you and left you to burn," Kerrigan whispered to himself. "He'll pay for tonight's work, Dixie. But he didn't destroy anything, really. You can't burn Truth."

Kerrigan hooked an arm around the old man's body and they headed in a wide circle to avoid the throng which was beating out grass fires in the lot adjoining the smoldering wreckage.

Back in his bedroom at the Trail House, Kerrigan rummaged in a closet for bandages and medicine.

"Reckon you saved my life tonight, boss," Dixie Whipple said, wincing as Kerrigan swabbed his bruised scalp with liniment. "We'll clean away the ashes an' rebuild the *Crusader,* you an' me. I've quit my rovin' ways, boss."

Cole Kerrigan grinned bleakly as he wound a turban of bandage around Dixie's skull. His mind was not dwelling on material losses now. The savings of a lifetime, the work of a decade here in Longhorn were now reduced to a sprawling rectangle of hot ashes and a pall of smoke that blotted out the Texas stars. But that was of little moment now.

Kerrigan went to a battered desk, pulled out a drawer and removed a gun belt with cartridges filling its loops. He buckled the shell belt around his lean midriff, settled the oak-tanned holster comfortably against his thigh.

Then he rummaged in the drawer and drew forth a Colt .45, wrapped in oily rags.

Dixie Whipple watched curiously as he saw Kerrigan unwind the wrappings from the Peacemaker. Lamplight glinted off the blued barrel, the cedar stock.

It was the first time Dixie had ever seen Cole Kerrigan handling a gun. He had never known Kerrigan so much as owned a weapon.

Austere lights burned in Kerrigan's eyes as he jacked open the .45 and spun the cylinder with a practiced thumb, checking the loaded chambers, filling the empty under the firing pin with a cartridge from his belt loops.

"I've been a newspaperman ever since I was fourteen," he mused aloud, speaking to himself, oblivious of the old printer seated on his bed. "Every year of it spent in hell-raising Texas cow towns. I've always preached against violence, urging men to obey the law instead of carrying it in their holsters. And yet, now that I get my own toes tromped on, I see where the old Western way of meting out justice has its merits."

He tested the hammer and trigger, slightly stiff from disuse, but there was a smooth grace in his lean hands which bespoke of long and intimate handling of firearms.

Whipple made no comment as he watched Kerrigan holster the Colt and don his gray Stetson. A sardonical smile twisted the man's lips as he turned to face the printer.

"You stick close by the room here, Dixie. McCord doesn't know but what your bones are cooking in the ruins. We'll let him keep on thinking that till we get him behind bars."

Dixie Whipple nodded. He knew better than try to stop this cold-eyed, determined man.

"Good luck, son," he whispered hoarsely.

Kerrigan gave his gun harness a hitch to settle the weight of the holster at its unaccustomed place on his flank. Then he stepped out into the corridor and closed the door behind him. Dixie Whipple shuddered slightly, listening to the measured thud of Kerrigan's boots as he walked down the stairs to the lobby.

CHAPTER THREE:
ARREST

The fire had spent itself and its audience was beginning to drift away, to homes which were no longer threatened by the flying sparks, or to saloons to resume interrupted poker games or finish hastily abandoned drinks.

A few onlookers lingered beside the glowing bed of coals, watching the heat fade from white to red on the iron skeleton of the Gordon press which had been Kerrigan's proudest possession. Kids plucked molten blobs of type from the ashes as souvenirs of this night's excitement. A few anxious property owners patrolled the surrounding ground, wetting down parched grass and keeping an eye on tar-paper roofs within a hundred-yard radius of the smoldering embers.

Speculation ran rife as to the cause of the fire. Pancho and Primotivo, the Mexican delivery boys, remembered that Dixie

Whipple had built a big fire in the potbelly stove that evening to melt a batch of glue so they could pad a stack of billheads on Saturday morning. Maybe a coal had popped out and ignited some wastepaper —

Older heads, reflecting on the editorial which had called for a showdown against the lawless element which ruled the trail town, pondered this evidence of Kiowa Mc-Cord's revenge and prudently kept their hunches to themselves.

One thing certain, Cole Kerrigan was ruined. He was but recently out of debt for fixtures and equipment. It would be many a day before the Longhorn *Crusader* was published again.

In the Jack of Diamonds saloon, drinkers lined the long pine bar of McCord's establishment, collecting free drinks. The half-breed was in an expansive mood tonight, rewarding the customers who had helped wet down the walls and roof of his place against the hellish temperatures of the fire directly across the street.

Folded copies of the *Crusader* jutted from many a pocket among the customers lining McCord's brass rail. The consensus of their remarks was the same.

Hell, what did Kerrigan expect, throwing

a challenge like that in McCord's face, naming names and demanding action to save the town from oblivion? Kerrigan was lucky he hadn't been bushwhacked, let alone seeing his print shop go up in smoke.

A few of the bolder ones, mostly gunmen in McCord's pay, openly congratulated the breed, speculating with profane witticisms on what Kerrigan's next move would be. But Kiowa McCord kept his own counsel. He vouchsafed no remarks in public regarding the origin of the *Crusader* fire, or his personal reactions to the challenge which its editor had thrown his way earlier in the day.

When the barroom crowd began to get noisy, McCord signaled his help to stop setting up the house, and retired to his private office where Sheriff Paul Palmquist was waiting.

The sheriff of Panhandle County made no secret of his alliance with Kiowa Mc-Cord. The breed's paid votes had elected Palmquist to office, three years before. Palmquist spent more time in McCord's saloon than he did at his jail office.

. . . Cole Kerrigan shouldered through the half doors into the barroom when the revelry was at its height, around three o'clock. His entrance was unobtrusive, but the editor's arrival brought an electric tension to the smoke-fouled room, stilled the raucous din, halted the various poker games.

The hush deepened as drinkers and gamblers caught sight of the revolver holstered at Kerrigan's thigh. This was the first time in the town's memory that the editor had discarded the pen for the sword.

The lean newspaperman stood in the doorway a moment, his face bleak, his slitted gaze inscrutable as it shuttled along the bar and the gaming tables, searching for a face there.

He moved away from the fanning batwings, thumbs hooked in shell belt, little knots of muscle gritting in the corners of his jaws. He halted beside a swamper who was scattering sawdust over the puncheon floor and his lips moved, his voice inaudible to the staring, paralyzed ranks of men lining the brass rail.

They saw the swamper jerk his head toward the door of McCord's office. Then Kerrigan moved in that direction, with the rolling, slack-jointed gait which had become familiar to the town.

He glanced briefly at the sign *Private — No Admittance* painted on the panels, then reached for the doorknob.

Men stirred nervously, their white faces reflected in the blemished backbar mirror. Apron-clad bartenders glanced at the sawed-off shotguns they kept racked at strategic intervals under the bar counter.

Before any man could move or speak a warning, Cole Kerrigan opened the door and stalked into the glare of lamplight in McCord's office.

The saloonman was in the act of pouring a drink into Sheriff Palmquist's whisky glass as Kerrigan eased the door shut with a boot heel and dropped a hand to the cedar stock of his Colt.

McCord stiffened, frozen in the surprised posture, his bottle poised over Palmquist's glass. Then they were staring at the black hole in the end of Kerrigan's six-gun.

"Tough break for you tonight, Cole." McCord grinned, setting the bottle down and hunching big shoulders under his broadcloth coat. "Sorry to see the *Crusader* burn down. A good newspaper is an asset to any town."

Kerrigan's eyes moved to Sheriff Palmquist, his gun leveled at the tin star on the man's vest.

"Belly over to the wall with your hands up, Sheriff," Kerrigan ordered. "McCord, you carry a derringer under your right sleeve. Don't try to unlimber it."

The color bleached from McCord's swart face, but he shared no part of the mounting panic which had seized Palmquist. The sheriff moved back his chair and stumbled around to face the wall, arms lifted to the level of his hatbrim.

"You don't know what you're doing, Cole," McCord said calmly. "Pull that trigger, and you'd never get out of my place alive."

Kerrigan crossed the room, ears alert to catch the slightest noise from the barroom door at his back. He reached out to seize McCord's right wrist, plucked a stubby-barreled .41 derringer from a clip under the saloonman's cuff. He tossed the hide-out gun into a woodbox in the far corner.

"You tackled the wrong man when you tried to bulldoze me, McCord." Kerrigan frisked a hand under the breed's swallowtail coat to make sure he was carrying no side-arms.

The breed ran his tongue over dry lips, alarm kindling in his hooded eyes as he saw Kerrigan step back, thumbing the milled gunhammer to full cock.

"You wouldn't shoot a man — when he ain't heeled —"

"There's a U. S. Marshal stopping over at

the Drover's Rest," the editor said. "I'm turning you over to Fitzharvey to stand trial for attempted murder, McCord. Sheriff Palmquist may wear your collar, but it isn't so easy to buy off a federal."

Kerrigan stepped over to where Palmquist stood trembling against the wall, reached out and removed the Navy Colt from the sheriff's holster.

"Attempted murder!" sputtered McCord. "Are you loco?"

Kerrigan laughed coldly, and played his ace.

"Dixie Whipple didn't die in that fire, McCord — Now head for the door. Sheriff, you stand pat."

With both guns jutting at waist level, Kerrigan headed after McCord as the saloonman, dazed and shaken by the editor's revelation, moved jerkily toward the door entering the barroom.

Kerrigan was close at the saloonkeeper's back as they stepped out into the deathlike hush of the barroom.

Saloon bouncers watched helplessly with hands on gunbutts as Kerrigan prodded McCord toward the street doors, too close to the saloonman for them to risk a shot in their employer's defense.

Bartenders stood impotently behind the

counter, unable to use their scatter-guns as Kerrigan prodded McCord out onto the porch, the slatted half doors swaying behind them.

A fine line of sweat dewed Kerrigan's lip as he directed his prisoner down the steps and across the plank sidewalk. One crisis was behind him. But death would stalk them during the next few minutes —

"Head for the Drover's Rest," Kerrigan ordered. "Keep to the middle of the street and don't try a break."

They were halfway down the block before shadows slipped from the Jack of Diamonds and moved in their direction, invisible in the clotted dark under awninged porches.

Ahead loomed the square outlines of the three-storied hotel where Ford Fitzharvey was staying, the dying glow of the *Crusader* ruins glinting weirdly from the window-panes.

"I wasn't born to stretch any hangrope, Cole," McCord boasted, a trace of his old arrogance returning. "You won't l—"

A crash of gunshots blasted and echoed down the false fronts lining the trail down street. Running men moved up fast along both sides of the street, gun-flashes winking.

Kerrigan held his fire, steering McCord

into the black maw of a blacksmith shop next door to the Drover's Rest. The wild shooting was intended to make him see the peril he faced, perhaps surrender his gun to McCord.

Crouched in shadow beside the brick wall of a cold forge, Kerrigan waited; gun muzzle in McCord's ribs. Another spate of shots volleyed out of the night, bullets rattling high on the blacksmith shop's false front.

Boots thudded on boardwalks. Shadows darted into alleys, paused on porches, hid themselves in the weeds of a vacant lot across the street. A steely silence settled down.

Gradually the night came alive with furtive sounds. Men were doubling back behind the blacksmith shop. McCord was a power in Longhorn, and his henchmen were out to rescue him before Marshal Fitzharvey was drawn into the picture.

"Are you all right, Kiowa?"

The yell went unanswered as McCord felt the pressure of Kerrigan's gun against his spine.

From a dozen angles, bullets hammered into the blacksmith shop, plucked slots in the shingled roof, clanged through the tin chimney canopy over the forge.

"The God-damn fools!" McCord raged

under his breath. "Overplaying their hand. They won't get anywhere with this —"

Kerrigan grunted in the darkness.

"Tell 'em that," he ordered. "Call off your wolfpack, McCord. If a slug as much as pinks me, I'll cut you down. This town isn't big enough for the two of us after what you did to old Dixie tonight."

McCord cleared his throat, and his shout arrested the stealthy movements of gunmen creeping up on the blacksmith house.

"Go back to the saloon, men! Kerrigan's fixin' to kill me if you don't call this off."

From the rear of the blacksmith shop, a Winchester opened up, its owner thinking to pick off Cole Kerrigan against the gray outline of the shop doorway.

A bullet struck a heavy anvil somewhere in the rear, ricocheted past Kerrigan's ear with a spiteful whistle.

Kiowa McCord uttered a soft exhaling sigh and settled face-down in the dust, his head and shoulders outside the door.

Kerrigan dropped belly down, wriggling forward alongside McCord's prostrate body, suspecting trickery. He thrust the sheriff's Navy .44 in the waistband of his pants and groped out a hand to touch the saloonman. "You hit, McCord?"

The breed lay motionless. So far as Kerri-

41

gan could tell, he wasn't breathing. The editor's exploring fingers encountered a warm, viscid substance guttering down over McCord's collar and coat lapel. He reached to the back of McCord's neck, examining the half-breed's thick nape hairs.

There was a bullet hole punched through the base of McCord's skull. A wild bullet had caromed off the blacksmith's anvil and killed his prisoner instantly.

Kerrigan wiped the blood off his fingers on McCord's steel-pen coat and crawled out of the blacksmith shop. Fifteen feet to the right was the porch of the Drover's Rest.

He heard men moving up along the wall of the shop, ignoring their leader's order.

Coming up to a racer's crouch, Cole Kerrigan leaped into motion. He somersaulted over a half-barrel of water used for cooling horseshoes, picked himself up, and vaulted the hotel railing.

No shots rang out as he ducked under the lighted windows of the hotel lobby and pushed through the door. The lobby was deserted, dimly lighted by a lamp over the clerk's desk.

Kerrigan headed down a hallway and paused at the door of Room K, where U. S. Marshal Ford Fitzharvey was staying. Light glowed under the crack of the door, but he got no answer in response to his light knock.

He tried the knob, found the door unlocked, stepped inside. The marshal's bed was in disarray, but Fitzharvey wasn't there.

Kerrigan drew a window blind, walked to a table, and poured a pitcher of water into a cracked bowl. He washed the sweat and soot from his hands and face, toweled himself dry, and sat down on the bed to wait.

Events had crowded too fast to be comprehended in their true perspective tonight. The *Crusader* was destroyed. Kiowa McCord was dead, accidentally slain by one of his own men. Tomorrow, Kerrigan would face the wrath of a town that was at least fifty-fifty on the side of the dead man.

Ford Fitzharvey showed up twenty minutes later. His mouth was a grim seam under his tobacco-stained mustache as he caught sight of Cole Kerrigan.

"Figgered you might have come here," the marshal grunted. "You know McCord's dead?"

Kerrigan nodded. "Hit by a ricochet," he explained laconically. "I was with him at the time."

The marshal pursed his lips thoughtfully.

"You were bringing him here when it happened, is that it? You figger McCord was responsible for burning your place?"

"Dixie Whipple caught him in the act. He slugged the old man and left him to fry. I got there in time to haul Dixie out."

Fitzharvey's eyes were troubled. "McCord's death puts you in a tight spot," the marshal said. "He ramrodded this town. His gun-hawks will be out to get you, Cole. You wouldn't have the chance of a snowball in hell if you stayed in Longhorn."

Boots rumbled down the hallway, halted outside Fitzharvey's door. The marshal dropped a hand to his gun as the door swung open to reveal Sheriff Palmquist and a burly deputy. The lawman's .30-30 swung to cover Kerrigan and the marshal.

"You're under arrest, Kerrigan!" snarled the sheriff. "Slap the bracelets on him, Koehler."

The deputy moved into the room, a pair of handcuffs dangling from his fist, his advance covered by Palmquist's Winchester.

"Hold on a second!" demanded Fitzharvey, stepping over to block Koehler. "What charge have you got against Kerrigan?"

Palmquist's teeth glittered in the lamplight.

"The murder of Kiowa McCord. The coroner says he was shot in the back of the head."

Fitzharvey hesitated, meeting Kerrigan's eye. Then he nodded. "Jail's the safest spot for you tonight, Cole," he advised. "We can beat this charge. Kerrigan didn't shoot Mc-Cord."

Palmquist grunted skeptically.

"I got eyewitnesses," he contradicted, "who saw Kerrigan put a hogleg against McCord's noggin and pull trigger. Shot him in cold blood when he figured the boys were closing in for the kill."

The deputy notched his manacles over Kerrigan's wrists.

CHAPTER FOUR: FRAMED

Dixie Whipple paced the floor of Kerrigan's hotel room like a caged animal. The old man curbed his mounting restlessness for an hour, and then rummaged in a closet and dressed himself in Kerrigan's shirt, pants, and shoes.

Feeling slightly ludicrous without his prized silk hat and Prince Albert — badges of gentility which had gone up in smoke tonight — the oldster moved down the hall to the banistered gallery overlooking the hotel lobby.

The Trail House was in the grip of an excitement which transmitted itself to Dixie Whipple and made him apprehensive, suddenly filled with a prescience that all was not well.

Within the minute he had picked up the news: Cole Kerrigan had been lodged in the Longhorn jail by Sheriff Paul Palmquist, accused of the point-blank killing of Kiowa McCord.

Dixie Whipple felt despair course through him. He knew the temper of this town, knew that Kerrigan's friends among the decent citizens of Longhorn were hopelessly outnumbered by the lawless element sympathetic to McCord's cause.

In fifty roving years as a journeyman printer, Dixie Whipple had seen sparks of hatred fanned into lynch fever more than once. He read those signs in Longhorn tonight.

Even in the Trail House, which drew a more sedate patronage than the saloons or the rooming houses on the outskirts of town where the harlots burned their red lights, Whipple heard men offering odds that Cole Kerrigan would never live to air his version of McCord's murder in the county courthouse.

Dixie left the hotel by a back stairs and ventured out on the main street. A crowd had gathered in front of Doc Kaarboe's shack, where the corpse of Kiowa McCord had been carried from the blacksmith shop.

Olav Kaarboe was the county coroner, and he had posted a bulletin stating that McCord had died as a result of a bullet in the brain, entering the skull from the rear. An inquest would be held Saturday noon.

The tramp printer walked with fear at his elbow, skirting the smoking remains of the *Crusader* building, crossing the rutted adobe street, and entering the Jack of Diamonds saloon.

Whisky was flowing like water across the bar. The rough crowd was here en masse tonight, and the barroom eddied with cross-currents of hate and mounting anger.

Scraps of talk fell on Dixie Whipple's ear, and the premonitory dread tightened its grip on his heart:

"McCord wasn't heeled. The stinkin' bastard plugged him without a chance."

"We'll tear down that calaboose brick by brick, by God. Cut Palmquist down if he tries to keep us away from Kerrigan."

Raucous laughter greeted this remark, high and fierce above the clamor of voices.

"Hell, Palmquist is after Kerrigan's scalp as much as we are. I'll lay odds he rips off his tin star and ties the noose around Kerrigan's neck."

Whipple had heard enough. He raced for the Trail House with panic dogging his heels, flung himself into Kerrigan's room and began stuffing clothing into a warsack.

Leaving the hotel, Whipple angled across town to the livery barn perched on a clay bluff overlooking the freshet-swollen waters of the Red.

He and Cole Kerrigan kept their horses here. The stable was deserted, its hostlers drawn to the main street by the fatal attraction which pervaded Longhorn tonight.

Whipple found a lantern and lighted it, going back to the stalls. He hauled their saddles off the rack, cinched them on Kerrigan's blue roan and the crowbait pinto which had brought Whipple to Longhorn eight months ago.

He lashed the warsack behind Kerrigan's cantle, and filled a nose bag full of oats to carry on his own mount. Then he led the horses out of the barn, swung into stirrups, and circled wide around the town, leading Kerrigan's horse with a hackamore.

At the northeast corner of the courthouse plaza, Whipple dismounted and hitched the horses to the fence, where a jungle of prickly pear cactus screened them from the jail.

Across the night came a dull rumble of sound, like remote thunder, meeting Whipple's ears as he threaded through the clumps of bull-tongue cactus in the courthouse yard.

Whipple's pulses raced as he saw a glimmer of lanterns bobbing down the main street, two blocks away. From sidewalk to sidewalk, the street was jammed with tramping men baying their hoarse calls of Cain. A lynch mob, heading for the plaza and the jail.

The door of Palmquist's jail office was open. Dixie Whipple saw the rawboned sheriff seated at his desk, ostensibly engrossed in a sheaf of reward posters. Keeping up a pretense of the lawman standing on guard to protect his prisoner.

Old Dixie scrabbled in the weeds by the pathside and found a broken brick. He drew back an arm and sent the missile hurtling toward the barred window of Palmquist's office.

The sheriff leaped from his chair as the brickbat smashed through the window with a jangle of flying glass. A six-gun was in Palmquists's fist as he lunged to the doorway and stared down at Dixie Whipple.

"You!" gasped the star-toter, as if he were seeing a ghost. "I thought —"

The tramp printer wore a clownish grin. He was weaving unsteadily, forward and backward, as if he were dead drunk.

This was no uncommon performance on Whipple's part. As regularly as clockwork, Whipple went on a spree after the weekly paper had been put to bed. As regularly, Palmquist would lock him up to sober over the week-end. And Kerrigan always bailed

50

him out on Monday mornings.

"Come here, you slobbering sot!" snorted Palmquist, glancing off past the courthouse to where the hang mob was moving grimly toward the plaza. Men crazed by liquor and hate and excitement, heading for Palmquist's calaboose with rope and club, knife and gun, men with death in their hearts.

Dixie Whipple staggered forward, babbling foolishly. When he reached the porch steps, Palmquist grabbed him by the collar and propelled him rudely into the office, slamming the door behind them.

As usual, Palmquist began the ritual of fumbling in a desk drawer for the keys to the cell block. As he did so, a swift transformation went over old Dixie.

Reaching toward the barrel stove in the corner, Dixie closed a gnarled fist over a thick iron poker.

Palmquist turned, a big ring of keys dangling in his hand. His ears registered the whistling sound of Dixie's poker swinging in an arc toward his head, but that was all.

Iron thudded on bone. The sheriff went down like a poleaxed steer, a livid bruise angling across his temple. Whipple worked fast. He drew the blind over the smashed-out window and bolted the front door to delay the oncoming mob. He pawed briefly through the sheriff's desk, found Cole Kerrigan's shell belt and holstered Peacemaker, looped them over his elbow.

Then he stooped, jerking the key ring from Palmquist's lax fingers. He stepped over the unconscious lawman and began testing keys in the iron door leading to the cell block.

The lynch mob had reached the far corner of the courthouse plaza by the time Whipple unlocked the door.

Cole Kerrigan was seated on a cell cot talking with U. S. Marshal Ford Fitzharvey. Palmquist had not locked the door during the marshal's visit. The two men looked up in surprise as the tramp printer strode across the floor, tossing Kerrigan his belt and gun.

"Dixie!" Kerrigan exclaimed, catching the gun harness. "What are you —"

Whipple gestured behind him.

"McCord's crowd," he rasped. "Sixty-seventy of 'em, headin' for the jail with a lynch rope, boss. We got to high-tail out of Longhorn while we can. I got hosses waitin'."

Kerrigan sprang out of the cell, headed for Palmquist's office. Before Fitzharvey could rise from his chair, Whipple clanged the iron door shut, twisted the big key in the lock and withdrew it.

"What's the idea?" bellowed the marshal, rage and bewilderment crossing his face. "Open that door, Whipple!"

The oldster shook his head. "You-all happen to be one of Uncle Sam's men," Whipple said. "You-all might get loco ideas about doin' your duty, standin' off that mob like Palmquist wouldn't have done. But it's too late for that, Marshal."

Fitzharvey gripped the thick iron grating with white-knuckled fists, his waterfall mustache twitching.

"You can't take the law into your own hands, you rebel!" raged the marshal, drawing a .45. "Unlock this cell before I throw down on you!"

Whipple ignored the lawman's threat, heading for the back door of the cell block.

Cole Kerrigan came back from the sheriff's office. His face was grim in the light of the cell lantern and his lean hands were buckling the gun around his middle.

"Dixie's right, Ford," Kerrigan said. "That hanging-bee crowd is crossing the plaza now, with a wagon tongue to bash the door in. We'd be shot like rats in a trap if we tried to make a stand."

Fitzharvey thrust his gun back into leather.

The marshal's face was suddenly gray and old.

"But you can't go on the dodge, Cole. You're innocent. If you run out on this charge, it'll look like admission of guilt. A couple shots into that crowd would scatter 'em."

The roar of the approaching mob was strong inside the jail now. Over at the rear door, Dixie Whipple was working with frantic haste to find the proper key to the lock.

"Do you think I'm the stripe who relishes running away from a thing like this?" demanded Kerrigan. "There's no other way left. You said yourself I couldn't stay around Longhorn with things like they are, guilty or innocent."

Their eyes met and locked, old friends gripped by indecision. A gunshot hammered on the front door of the jail, a raucous voice demanding that Palmquist open the door and deliver the prisoner in his custody.

"You know where my duty lies, Cole," Fitzharvey groaned in an almost inaudible whisper. "Palmquist will press charges and force me to trail you. And I'd have to do it — if it took me to the ends of the earth. You know that."

Dixie Whipple had the back door unlocked

now. Kerrigan hesitated, then moved toward it, his eyes bitter.

"You got a gun, Ford," Kerrigan whispered. "Now's your chance to use it, if you see things that way."

Fitzharvey's face jerked as he saw Kerrigan follow Dixie Whipple out into the night.

The lynch mob had not yet surrounded the jail as Kerrigan and Whipple crossed the plaza to their waiting horses. In saddle, they spurred through the deserted outskirts of the town, toward Kiowa McCord's log toll bridge which spanned the Red.

The toll gates were untended tonight, as they had expected. Kerrigan felt the irony of it as they galloped across the hoof-splintered puncheons of the bridge Kiowa McCord had built, the bridge which the *Crusader* had fought to make free to traffic.

They reined up on the north bank, staring back at the smoke-shrouded Texas town. Flight would close a chapter in Cole Kerrigan's stormy life. Ahead lay an empty and unfathomable future as a wanted man.

Dawn was staining the east as the two riders headed into Indian Territory, to put Texas below the horizon forever.

CHAPTER FIVE:
ADVICE

The cloven hoofs of millions of cattle had blazed a broad trail to link the horizons. Kerrigan and Whipple followed it as a line of least resistance, a blueprinted highway made to order for their flight.

Hunted men, wise in the artifices of the owlhoot gentry, might have backtracked and looped in wide detours to confuse pursuit. But Kerrigan discounted the chances of Longhorn organizing a posse to trail them across the Nations into Kansas.

Their one concession to prudence was to avoid the trail towns on the 250-mile route out of Texas. They rode the grubline of northbound herds, giving their horses free head and arriving, as a matter of course, at the ultimate end of the Chisholm Trail — Dodge City.

Roaring cowboy capital of the West, famous for its town-taming marshals and original Boothill cemetery, they found

Dodge in a turmoil of seasonal activity.

Vast cattle herds were bedded down on the holding grounds south of the town, awaiting their turn at the teeming stockyards and loading chutes, where endless rows of cattle cars waited on the Santa Fe sidings to start the long haul to eastern slaughterhouses.

Kerrigan and old Dixie had exactly four bits between them when they hit Dodge. A livery barn held their saddles as security for grooming and graining their mounts. Kerrigan hocked his six-gun for the price of a square meal, a shave and a haircut, and a bath for the two of them — the latter ablutions being a rarity in Dixie's odoriferous life.

They engaged a room in a back-street flophouse near the stockyards and held a council of war.

"I know the editor of the Dodge City *News*," Kerrigan said. "Jimmy O'Neil, an old friend of my dad's. I'll take a *pasear* over there and see about landing you a job, Dixie."

Whipple fixed suspicious blue eyes on the editor.

"A job for me? How about you, boss?"

Kerrigan shrugged, dipping a comb in the

water bowl and drawing it through his brown cowlick. His image in the blistered mirror revealed harsh lines and a sprinkling of gray along his temples which hadn't been there three weeks before, in Longhorn.

"Kansas wouldn't be healthy for a man with a Texas murder charge hanging over his topknot, Dixie. Too many drovers coming up the Trail who'd spot me. Bounty hunters."

Whipple stretched out on the sagging bedstead and watched flies sipping at a poisoned blotter in a saucer on the window sill. His gaze was drawn to an empty whisky bottle which held up the sash, and its label roused old appetites in the printer's belly.

"I'm ridin' the river with you, boss," Whipple said finally. "You owe me a couple weeks' wages. I aim to stick to you like a tick until you pay off."

Kerrigan laughed, touched by the old gaffer's stubborn loyalty. He swatted dust from his Texas sombrero and settled it at a jaunty angle across his head.

"I'll be back in an hour," he said. "Don't drift off to some saloon while I'm gone. We might be leaving in a hurry." Kerrigan headed for the *News* building on Front Street with an easy familiarity which came from prior visits to this hell-roaring railhead town on the Atchison, Topeka & Santa Fe.

Dodge might have been the pattern from which Longhorn and lesser trail towns had been cut. Certainly its streets were jammed with the same heterogeneous off-scourings of humanity.

Bearded buffalo hunters, relics of a past era. Texans, dusty from the long trail drives. Broadcloth-coated gamblers and sleek cattle speculators. Beef buyers from the East, whiskered in the imperials and burnsides and Dundrearies of their ilk.

Painted Jezebels promenaded the sidewalks, gaudy in crinolines and parasols. An occasional Indian, stagecoach jehus and bullwhackers and merchants, gathered in this wild melting pot on the Kansas plains.

Kerrigan's blood stirred to the tempo of the cattle town. His senses responded to the rumble of wheel and hoof and boot on its crowded streets, to the bawling cattle confined in the Santa Fe pens, to the tinpanny jangle of dance-hall pianos and the myriad sights, sounds, smells, and emotions of this lodestone of his world.

He felt, too, a sense of exile, of being a part and yet apart from this bustling life. He curbed an impulse to cross the street to avoid meeting a lanky marshal with a star on his vest. The lawman caught his eye, walked on past.

Then Kerrigan reached O'Neil's newspaper office, and his depression cut deeper as he saw the familiar bustle and clatter and clutter that went with his profession.

He found Jimmy O'Neil as he remembered him last, a lean, balding, energetic little man with nose glasses and ill-fitting false teeth, a celluloid eyeshade cowling his brow and casting a greenish pallor over his appleskin cheeks.

O'Neil handed his guest a cigar and settled back in the ancient Morris chair which had been his throne for thirty tempestuous years in this cattle town. At his elbow was the desk littered with proofsheets and paste pot and big shears, where his pen had helped shape Kansas opinion for a third of a century.

O'Neil laced his fingers over an up-pulled knee and tried to appraise the restlessness in Kerrigan's manner. Here was a man not wanting to admit defeat, but bedeviled by concealed fears or circumstances.

"Didn't make a paying thing of the *Crusader,* Cole? A job's always open for you with the *News,* like I told you before. You'll go far in this business. You've got printer's ink in your veins, just like your dad before you."

Kerrigan smiled without mirth, letting the rich cigar smoke fork from his nostrils. It was the first time in three weeks he had let himself relax. "I came," he said ruefully, "to brace you for a grubstake, Jimmy. You are looking at a wanted fugitive. Worse yet, you are looking at an editor without a newspaper."

Jimmy O'Neil listened attentively to Kerrigan's story, recalling the struggles of his own youth when the *News* had backed Wyatt Earp and Bat Masterson in an era when Dodge City had been the sinkhole of frontier outlawry.

"And so," concluded Kerrigan, "I come seeking money — and to ask your advice. I'm at loose ends. I can't return to Longhorn and buck a stacked deck there. I don't know which way to drift from here, Jimmy. Obviously I can't accept your offer. Dodge is too close to Longhorn, visited by too many people who know me."

O'Neil rotated his thumbs around each other and tongued his cheek thoughtfully.

"Lynch law is no respecter of a man's guilt or innocence," the old publisher agreed. "So far as Longhorn is concerned, I'm glad you've left the place. The Chisholm Trail has been going downhill since eighty-four.

Your *Crusader* was built on sand. Longhorn has no future. Five years from now it'll be a ghost town."

O'Neil hitched his Morris chair around and contemplated a big wall map of North America which hung over his filing cabinets.

"Paraphrasing the immortal advice of our contemporary on the New York *Tribune,* Horace Greeley," O'Neil observed half-seriously, "I'd say 'Go West of Texas law, young man.' There's still plenty of opportunity for a man of your talents beyond the reach of misguided justice. Make a fresh start on a new frontier."

Kerrigan smiled dryly, tapping cigar ash into a cuspidor.

"West of Texas law," he repeated musingly. "I don't know where that would be. This is eighty-nine, Jimmy. I have no doubt but what Palmquist will circulate reward posters all over the country, with my description on them. Some bounty hunters would spot me eventually, no matter how far away I went — Oregon or Montana or California."

O'Neil started to whistle a tune, turning back to his desk and riffling through a sheaf of news dispatches impaled on a spike. He tore a sheet off the spindle and handed it to the Texan.

"I didn't mean go West in the accepted sense, Cole," he said. "I know what I'd do if I had your youth. Read that."

Kerrigan scowled curiously. O'Neil had handed him a news dispatch bearing a Skagway, Alaska, date line.

It told of the need for permanent citizens in the northern Territory to replace the sourdoughs who had joined the Sitka gold rush, attaining its peak in 1887.

It was an appeal from the Territorial Legislature for men and women who could profit from Alaska's potential riches — the virgin fields of fishing, lumbering, mining, whaling, seal fishing. Plus the need for merchants and lawyers, teachers and newspapermen. O'Neil waited until Kerrigan had read the dispatch over a second time. Then he reached for the knob of his iron safe.

"How much *dinero*," he asked, "will you need?"

When Cole Kerrigan left the *News* office an hour later, his eyes were alive with the resolution of a man with new horizons to cross, fresh opportunities waiting beyond the reach of Texas law.

He walked with a springy stride, free for the first time since his exile of the sense of outraged justice and being at loose ends, which he had carried to his interview with O'Neil.

Dixie Whipple was waiting for him at the flophouse.

"A mail steamer leaves Seattle the third of May," he told the astonished printer. "I aim to be aboard her, Dixie. There's a big field for newspapermen in Juneau, Sitka, Ketchikan. And the north country is a paradise. Green and cool and fertile, not like this sagebrush and cactus desert we're used to."

Dixie Whipple shivered. His mental picture of the Alaskan country was typical of his day — a land of Eskimos and icebergs, trackless glaciers and midnight sun, a land fit only for walrus and reindeer.

"O'Neil's got a job for a compositor," Kerrigan continued, taking a roll of bills from his pocket and counting them into two equal stacks. "I borrowed enough to settle our accounts, Dixie. Plus enough to get me to Alaska."

Dixie Whipple crowded the picture of snow and ice and dog teams out of his head and drew himself up haughtily.

"You ain't hintin' that we split our partnership, are you, boss?" he demanded in offended tones. "You got enough *dinero* there for two steamship fares, ain't you?"

Kerrigan laughed and scooped the green-backs into a common pile. "You're an incurable old drifter, Dixie. What'll you do if your feet get to itching, up there on the Arctic Circle?"

Whipple snorted. "I'll have Alasky chilblains on my heels first!" he retorted, composing his dignity. "When do we leave Dodge?"

Kerrigan consulted an A.T.&S.F. timetable which O'Neil had given him.

"An express pulls out for Denver in two hours," he said. "We take the Union Pacific from Cheyenne, follow it to Spokane, and cut across Washington Territory to Seattle. We'll have just time enough to buy winter duds before the steamer pulls out for Juneau."

There was much to be done in the short time left to them. Dixie Whipple headed for the Santa Fe station to purchase their tickets, leaving Kerrigan to attend to the sad business of selling their two saddle horses.

Kerrigan sacrificed the horses for a fraction of their worth, doing so with the feeling that he was burning his bridges behind him, leaving his old life forever. When a Texan sells his saddle —

He redeemed his six-gun at the pawnshop,

wondering at the strange prescience which impelled him to carry a weapon across his new horizon, yet knowing the gun would be tied inexorably to his fate.

A half-hour before train time, Dixie Whipple hustled into the big Lone Star saloon on Front Street, meeting place of Chisholm drovers up the trail from Texas. He was resplendent in a new Prince Albert and a glossy stovepipe hat, purchased at a second-hand haberdashery which catered to gamblers.

His intention was to lay in a stock of red-eye, which might come in handy for medicinal purposes when they got into the blizzard-whipped Arctic country.

Old Dixie sampled the bartender's stock rather generously before deciding on what brand of poison he would carry with him into snowbound exile.

The old man was torn between a desire to go on a crying jag at the prospect of leaving the cattle country, and an impulse to celebrate his travels to a distant clime.

He was wavering between the two when a familiar figure entered his limited and somewhat blurry line of vision. It was Billy Pearson, who ran the Diamond P spread not ten miles out of Longhorn, Texas.

"Well, if it ain't my old drinkin' pardner

from the Deep South!" boomed the cattleman, moving alongside Whipple at the crowded bar. "If I'd known you were sashayin' up to Dodge I'd have run you in as a cavvy wrangler on my drive, Dixie. Just got in yesterday with two thousand head of mossy-horns."

Dixie Whipple signaled the bartender for an extra glass. He pulled Pearson closer to him and said confidentially, "Me and Cole Kerrigan are pullin' out for Alasky, Bill. Yep. We're ketchin' us a steamboat at Seattle the third o' next month. We're leavin' this rattlesnake an' coyote country for the land where the tall timber grows."

Billy Pearson's jaw dropped in amazement.

"Alaska!" he ejaculated. "Lo an' be Gawd, you ain't joshin', are you? Wait till the boys hear this down in Longhorn. A dried-up old Johnny Reb like you, up to his top hat in a snowdrift. You're killin' me, Dixie!"

A warning tocsin rang somewhere in the recesses of Dixie Whipple's brain, bidding him hold his tongue. But he was mellowed by the warm liquor in the pit of his belly, and Billy Pearson was lifting three fingers of amber whisky to drink to his luck.

"Here's hopin' the Aurora Bory Alice will never melt your igloo, Dix!"

"Here's ticks in your bedroll clean back to Texas, Bill!"

Dixie Whipple made his circuitous way back to the rooming house by dead reckoning and the blind luck which Providence gives to homing drunks, a bare ten minutes before their train was due to pull out for Denver on the first lap of their journey.

Not until Kerrigan had the old man safely aboard the westbound passenger train and the flat plains were wheeling past to leave Dodge City on the far horizon did Dixie Whipple's brain clear sufficiently for him to reflect on his loose talk at the Lone Star saloon.

"If I'd been blessed with the sense God give a crowbar," he castigated himself, "I'd have steered clear of them Texicans —"

Whipple unbuckled the new carpetbag which Kerrigan had purchased in lieu of their warsack, and retrieved three bottles of rye whisky therefrom.

A trifle unsteadily, he made his way back to the rear platform of the coach.

He dumped the whisky bottles over the rail, saw them shatter on the crossties behind the speeding train.

Cole Kerrigan's laugh sounded over his shoulder, broke into Whipple's thought-stream. "Swearing off Demon Rum again,

Dixie?" chided the Texan.

Whipple shuddered under his outsized Prince Albert. "Never lettin' a drap of the stuff touch my tongue as long as I live," Dixie vowed solemnly. "Likker loosens a man's tongue. Makes him go besmirk an' talk when he should listen."

Whipple decided to keep his guilty secret for the time being. He felt a little sick inside, wondering how long it would take Billy Pearson of the Diamond P to carry the news back to Longhorn that he and Cole Kerrigan were heading for Alaska.

Longhorn would take their flight as clear proof that Kerrigan was guilty of Kiowa McCord's murder now. Sooner or later, old Ford Fitzharvey would pick up the scent like the stubborn old law dog he was.

The threat of the bloodhound marshal sniffing their back trail would lie uneasy on Dixie Whipple's conscience for a long time to come, be he asleep or awake. But there was no use adding his indiscretion to the burden of Kerrigan's worries.

CHAPTER SIX:
FRONTIER

The day coach was fetid with the mixed odors of spilled lamp oil and blistering varnish, tobacco smoke, and perspiring passengers. Its grimed windows were sealed against the volcanic dust which a dry, hot wind was scouring across the vast plateau of eastern Washington Territory.

Cole Kerrigan wedged his shoulder blades against the hard corner of the wicker seat and wished he could swap places with a bronco-buster on the hurricane deck of a Texas mustang. The coach jounced over the unsettled ballast of the new roadbed like a ship crossing troubled waters.

Dixie Whipple shared the seat opposite with a pompous, slick-shaven politician who had informed the passengers, the moment he boarded the train at Spokane, that he was a member of the Territorial Legislature.

With little in common but their garrulity and their silk toppers, Dixie and "the Senator," as Kerrigan had mentally dubbed the potbellied legislator, had spent the past 100 miles in an animated debate on the relative merits of Texas and Washington Territory.

Ten days of frontier travel lay between them and Dodge City. The train was winding its tortuous way through the rolling hills of the Palouse country, having virtually left civilization behind at Spokane this morning.

Kerrigan wallowed in a slough of boredom insofar as his traveling companions were concerned; but the passing landscape outside commanded his interest.

He scanned the desolate but somberly beautiful reaches of arid country with the keen and analytical eye of a journalist, cataloging its strange aspects, wondering at his own abysmal ignorance of such a vast and spectacular land.

Only ten days ago he had aired the naïve opinion to Jimmy O'Neil that there was no frontier left in America. Yet this broad tableland that was southeastern Washington was but little altered from the days when the prairie schooners of the Oregon Trail had touched its borders, when the martyred Whitman had sought to bring Christianity to its Indian tribes, when America and the British Empire had quarreled over its pos-

71

session and "Fifty-four-forty or fight" had been the watchword of the day.

This was not the direct route from Spokane to the Puget Sound seaports. Sandwiched between the coach and the lone baggage car was a flatcar laden with a huge harvesting machine whose vertical dimensions made certain tunnels impassable. As a result, Kerrigan's train had been shunted into the Snake River country far to the south, giving the Texan an unscheduled lesson in geography.

The elemental thrill of exploring the new and unknown stirred Cole Kerrigan, made him forget the stuffiness of the coach, its boring passengers, the incessant wrangling of old Dixie and the politician.

A stranger to mountains as the Far West knew them, Kerrigan found himself intrigued by the ranges indicated on the map, obsessed with regrets that he was rushing through a country he would have liked to explore at closer hand.

Behind were the snow-clad Bitterroots and the Rockies; to the south the Blue Mountains. Ahead to the west, the mighty Cascade Range, its volcano-peaked horizon soon to come into view. And completing the circle to the north, the unsettled reaches of the Okanagans.

Accustomed to investigate what interested him, this trip through enthralling new country was to Kerrigan like leafing through the pages of a book which commanded his interest but with the reading denied him by the pressure of time.

As the snorting wood-burner flung back the miles, Kerrigan became aware of a subtle change in the scenery, an altering expression on the face of the plateau. Cattle grazed on the brushy hillsides, but here and there, with increasing frequency, a home-steader had plowed a field and strung a fence, the rich brown soil forming an orderly, man-made patchwork against the landscape.

The fields increased in size to encompass thousands of acres. Kerrigan noted that half of these fields lay fallow to the weather, their furrowed slopes checker-boarding vivid green squares where spring wheat was leafing up through the coffee-colored clods.

The cattle range lay to the rougher country on the south, toward the Snake River. Here on the plateau proper, wheat seemed to reign unchallenged, with barbed-wire fences marching off into hazy distances, their posts clogged with last year's tumbleweeds.

It was a grand and thrilling spectacle, even

to Kerrigan's eyes, which were used to the unfenced vistas of the Texas Panhandle. This was dry, high, desert country. Yet this soil, the settled ashes of volcanoes which had reared up the lofty mountain ranges on all sides, was incalculably fertile. The broad, lush fields of growing wheat testified to that.

Dixie Whipple and the Senator joined him on the swaying platform. The politician waved a fat, beringed hand at the landscape wheeling past.

"Your friend has been regaling me with accounts of the Wild West aspects of your native Texas, Mr. Harrigan," the Senator remarked fatuously. "I assure you this very country unfolding before your eyes is not without its elements of melodrama and frontier violence. Yes indeed, Mr. Harrigan."

Kerrigan met the beam in the Senator's wet, fat-lidded eyes and a deep ennui poured through him.

"This country was given over to rattle-snakes and jack rabbits before the cattle-men came," the Senator droned on, lifting his voice above the sedative click of the trucks over rail joints. "Not a little blood was shed when the first wheat farmers began to fence the land and break the sod with their plows. In fact, only two years ago one of the former governors of the Territory, Paul Richard Prescott, was shot from ambush a few miles from here —"

The man reminded Kerrigan of a stump speaker campaigning for election.

"I understand you are a journalist, Mr. Harriman," the politico went on. "A pity you cannot catch some of the human drama unfolding on these ancient hills. The bitter feud between the solidly entrenched cattlemen and the encroaching wheat growers, advancing behind their phalanx of plowshares and reapers. The decisive battle in this range war is yet to come. The clash of arms will yet resound over these —"

The deep-throated whistle of the locomotive cut off the Senator's flowery discourse. Brake shoes bit suddenly against spinning wheels, and the three men on the coach platform had to grip the iron railing to keep their feet, as locked wheels began screeching over the uneven rails.

Kerrigan stepped to the platform edge, gripped the grab bars and leaned out, slitting his eyes against the beat of cinder-laden wind.

The engine was about to enter a series of cuts and fills where the railroad knifed across upflung badlands gashed with brush-choked coulees.

An oath escaped Kerrigan's lips as he saw

the engineer's reason for halting the train. At the mouth of a cut, a pile of brush and boulders blocked the tracks.

The funnel-stacked locomotive ground to a halt with its cowcatcher nudging the barricade. Simultaneously, a group of mounted men spurred out of the thick brush flanking the right of way and headed for the stalled engine, sunrays glinting off six-guns and rifles. Each rider wore a bandanna mask.

"Trouble?" inquired the Senator, clipping the end off a Cuban perfecto and jabbing it between his thick lips. "A hotbox, probably. These back-country trains —"

Kerrigan glanced back across his shoulder.

"More like the cowboy and Indian stories Dixie has been telling you about," the Texan replied. "Desperadoes appear to have designs on our train, Senator. Be prepared to lose that gold watch and chain of yours."

The cigar dropped from the Senator's lips. His florid cheeks bleached to the color of banana meat.

"D-Desperadoes? Train robbers?"

The politician's wail receded in his fat throat and he plunged back into the coach to wedge himself in the conductor's closet.

At the same instant hoofs clattered over crossties behind the coach and Kerrigan turned to see a rider spur out of the brush, covering the two men on the platform with a Colt .45.

The two Texans raised their arms, staring at a pair of gooseberry-green eyes between the brim of a flat-crowned Stetson and a red bandanna knotted over the outlaw's face.

"Oblige me by climbin' down so I can keep an eye on the door, gents," a throaty voice issued behind the bandit's mask. "Just stand hitched and we won't have any trouble."

Kerrigan and Whipple dismounted from the coach steps and stood beside the car. Up the tracks, they saw a masked rider covering the engineer and fireman, who had climbed out of the cab.

There were six riders in all up ahead. Four of them took stations at either end of the baggage car. The remaining pair spurred over to a flatcar and dismounted, untying gunny sacks from their saddles.

They worked without haste, apparently knowing exactly what job they had to do. They clambered up on the flatcar, gripping the timbers which helped secure a big harvesting machine in place.

Kerrigan scowled curiously, studying the machine. Its bull wheels were painted a vivid red. Galvanized metal sides glinted in the sunlight with a pristine sheen which revealed that the harvester had been recently shipped from the factory.

The two outlaws fished inside their sacks and deposited objects deep in the innards of the machine. They struck matches, poked arms into the harvester.

Their job done, the riders made haste to leave the flatcar, vaulting into saddles and spurring away.

Kerrigan jerked his head around to stare at the guard whose guns covered the rear of the coach. A vagrant dust devil whisked its skirts across the right of way at that moment, lifting the outlaw's mask for a brief instant.

Kerrigan and old Dixie caught a whisked-off glimpse of a wide, hard mouth, with tobacco-stained teeth under a dark mustache. A blocky, blue-shaven jaw, a nose with a curved bridge like a bowie blade. Then the wind passed and the bandanna settled back into place.

The rider appeared not to have noticed the momentary revelation of his features, his eyes fixed on the flatcar and its freight.

A sense of impending disaster shot through Kerrigan as he saw wisps of smoke leaking from inside the harvesting machine. The six riders were spurring up the hillside to vanish in the brush like a covey of quail.

Then a series of three closely spaced explosions ripped through the length of the new harvester. The big machine lurched against its scantlings like a convulsed monster in a cage.

Yellow and white smoke erupted violently in all directions, spraying iron fragments and splintered planking hundreds of feet in the air to pepper the surrounding slopes under a barrage of scrap.

Then the smoke swirled down to obscure the train, still rocking under the concussion. The smoke bore to Kerrigan's nostrils the biting fumes of dynamite.

He twisted his head to see that the masked guard behind them had vanished into the coulee mouth. Somewhere inside the coach a woman screamed, peal on peal.

Mail clerks poked their heads timidly through portholes in the sliding steel doors of the baggage car.

The smoke thinned and lifted under the hot wind. The gleaming harvester now lay in shattered ruin on the splintered platform of the flatcar, its twisted steel and shattered gears settling like the fractured bones of a beast disemboweled by a springing trap.

The train conductor brushed past Kerrigan as he and Dixie ran up the roadbed to meet the engine crew beside the car. The conductor shook an impotent fist at the smoke-obscured hillside where the dynamiters had vanished.

"Them damned Snake River cattlemen did this!" bellowed the railroader. "This here's the first combined thrasher an' harvester ever shipped to Washington Territory. It was consigned to Gov'nor Prescott's ranch down in Wheatville. The Y & E will be sued from hell to breakfast —"

There was little to be done. A brakeman inspected the damage and pronounced the flatcar ready to roll. The hoghead issued an appeal for all male passengers to help clear the barricade from the tracks.

Every man in the coach responded, with the exception of the Senator, who was found slumped in a dead faint in the conductor's closet. As Kerrigan helped roll boulders off the tracks, he recalled the Senator's half-boastful words telling them about the wheat-cattle feud raging on this frontier.

He was remembering, too, how Jimmy O'Neil had told him, back in Dodge City, to head West of Texas law. Well, he was here now.

Dixie Whipple fell in step beside Kerrigan as the passengers headed back to the coach.

"Did you see that owlhooter's face, boss?"

Kerrigan nodded. "I'd recognize it if I ever saw it again. A pity that we hold the only clue to the gang that did this dirty work, Dixie. And us heading for Alaska."

CHAPTER SEVEN:
DESTINY

Heading straight into the red glare of a setting sun, the Yakima & Eastern train pulled into a town cupped in a fold of green, wheat-carpeted hills, and drew to a halt before a ramshackle depot painted a grotesque maroon.

A weathered white signboard on the gable caught Kerrigan's eye through the coach window as he stood up to stretch his cramped muscles:

WHEATVILLE

Population	Elevation
488	1822 Ft.

"Twenty-minute stop here, folks!" announced the perspiring conductor, consulting a turnip watch. "Yes, lady, we've missed connections at Pasco Junction. You'll have to lay over there until tomorrow afternoon."

Dixie Whipple elected to remain aboard the coach to fan the Senator's face, who confessed to a mild heart attack while hiding in the conductor's closet. Cole Kerrigan, however, followed the other passengers out on the cinder platform to get a breath of fresh air.

He surveyed the isolated, drab little settlement with a faint nostalgia. In many respects Wheatville resembled the trail town of Longhorn, Texas.

Its main street, crossing the railroad at right angles, was flanked by the same ugly assortment of false-fronted saloons and mercantile stores, livery stables, and feed barns. He saw signs identifying blacksmith shops, saddle makers, a wheelwright, and a county courthouse.

In one respect, however, Wheatville was unique. The towering wooden column of a grain elevator was the dominating landmark of the town, flanked by long rows of wheat warehouses skirting a side track. There were loading chutes and cattle corrals further down the tracks, but, as its name implied, this was a wheat town.

A sizeable crowd of Wheatville's citizens was on hand to greet the train. They joined the passengers who stared with morbid interest at the dynamite-wrecked machine on the flatcar, smugly aware of their intimate part in the drama.

Kerrigan saw in the shocked dismay with which Wheatville's residents surveyed the wreckage that the coming of this train was an event long anticipated; that the loss of the harvester was as staggering a blow as if the flatcar had borne the crepe-hung catafalque of a deceased celebrity.

Wheatville had taken a community pride in being the first town in the Territory to take delivery on a combined harvester, the mechanical marvel which had only been invented a year before.

A withered ranch wife in challis sacque and gingham sunbonnet stood beside Kerrigan. Tears were trickling down her seamy cheeks as she surveyed the twisted wreckage, a palm cupped around an ear to catch the conductor's version of the outlaw band's attack in the wastelands fifteen miles east of the town.

"Wait till Miss Rona sees this," groaned the woman in funereal tones. "They do say she borried five thousand dollars from the Baker-Boyer Bank down in Walla Walla to buy this contraption. You reckon it's covered by insurance, stranger?"

Kerrigan paused in the act of shaking tobacco into a thin husk.

"Beats me, ma'am. You say that machine belongs to a woman? The conductor said it was consigned to Governor Prescott's ranch."

The old woman tucked a wisp of salt-gray hair under her bonnet. "He uster be our Territorial Gov'nor, Dick Prescott did. But he was 'sassinated two year ago over on the Snake. They do say Giff Ogrum's cowboys done it. Leastwise, his datter Rona —"

A stir ran through the crowd. A barefooted kid who was chinning himself on the tilted bull wheel stared over the heads of the crowd and piped up excitedly, "Here comes Rona Prescott now, ridin' over from Torv Trondsen's bank!"

The ranch woman poked Kerrigan in the ribs with a thumb, speaking with the familiarity of a recluse hungry to talk with someone from the outside world.

"Rona's goin' to throw a conniption fit when she sees what happened to her machine, stranger," his informant whispered. "She's perty as a little red wagon, but don't let that fool ye. Rona Prescott's a heller when she gets her dander up."

From his position on the outskirts of the crowd, Kerrigan saw a girl ride up to the edge of the platform, mounted on a leggy pinto. She ground-tied the horse and swung

85

lithely out of stirrups.

The crowd moved back, facing her, sober, expectant. Cole Kerrigan licked his quirly cigarette abstractedly, his interest whetted by this daughter of a murdered ex-governor. She was a slim young girl, barely past twenty, he judged; wearing bibless Levis and a flat-brimmed white Stetson to match her rolling, mannish gait. This would be Rona Prescott, the girl who had ordered the first combine ever to reach the West Coast. That fact alone set her apart in Kerrigan's eyes.

She paused at the edge of the crowd, sensing that some disastrous news awaited her even before she lifted her candid brown eyes to the wreckage on the flatcar.

The cigarette dropped unnoticed from Kerrigan's lips as he watched Rona Prescott's hands ball into fists inside her beaded buckskin gauntlets, saw the color slowly recede from a sun-bronzed face that would have been wistfully beautiful under happier circumstances.

In contrast to the drab and work-hardened womenfolk who moved toward her in sympathetic silence, Rona Prescott appeared lovely and feminine in spite of the masculinity of her garb.

Her slim, curved body was not flattered by the austerity of blue workshirt and buckskin vest, fringed and beaded in the Indian fashion. A pleated chin strap held the white Stetson at a rakish angle across her head, complementing the rich, golden wealth of hair that fell in thick waves to her shoulders.

"Why doesn't somebody say something?" the girl demanded. "What's happened? Is that my — my new combine?"

The Wheatville stationmaster shuffled out of the crowd, twisting a suppliant hat in his fingers.

"This warn't the railroad's fault, Rona," the agent said. "Six-seven masked bandicks teched off dynamite inside your thrashin' machine, over in the Horse Heaven breaks."

Kerrigan saw the girl stiffen under the impact of the news. Color flooded back into her cheeks now, and her amber eyes glinted with swift and outraged wrath.

"Masked bandits — fiddlesticks!" she said hotly. "You know as well as I do who wrecked my harvester, Ed Chellis. A blind man could see Gifford Ogrum's hand behind this outrage!"

Couplings jangled as the locomotive chugged away from the platform, leaving the passenger coach behind as it shunted the flatcar onto a siding. The crowd followed it, turning to cast awed glances at Rona

Prescott, who remained where she was, slapping a denim-clad knee with a riding quirt, her eyes staring after the flatcar without seeing it.

The old lady who had attached herself to Cole Kerrigan went scuttling off in the wake of the train, as a mourner would escort a coffin to a cemetery.

Kerrigan found himself alone on the platform with the girl who, in the space of a few brief minutes, had assumed a definite entity in his eyes.

He removed his wide-brimmed Texas sombrero and walked over to where Rona Prescott stood, her face unnaturally flushed in the ruby glow of the sinking sun.

"Begging your pardon, ma'am." His Texas drawl cut through her abstraction. "I was a passenger on this train when your combine was blown up. I overheard you say you believed you knew who stopped the train."

The girl's wide amber eyes ranged up and down his tall frame, came to rest on his own.

"Of course I do — but proving it is something else again!" flared the girl. "Giff Ogrum and his Rafter O hellions are out to destroy anyone who plants a grain of wheat in these hills. He and Mizzou Howerton and Rip Hoffman — all those cowmen think they own every acre north of the Snake."

Kerrigan fingered his Stetson.

"The reason I asked, ma'am, was because I happened to get a quick look at one of —"

A discreet cough interrupted Kerrigan. He turned to see a mousy little individual facing the girl, myopic eyes scared-looking behind thick spectacle lenses. He wore an ink-stained apron and sateen sleeve guards which told Kerrigan that he was in the presence of a fellow newspaperman.

"I — I was all set to print a big story in the *Spectator* about this new contraption you shipped in, Rona," the little man said, twisting a sheaf of copy paper in his inky fingers. "But after what's happened, I don't feel so skookum. I'm jiggered if I know just what to write —"

Rona Prescott tossed back her head and planted gloved wrists akimbo on slim hips. Her eyes flashed with a sudden exasperation which caused the little man to fall back a step before her scorn.

"This is Jay C. Ellison, the great scribe!" she told Kerrigan, controlling herself with an effort. "I can well imagine what your brave little sheet will print about this, Jay." Her voice took on a simpering, high-pitched mockery. " 'The long-awaited arrival of

Miss Prescott's combine harvester took place on Monday last. Unfortunately, it had been slightly damaged in transit.' "

Jay C. Ellison retreated another step, lifting an arm as if fending off a blow.

"Now, Rona, don't you get riled at me. You're just like people say you are, a rowdy and a tomboy. You can't blame me for treading cautiously when —"

The girl stamped a spurred boot heel on the cinder apron with a vehemence that made Ellison's voice subside into a whisper.

"You listen to me, Jay Ellison!" she stormed, annoyance taking possession of her, making her oblivious to Kerrigan's presence. "Why don't you print the truth in your sniveling paper just for once? With the wheat and cattle interests locked in a death struggle — with the very future of Wheatville at stake — what do you do? Fill your columns with tripe about how Buster Stevens has a new baby sister or Ed Hickey's reshingling his privy. You make me sick!"

Kerrigan was vaguely aware that the locomotive had been coupled onto the coach and that his fellow passengers were being herded back aboard by a conductor eager to put Wheatville and the wrecked combine behind him.

But he remained rooted to his tracks, caught in the spell of Rona Prescott's tirade.

"If you're so afraid of publishing the real news, why don't you quote me, Ellison? Why don't you say that Giff Ogrum and his paid gun-toters dynamited that combine — as part of their scheme to destroy me and my ranch and intimidate every other wheat-man in Palouse County? Why don't you print that — over my signature? I dare you!"

A slow grin spread across Kerrigan's lips as he saw Jay C. Ellison put a placating hand on the girl's sleeve. In the background, Dixie Whipple's gnomelike face was pressed against the coach window, making frantic pantomime, urging him to get back on the train.

"Now, Rona — you know I can't print libel like that!" whined the Wheatville editor. "You got no proof it was Giff Ogrum who stopped the train, not a speck o' proof. I can't afford to get the cowmen down on me —"

Rona Prescott shook off the editor's hand and whirled on her heel, crossing to the edge of the platform and vaulting astride her waiting pinto like a circus acrobat. A group of hawk-faced womenfolks clucked their tongues disapprovingly as the girl reared her frisky pony and curvetted away from the platform.

"All abo-o-oard!" bawled the conductor, above the clangor of the locomotive bell. "Bo-oard for Pasco an' points west!"

Jay C. Ellison ran helplessly to the end of the platform.

"Write anything you like, Jay!" the girl dismissed him. "I'm sure whatever you print about this business today will be a masterpiece of courageous journalism. In a pig's eye!"

Smoke snorted from the engine's diamond stack and the train slid away from the Wheatville platform, the conductor clutching the grab rails and swinging up on the coach steps.

Cole Kerrigan stood beside Jay C. Ellison, staring after Rona Prescott as she spurred high, wide, and handsome down a country road which ribboned over the southern hill, dismissing Wheatville in the dust of her pinto's hoofs.

"That — that hoyden!" sputtered Ellison, catching Kerrigan's amused glance. "The man was never born who could outargue that tomboy of the gov'nor's. She needs a good spanking —"

Kerrigan snapped out of his trance then, as the outbound train rattled over the sidetrack frogs onto the main line. He saw

Dixie Whipple on the rear platform of the coach, his anguished wail floating back to Kerrigan's ears.

"Run, you damn fool! Rattle your hocks!"

Kerrigan started forward, limbering his legs for a sprint. The train had not yet begun to pick up speed. Catching it would be a simple matter. But at the end of the station platform something impelled the Texan to slack up and halt, waving a hand at Dixie Whipple's dwindling form.

Old Dixie squalled an indignant oath and, clutching his silk hat, did a frog-hop off the coach steps. He landed in a bed of Russian thistles, bounced to a stop with the tails of his Prince Albert flying all directions, and climbed to his feet spouting epithets and swatting clinkers from the seat of his breeches.

Kerrigan waited beside the station as the old printer limped back through the dusk, his topper askew and his sunken mouth sucked in until his chin and nose nearly touched.

"Have you gone completely besmirk, boss?" croaked the old gaffer, bruised and scratched and mad as the bantam rooster he resembled. "Damn it to hell, our carpetbags are on that blasted coach. And we've missed our boat at Se-attle!"

Kerrigan put a placative arm around Dixie's shoulder. "We're stuck here until Saturday night now," the Texan chuckled, consulting the Wheatville train schedule board. "It won't hurt us to light and cool our saddles a few days, *amigo.* There'll be other boats leaving for Alaska."

Dixie Whipple smoothed his dusty silk hat along a sleeve. "Sometimes," he fumed, "you act like a damyankee idjit, boss. I'm damned if I know why I put up with your foolishment."

Kerrigan stared off at the rimming wheat fields, filling his lungs with the cool, wine-like air of dusk.

Wheatville lost its drabness under the violet veil of twilight. Along the wagon road south of the town, the dust of Rona Prescott's departure still lay on the heavy air, drifting slowly to settle on the waist-high wheat beside the road.

CHAPTER EIGHT:
COWMAN

The ornate lettering across the warped clapboards of the false front had originally spelled *Pacific Saloon — Billiards*. Someone had given the ramshackle building an over-all coat of barn paint, and a new sign now proclaimed:

Palouse County Spectator
Jay C. Ellison, Editor
See Us For Job Printing

Across the street from the newspaper office, Cole Kerrigan and Dixie Whipple were having breakfast on the screened porch of the bug-ridden hotel where they had spent the night.

Kerrigan was surveying the wheat town with keen interest, noting things under the intense morning sun which had escaped his attention from the train window yesterday evening.

Wheatville was a county seat — though Palouse was a misnomer, according to the drummer who sipped his morning coffee with them. The true Palouse County lay beyond the river of that name, which meandered along the eastern boundary of the county.

As the seat of local government, Wheatville boasted a courthouse, a jail presided over by a sheriff, and a land office.

A church steeple, bald patches showing on its frayed shingled pinnacle, lifted a weather-beaten finger toward heaven from a grove of box elders and locusts beyond the railroad yards. A one-room schoolhouse with a bell in its cupola perched on the alkali-mottled slope overlooking the town on the north, proof that Wheatville was no fly-by-night boom town, but a settlement that had taken permanent root.

A Walla Walla bank had established a branch here, the only brick structure in Wheatville. It being Saturday and shopping day, the board sidewalks were unusually crowded.

Kerrigan found himself contrasting these hardy dwellers of a semidesert land with the equally hardy pioneers who frequented the cow towns of Texas.

Wheat farmers and their families, in town

to buy provisions and swap the week's gossip, were arriving in buggies and buckboards, the size of their wagons and teams varying with their distance from town.

Their women were decked out in their best bustled gowns and flaring sunbonnets, and carried parasols against the dry, penetrating heat. The wheatmen themselves were a sturdy, taciturn breed for the most part, wearing denim jumpers and bibbed overalls, their faces red as turkey wattles under ragged straw hatbrims.

There were cowboys here too, wearing brush-scuffed chaps and stilt-heeled boots, hitching their ponies along the chewed racks in front of saloons and outfitting stores.

They walked with the same bowlegged swagger as did their fraternity in Texas or Kansas or Wyoming. But these Washington punchers were less affected by the Spanish *vaquero* influence which accounted for the ten-gallon hats, silver *conchas,* and jingle-bobbed spurs of their Texas counterparts.

These cowhands were less picturesque than border riders, but most of them packed holstered six-guns as an integral part of their costumes.

Dixie Whipple eyed the gaudy labels of whisky bottles racked in a saloon window next door to the *Spectator* office, and rubbed his stomach forlornly. A slug of rot-gut to cut this infernal volcanic dust from his craw — but he recalled his last drink at Dodge, and a mental picture of Marshal Fitzharvey picking up their trail reminded Whipple sharply of his pledge to ride the water wagon.

Dixie hadn't confessed his dereliction to Kerrigan as yet. Time enough for that when they were safe in Alaska.

Kerrigan tipped back his chair and loosened his belt, a toothpick waggling between his lips as he grinned down at the bald-headed printer.

"Straighten that string tie, *amigo.* We've got to look sharp when we brace Jay C. Ellison for a job."

They strolled across the street through wheel-churned dust that lay thick and powdery under heel. Curious glances bent their way, amusement in the stares which surveyed Dixie Whipple's pygmylike stature under the ridiculous stovepipe hat, admiration and curiosity in the eyes of women who were vaguely stirred by Kerrigan's rangy height and conspicuous Texas sombrero.

They entered the newspaper shop that had formerly housed a saloon. Their first glance was enough to inform them that the Palouse

County *Spectator* was hardly a flourishing concern.

The former barroom was now jammed with tools of their trade — stone tables, untidy cases of type, a foot-driven Pearl platen job press.

In the rear, where billiard balls had once clicked, a Country Campbell drum cylinder press squatted under belted pulleys, the driveshaft going through the wall to the steam engine out back.

Country newspapers were traditionally untidy, but the *Spectator* building was littered with wastepaper that a cow could have bedded down in. The brass-railed mahogany bar was still in place, its backbar shelving now utilized for the haphazard storage of varicolored paper stock, exchanges, and junk.

At first, Kerrigan and Whipple thought the shop was deserted. Then, as their eyes became accustomed to the wash of daylight through the ex-saloon's stained glass windows, they saw a sad-eyed printer's devil busy in the back of the shop, lackadaisically scrubbing forms of type in a vat of lye water to clean off the ink.

And in a front corner to their left, Jay C. Ellison was snoozing in a chair beside an untidy roll-top desk, his feet propped up on a rusty Franklin stove topped by a glue pot.

Kerrigan walked over and tapped the dozing publisher on the knee. Ellison sat up with a start, thrusting a pair of steel-rimmed spectacles back on his nose.

"Eh?" grunted Ellison, staring at them without recognition. "What can I do for you?"

"We're a couple of stranded knights of the fourth estate," the Texan said jocularly, introducing himself and old Dixie. "Whipple here is a compositor and pressman of many years' experience. I am somewhat handy at all phases of country newspaper work — advertising, reporting, editorial. We come in search of temporary employment."

Ellison straightened his soiled collar and cleared his throat, composing his features into an expression intended to convey the fact that he was an important personage in Wheatville. His gentility was somewhat nullified by a two-day stubble of beard and the strong odor of whisky on his breath.

"The *Spectator* is — uh — shorthanded at the moment," Ellison admitted. "Unfortunately the controlling interest in this publication is owned by Torv Trondsen, the banker across the street. I hardly feel his budget would stand an addition to the staff at this time. You might try the *American* over at Prosser —"

Kerrigan grinned, his eyes following Dixie Whipple as the frock-coated printer stalked down the alley of type cases. The oldster's nostrils were twitching as if there was a fetid smell in the shop, his sparky eyes surveying the disorganized plant with obvious disapproval.

"Don't worry about straining the pay roll, Mr. Ellison," Kerrigan said reassuringly. "As a matter of fact, we'll only be in your fair city until the next train provides us with a means of continuing our journey to Seattle. Mr. Whipple and I would be glad to work for the fun of it — to help pass the time, you might say."

Ellison got to his feet, new interest kindling in his myopic eyes. He rubbed his palms avariciously.

"As a matter of fact," he remarked with a sly inflection, "I've been needing to ride over to Ritzville for quite a spell to — uh, collect for some advertising. If you think you could take over for a day or two I am sure Mr. Trondsen would have no objections to my letting you get out next Friday's paper during my absence."

"It's a deal. When do we start?"

Ellison led the way to the rear of the shop.

"This is Horsey Flathers, my assistant," Ellison introduced, gesturing toward the sleepy-looking youth who was pouring buckets of rinse water over the lye-cleaned type. "Horsey, Mr. Kerrigan and Mr. Whipple are going to help us out for a few days. I'm going to run over to Ritzville."

"To see the widder Spear?" Horsey inquired innocently.

"Don't be impertinent!" coughed Ellison, turning purple. "I have business over there. I want you to show our friends the ropes, understand?"

The young Texan and his partner took over their temporary management of the *Spectator* with such brisk efficiency that Jay C. Ellison felt a pang of jealousy when he hitched up his buggy that afternoon and headed for the neighboring county seat to the north, where he had a matrimonial interest in a certain bereaved lady.

Never in the three years Ellison had published the Wheatville weekly had the shop buzzed with so much industry. He was thankful that his mortgage holder, Torvald Trondsen, was absent in Spokane at the time.

Dixie Whipple took over the renovation of

102

the printing plant with the crisp efficiency of a housewife cleaning up a neglected kitchen.

Horsey Flathers, the combination printer's devil, pressman, part-time reporter and janitor, soon found himself buried in the tedious job of restoring the cluttered type cases to something approximating their proper order.

An upper story in the rear of the former saloon building contained rooms which had once been devoted to private gambling, and the two Texans purchased blankets and took up lodgings there to escape the louse-infested hotel across the street.

Kerrigan spent his second day in Wheatville getting acquainted with the town's fifty-odd businessmen. He scribbled down pertinent news squibs concerning their respective families and friends, and acquired a liberal education in the manners and customs of the wheat country at the same time.

He was impressed by the vast potentialities of this new frontier, which within the memory of a middle-aged man had been a scantily populated, semidesert wilderness, harried by Indian uprisings, handicapped by lack of roads, alternately parched by droughts and mantled by winter blizzards.

But Washington Territory was now on its way to becoming a full-fledged state. In February, Congress had passed an Enabling Act which provided that the peoples of Washington — together with the Dakotas and Montana — should adopt constitutions and be admitted to the Union on equal footing with the other states, and to make donations of public land to such states.

Of more immediate interest, Kerrigan sought details of the range war which now raged between the wheat growers of Palouse County and the cattlemen whose ranges flanked the Snake River on the southern boundary of the county.

The name of Giff Ogrum hung like a sinister shadow over Wheatville and its residents. Kerrigan's informants were reluctant to discuss the Rafter O boss, who lived with a Umatilla squaw wife down on the Snake, and who was generally agreed to be the leader of the cow combine which was pledged to destroy the wheatmen by whatever weapons lay at hand.

Wheatvillians were more eager to answer his discreet inquiries about Rona Prescott, however. She farmed 6,000 acres known as Pleasant View, in a broad valley called Eureka Flat, directly adjoining Giff Ogrum's range.

Governor Paul Richard Prescott had originally brought Eureka Flat under cultivation. He had pioneered in putting wheat ranching on a businesslike basis. Governor Prescott had been the first rancher to abandon the old idea of sowing crops by hand broadcasting, importing horse-drawn drills for the purpose.

He had spurned volunteer crops, whereby stubble remained unplowed over a season, and the volunteer stand of wheat was allowed to head and be harvested.

Then, two years ago — although Kerrigan found but passing mention of the tragedy in Ellison's files of the *Spectator* — Governor Prescott had been killed by ambushers while crossing the Snake River on his way to Walla Walla.

Rona Prescott, then only nineteen and an orphan, had left her college career to take over Pleasant View ranch. The saga of her courage and resourcefulness was brought to Kerrigan's ears by every businessman he interviewed.

"In a nutshell, Mister Kerrigan," explained Charlie Fitzpatrick, who ran a photo studio down the street, "it b'ils down to the cattlemen along the Snake tryin' to scare the wheatmen out of the county. Some of 'em almost quit last year, too, when their wheat was fired and some of their harvest hands killed in saloon brawls here in town. But Rona Prescott, she rallied the wheatmen, made 'em fight back."

Art Matthews, who was the county coroner and ran a combination furniture store and undertaking parlor, was more frank in his discussion of the feud.

"This summer's harvest will be the showdown, Kerrigan. Giff Ogrum and his sidekicks — Rip Hoffman and Mizzou Howerton — they've imported gun-hands from Pendleton and the Jackson Hole country over in Wyoming. They aim to get back this wheat land for grazin' range. Bein' from Texas, you prob'ly sympathize with that. Bob-wire fences are pizen to a Texan, I understand."

Publisher Jay C. Ellison returned from his amatory jaunt to Ritzville on Saturday morning to find that the *Spectator* published in his absence had caused a minor sensation in town.

Not in years had its front page been so crammed with news items of general interest. Dixie Whipple's expert hand was seen in the professional layout of display ads and headlines, and in the hand-set columns of type, strangely free of Horsey Flathers's spelling and punctuation errors.

A banner headline on the front page carried an accurate account of the bandit attack on the Yakima & Eastern train and the dynamiting of Rona Prescott's combine.

Although Kerrigan's article ventured no personal opinions regarding the outrage, it concluded with a paragraph which prickled the hairs on Ellison's necknape:

The perpetrators of the outrage are secure behind the anonymity of their masks. However, local opinion believes that cattle interests opposing wheat ranches were responsible.

"He'll ruin me!" groaned Ellison, discussing the paper with Ed Chellis, the station agent. "Giff Ogrum will be mad as a rattlesnake in dog days when he sees that!"

"Ruin you?" scoffed the railroader. "Hell, Jay — that Texas feller has put life into your dead paper. You better fire him before Trondsen gets back from Spokane and gets a notion to hire himself an editor with some backbone."

Ellison stared at Chellis's copy of the *Spectator* with a grudging admiration. "I can't very well fire the booger — him and his tilikum are workin' for free," whined the editor. "Besides which, they are pullin' out of town on tonight's train anyhow."

That evening, with traintime limiting their Wheatville interlude to less than an hour, Cole Kerrigan escorted Dixie over to the Last Chance saloon and insisted on his downing a stiff jolt of whisky.

"You deserve a reward for setting the *Spectator* to rights, Dixie," Kerrigan laughed. "Besides, an old tippler like you should climb on the wagon by degrees."

Dixie, his innards warmed by corn whisky after the most prolonged drought his stomach had experienced in sixty-odd years, accepted Kerrigan's viewpoint philosophically. "Mebbe there's too much snow an' ice in Alasky this time of year nohow, boss. Wheatville wasn't a bad place to hole up for a week. Old Fitzharvey ain't apt to —"

Whipple was interrupted by a thunder of hoofbeats on the street outside, mixed with wild cowboy whoops and a popping of six-guns.

"Looks like Giff Ogrum an' his Rafter O bunch are aimin' to tear the town apart again," grunted the bartender, filling Dixie's glass again. "Them orey-eyed bronc stompers paint this burg red every Satiddy night."

The batwings burst open to admit a troupe of gun-hung, boisterous cowhands, led by a towering figure in a ten-gallon Stetson which matched Kerrigan's own.

"Set us the house, Baldy!" the big rider ordered, slamming a gold coin on the pine counter. "We aim to hunt ourselves a curly wolf an' skin him wrongside out!"

"Comin' up, Mister Ogrum!" chuckled the barkeep, hustling to provide glasses for his roistering customers.

Cole Kerrigan's eyes narrowed to pin points as he stared at Giff Ogrum's reflection in the blistered backbar glass.

Here was the gun-boss of the Snake River cattle faction, the squaw man of whom he had heard so much and yet so little. The outlaw bent on crushing the wheat growers whose plows and fences had encroached on the cattlemen's traditional grazing lands.

Ogrum was a towering, barrel-chested man, handsome in a swashbuckling sort of way. Something in the cast of his face, the cruel droop of the wide mouth and the belligerent outthrust of blue-shaven jaw, reminded Cole Kerrigan of another range tyrant out of his past — Kiowa McCord.

He was decked out in checkered hickory shirt and calfskin vest, bullhide chaps and spurred Coffeyville boots. Rubber-stocked Colts swung from his flanks, holstered for cross draw.

A train whistle cut through the dusk, and

Kerrigan sunk hard fingers into Dixie Whipple's wrist, leading him out of the barroom.

"Did you see Giff Ogrum, Dixie?"

The old journeyman printer nodded, wiping his mouth with the back of a blue-veined hand.

"I did. You-all ever see a meaner lookin' customer? A damyankee if ever I saw one."

"Haven't you ever seen Ogrum before, Dixie?"

The oldster paused, understanding flashing across his face as he stared back at the saloon.

"By God! You mean —"

"Giff Ogrum was the masked hombre whose gang dynamited Rona Prescott's combine the other day."

Rounding the curve of the hill came the growing yellow eye of the locomotive headlight, rolling into Wheatville to take them on to Seattle.

CHAPTER NINE:
WARNING

Jay C. Ellison appeared at the *Spectator* office Monday morning with a hangover and a nasty temper for so diminutive and mousy a man.

He intended to work out his grouch on the world by chastising Horsey Flathers, the printer's devil who absorbed Ellison's punishment with the satisfying meekness of a puppy.

His headache was not helped out by what he found. Horsey Flathers was busy washing down the press with coal oil, while Dixie Whipple dismantled the dirt-incrusted machinery.

And at his neatly ordered roll-top desk, Cole Kerrigan was scribbling on a pad of copy paper, having usurped Ellison's chair.

"You!" gulped Ellison, taking off his glasses. "I thought you two pulled out for Seattle Saturday night!"

The lean Texan grinned, vacating the

editor's throne with a flourish.

"We missed the train," Kerrigan chuckled. "Ellison, I want you to take a look at this editorial I wrote for you. It will boost circulation all over the county."

Ellison picked up the top sheet, adjusted his glasses, took one look, and gave vent to a gagging moan. He slumped into the chair with the loose-jointed manner of a man recently kicked by a Missouri mule.

GIFF OGRUM WAS RESPONSIBLE FOR THE DESTRUCTION OF THE PRESCOTT COMBINE LAST WEEK! the headline read.

"You stupid fool!" groaned Jay C. Ellison, his face chalky. "Are you asking me to commit suicide? You would dare to print such a — such a calumny on an influential citizen like Ogrum?"

Kerrigan pointed to the other pages.

"Read on, *amigo,*" he invited. "We're not barking at the moon. I personally saw Giff Ogrum guarding the passenger coach at gun's point when that harvester was dynamited. Dixie and I can testify to that under oath when Ogrum is brought to trial!"

Ellison struggled to his feet, his face mottled.

"Get out of my shop!" he shrieked. "Take that broken-down rebel of a printer with you. You're fired! Get out before I have Sheriff McCaw lock you up!"

Kerrigan shrugged. Before he could speak a shadow fell through the open doorway behind him, and he saw Ellison's face change into a servile mask of humility.

"Mornin', Mister Trondsen."

Kerrigan turned to see a yellow-haired giant in a gray business suit standing in the doorway, his square Nordic face framed in straw-colored Dundreary whiskers. The man held a copy of the *Spectator* in his left hand. The right was extended to Kerrigan.

"I'm Torvald Trondsen," the stranger said gravely, his voice burred with a slightly Norwegian accent. "I presume you are Mr. Kerrigan? I heard about you the moment I got back from Spokane Saturday night."

Jay C. Ellison made gagging sounds in the background as Kerrigan shook hands with the banker.

"The *Spectator* has been losing money for years," Trondsen went on, ignoring the editor. "If it could be published every week on a par with this issue you put out in Ellison's unauthorized absence, things might be different."

Jay C. Ellison scrabbled among the papers on the desk and thrust Kerrigan's editorial

113

in the banker's hands. "Take a look at this, Mister Trondsen!" implored the editor. "This — this stranger is trying to ruin us. He'd have Ogrum suing us for defamation of character. He'd have —"

"Quiet, Jay — quiet!" snapped the banker impatiently. "What have we here?"

When he had finished reading, Trondsen gave vent to a low whistle.

"I see why this upset you, Jay," the banker commented. He stared at Kerrigan thoughtfully. "No doubt you've got a case on Gifford Ogrum, young man. However, I'm afraid the time isn't ripe to publish such a — bombshell as this."

Kerrigan's brows drew together as Trondsen hurried on.

"You see, we who have Palouse County's future at heart feel the time will come when Ogrum will stick his head into a hangrope. If we smoke him out into the open with this relatively minor charge, it might defeat our purpose."

Trondsen turned to Ellison, brows knitting as if he were pondering a decision. The mousy editor wore a triumphant smirk, gloating at what he considered a moral victory over Kerrigan.

"I overheard you dismissing Mr. Kerrigan from our employ, Jay. I don't advise that."

"But," sputtered Ellison, "we can't afford —"

"We can't afford to lose a good man, Jay. If Mr. Kerrigan and his partner will consider working for such a run-down paper as the *Spectator*, I want them to stay. How about it, Kerrigan?"

The Texan hesitated a bare fraction of a second.

"We could see how it works out," he temporized.

Ellison appeared on the verge of apoplexy as he saw a rare smile bend Trondsen's lips.

"If I'm to be responsible for this paper," he began, "I —"

"Don't get your dander up, Ellison," consoled the Texan. "You're still the kingpin around here. Dixie and I will take our orders from you and our wages from Mr. Trondsen here. It ought to work out *muy bueno* all around."

In such fashion, without so much as a written news item in the *Spectator*, Kerrigan and Dixie Whipple transplanted themselves into the woof and warp of Wheatville's somnolent life.

Whipple agreed to Kerrigan's decision with an alacrity which the Texan failed to interpret. In the back of his head, the little

115

printer believed that Wheatville was as safe a hideout as any, if Ford Fitzharvey was on their trail.

That afternoon the *Spectator* was visited by one of Wheatville's most influential citizens — Scotty McCaw, the sheriff of Palouse County. A grizzled veteran of Indian-fighting days, McCaw walked with a limp caused by an old arrow wound, and he struck Kerrigan as being a lawman of keen integrity, with a reputation for being as square as a section corner.

Accompanying McCaw back to his office in the county jail, Kerrigan informed the sheriff, in confidence, of his accidental discovery that Giff Ogrum had had a part in the destruction of Rona Prescott's combine.

"You got grounds there to swear out a warrant so I could drag Ogrum out of his den," McCaw admitted gravely. "Personally, there's nothing that would please me better than notch my gun sights on that killer. But I agree with Torv Trondsen. It won't do to print your story just yet."

"Is Ogrum so big he's buffaloed you too, Sheriff?"

McCaw colored. He had been a hero of the Battle of Steptoe Butte, thirty-odd years before. Never in his stormy career had Mc-

Caw's courage ever been questioned.

"Ogrum's big, yes. But don't misunderstand me, Kerrigan. We got to play our cards close to the belly, wait for Ogrum to make a really wrong step. This wheat-cattle feud has got to come to a head this summer, before Washington becomes a state. Ogrum knows that. He'll make a mistake, fail to cover his tracks — and I'll have the deadwood on him."

Kerrigan shook his head in disagreement.

"Harvest is only a few weeks away," he pointed out. "If Ogrum plans to destroy that harvest as people hint he will, blood is liable to flow. I'd like to see Ogrum put behind bars on any excuse we can trump up before any wheatmen lose their lives or their crops."

McCaw rubbed his game knee and shook his head.

"I see your point, Kerrigan. But there's other men to consider, like Mizzou Howerton an' Rip Hoffman and their crews. They're birds of a feather."

Kerrigan found himself staring at the piles of reward posters stacked on the sheriff's desk. Most of them appeared to be from near-by territory — Oregon and Idaho, a sprinkling from as far away as Utah and Arizona.

The day might come when a poster bearing Kerrigan's picture and description would arrive on Scotty McCaw's desk. Against that eventuality, Kerrigan decided to tell his story to the Wheatville sheriff, after they got better acquainted.

"Okay, Sheriff," Kerrigan drawled, rising. "I'll pigeonhole what I know about Giff Ogrum for the time being. But if you ever need my testimony in court — don't hesitate to call on Dixie and myself."

The old Indian fighter followed Kerrigan to the door, fingering his ropey mustache thoughtfully.

"I'm glad you've hung your hat here, son. You strike me as a man to ride the river with."

Kerrigan flung himself into his new life with a tireless zeal which found him on the job from dawn until far into the night. The *Spectator* was sadly in need of advertising revenue and its news columns needed a transfusion of new blood. A four-pager, its inside pages were known to the trade as "boiler plate," mostly patent medicine advertising, recipes, and other trivia which Ellison published in trade for his stock of newsprint and ink.

The last scant rainfall came to the wheat

country as May was drawing to a close, and the far-flung hills were mantled in an ever-rising stand of ripening wheat. Ranchers were unanimous in predicting that '89 would be a bumper year. Their excitement and anticipation transmitted itself to Kerrigan, bringing him to the realization that he was no longer an alien here, an itinerant passing through.

Under the palliative effect of long hours and hard work, Kerrigan gained surcease from the nagging sense of injustice which had goaded him ever since his exile from Texas.

The sinister Longhorn episode was fading in his memory when, a month after their arrival in Washington Territory, Kerrigan received a registered letter stamped *deliver to Addressee Only.* It bore the letterhead of the Dodge City Kansas *News.*

After being placed on the *Spectator's* payroll, Kerrigan had mailed Jimmy O'Neil the unused portion of the money he had borrowed from the Kansas editor. Now, receiving his first contact with the outside world since heading west of the law, Kerrigan felt that O'Neil's letter held portentous tidings for him.

He had received the letter just before saddling up a rented horse for a circuit of outlying communities in the north end of Palouse County, where he hoped to establish correspondents who would give the county's more remote areas a fuller news coverage in the *Spectator.*

He waited until he had put Wheatville behind the first row of hills before reining up and opening O'Neil's letter. A lanky knee hooked over the pommel, his eyes raced over the Kansan's copperplate Spencerian script:

Dear friend Cole:

Thanks for the money received in yours of the 19th inst. There is no rush in repaying this loan, as you know. I am not surprised to learn of your decision to postpone your journey to Alaska. Washington Territory, the northwesternmost cornerstone of our expanding commonwealth, is undoubtedly a land of golden opportunity.

I regret that I cannot continue in this optimistic vein, Cole. But word of a disturbing nature has reached me which I feel I must pass along.

Through roundabout sources, mainly hinging on the news of the Crusader's demise in Longhorn, I have learned that your intended "flight" to Alaska is now common gossip in your old Texas haunts.

It pains me to divulge that your bibulous partner, Dixie Whipple, got in his cups at a Dodge City saloon while you were here, and spilled the beans regarding your plans to a rancher who lives in the vicinity of Longhorn.

This individual reported your seeming "escape from justice" when he returned to Longhorn. Trail gossip has it that you are presumed guilty of Kiowa McCord's murder, and that the Longhorn sheriff — Palmer or whatever his name was — has prevailed upon Marshal Ford Fitzharvey to apprehend you.

This may be mere trail gossip, true or untrue. This I do know: Fitzharvey registered at a local hotel this week. He can easily trace you as far as Seattle. There he will learn that you and Dixie did not book passage on any Alaska-bound steamer.

It is my sincere hope that the marshal does not ferret you out in Wheatville, for that frame-up in Texas might prove dangerous. Feel free to write me at any time, but in the interests of prudence, I will not write you again unless you supply me with an assumed name or a secret address of some sort.

Your obedient servant,
Jas. M. O'Neil

Kerrigan's first impulse was to ride back to Wheatville and confront his partner with the dangerous consequences of his indiscretion.

Then, after the first cold shock of dismay had spent itself, the Texan felt only a poignant tolerance for old Dixie mellowing through him.

This, no doubt, explained the old gaffer's mysterious reformation, his total abstinence from hard liquor. Dixie's burden of guilt must be considerable, if indeed he recalled his dereliction in Dodge City at all. Certainly, there was no disputing Whipple's fierce loyalty.

Kerrigan swung out of stirrups, seeking physical release while he threshed this thing out.

The brand of Cain was on him, so far as Texas was concerned. By now, U. S. Marshal Ford Fitzharvey had had time to be checking steamship line offices in nearby Seattle.

Further flight was still possible. A multitude of alternative plans swarmed through Kerrigan's head. He could change his name, even his profession. The wilds of British Canada beckoned, or he could even seek his destiny in South America, haven of many a wanted man.

Kerrigan moved over the fringe of a wheat field bordering the road and knelt down to touch a match to O'Neil's letter. He watched the paper curl into ash and disintegrate in the breeze.

He ground out the remains in the flinty brown clods. He felt close to this hard, dry, fertile earth, somehow; he claimed a kinship to this wild, free, growing empire.

The little big things he had experienced in one brief month — the flaming red sunsets; the simple, earnest, unwavering determination of the pioneers who had conquered this desert wilderness; the cool twilights after the punishing heat of the long summer days — these things loomed now as precious and indispensable to him, a part of his blood.

Washington had become his new, but his ultimate horizon. His roots were here. He knew that with an irrevocable finality that stemmed from somewhere deep within him. It was a gamble to remain at the end of a trail that the Texas marshal could easily follow to his door, in time. But that was in the lap of the gods.

Kerrigan ground the ashes of O'Neil's letter in the dirt and walked back to his waiting horse with an exhilaration he could
hardly analyze.

CHAPTER TEN:
STRATEGY

Horsey Flathers had picked up another trick of the trade from his tutor, Dixie Whipple. In the past Horsey had more than once received a stiff jolt of static electricity while feeding paper to the drum cylinder press, despite the fact that it made only 700 revolutions to the hour.

He was now wetting down sheets of newsprint with a damp sponge in takes of 50, a wrinkle of craftsmanship which Dixie had explained to him. It eliminated the static electricity which often made presstime a nightmare.

In Horsey's eyes the wizened little hobo printer was a demigod, a savior who had brought a fresh zest to his humdrum world, filling him with a budding ambition.

"Mist' Ellison will be wantin' his morning glass of beer, Mist' Dixie," the printer's devil spoke up, having sponged off the 350 pages of the press run.

Dixie Whipple looked up from the lead and slug rack.

"From time immemorial," the printer said in pedagogical tones, "a sharp line of demarcation has existed between the printing department and the front office, be it a country weekly or a city daily. Never forget that, Horsey. You-all take your orders from me, as shop superintendent. Ellison runs the business office."

"But Mist' Ellison likes his beer reg'lar at ten o'clock —"

"Let that damyankee stone-of-a-peach fetch his own suds. You got to mix up a batch o' glue an' block them tickets for the Baptist sociable. An' tear down that stud-horse bill I run off this mornin'. You got no time to be runnin' damfool errands for anybody durin' workin' hours, Horsey. Especially for that there damyankee Ellison."

"Yes, Mist' Dixie." Horsey Flathers felt a delicious ripple go down his spine. He hated Jay C. Ellison with the hate a slave knows after repeated lashings from a vitriolic master. It had never occurred to him to defy Ellison's tyranny. He had never been schooled in the inviolate traditions of the typesetting fraternity.

Old Dixie was stacking up a pile of letterheads under the guillotine blade of the paper cutter when Jay C. Ellison came into the back shop with his prancing stride.

Little love had been lost between Ellison and Dixie from the moment the opinionated little tramp printer first set foot in the *Spectator* office. Conditions had worsened rapidly when old Dixie overheard the bombastic little editor boasting to a visitor in the front office that his father had been a petty official in the Reconstruction regime that had descended on a prostrate South like a flock of vultures.

That, so far as Dixie Whipple was concerned, branded Jay C. Ellison for all time to come as a bluenosed carpetbagger. From that moment forward the mere proximity of the officious little editor affected Whipple the same as a red flag waved in front of a brimmer bull.

"Horsey!" called Ellison, halting beside the job press. "Hor-sey! You're late with my beer. Get a move on, you lazy rapscallion!"

Horsey Flathers, busy stirring a pot of glue, flashed a look at Dixie Whipple and drew strength therefrom.

"Mist' Dixie says I got to take orders from him."

Ellison stared, unable to believe his ears.

He was unused to anything but servile obedience from his browbeaten helper.

"Did I hear you right, Horsey? Is this — this unwashed Johnny Reb inciting you to mutiny?"

Dixie Whipple took a malodorous corncob pipe from his toothless gums and gestured with the stem.

"Skiddoo back to your chair-warmin', Jay C. Horsey's busy. We got no time for monkey business with no carpetbagger."

Ellison purpled. He was a head taller than the diminutive printer, and had an advantage of 30 years. This made him bold.

"You're both fired!" shrilled the editor. "Come to the office and draw your time. This is once Cole Kerrigan ain't here to intervene in my affairs."

Dixie Whipple carefully wiped his hands on his apron. An unholy gleam appeared in his little blue eyes.

"Stay around and watch this, Horsey," the printer said. "You're goin' to see how me an' Stonewall Jackson an' Robert E. Lee put the kibosh on the Yankees at Bull Run."

One minute later the startled pedestrians on Wheatville's main street were treated to the spectacle of Jay C. Ellison, gripped securely by the collar and the seat of his pants, being propelled into the gutter by a veteran half his size.

Too dazed for speech, Ellison picked himself out of the dust and headed for the bank to enlist Torvald Trondsen's support. Dixie Whipple, bluing the air with Confederate invective, stalked back into the newspaper office and sat down in Ellison's chair to cool off while he discoursed on Ellison's dubious canine ancestry.

The printer's roving eye chanced to land on Ellison's wastebasket. On top of the heap of discarded proofsheets and copy paper he saw an article in Cole Kerrigan's handwriting which he hadn't recalled setting into type. It was the editorial condemning Giff Ogrum for his connection with the dynamiting of the Prescott combine.

Ellison had taken advantage of Cole Kerrigan's field trip to get rid of the pigeon-holed document. Sight of his boss's plain-spoken editorial planted the seeds of a very radical idea in Dixie Whipple's head.

"By crackies," opined Dixie, his rage retreating before the advent of a wide and wicked grin, "there's more than one way of cooking a damyankee's goose. Yes siree."

Dixie retrieved the editorial from the wastebasket and stomped back into his print shop domain with the air of a conquering hero, shooting Horsey Flathers a reassuring wink. He had the editorial half set up in Long Primer when Jay C. Ellison arrived on the scene with Torvald Trondsen in tow.

"Dixie," called the banker, "come here. We've got to have a talk."

Whipple listened with abject humility to Trondsen's defense of Ellison's authority. He went so far as to proffer a meek apology to the ruffled editor.

"We'll keep Horsey on the job," Trondsen wound up his referee's decision. "Henceforth, don't send a minor into a saloon after your beer, Jay. The sheriff wouldn't approve."

Torvald Trondsen returned to his bank office with the feeling that his diplomacy had poured oil on the troubled domestic waters in the *Spectator* office. Ellison was mollified, his authority re-established. Dixie Whipple seemed properly contrite about his insurrection.

That night Jay C. Ellison approved the proofs of the weekly edition and retired to his boardinghouse with a quart of Scotch, leaving Dixie and Horsey Flathers to run off the edition.

Ellison had hardly left the building before Dixie Whipple had removed the front-page form from the press and set about making certain changes in the layout which Ellison had okayed.

. . . Next morning the village of Wheatville was set agog by the most sensational issue of the Palouse County *Spectator* which had so far left the press.

Squarely in the center of page one, set off by the thickest border Dixie Whipple could find in his font cabinets, was an editorial. It occupied the space which Jay C. Ellison had earmarked for an innocuous article of his own, demanding new textbooks for the Wheatville grammar school.

Granting the worthiness of any educational institution to the support of the press, Dixie Whipple had replaced Ellison's screed with an editorial which was anything but innocuous:

GIFF OGRUM WAS RESPONSIBLE FOR THE DESTRUCTION OF THE PRESCOTT COMBINE
Newcomer to Wheatville, Present at Holdup of Train, Saw Snake River Cattleman as Member of Masked Bandit Gang!

Dixie Whipple was conspicuous for his absence. Somewhat awed by the enormity of his deed and its reception by the town's startled citizenry, he had accepted an invita-

131

tion to board the R.F.D. mail wagon which made a circuit of the county and which was not due back into Wheatville until Sunday afternoon.

The wheat town buzzed like a jostled beehive. The news spread on the wings of the wind, drawing an unusually heavy shopping crowd to Wheatville.

In his office at the county jail, Sheriff Scotty McCaw paced the floor and debated whether to padlock the town's saloons before Giff Ogrum and his Rafter O hands arrived for their weekly drinking spree.

Torvald Trondsen, as owner of the *Spectator* and indirectly responsible for its contents, was even more perturbed. He saw in Kerrigan's abortive editorial the makings of disaster.

Editor Jay C. Ellison reacted in a less passive way. He appeared at the Y & E station during the noon hour, carrying two carpetbags and followed by Horsey Flathers, who had been drafted for porter duty and was carrying Ellison's horsehide trunk with a suspicious alacrity.

Ellison deposited the baggage with station agent Ed Chellis, with explicit orders to get them aboard the seven-forty passenger train that night as unobtrusively as possible.

"I'm getting out of this madhouse," Ellison groaned as he purchased a one-way ticket to Tacoma. "I'm the first man Giff Ogrum will look up when he hits town tonight. He'll think I'm responsible for that scandalous write-up. Is there any way you could smuggle me aboard the seven-forty, Ed? It's a matter of life or death."

The station agent smothered a grin. "Well," he drawled seriously, "you might rent a coffin from Art Matthews's undertakin' parlors. We could load you on the baggage car, right under Ogrum's guns."

CHAPTER ELEVEN:
CHALLENGE

Unaware that Wheatville's serenity had been violently disrupted by the power of his pen, Kerrigan returned from his junket of the north-county ranches shortly before sundown.

Results of his field trip had been gratifying. He had recruited a corps of amateur reporters, who would mail in their weekly news items, payment by space rates amounting to a dollar a column.

In addition, Kerrigan had widened his acquaintance with Palouse County wheatmen and on the side, without making any special effort, he had garnered in over 40 subscriptions to the *Spectator* — an increase in circulation of over ten percent.

"You run across your partner on your way in, Mister Kerrigan?" inquired the hostler at the Black Stallion livery barn where the Texan rented his horse.

"Dixie? Yes, I passed him this morning,

riding deadhead on the R.F.D. mail wagon. Getting himself some fresh air and looking over the country."

The stable tender grinned slyly.

"Did Whipple show you a copy of this mornin's *Spectator*?"

Something in the hostler's voice pricked Kerrigan's curiosity. He recalled how Jeb Linklater, the mail carrier, had been in too much of a hurry out on the county road this morning to give Kerrigan a quick look at the paper got out in his absence.

"No, I haven't seen the paper," Kerrigan said warily. "Dixie didn't have any extra copies along."

The hostler ducked into the stable office and came out with his own dog-eared copy.

"Dixie foxed old Jay Ellison plenty, Mister Kerrigan. Take a squint at this."

Kerrigan eyed the sprawling headlines and uttered a groan.

"Jumpin' Jehoshaphat! Old Dixie has gone besmirk again —"

The hostler chuckled. "He's turned Wheatville upside down an' shook it. Mothers won't let their kids on the street. Ellison's in a lather. The whole town figgers lead will start flyin' when Giff Ogrum an' his Rafter O bunch get to town. Did you actually see him robbin' that train, Mister Kerrigan?"

But the Texan strode out of the livery barn without answering, his brain crowded with speculation. He saw through Dixie Whipple's scheme. The old tramp had lighted a fuse under Jay C. Ellison's coattails and had skipped out of town while events took their course.

Old Dixie's coup had its humorous angles, but the situation was not without promise of serious consequences. This was the first time anyone had called Giff Ogrum's bluff. It might well force a bloody showdown in the wheat-cattle feud which had been festering in Palouse County, and Cole Kerrigan knew he carried the burden of the responsibility for whatever events lay ahead.

A girl was waiting on the porch of the *Spectator* office when the Texan arrived there. For a moment Kerrigan did not recognize his visitor. Then he realized, with a strange leap in his veins, that the girl was Rona Prescott.

She was garbed, as on the occasion of their first meeting, in bibless Levis and spurred riding boots; but she was wearing a blouse of apricot silk which accentuated the swell of her firm young breasts and the smooth skin of her throat.

Rona laughed softly as she pulled off a gauntlet and extended a slim hand.

"I just wanted to shake the hand of an editor with the courage to print the truth!" she greeted him. "I had ambitions to be a newspaperwoman myself, back in college. I'm afraid Ellison's writings haven't inspired me to follow such a career."

Kerrigan smiled, unlocking the front door and standing aside as she entered the dimly lighted office. He pulled out Ellison's chair for her.

"I'm glad to see you again, Miss Prescott," he said. "Or do you remember that we have met before?"

Her amber eyes went grave as she regarded him.

"Of course," she said, her bantering tone gone now. "I have been meaning to apologize for riding off so rudely that day, Editor. I'm afraid I was — too upset at the time to realize you were about to tell me something when Ellison interrupted."

Kerrigan pulled up a chair and sat facing her.

"As a matter of fact," he said, "I was going to tell you I saw one of the outlaws when the wind lifted his mask. Now it seems you've read about it first."

"You've put Giff Ogrum on the defensive for the first time since this feud started, Editor. I thank you for that."

"You don't think it was published prematurely? This won't drag you into anything unpleasant?"

The girl tossed back her wheat-colored curls.

"Giff Ogrum has tried to buffalo me before this," she told him flatly. "I might warn you, Editor, that Ogrum is a vindictive man. Don't turn your back to him. And be on the alert tonight. He's dangerous when he gets liquored up."

She stood up to go, and Kerrigan was conscious of a wave of emotion he had never experienced in his 32 years.

"Thanks for dropping around, Miss Prescott. I'll remember what you said if Ogrum shows up."

She lingered a few moments, exchanging pleasantries. Her nearness seemed to put a spell on his senses, and after she had gone the aura of her personality seemed to tarry with Kerrigan.

As dusk pooled over the town, Wheatville's tension mounted. Giff Ogrum and the Snake River cattle crowd were due any moment.

The seven-forty train from Spokane was

rounding the bend when Ogrum and twenty-odd cowpunchers swept into view, racing the headlight of the locomotive. According to custom, they reined up in front of the Last Chance and trooped inside.

Within a minute of his coming, Giff Ogrum had the news which had thrown Wheatville into a turmoil of suspense throughout the day. Within another five minutes, the Rafter O boss was climbing aboard the lone passenger coach of the seven-forty, which was halted at the station while its locomotive took on water.

The glare of the coach oil lamps glinted off Ogrum's shell-studded gun belts and the blued backstraps of his Colts as he stalked down the aisle to where Jay C. Ellison cringed in his seat, vainly seeking to hide behind a farm journal.

A crumpled copy of the Palouse County *Spectator* was in Ogrum's fist as he halted alongside Ellison's seat and jerked the magazine from the editor's hands. The abdicating man seemed to shrivel under Ogrum's glare.

"Leavin' town, Jay C.?" inquired Ogrum softly. "I'd think you'd explain this little write-up you gave me. It's man-sized talk, coming from a sawed-off runt like you."

Ellison's eyes rolled grotesquely behind his magnifying spectacle lenses. He pressed back against the wicker seat, a clammy sweat beading his pores.

"I — I didn't write that story, Mister Ogrum — on my word I never!" whimpered the editor. "It was that gangly Texas man that Trondsen hired a couple weeks back. Cole Kerrigan, his name is. He claims he saw you the day Rona's combine was blown up —"

Ogrum's face darkened. For the first time since the special train from Spokane had been halted out in the Horse Heaven breaks, the Rafter O outlaw recalled the two men he had covered with his six-gun on the rear platform of the coach.

"Kerrigan, eh? Where can I find him?"

Jay C. Ellison pointed a trembling finger through the open window beside him.

"He's due back in town tonight. You can find him over at the office."

. . . Seated in the glare of a shaded lamp in the *Spectator* office, Cole Kerrigan heard the Saturday night train pull out for Pasco Junction, unaware that it was carrying Jay C. Ellison out of his life.

He was re-reading the editorial which Dixie Whipple had slipped into print, when hoofbeats sounded on the hardpan street outside, followed by a swift rataplan of spurred boots racing up the porch steps.

Rona Prescott flung open the door. Her eyes were wide and fearful as a hunted doe's.

"Editor, you've got to get away — let this thing cool down," she panted frantically. "He's coming — to kill you —"

The Texan stood up as the girl crossed over to him and put her hands on his, staring up at him wildly, her bosom heaving.

"Who's coming to kill who, ma'am? Suppose you sit down and catch your breath and start all over again."

She sucked in a deep breath.

"Giff Ogrum. That sniveling rat Ellison has sicked him onto you for writing that story, Editor. The whole town knows it. He's on his way here now — with his Rafter O bunch and Rip Hoffman of the Flying H. He's bragging that he'll make you eat the *Spectator* and then run you out of the county."

The Texan braced his shoulders, pushed by Rona Prescott, and stepped out on the porch.

A crowd was moving down the main street from the direction of the Last Chance, paced by the towering figure of Giff Ogrum.

141

"Thanks, Rona," Kerrigan muttered. "If he wants a showdown, we might as well settle it here and now. I don't aim to leave Wheatville till I'm good and ready."

The girl gasped out something as she saw the rangy young editor stride out across the porch. Without a gun at his hip, Cole Kerrigan leaned against a porch post, his lean body silhouetted against the lingering sundown glow which turned the street to a ribbon of tarnished silver.

Standing at ease, thumb hooked through his belt, Kerrigan waited for Ogrum to arrive.

The Rafter O boss swung off the street and halted on the plank sidewalk in front of the *Spectator* office, the crowd milling in a half-circle behind him.

For the space of a dozen clock-ticks, the cattleman stared up at the lean, wiry man who stood bareheaded under the wooden awning, scratching his shoulder on a post.

In the red glow of dusk, Ogrum's flushed face had a recklessly handsome look. He was a prime figure of a man, scaling over 200 with a chest like a Texas bull and legs as thick and hard as oak posts.

The curved handles of Colt revolvers swung from Ogrum's thighs. By comparison, Kerrigan's unholstered flanks advertised his unpreparedness. The crowd, noting the fact that Kerrigan was unarmed, whispered tensely along its perimeter.

"You Cole Kerrigan?"

Ogrum's voice was deceptively soft, but it held a sharp edge.

"The same. What's the burr under your saddle, Ogrum?"

Kerrigan's voice was low-pitched also, barely reaching the forefront of the crowd.

White spots appeared over Ogrum's cheekbones. He whipped a hand to the pocket of his shirt and drew out a folded square of newspaper.

"You ain't denyin' you wrote these lies about me?"

The crowd held its breath, awaiting the Texan's answer.

"No-o," Kerrigan drawled. "I wrote that story. I saw you the day the Prescott combine was dynamited."

Ogrum sneered. He turned, eyes raking the crowd, searching the faces of the cowhands.

"You, Dave Beechey!" gruffed the rancher. "Where was I on April twenty-third — the day that wheat thrasher was blown up?"

A lean, hook-nosed buckaroo who was foreman of the Rafter O spread moved out of the crowd, leering confidently.

"You were ferryin' a herd o' feeders an' she-stuff over onto our summer range this side o' Starbuck, Giff. And there was ten-twelve of us rannies who can testify you was with us all day."

Giff Ogrum swung back to face Kerrigan. The Texan was regarding Dave Beechey with a contemptuous grin.

"So much for that," Ogrum said. "Kerrigan, I don't cotton to have no stranger print a bunch of damned lies about me. I aim to cram this paper down your craw and make you spit it out in little bitty pieces. Here an' now."

Kerrigan moved to a lower step, a slow grin peeling back his lips to expose even white teeth.

"A Texican can eat beef with the hair on it an' digest it, Ogrum," he said. "But there's two things my belly can't take a-tall. One is eatin' paper an' spittin' it out. The other is being called a liar by a man with a wolf-pack backin' his play and packing two guns to my none."

A stir went through the street crowd as Giff Ogrum ostentatiously untied the thongs at the toes of his holsters and unbuckled his twin gun belts, his eyes never leaving Kerrigan's face.

Ogrum tossed the guns to one side and

144

spat on his palms, rubbing bunched knuckles up and down his chaps. "I'm ready whenever you are, Texas man. You called the play. I'm copperin' your bet."

Chapter Twelve:
Showdown

Cole Kerrigan was not aware of the crowd surging forward in the dusk. He ignored the fact that this burly giant outweighed and outreached him. He forgot everything except the gloating challenge in Ogrum's eyes and the hot blood pounding through his own temples.

Stepping catlike to the sidewalk, Kerrigan stripped off his shirt to expose wedge-shaped shoulders and a back and chest plated with sinewy brown muscle.

Ogrum dropped into a crouch, circling like a range wolf closing in for the kill.

"It's your move, Ogrum. I'm ready to settle this thing."

Ogrum lunged, launching a haymaker from his bootstraps. The crowd roared as the Texan blocked the punch and danced back before the bigger man's rush, lancing out a piston-thrust which clipped Ogrum's jaw and set him back on his heels.

Schooled in the brawling technique of the barroom, Giff Ogrum pressed in behind sledging fists, jaw down, teeth locked. The crowd swayed back as Kerrigan sparred off the blind fury of Ogrum's assault, finally halting in midstreet to slug it out toe to toe.

The frenzy grew to pandemonium as the crowd saw Cole Kerrigan draw a gout of blood from the cattleman's nostrils with a lightning hook. They heard Ogrum counter with a hammer blow to the belly which staggered Kerrigan. He was hurt. Hurt bad.

Sensing a quick finish, Ogrum came in like a wild bull. But he was swinging at a phantom that bobbed and feinted just out of reach of his flailing fists, an adversary that ducked and parried, nimble on his feet, lancing in a right cross or a left uppercut whenever he saw an opening.

Gradually Ogrum's superior weight and reach began to tell. Kerrigan managed to close the cowman's left eye with repeated jabs to the head, but lefts and rights were breaking through his defense to jolt Kerrigan's ribs and belly.

Catching the Texan off balance for an instant, Ogrum bored in with his shoulders bunched and his head lowered, his skull butting Kerrigan's chest with the impact of a ram.

Knocked sprawling, Kerrigan crashed heavily on his back. Through the blood and dust and sweat he saw Ogrum diving in on top of him, shovel-like hands locking on his neck, gouging thumbs questing for his windpipe.

Kerrigan rolled, whipping his legs in a scissors grip around Ogrum's beefy midriff. He knew he was licked if this brawl developed into a barroom wrestling match.

His one chance was to outbox Ogrum, tire him down, chop his face to a beefsteak, and bide his time for the pay-off punch.

Ogrum was astraddle his body now, his shoulders seesawing as he drove lefts and rights, rights and lefts into Kerrigan's face. The Texan drew back his right leg, managed to grasp Ogrum's pummeling wrists, and then drove his boot heel under the cowman's jaw.

The kick stunned the Rafter O boss, gave Kerrigan his chance to wriggle out from under and gain his feet. His lungs were heaving, his arms hanging at his sides like dead weights.

Through a tousled screen of hair he saw Ogrum come up, grabbing a double handful of talcum-dry dust. There was no time to dodge. The stinging dirt caught him squarely in the eyes.

Choked and blinded, Kerrigan didn't see the kick coming. It caught him in the pit of his stomach. Blackness swirled in a tight vortex around him as he sagged to his knees and fell back under another kick to the shoulder.

He saw Ogrum lunge forward, a boot drawn back for the classic *coup de grace* of the rough and tumble school — a kick to the crotch.

But a third figure intervened then, blocking the foul and whirling to drag Kerrigan to his feet. It was Sheriff Scotty McCaw, his hard-bitten face twisted with rage.

"I got no objections to men settlin' their differences fair an' square with their fists," roared the old Indian fighter. "But you try any more Injun tricks an' I'll break this up, Ogrum!"

The brief respite eased the nausea in Kerrigan's stomach. Tears washed the stinging dirt from his eyes. He flung hair back off his forehead, braced himself to meet the renewed fury of Ogrum's assault. The cowman was out to finish the fight now.

Kerrigan met the onrush with a lucky punch that split the skin over Ogrum's right cheekbone. He followed with a jarring one-two that staggered Ogrum for the first time since the fight had begun.

The crowd roared for a knockout as Kerrigan ducked his jaw and bored in, following up his advantage with a punishing barrage of lefts and rights.

The squawman's eyes held yellow glints of fear. He was beginning to breathe heavily. He was chunkier, thicker-boned, and consequently slower than his whipcord opponent.

For the first time, the staring Rafter O cowhands realized that this duel of brawn against scientific boxing might have a different end than the one they had presumed inevitable. Never had Giff Ogrum emerged the loser from a rough-and-tumble brawl where no holds were barred.

A haymaker with all the rancher's welling desperation behind it caught Kerrigan on the point of the jaw and dropped him again.

Sheriff McCaw's hands hovered over gun butts as he saw Ogrum leap into the air with bunched heels, aiming to stomp his full weight on Kerrigan, spill out his entrails with sharp spike heels.

But the Texan rolled out from under and bounced to his feet. For a fraction of a second Ogrum was off balance, his defenses down. Kerrigan whipped up an uppercut which seemed to explode behind Ogrum's left ear. The rocky fist smashed against bone with a sound like an ax hitting an oak knot.

Ogrum's head snapped sideways. His knees hinged, and he pitched sideways in the dirt.

For a moment Kerrigan believed he had won. Ogrum crouched on all fours, head down, blood dripping into the sand, shaking his head like a poleaxed bull.

Then he summoned his strength. His great back arched. Sinews bulged in corded arms, naked now in the ribbons of shredded sleeves, as he tried to lift himself.

He came to his knees, bawling an oath. In the murk the crowd saw Ogrum stab a hand to his right boot. Starlight glinted on a bowie blade which leaped from a concealed sheath.

Ogrum jumped up and forward, the knife lashing out in a stabbing arc toward Kerrigan's chest. The Texan fell back, felt the blade razor harmlessly across his breastbone. Then, before Ogrum could draw his arm back for a second thrust, Kerrigan drove a pile-driver punch to the cowman's heart.

Ogrum reeled, the knife sliding from his fingers. Then he dropped on his face, his legs gouging furrows in the dirt behind him. A shudder racked the man's frame and he lay still.

Rip Hoffman of the Flying H had a gun in his hand, but hastily pouched it as he saw the sheriff move toward the compact group of cowmen, a Colt in either fist.

"I think Ogrum's been whupped to a finish, men," the veteran spoke. "Don't none of you waddies try to take up his fight where he left off. I'll gut-shoot the first man who draws."

Cole Kerrigan lurched over to where Ogrum lay and rolled him over on his back. The man's face was a bruised jelly, his eyes filmed over with dust.

The Texan stood there a moment, looking down on the unconscious hulk of the man he had beaten insensible. The savage conflict was over. Kerrigan turned to stare bleakly at Dave Beechey.

"Carry Ogrum to his horse," he ordered the Rafter O foreman, his voice low and thick through swollen lips. "Pick up his guns over yonder. This town isn't big enough to hold the two of us after tonight."

Dave Beechey grunted. He and Rip Hoffman lifted Ogrum by the arms and legs and started off down the street toward their waiting horses. Sheriff Scotty McCaw moved with them, guns alert to curb a riot at the outset.

An aisle formed in the panting press of humanity in front of the *Spectator* office as Cole Kerrigan dragged his feet up the steps.

He paused a moment, arm hooked around a porch post, resting his head against the sharp corner of the wood.

He had met Ogrum's challenge and bested it. From now on hate would fester rather than heal between them. Knowing Ogrum's breed, Kerrigan knew that tonight's brawl had settled nothing. Another meeting was inevitable, perhaps above smoking guns.

He picked up his shirt and thrust his arm through the sleeves before heading into the office.

Rona Prescott waited for him there, her face chalky white, a suspicious moisture on her cheeks.

"I — I'm sorry you had to see such a — disgusting spectacle, Rona," he apologized, conscious that his mouth was puffed and bleeding.

The girl pressed his torn and bruised hands between her own, looking up into his eyes with all the pride and adoration of a woman's heart mirrored there for him to see.

"I'm proud — proud, Editor," she whispered. "I'm going back to the ranch with a new faith tonight. This is the first time anyone ever called Ogrum's bluff."

His eyes clouded. "You're going back home — tonight? Alone? I'll saddle up a horse and go with you."

She shook her head, her eyes glistening. "No — Veryl Lasater's with me. My foreman. And some of my boys. They were pulling for you out in that crowd tonight."

She paused at the doorway, and between them coursed a new understanding which had no need of words.

"You've never been out to see my ranch yet, Editor," she reminded him. "I wish you would. Soon. Won't you come?"

He nodded, somehow ill at ease before her tenderness. "I promise," he said huskily. "I've been wanting to have a look at Pleasant View."

CHAPTER THIRTEEN:
WHEAT

The R.F.D. mail wagon got back to Wheatville Sunday evening just as the bell in the Baptist steeple was summoning the town's devout to vesper services.

Dixie Whipple alighted somewhat reluctantly from the wagon, in front of the *Spectator* office. His Prince Albert and silk topper had lost their sable hues under a neutral coating of gray dust during the course of his overnight tour of the wheat country.

The tramp printer dreaded his next meeting with Cole Kerrigan. At the outlying ranch where they had spent the night, Dixie had listened to a somewhat embroidered narration of the classic fist-fight and Ogrum's banishment from the town. In a way, Kerrigan had fought Dixie's battle.

The invitation of the church bell reminded the old gaffer of the half-hearted promise to attend church which he had given the Reverend Harold Dixon, when that worthy had called at the print shop a week before to pick up a batch of printing.

Dixie stared off at the looming church steeple with a wistful eye. He recalled that he hadn't been inside a church for 40 years, a regrettable thing for a man who was inherently God-fearing and whose pungent profanity was, to say the least, an excuse for an hour's penance.

"Dixie!"

The gnomelike little printer shuddered as he heard Cole Kerrigan's call from the open door of the newspaper office. The Texan was slow to anger, but his voice boded no good.

Assuming his most cherubic air, Dixie Whipple walked over to the *Spectator* building and went inside, removing his stovepipe hat with contrite humility.

"Howdy, boss. You-all look like you come off second best with a meat grinder."

Kerrigan tilted back in Ellison's swivel chair, stern lines forming on the black-and-blue cartoon of his face.

"Have a nice jaunt with the mailman, Dixie?"

Whipple essayed a feeble grin. "Tol'able. Well, I guess I'll take in the evenin' services over at the Baptist Church, boss. I promised Rev'nd Dixon —"

Kerrigan's beckoning forefinger arrested

Dixie Whipple's good intentions on the threshold.

"You've got plenty of sins to repent for right here and now, Dixie. It isn't like you to high-tail out of town and leave another man to do your fighting for you. You don't even have the excuse of being drunk."

Whipple sank into a chair, his big spaniel eyes avoiding Kerrigan's glare.

"It was either Ellison or me, boss. Ever' time that damyankee got in my way I seemed to go besmirk."

Before Kerrigan had a chance to unload what was on his mind, Torvald Trondsen dropped by the office on his way to church.

The news he brought nullified in advance whatever moral Kerrigan had intended to put over to his recalcitrant partner.

"Our friend Jay C. Ellison has skipped for parts unknown, boys," the banker said, adding his blackest scowl to the burden of Dixie Whipple's misery. "I strongly suspect that was Dixie's motive in printing that editorial behind our backs, Kerrigan."

Old Dixie hung his head, but a vast contentment flooded through the little man. His strategy had worked. Whatever verbal punishment Kerrigan had to mete out now would be an anticlimax.

"I'm without an editor, any way we look

at it," the banker went on. "Before Ellison drew his final pay yesterday, he relinquished what little equity he had in the *Spectator.* I'd like to offer you a ten percent interest in the paper, Kerrigan, as an inducement to stay on as its publisher."

Kerrigan hesitated. "Dixie and I had planned only a few months' stay, Torv," he said. "I don't know —"

"A Texan rides better if he owns his own saddle," pursued Trondsen. "I'm no newspaperman. I took over the *Spectator* before Ellison came to Wheatville, as the result of a foreclosure. Think over my proposition, anyway."

Kerrigan flexed his bandaged knuckles. The abdication of Jay C. Ellison put Trondsen in a dilemma. Perhaps Trondsen had come to them in the guise of Opportunity.

"Suppose we put it this way, Torv," Kerrigan said. "Dixie and I will stay on the job until the *Spectator* is on a paying basis and this cattle feud is settled. With an option to buy out the *Spectator* sometime in the future."

Torvald Trondsen looked grave.

"We've got to face facts, Kerrigan. You've incurred Giff Ogrum's enmity now. Especially since you disgraced him in front of the whole town last night. I'm afraid you — and Dixie too — have drawn a personal share in this wheat and cattle feud of ours."

The Texan stood up, grinning down at Dixie Whipple. "You run along to church, Dixie. You've got a lot of repenting to catch up on, you old scoundrel."

Two days later Cole Kerrigan saddled up a sorrel gelding he had purchased from the Black Stallion livery stable, and headed south along the country road which ribboned over the rolling wheatlands toward the broad valley of Eureka Flat.

He planned to justify his hasty acceptance of Rona Prescott's invitation to his eagerness to pass on the news of his accession to the editorship of the *Spectator.* Secretly he admitted to a growing desire to know the girl more intimately.

His travels in the interests of the paper had not carried him, as yet, into the country between Wheatville and the Snake River. He was aware that the late Governor Prescott had taken title to the richest belt of wheatland in Palouse County, but he was unprepared for the grandeur of the Prescott ranch when he topped Skyrocket Hill and looked down over the broad expanse of Eureka Flat.

Pleasant View's flowing acres of summer

fallow and lush summer wheat had been aptly named. Eureka Flat's thousands of acres — the bulk of them level as a billiard table between the rolling foothills — stretched off and away into purple distance, to the rugged uplands flanking the Snake.

Within range of his vision now, Kerrigan knew he was scanning the vast grazing lands of Giff Ogrum's Rafter O range, flanking Rona Prescott's fences on the south. Those frowning rocky hills, eroded with canyons and crisscrossed with timbered coulees, were ideal for sheep and cattle.

He dipped down the rutted wagon road toward the blotch on the landscape marking Pleasant View ranch. As he drew nearer, the blotch resolved itself into red barns and whitewashed corrals, clumps of box elder, and lofty green locust trees.

Pleasant View was an oasis in a desert of wheat, in no way resembling a Texas cattle ranch.

Sleek milk cows grazed in an alfalfa patch irrigated by power from a big windmill at the edge of the corrals. Swine grunted in noisy competition around an empty corn crib on Kerrigan's left. The cackle of chickens and the gobble of turkeys issued from a fenced-off enclosure to the right of the main gateway.

Governor Prescott's ranch house was a square, cupolaed structure, ornate with the Victorian gingerbread and pillared portico in vogue with wealthy country gentlemen of the day. Its white walls gleamed in the beating sunshine, broad lawns glistening under sprinklers which whirled lazily under the fruit trees surrounding the house.

Rona Prescott, mannish in overalls and blue workshirt, emerged from a blacksmith shop where she was helping ranch hands shoe horses in preparation for the coming harvest season. With her was a bony, red-headed man Kerrigan remembered having seen in Wheatville.

"Hi, Editor!" the girl called in greeting, waving a farrier's rasp. "Cole Kerrigan, meet my foreman, Veryl Lasater. Veryl, you take care of the editor's horse while I show him around the ranch."

To Cole Kerrigan, accustomed to the adobe buildings and brush corrals and the cactus and mesquites of the Texas *brasada* country, this close-hand view of a flourishing Washington wheat ranch was a rare and thrilling experience.

"We'll start off with our proudest possession — The Well," Rona said, linking her arm through the Texan's. "Yep, even when

Dad was living we were prouder of The Well than we were of the big house he built before Mama died. It's the deepest well in the county, and the first one. It was Dad's boldest gamble."

Water was the most priceless commodity in this arid land, as it was elsewhere in the frontier West. Kerrigan recalled, as he saw the bubbling tanks surrounding the Prescott windmill, that Wheatville depended for its water supply on cisterns replenished every two weeks by tank cars brought in by the railroad.

The ranches he had visited in the northern portion of the county each had its seven or eight cisterns, holding as much as 6,000 gallons each, for the catchment and storage of melted snow during the winter season.

"Dad brought an oil rig up from California to make this bore," the girl explained, warmed by Kerrigan's obvious interest. "You'd have thought it was a Roman holiday, the way men came from all over — from Pendleton and Waitsburg and Prosser and Ritzville. They all told Dad he was crazy. But he hit water at 1,800 feet. Even in drought years the supply never fails."

They moved on past the horse barns and the granaries to a quadrangle of vast machine sheds crammed with implements, the functions of which Kerrigan was but vaguely aware.

He saw headers and peg-tooth harrows, drawn in tandem behind eight-horse teams; disk plows and seeding drills, weeders whose eight-foot steel blades were designed to skim under the surface of a field and sever the roots of Jim Hill mustard and Russian thistle and China lettuce. It was an invention peculiar to Eureka Flat, she told him parenthetically, and was known as a "slicker."

There were two Case threshing engines, self-propelled, for running the big galvanized iron separators with their spouts for threshed chaff; huge wagons for transporting sacked grain to the warehouses in Wheatville; three-bottom gang plows, mowing machines, and a multiplicity of smaller machines.

"In flat country like we have here — like those two sections of Turkey Red yonder, or all that Jenkins Club wheat in the north eighty — a combine harvester is the quickest way to thresh," the girl explained, as they moved on toward the outskirts of the ranch, where growing wheat crowded close to the fences. "That's why Giff Ogrum dynamited that combine I ordered."

It was the first time Rona had mentioned

the Rafter O boss. She had discreetly ignored Kerrigan's bruise-mottled face and bandaged knuckles, mute reminders of the street fight she had witnessed on Saturday night.

"But now you won't have a combine?" he asked.

Rona laughed. "But I will, Editor. The railroad insurance will keep the bankers from breathing down my neck, and I've got a new combine ordered from the East. I'll get it here intact if I have to call out the Territorial Militia to ride herd on the train!"

She showed him the dipping vats where sacked seed wheat was treated in formaldehyde or blue vitriol solutions as protection against smut. She explained the theory of summer-fallowing the fields, rotating crops every other season — an agricultural innovation introduced to Washington Territory by her father.

"We don't get much rain on this edge of the Columbia Basin," she explained. "Nothing like they get farther east in the Palouse country, or even down in Walla Walla County. But this soil is tremendously fertile. We get a yield of 30 bushels to the acre in normal years. And some day, when the government dams the Columbia, we'll see this desert blossom like a garden. You have the vision to see its future, don't you, Editor?"

They were leaning against a fence, watching polka-dotted guinea hens scratching for bugs under the wild rosebushes.

Never had Kerrigan felt more keenly the vibrant personality of this girl, who had picked up where her martyred father had left off, refusing to surrender this teeming land to the foe that lurked in the cattle range to the south.

"Of course I do," he mused, watching wind-billows surge across the vast green ocean of wheat. "This country gets into a man's blood. It's —"

He broke off, aware of the keen scrutiny of her eyes.

"Let's get acquainted, Editor," she suggested with girlish impulsiveness. "You're a lean and quiet-mannered Texan, a stranger who dropped in from the blue on a day when I — I was wondering if it was worth the struggle. Beyond that, you're still a stranger, Cole Kerrigan. Must you be?"

He averted his face, lest his eyes betray the bitterness which seized him at the thought of having to evade any direct answers to her entirely innocent questioning.

"There isn't much to tell," he said. "My

dad was a newspaperman of the old school — the tumbleweed kind. I was weaned on printer's ink, born with a composing stick in my hand. That was back in Texas, thirty-three years ago come July tenth."

"And your mother?"

"She taught school until the hard work killed her. Drumming knowledge into the heads of Mexican peons and rowdy ranch younkers, in a one-roomed adobe overlooking the Pecos River."

He broke off, laughing, remembering his elaborately rehearsed explanation for having visited her ranch so soon.

"I forgot to tell you — Trondsen's made me publisher of the *Spectator,* Rona. It seems that Jay C. Ellison has retired to a more peaceful clime."

She gripped his hands in her, her face radiant.

"Oh, that's wonderful news, Editor!" she exclaimed. "It means you'll be staying to see the harvest — It's a vast, breath-taking thing, a Washington harvest. Nothing on this earth is quite like it. To see these green fields slowly turn yellowish, and then a vivid, blinding gold under the sun —"

An awkward silence fell between them. Kerrigan elected to bridge it with a question of his own, to divert her interest from the closed book of his own past.

"Turn about's fair play," he reminded her jokingly. "I know you're the daughter of an ex-governor of the Territory. I've heard the biddies over in Wheatville remark that every eligible bachelor in the county wants to marry you. And Jay Ellison claims you're a hoyden whom no man could ever tame."

A brooding mystery crossed her face as she tossed back her rich, wheat-colored hair, letting the sunshine beat down on it, toying with the battered work hat in her hands.

"Men?" she mused. "I guess I haven't room in my life for marriage and babies. The Ladies' Aid women say I won't wear dresses or use a side saddle as any real lady should. Maybe they're right, Editor. Perhaps I'm just a tomboy no man would look at twice."

Kerrigan devoted himself to building a cigarette.

"But you're not really as masculine as all that. Didn't you tell me you studied journalism at college?"

She nodded, seeming to withdraw deeper within herself.

"Yes — I was on my last semester as a sophomore at the university over in Seattle when — when Daddy was ambushed. Not long afterward Giff Ogrum came over to

167

the ranch, wanting to buy Eureka Flat for a song and turn it back into winter pasture for his cattle. I knew then whom I was fighting. That's been over two years now."

Across the noon quiet came the clang of a suspended wagon rim beaten with an iron bar. The girl shook herself out of her mood with an effort and took his hand.

"Dinner call," she said. "We're having fried chicken and new potatoes today. Our cook is worthy of the Waldorf."

The Prescott ranch hands came trooping over from the bunkhouse, boisterous and exuberant. Young and strapping specimens, most of them; others bearded and graying, veterans who had come to the Flat with "The Gov'ner" to help found this oasis in a dry and promising land.

They were midway through the meal when the wizened cook emerged from his kitchen, flushed and excited.

"There's heavy dust risin' over the South Strip, Rona!" the cookee declared solemnly. "It ain't a dust storm, neither. An' I see a rider kitin' acrost the summer faller, hell bent for election. Either the Grumheller boy or maybe Joe-Ed Bainter, near as I can make out without my glasses."

Meal forgotten, the ranch hands followed Rona Prescott out on the cool porch, tense under the portent which the cook's news left hanging ominous in the air.

A lone horseman was beating up the valley toward the ranch, a yellow plume of dust drifting unbroken along his trail for a mile across the summer fallow.

"It's Bainter," Rona said. "Boys, rustle out to the corral and saddle up. Joe-Ed's got something serious on his mind, quirting old Nellie in this heat. And saddle my pinto while you're at it."

Cole Kerrigan ducked back into the house for his Stetson. When he emerged, it was to see a jumper-clad wheatman riding a gaunted mare across the yard, trampling a garden patch, so imperative was his haste to reach the porch where Rona Prescott stood waiting.

"What's up, Joe-Ed?"

"There's hell to pay over on yore South Strip, Rony!" panted the rancher, sliding exhausted from his saddle. "More damn' sheep than you can shake a stick at, a-swarmin' acrost that young Bluestem o' yourn."

"But Joe-Ed!" protested the girl. "The Strip's under fence —"

Bainter shook his head, dragging off his straw hat.

"Not any more it ain't, Rony. That bob-wire's been cut in forty places along Giff Ogrum's range."

Joe-Ed Bainter poked a horny finger through a perforation in his hat crown.

"One of his hellions chased me off with a Winchester."

Cole Kerrigan, tarrying on his way to saddle his own horse, saw fighting glints kindle in the girl's eyes.

"We'll fight, Joe-Ed. Ogrum can't get away with this."

"Better tell your boys to carry plenty o' ammunition if you aim' to run them bleaters back onto their own grass, Rony," the rancher counseled. "I got a hunch Ogrum's wild bunch is waitin' in the bresh, sp'ilin' to give your boys a battle."

Chapter Fourteen: Trouble

The boisterous ranch hands had lost their gay-heartedness and the easy camaraderie they had exhibited at the dinner table. Returning from the bunkhouse with rifles and side arms, their faces wore the grim anticipation of men ready to come to grips with death.

A line of worry gathered between Cole Kerrigan's brows as he saw a roustabout throwing a saddle on Rona Prescott's calico pony. The girl was coming out to the corrals to meet them, a Winchester in her hands.

"Miss Prescott isn't riding with us!" protested Kerrigan, as he led his own mount over to join the waiting riders. "This is no job for a woman!"

Veryl Lasater chuckled bleakly as he watched the girl scabbard her .30-30 and swing into stirrups.

"You don't know the boss very well, Kerrigan," retorted the Pleasant View foreman.

"She can beat any man here. We'd have to rope an' hog-tie Rona to keep her from going along."

They swung in dusty calvalcade past the Prescott home, with Joe-Ed Bainter leading them on a fresh saddle horse.

Dust rose in stifling layers from the brown summer fallow, forcing the riders to fan out on a wide front, with Rona and old Bainter slightly in the lead.

Cole Kerrigan was carrying a .25-3000 carbine under his saddle fender, a light but long-range piece he had borrowed from Horsey Flathers against the chance of potting a coyote or a cottontail on his ride over from Wheatville.

He rode with the carbine across his pommel now, his eyes focused on the burned brown line of the southern hills.

The riders swept up to the crest of the first low ridge and pounded into the valley beyond, swinging wide to the west to avoid trampling a lush stand of Turkey Red.

Ahead of them, beyond the next hogback, the sky was blemished with rising dust, billowing toward the zenithlike smoke from a Texas prairie fire.

Heat punished the riders as they gained the sky line and looked across the rugged, rock-strewn plateau of the Snake River cattle country.

Kerrigan's mouth compressed into a harsh line as he stared down the slope ahead. At the foot of the hill stretched a long ribbon seeded to Bluestem wheat, now at its tenderest and most vulnerable stage. This, then, was Rona's South Strip.

The field was mottled with dirty gray patches marking flocks of sheep, their sharp hoofs beating the young wheat into the soil, the cacophony of their bleating reaching the ears of the riders poised on the plowed hilltop.

The milling sheep were fast ruining the Strip's virgin crop. Through the dust which rose up from the trampled wheat, Cole Kerrigan saw where whole sections of boundary fence were down. Human hands, wielding keen pincers, had cut the rusty strands of barbwire. But no sheepherders or mounted cowboys were to be seen.

Kerrigan's gaze lifted to the brushy, lava-sown badlands beyond the broken fence. Here was an ambuscade made to order. From any one of a thousand boulders or brush clumps, gunmen might be waiting to open fire on Rona Prescott's crew.

They charged down the plowed slope, trailing streamers of yellow dust. The riders bunched up at a wire gate on the north fence. Joe-Ed Bainter hopped from stirrups and unhooked the wire fastenings, dragging the gate back to admit the riders. Then they were streaming out across the young wheat, firing guns at random, yelling like banshees as they bore down on the drifting sheep. The woollies scattered, circling crazily, darting this way and that as the Pleasant View riders fanned out to drive them back onto their graze.

Then, above the bedlam of bleating ewes and yelling riders and thudding hoofs, Kerrigan's ears caught the flat, far-off whipcrack sound of gunshots.

Bullets whipped through their ranks, unnoticed in the confusion. The screening dust was their best protection. If the drygulchers were invisible, so were their targets.

Kerrigan glimpsed Rona Prescott, bent low in saddle and waving her shapeless Stetson, cutting down on an isolated band of sheep, swinging them southward out of her bespoiled grain.

Bullets from hidden sharpshooters cut the dust, but failed to deter the reckless, headlong advance of the Pleasant View riders.

Cole Kerrigan spurred through the blinding dust, tying a neckerchief over his face. Sheep scattered like chaff before him as he sent his mount vaulting over a tangle of snipped barbwire to put the boundary fence behind him.

Cutting wide to the left, the Texan spurred into a clay-banked coulee and followed it to the crest of the highest knob of ground on Ogrum's range.

He reined up at the summit, scanning the rough brush country between him and the meandering, green-black line of the Snake, only a mile to the south. His elevated position put him beyond effective rifle range of the melee that surged along the South Strip.

Through clouding dust, he caught sight of squatting figures behind lava boulders midway down the scabrous slope, and 200 yards west of his position.

The gun-hawks, shooting at random at the madly circling targets of Rona Prescott's ranch hands beyond the violated fence line, would be Ogrum riders.

Kerrigan levered a shell into the breech of the .25-3000 and drew a bead on a rock pocket which concealed four of Ogrum's bunch. The carbine recoiled sharply against his shoulder and the slug spat into the rubble between the sprawled figures.

They leaped to their feet, unaware that a rifleman had outflanked them under cover of the shallow gulch.

Kerrigan triggered the carbine as fast as he could jerk the lever, following the ambushers as they left their hillside pocket and scuttled for a near-by coulee.

Sporadic gunfire crackled from further along the slope, and Kerrigan saw short-gun bullets pick up dust puffs down the ridge as Ogrum's riders returned his fire. He reined back along the ridge to the shelter of a granite outcrop, keeping a sharp eye on the country behind him.

Then the firing died off abruptly, and Kerrigan realized that Ogrum's fence cutters had achieved their main purpose when they had hazed the grazing flocks of sheep onto Pleasant View wheat, and were now withdrawing.

Kerrigan dismounted, weighted the reins of his blowing mount with a handy rock, and maintained his lookout post, wary against the chance of Ogrum's drygulchers cutting around to encircle him.

Feathers of dust lifted above the far end of the coulee where the gunmen had disappeared, and he caught a brief glimpse of seven riders heading toward the Snake, out of range of his .25-3000.

To the north, Rona Prescott and her frenzied crew had stampeded the last of the sheep out of the grain, scattering them in a tattered gray tide across the tawny brush-land.

Now the ranch hands were gathering along the broken fence, waiting for the dust to settle and give them an idea as to how extensive the damage was.

Kerrigan waited until the dust of Ogrum's departing fence cutters had thinned in the shimmering heat-haze to the south. Then he reloaded the carbine from shells carried in his saddlebags, mounted, and picked his way back down the slope to rejoin Rona Prescott and her men. The crew was busy trying to repair the damaged fence as Kerrigan rode up. Rona Prescott and Joe-Ed Bainter sat their saddles off to one side, their faces grim and heartsick as they surveyed the sheep-trampled wheat.

"You can see what's back of this job, Editor," the girl remarked, as Kerrigan drew rein alongside her stirrups. "The lost wheat is nothing. Ogrum knows the South Strip is just an experimental field so far as I'm concerned, testing out some Dakota seed wheat. But he's trying to intimidate my men with his stupid pot-shooting, aiming to leave me stranded without a harvest crew."

Joe-Ed Bainter snorted contemptuously, a spear of green wheat wagging from his lips.

"He must think us wheatmen are a gutless bunch," the rancher grumbled. "Ain't ary a man on Rony's pay roll who wouldn't ride into the jaws o' hell to save her wheat."

Kerrigan stared off to the southeast, his spine stiffening as he spotted a lone rider coming up the Strip fence at a gallop.

Rona Prescott saw his knuckles harden on the stock of his carbine, and shook her head to allay his alarm.

"That's the sheriff, I think," she said. "McCaw's been over in this end of the county collecting taxes this week. Mostly likely saw the dust and heard the shooting and is drifting over to investigate."

Bainter's dust-caked lips curled in a bleak grin.

"And, as usual, we ain't got much proof that Ogrum was back of this job," he said bitterly. "Them sheep weren't his'n. They belonged to a couple old herders named Jawn Morehead an' Les Wilson. They only lease this range from Ogrum."

Sheriff Scotty McCaw raised an arm in greeting as he jogged up. The old Indian fighter's eyes were blazing as he saw Rona's men patching up the snipped wire, saw the sheepsign in the trampled Bluestem.

"Ogrum's at it again, eh?" grunted the Wheatville lawman, chewing at his bushy mustache.

A film of dust cascaded from Rona Prescott's shirt as she lifted her shoulders.

"Those sheep belonged to Morehead and Wilson, Scotty. It wouldn't do you any good to arrest those old codgers. But you can bet your bottom dollar Giff Ogrum cut my fence."

The sheriff's weathered face reddened.

"Neither Wilson nor Morehead would risk their woollies founderin' on that young Bluestem, Rona. I aim to read the riot act to Ogrum for this deal."

Kerrigan's horse shied nervously as the Pleasant View hands joined them, leading their mounts. The Palouse County sheriff regarded the harvest hands soberly. "I heard shootin'," McCaw said. "Was that you boys tryin' to booger the sheep? Or were bushwhackers firin' on you?"

"Both," put in Cole Kerrigan. "There were seven riders 'bushed back up on the hill yonder, taking pot shots in this direction. They were aiming to scare off Miss Prescott's men."

Joe-Ed Bainter offered his bullet-punched hat for the sheriff's inspection.

"Only an accident they didn't kill somebody," stormed Bainter. "What are we goin' to do about this, Sheriff?"

McCaw hipped over in saddle, his first

wrath cooling to give way to a slow, smoldering resolve.

"I'll ride over to the Rafter O this afternoon an' see what Ogrum has to say about them bushwhackers Kerrigan seen."

The sheriff's gaze flitted over the solemn faces ranged before him.

"It'd be invitin' suicide to jump Ogrum at his home ranch by my lonesome," he admitted practically. "I'm calling for a volunteer to go with me, men."

There was a brief moment of silence. Then Rona Prescott nudged her pinto toward the sheriff, matched almost at the same instant by Kerrigan and Bainter. Of one accord, the Pleasant View hands pressed forward to indicate their willingness to visit the Rafter O with Scotty McCaw.

"We'll all go, Scotty!" spoke up Rona Prescott.

McCaw shook his head.

"Ogrum would spook for certain if a young army invaded his spread," the sheriff pointed out. "We don't want to give that squawman no excuse for a massacre. No — I'll take along one man. Which don't include you, Rona, so pull in yore pert little chin."

McCaw's ice-blue gaze studied the group before him and finally came to rest on Cole Kerrigan.

"Your face still looks like a raw beefsteak from the other night, Kerrigan. I think I'll take you along. You ain't exactly in love with Giff Ogrum."

A chorus of protest went up as Kerrigan reined out of the group and swung alongside the sheriff.

"But Kerrigan isn't in this thing, Scotty!" Veryl Lasater spoke up. "Take me along. I'll help you slap your brand on that no-good son."

Kerrigan gathered up his reins, jerked his head toward McCaw.

"The sheriff's chosen his man," said the Texan, grinning. "Put it this way: I'm a newspaper reporter covering a hot story. Let's rattle our hocks, Sheriff."

They spurred off toward the southeast at a long lope. The sheriff waited until they had put a hogback between them and Rona Prescott's ranch before reining up. "We'll be rammin' our horns into a rattler's den, Kerrigan," observed the old lawman. "You ain't goin' along as no observer. Suppose we make this official, huh?"

As he spoke, McCaw fished a gnarled hand in the pocket of his shirt and drew out a nickel-plated star, which he flipped over to the Texan. It was a badge engraved with the words *Deputy Sheriff.*

"I'd be right pleased," McCaw said, "if you'd hang onto that star as long as you stay in Wheatville. I need a good man."

Strange emotions were windowed in Kerrigan's eyes as he looked up at the sheriff.

"Before you swear me in, Scotty, you might as well know I may be packing a bounty on my topknot. For a killing I didn't commit, but you only got my word for that. One of these days a U. S. marshal may be dabbing his loop on me and hauling me back to Texas. That wouldn't look so good, being your deputy."

McCaw waved a knotted hand.

"I'm a good judge o' men an' hosses, Kerrigan. Your say-so is gospel for me. Consider yourself swore in as a bony-fide law enforcement man."

Kerrigan pinned on the deputy's emblem thoughtfully. It was no idle gesture, but a thing which made him a vital part of this rangeland drama he had heretofore witnessed as an alien.

"The Rafter O is yonderward, about an hour's ride," McCaw said briskly. "Ogrum built his ranch beyond that notch in the hills. And from here on in we probably got a gunsight notched on our briskets, Kerrigan, so keep your stirrup-eye peeled for trouble."

CHAPTER FIFTEEN:
DEFIANCE

A deceptive quiet hung over the Rafter O home ranch as McCaw and Kerrigan fox trotted along the tree-bordered lane which skirted the rocky, nearly dry bed of the Snake.

Riding with one hand gripping his carbine, Kerrigan's first view of Giff Ogrum's ranch reminded him of a pastoral painting that hung in the *Spectator* office.

She-stock and heifers grazed on a patch of bottomland clover, lowing apprehensively as they rode past. Horses galloped across a riverbank pasture, frolicking and prancing as they followed the jogging riders toward the ranch grounds.

Up ahead, sheep dogs were yapping a warning of their approach. Fat red hens fluffed dust through their feathers by the roadside.

Somewhere beyond the unpainted hay-barns, a hammer was ringing on an anvil.

Cicadas trilled their sedative melody from flowering mustard which fringed the lane with saffron blooms. It was a quiet scene, a sylvan masterpiece.

Yet the riders were keyed to a fine pitch, knowing that hostile eyes covered their approach from behind shuttered windows. It was a quiet that brooded evil.

Now they were in the barn lot, splashing over a pebbly creek that spilled a trickle into the river. The sheep dogs had set up a deafening clamor now. The clang of iron ceased from the hidden blacksmith shop. The Rafter O was alerted, waiting, watching.

A slovenly Indian woman, her elephantine body overflowing a slatternly flour-sack dress, was making lye for a batch of soap in the untidy yard back of Giff Ogrum's sprawling, unpainted ranch house. She waddled into the house as they came across the barnyard.

"That's Big Yoom, Ogrum's squaw," muttered Sheriff McCaw through the corner of his mouth. "She's a Umatilla, an' mean as a sheddin' rattler. Big Yoom's gone to tip off Giff that a couple tin-stars are ridin' in."

They reined up alongside a sagging gate which broke the line of a picket fence in front of the house. The sheep dogs were swarming around their horses, barking.

A yell from the house silenced the dogs, sent them kiting under the shade trees bordering the unkempt yard, pink tongues lolling.

Giff Ogrum stepped out on the porch, yawning as if he had been interrupted from a nap, thumbing gallus straps over his beefy shoulders.

Ogrum's face was bruised and scabbed, even as Kerrigan's. He was shirtless, but a black-butted Colt hung from his thigh, the rawhide thongs dangling untied from the toe of his holster to indicate that the Rafter O boss had buckled on his gun harness in some haste.

The rancher's face was inscrutable as he strolled out to shove open the gate, weighted by a bucket of rusty bolts. A slow menace kindled in his eyes as he stared at the badge on Cole Kerrigan's shirt.

"One o' McCaw's flunkies, eh, Kerrigan?" asked the cowman. "You didn't ride out here to see if I'd shake hands, did you — seein' as I was in no shape the last time we met?"

Kerrigan stacked his hands on the saddle horn.

"Hardly. A street brawl won't settle our differences, Ogrum."

185

Ogrum leaned against the gatepost, shifting his gaze to the sheriff.

"Then why are you here? You an' me settled our tax business last week, Scotty."

A flicker of movement off to the left, in the direction of the Rafter O bunkshack, drew Kerrigan's eye. A rider was heading down the riverbank road, spurring at a hard run despite the sweltering heat of the afternoon.

"Sendin' a man out to head off them seven riders who cut the Prescott fence, eh, Giff?" McCaw said evenly.

Ogrum scowled, slightly taken aback by the bluntness of McCaw's word. "Meanin' what?"

McCaw hunched over in saddle, his bony, blue-veined hand resting on his thigh within quick reach of his shiny holster.

"You were always a hand for beatin' around the bush, Giff." The sheriff's voice held a raw edge. "You know damn' good an' well why we're here. A band of woollies strayed onto Rona Prescott's wheat in the South Strip. Your men cut her fences an' fired on her ranch hands from ambush. I rode over to find out the answers."

Ogrum spread calloused palms in an arrogant gesture betokening his utter ignorance of what McCaw was driving at.

"What few sheep I run are up-river toward Lyon's Ferry," he countered. "You're barkin' up the wrong tree, Sheriff. If any sheep busted into Prescott grain, they belonged to Les Wilson an' old John Morehead."

Ogrum's squaw waddled out of the screen door and settled herself like a dissolving mountain of flabby lard on a rocking chair on the porch. She carried a basket of peas and a pan for shelling them, but Kerrigan noticed that a deer rifle was leaning against the clapboard wall within reach of the Indian woman's plump brown arm.

Remembering McCaw's warning that she was dangerous, Kerrigan decided to keep an eye on the corpulent squaw.

"I grant that you leased your sheepland to Wilson an' Morehead," admitted the sheriff, glowering, unaware of Big Yoom's presence. "But how about the seven riders Kerrigan saw shootin' at Rona's crew? How about the fence cuttin'? Wilson an' Morehead ain't that stripe. They wouldn't risk bloatin' their lambs on green wheat that-a-way."

Ogrum focused his attention on Cole Kerrigan now, as if to draw his gaze away from Big Yoom.

"The boys tell me you're the hi-you-mucky-muck on the paper now, Kerrigan. You don't aim to print anything about this business on the South Strip, do you?"

McCaw's deputy colored under the cowman's indolent stare.

"I always print the truth as I see it, Ogrum," he said. "I haven't been in Palouse County long enough to get the whole picture of this wheat-cattle feud, but from what I've seen so far, there's no basis for a feud at all. There's room enough in Washington Territory for sheep and cattle too."

Ogrum exposed tobacco-stained teeth in a wintry grin. He waved a big hand toward the Snake River.

"South of the river yonder, wheatmen are plowin' their way up from Walla Walla an' Dayton an' the Touchet," Ogrum snarled. "North of the Snake they're spreadin' acrost the Palouse and into the Big Bend. That's country that cattle have ranged over since the days when McCaw here was fightin' Injuns."

"I don't follow you, Ogrum," Kerrigan interrupted coolly.

"You're from Texas, Kerrigan. You ought to know why a cattleman can't squat on his hams an' do nothing while sodbusters fence off his range."

"Land should go to the greatest good of all concerned," the deputy countered. "I repeat what I said before — there's range

aplenty for you stock breeders and cattlemen, but land as rich as Palouse County
wasn't intended to pasture a few thousand
head of skinny beef critters. They grow the
finest wheat in America out here. The
wheatmen are entitled to —"

A gleam of moving metal over on the
porch made Cole Kerrigan jerk his head
around.

He whipped his carbine up, sighting down
the barrel at the obese Umatilla squaw
seated in her rocker. Big Yoom had the deer
rifle in hands which resembled inflated rubber gloves. The muzzle was aimed at Scotty
McCaw.

"Tell your woman to get back to shelling
peas, Ogrum!" Kerrigan warned grimly. "I'd
hate to wing a female —"

Ogrum turned, his ear catching the rasp
of McCaw's six-gun clearing leather as he
bent a glare in the squaw's direction.

Big Yoom's eyes flashed like an animal's
behind hammocks of greasy fat, as she held
her bead on the spot where McCaw's suspenders crossed.

Swift words in the Umatilla jargon
tumbled from Ogrum's lips. The squaw
grunted in her fat throat, uncocked the rifle,
and leaned it carefully beside her rocking
chair. Then she heaved laboriously to her

feet and waddled back into the house.

"The woman didn't mean nothin'," Ogrum grumbled. "Boot that carbeen of yours, Kerrigan. If I wanted you bush-whacked, you'd be cold turkey by now. You're already covered from the bunk-house."

Sweat pearled on Kerrigan's forehead as he shoved his rifle through the rawhide loops on his saddle fender. His flesh crawled under the threat of swift doom which Ogrum had implied, no doubt with truth, and he awaited the signal to ambushed gun-men in the vicinity.

He saw now the wisdom of McCaw's wish to visit Ogrum's place with another rider. One man might meet with an "accident," but hardly a pair.

McCaw jabbed his six-gun back into leather with a savage thrust of his arm. He picked up his reins, meeting Ogrum's taunt-ing smile.

"I realize you covered your tracks on that sheep deal this mornin'," he acknowledged. "I didn't come out here to arrest you. But I got something to tell you before we leave this powwow, Ogrum. Something in the nature of a last warning to you."

The nasty smile widened on the rancher's mouth as he waited for the sheriff to go on.

McCaw's mustache fluttered as he sucked in a deep breath.

"I've got a bellyful of the trouble you're causin' my county, Ogrum," the sheriff said flatly. "You started it with the murder of Gov'nor Prescott — which I can't prove ag'in you. You've carried it right up to this fence-cuttin' deal on the Prescott strip today. It's got to stop, Ogrum. Next time I visit the Rafter O I won't come talkin'. I'll aim to wipe you an' your kind off the face of the earth."

Ogrum started to speak, but McCaw rushed on, his words a hot torrent with the passion of his unbridled temper.

"I'm going to authorize every wheatman in the county to pack a gun in the defense of their property, Ogrum. From here on out, I'm backin' the wheatmen to win this feud you forced on 'em. Wheat's here to stay. If you want to keep raisin' cattle in this Territory, it depends on you. And you can pass the word along to Mizzou Howerton and Rip Hoffman."

Giff Ogrum folded his arms, teetered on the balls of his feet as his eyes shuttled between the sheriff and his deputy.

"Before you two rannihans get off my ranch and stay off," Ogrum grated, "I've got a little ultimatum of my own to ram down *your* throats. This country ain't big enough for wheat an' cattle both. We're in this fight to the finish."

Cole Kerrigan caught the intensity of the rancher's threat. He knew he was witnessing the first out-in-the-open declaration of bloody and final war.

"I can quote you," he asked, "in the *Spectator?*"

Ogrum whirled toward the Texan like a striking reptile. "What I'm saying ain't for publication, Kerrigan. Print it, and Gawd help you."

The Texan straightened in saddle. He was recalling the almost identical words flung at him a few months ago in Texas by Kiowa McCord.

"I'll be the judge," he flung back, "of what I print or don't print."

Ogrum drew himself up to his full stature, his green eyes reminding Kerrigan of a rabid dog's.

"There ain't a wheat rancher with a kernel in the ground," Ogrum raged, "who'll cash in on a harvest this summer."

So saying, Ogrum slammed the gate shut and stalked back toward the house.

Kerrigan reined around and spurred after the sheriff as McCaw lined out down the tree-fringed lane, showing Giff Ogrum his back with a cool disdain for bushwhack lead.

Staring after the departing riders, Ogrum fanned his arms behind him in a restraining signal to the henchmen who crouched at vantage points around the ranch grounds, fingers waiting on triggers.

"I talk too much," Ogrum growled. "I talk too damned much."

. . . The thud of hoofs thinned and died on the heavy air as McCaw and Kerrigan rode grimly out of the Rafter O and veered north toward Wheatville.

Ogrum's challenge still echoed in Kerrigan's head. The chips were down. The reverberations of Ogrum's ultimatum would ring throughout the county if Kerrigan published it.

But would it be wise to do so, this close to harvest? He knew the reprisal Ogrum would unleash against him personally. He also knew where his duty lay, as editor of a paper which decent citizens had come to rely upon as their mouthpiece. He hoped Torvald Trondsen would see eye to eye with him on that.

CHAPTER SIXTEEN: STORM

Torvald Trondsen sat in his office at the Wheatville bank, a copy of the latest *Spectator* spread out on his desk. It was the first to appear under the editorship of Cole Kerrigan, and its contents had been approved by Trondsen before Dixie Whipple ran off the edition.

This issue was a bombshell. The banker wondered now if he had not let Kerrigan's crusading zeal get the better of his judgment.

If the *Spectator* was to represent the interests of the majority of Palouse County's population, Kerrigan had argued, then the paper had a solemn obligation to warn the wheatmen of Giff Ogrum's warlike intentions, just as it would advertise the presence of a rabid animal running amuck in the community.

Yet Trondsen knew, with a sickening

premonition he could not shake off, that the *Spectator's* headlines this week would fan into open flame the smoldering feud between cattle and wheat factions.

But the die was cast. A banner headline on page one was now being read throughout the county:

OGRUM THREATENS PALOUSE COUNTY WHEAT HARVEST

The news story which followed, phrased in Kerrigan's crisp style, was virtually a verbatim report of his visit to the Rafter O headquarters with Sheriff Scotty McCaw.

Kerrigan subscribed to the time-honored credo that editorial opinion should not tincture his news columns. His account of the sheep invasion of Rona Prescott's South Strip, therefore, had named no names, made no accusations as to the identity of the riders who had cut the boundary fence or fired on the Pleasant View hands.

In his editorial page, though, Kerrigan pulled no punches. He had given his views the prestige of a byline. The Texan's first editorial since taking over Ellison's job on the *Spectator* would shake Palouse County to its core.

PALOUSE COUNTY IS AT THE CROSSROADS
By Cole Kerrigan, Editor

This writer has been a resident of Wheatville less than two months. Heretofore, his role has been that of a newcomer, observing events without bias or prejudice. Now, as editor of this paper, he makes bold to consider himself a citizen of Washington Territory, with the best interests of its people his prime desideratum.

The writer was born and bred in the tradition of the open range, where "cattle was king." He was nurtured in the belief that plow and fence were unnatural encroachments on soil Nature intended to remain public domain.

His studied opinion of the Washington scene brings about a complete reversal of these views. The Columbia Basin, fertilized by the volcanic dust of countless ages, holds vast potentialities as a wheat empire. As grazing land for stock, it can be appraised as mediocre. If the choice lies between cattle and wheat, the answer for Palouse County must be overwhelmingly for the latter.

The Spectator believes that Washington Territory is big enough for both wheat and cattle. Geography backs this premise. The rugged country bordering the Snake River is unfit for cultivation, ideal for stock forage. By the same token, the majority of Palouse County is more suitable for wheat culture.

As reported elsewhere in this issue, lawless interests representing the cattle industry are determined to crush out the wheatmen at any cost. Against this threat, this week Sheriff Mc-Caw has advised all wheatmen to protect their coming harvest with force if necessary. The Spectator applauds this fearless decision.

This summer's harvest will be the most critical period in the history of Palouse County. The threat of fire and bloodshed is already rampant. Wheatmen, stick up for your inalienable rights to defend your homes and property! Before another harvest season comes, Washington will be a state, coming under the protection of the federal government. Until that time, the solution of your problems must be handled in the pioneer way.

Palouse County is at the crossroads. The loss of your wheat harvest would mean bankruptcy for most of our county. The right lies on your side. Fight force with force if the necessity arises. Only by such tactics will the county achieve its rightful heritage.

Trondsen shook off his sense of depression and moved to the window overlooking the street. It was midafternoon, but Wheatville appeared almost deserted.

Ranchers' families had come to town in their buggies and spring wagons, had done their weekly shopping and then had left town, despite the allurement of a dance at the I.O.O.F. Hall and a sociable scheduled by the Baptist Church.

These things hinted of trouble in the air.

The hitchracks in front of the Last Chance saloon, on the other hand, were jammed with saddle horses. The majority bore the Rafter O brand, but Mizzou Howerton's Slash M-H Connected and Rip Hoffman's Flying H were also represented.

Trondsen read the evidence and found it bad. Kerrigan's editorial had emptied the town of its usual Saturday visitors from the outlying wheat ranches, but it had drawn the cattle faction to Wheatville as a magnet attracts iron filings.

Clearly, Wheatville was clearing the decks for action of some sort. Mothers were seeing to it that their menfolk and children kept off the streets. Menace hung heavy on the air.

Trondsen locked up the bank and walked down the deserted street. He knew the saloon was crowded with sullen cowpunchers, arrived in town hours before their usual time. All the ingredients of catastrophe were gathering in Wheatville today.

The whiskered banker felt a chill coast down his spine. As owner of the Palouse County *Spectator,* he knew he was marked for reprisal as surely as was Cole Kerrigan.

Nature itself seemed to be under the brooding spell of impending doom which cast its pall over the wheat town. The sky was cloudless, as was usual for early June. But the sun was a bloody red eye in the west, and the atmosphere held a brassy, neutral hue which obscured the normal blue.

To the southwest, vast brownish-yellow clouds were racking over the horizon. The air was heavy, oppressive. Not a breath of wind stirred.

Trondsen crossed over to the *Spectator* office. Going inside, he saw Dixie Whipple busy in the back of the shop, hand-pegging a display ad for some county legal business. Horsey Flathers had left for the day.

The banker found Cole Kerrigan standing at a side window, staring at the menacing clouds which were marshaling over the rolling hills.

"Looks like a hell of a rainstorm is on the way," Kerrigan said. "That won't help the crops at this stage, will it? I understand you never had rain this late."

Trondsen drew an uneasy hand through his cornsilk Dundrearie beard. "It's a dust storm, Cole. They hit Washington occasionally. Something like your cyclones back in Texas."

A heavy silence lay between them for a few minutes. Then Trondsen spoke up again, his voice shaky. "I don't like the looks of things, Cole. The cattle faction is gathering in town. Your story is going to cause trouble."

Kerrigan stepped over to his desk and ripped a ribbon of proofsheet off a spindle. Printed thereon was a short news item which had been turned in by a local housewife.

Mrs. Bess Trondsen and her children, Barbara, Johnny, Dorothy, and Beverly, left Friday evening for their vacation over at Ocean Park, on the beach. This is a month earlier than usual for the Trondsen tribe to leave us. Enjoy some of those luscious razor clams for us, folks.

"You didn't tell me you'd sent your family away, Torv," Kerrigan remarked. "It's none of my business, but are you afraid of some sort of personal reprisal?"

Trondsen avoided Kerrigan's gaze.

"I always send the wife and kids over to Ocean Park to escape the hot weather. It doesn't mean anything."

"But you sent them to Ritzville by wagon. That's a tiresome trip. Why didn't they wait for tonight's train?"

Before Trondsen could reply, a funneling roar of sound came out of the southwest on the wings of a tornadolike gust which shook Wheatville's frame buildings.

"She'll be a ripsnorter," the banker said, lifting his voice above the sudden wail of wind under the eaves. "It'll be like this most of the night, most likely. I hope it puts a crimp in Ogrum's plans. Perhaps the Almighty sent this storm to protect us both —"

Kerrigan accompanied Trondsen out on the porch. The dust canopy was tumbling like a brown tidal wave across the wind-flattened wheat fields to westward, darkening the land with premature twilight.

Somewhere on the outskirts of town a big locust tree bent, splintered, then uprooted under the fury of the wind. The cottonwoods around the railroad tank plunged like frightened cattle. Flying debris raced over the roof tops.

The streets were broomed clean of their three-inch carpet of powdery dust, exposing the rutted hardpan beneath, solid as paving blocks. The straw-stuffed horse on the ridgepole of the Black Stallion livery barn tore loose and went boomeranging in a wide arc, to rupture grotesquely against the brick walls of the bank, like a Pegasus arcing across the heavens.

The two men clung to the porch pillars as the wind whipped at their clothing with savage fury. The oncoming dust blacked out the sun, obscured the post office 40 feet across the street. Cow ponies lining the racks in front of the Last Chance turned their rumps to the gale, snorting with terror.

Then the full force of the dust storm hit Wheatville. Before Kerrigan and Trondsen could retreat inside and bolt the door, the air was freighted with stinging particles of lava ash. Lighted windows became pale glowing patches in murk which resembled the unearthly light of a solar eclipse. Shingles were stripped from roofs and driven across the town like autumn leaves.

Uprooted weeds bounded along the board sidewalks like animals hastening for shelter. The interior of the print shop went suddenly pitch dark. Dixie Whipple, his cussing unheard above the roar of the gale, lighted a lantern in the back of the shop and went on with his work.

Kerrigan hurried along both walls of the building, checking window fastenings. But it was impossible to keep out the dust. Talcum-fine, it seeped between cracks in the clapboards, sifted through tightly closed windows, filtered between the shingles overhead, and covered everything in the room with a powdery coating. Kerrigan groped back to the railed-off editorial office up front, fumbling for a match.

Above the fury of the storm he heard someone shouting his name outdoors, pounding on the bolted door.

"Sounds like Horsey Flathers!" shouted Torvald Trondsen. "I'll let the kid in."

Kerrigan was groping for the lamp when Trondsen unbolted the front door. A grit-laden blast of air ripped into the building, causing a snowstorm of loose papers.

Trondsen stood back from the door, staring at a figure silhouetted on the threshold against the pale gleam of lighted windows in the post office across the street. It was not Horsey Flathers.

A spurt of flame cut through the whorling dust. The muffled crash of a gunshot smote Kerrigan's eardrums.

He saw Torvald Trondsen lurch back, doubling over, hands hugging his middle.

His knees buckled and the banker pitched to the floor.

Kerrigan leaped to the door, looked out. The world was a void of flying dust. He saw no trace of the gunman. The Texan jammed the door shut and shot the bolt against the fury of the gale. He found a match, struck it on a pants leg, sprang to Trondsen's side.

The banker was dying. A crimson stain was spreading over his shirt, welling thickly between his clutching fingers.

The match flickered out between Kerrigan's fingers and darkness hid the horror which convulsed the Texan's face. He knew, in that shocked instant, that Torvald Trondsen had taken a point-blank bullet intended for him.

CHAPTER SEVENTEEN:
DEATH

Dixie Whipple came up with his lantern, his lips moving soundlessly against the fury of the dust storm. Kerrigan lifted the wounded banker off the floor, yelling for the printer to lead the way to their living-quarters in the rear upstairs.

Blood dribbled from the bullet hole in Trondsen's midriff as Whipple preceded them up the stairs, weird shadows wagging against the vibrating walls.

Kerrigan stretched Trondsen out on his bed and turned up the lantern wick. Dixie produced a pair of shears from his apron and snipped the blood-soaked shirt away from Trondsen's chest to expose the wound. It was directly under the fork of the breast-bone.

"Run over to Doc Strang's, Dixie!" ordered the Texan. "I'll do what I can to make a poultice and stem the blood. Tell Doc to fetch his chloroform."

Torvald Trondsen's eyes fluttered open. His usually ruddy Nordic features were now bleached paper-white with the pallor of approaching death.

"Don't send Dixie — outside," gasped the banker, his words faintly audible in a lull of the wind-borne sand which was pelting the shingles over the bed. "Ogrum's bunch — is out to — destroy the *Spectator* and you — with it. Doctor — do me no good now. Cole, I want to — send for Bess and the kids."

Trondsen's voice trailed off. He had lapsed into a coma.

"You stay here," Kerrigan told Dixie. "I'll duck out the back way and fetch a medico. It's the least I can do. Trondsen took a slug intended for me. The killer mistook him for me in the darkness —"

Kerrigan ducked out of the bedroom, sliding his hands along the balustraded gallery.

He was halfway down the staircase when his ears registered a jangle of breaking glass on a window facing the side street. His first thought was that the storm had found a pane where the putty had broken away. Then he saw a blazing ball of rags fly through the broken window and land on the paper-littered floor like a rocket.

His mind sped back to Longhorn. This was history repeating itself. Kiowa McCord and the *Crusader,* Giff Ogrum and the *Spectator* — the play was the same, only the scenery different. The enemy was out to destroy the newspaper that opposed them —

Kerrigan grabbed a water bucket off a wall shelf near the printing press and doused the burning rags, stamped out the blazing wastepaper.

Then he raced for the front of the office, threading his way past stone tables and type cases in the darkness, finally reaching his roll-top desk.

He ripped open a locked drawer with strength born of desperation, clawed there for his shell belt and the .45 Peacemaker he had redeemed from the hock shop in Dodge City and which, until this moment, had never been belted around his waist.

A second ball of flaming rags arched through the broken window like a red comet, landing on the platen disk of the job press. The ink burst into flame, but the confining roller had wedged the fireball in a harmless position well off the floor.

Kerrigan leaped to a window nearer the front of the building, smashed out a pane of glass with his Colt muzzle, raked the sharp fragments from the frame, and poked his head outdoors.

Sand scoured his face like grit from a whetstone. He saw dim figures take shape farther down the building, trying to ignite another bundle of oily waste.

Kerrigan thrust his gun outside and tripped the hammer. The shadowy figures scattered.

Then a vicious cross-draft swept through the newspaper office behind Kerrigan as a window behind the former saloon bar was smashed by a rifle barrel.

The flaming rags on the job press illuminated the room, exposed Kerrigan as a target. He saw the Winchester muzzle swing toward him, saw flame spit from the bore.

The bullet was intercepted by the corner of a type cabinet. Flying bits of metal showered the room as Kerrigan backed against the wall and emptied his six-shooter at the rifle perched on the sill of the window opposite. The Winchester teetered there a moment, then vanished outside.

The job press was like a torch, filling the print shop with a satanic red glow. Dust was clouding into the building, guttering the flames, smoking up the atmosphere.

Kerrigan dived for the shelter of the potbellied stove, broke open his Colt and reloaded from his belt cartridges. He saw Dixie Whipple rushing down the balcony stairs, waving his arms and yelling in soundless pantomime.

A window at the far end of the shop caved in before the assault of gun muzzles and two men, their faces masked behind bandannas, forked over the sill and jumped down to the floor behind the drum cylinder press.

Dixie Whipple scuttled to the opposite side of the press and grabbed an iron pot of lye water which Horsey Flathers had mixed for the type-cleaning vat.

Yelling like a banshee, Dixie Whipple scrambled up on the frame of the press and sent the potful of caustic solution flying over the top of the cylinder. It clanged off a pulley overhead and sprayed its contents across the crouching gunmen.

Their agonized yells reached Kerrigan's ears above the cacophony of the storm outside. Before he could weave his way through the maze of printing equipment, the two outlaws dove out the window, drenched with a liquid which could eat the skin from their flesh.

Dixie Whipple came out from behind the press, gripping an extra blade from their Advance paper cutter. In his hands the razor-edged steel looked like a cutlass. "We'll beat the bastards!" the old printer screeched in Kerrigan's ear. "That lye bath wasn't exactly attar o' roses."

Kerrigan grabbed Dixie's arm as the old man was heading toward the window to station himself there with the guillotinelike blade.

"You get back up there and stay with Trondsen. I'll hold the fort downstairs."

Whipple's answering shout was a reedy whisper above the organ wail of the dust storm raging outside. "No need for that, boss. Trondsen's dead. He never regained consciousness, pore devil."

The news, expected though it was, stunned Kerrigan. The stocky Norwegian had been his stanch supporter and loyal friend. He had sacrificed his life to the cause of his ideals.

Kerrigan groped his way to the back door of the building and let himself out into the fury of the storm. The intensity of the wind precluded any possibility of the attackers firing the building from the outside, unless they obtained oil from somewhere to slosh over the clapboards. He rounded the rusty boiler of the steam engine and worked his way down the alley between the *Spectator* office and an adjoining building.

Midway to the street, he stumbled over a barrier crumpled under the smashed-out window.

His groping hands encountered the Winchester which had so narrowly missed bringing about his own doom. Then his fingers brushed across a human head, the face masked behind a bandanna.

It was jet black in the alley. The dust-laden wind sucking and howling between the confining walls made striking a match out of the question.

Kerrigan's exploring fingers encountered a bullet hole in the man's forehead. The knowledge that his bullet had struck down a human being put an icy tremor through Cole Kerrigan. He had never taken a life before.

Other than that the dead man wore batwing chaps and spurred boots which branded him as a cowboy, Kerrigan could make no further identification in the darkness. Probably one of the whisky-crazed bunch from the Last Chance, up the street.

He dared not risk climbing in the window, knowing that Dixie Whipple was patrolling the interior of the shop with the two-foot blade from the paper cutter. One swipe of that formidable weapon could decapitate a man.

A complete circuit of the *Spectator* building revealed no sign of prowling foemen. Kerrigan let himself back in the rear door and locked it.

The dust storm was abating slightly, and Kerrigan's yell brought Dixie Whipple groping out of the darkness. He had his corncob pipe going and still clutched the blade of the paper cutter like a giant saber.

"Looks like I tallied a buckaroo out in the alley," Kerrigan reported. "Maybe they're gathering their forces for another attack, Dixie. You better put that pipe in your pocket."

Dixie knocked the dottle from his corncob and headed for the alley window to stand guard with his steel blade. Cole Kerrigan went to the opposite side of the building to keep vigil against any renewed attempt to destroy the newspaper plant.

Around midnight the storm blew itself out, passing on with the suddenness that had characterized its arrival. It revealed a night sky aglow with myriad stars and a sickle of butter-yellow moon.

Peering out the front door, Cole Kerrigan saw that the hitchracks in front of the Last Chance saloon were completely deserted.

Giff Ogrum and his cowprods had ridden out of Wheatville under cover of the storm.

Sheriff Scotty McCaw hammered on the front door a half-hour later, and Kerrigan admitted him.

The lawman shook his head sympathetically as he surveyed the shambles of the print shop, exposed now in the glare of ceiling lamps. The floor was covered with loose paper and a half-inch layer of fine dust, rippled by occasional gusts of wind through the broken windows.

"I been sittin' out the storm over at the Last Chance," McCaw said. "Makin' sure Giff Ogrum an' his hard cases stood pat. I didn't want them usin' the storm to cover any orneriness."

Cole Kerrigan, his face grimed with dirt and sweat, jerked a thumb toward their upstairs quarters.

"Some of Ogrum's men must have given you the slip, Scotty. They shot Torv Trondsen in cold blood from my doorstep."

Shock and disbelief contorted the old Indian fighter's countenance. He had counted the Wheatville banker among his closest friends.

"The hell you say! I stuck right by Ogrum's elbow all evenin', until they pulled out of town just before the storm quit. I

213

wonder who killed poor old Torv?"

Kerrigan picked up Dixie's lantern. "Come outside, Sheriff. I've got another customer for the morgue."

McCaw followed the Texan out onto the front porch and down the narrow alley.

The sprawled corpse, mantled under a thick layer of dust, resembled a grotesque mummy propped against the wall. McCaw stooped to fumble at the bandanna mask which concealed the face of the dead man. He drew it aside to reveal a hard, narrow face, smoothshaven to the blue roots of a heavy beard.

"Rip Hoffman," McCaw said. "One of Ogrum's sidekicks. I wondered why I hadn't seen him in the saloon this evenin'."

Kerrigan clamped his jaw grimly. The Flying H boss had attempted to murder him with the rifle which lay alongside the corpse. This was damning proof that the Snake River cattle faction had been behind to-night's raid on the *Spectator.*

"I'll have to send a wire to Mrs. Trondsen and the kids," Kerrigan said miserably. "They're on their way to Torv's summer place down on the beach. I'd rather be stirrup-drug through the gates of perdition than have to write that telegram."

Scotty McCaw tugged at his mustaches

thoughtfully. He stared down at Rip Hoffman's corpse with a blind, impotent rage seething through him.

"I hope it was Hoffman who killed Trondsen," the sheriff said. "But I don't reckon we'll ever know for sure."

CHAPTER EIGHTEEN: LEGACY

Wheatville dug itself wearily out of a thick veneer of gray dust next morning, shook itself off, and set about the tedious business of cleaning house.

At the *Spectator* office this was an ordeal which forced Kerrigan to cancel the weekly edition, since Dixie Whipple had to dismantle and wash in coal oil every item of movable machinery in the place. Horsey Flathers was set to work with a pair of blacksmith's bellows, blowing a half an inch of dust from every compartment in the type cases. Every upper-case and lower-case letter, every comma, quad, and column rule had to be exhumed separately from a bin of powdery grit.

The funeral of Torvald Trondsen was delayed until midweek, pending the return of his widow and children from their summer place at Ocean Park.

The community church was jammed to overflowing when the Reverend Dixon preached a eulogy over the banker's remains. And the funeral cortege of buggies and democrat wagons and mourners afoot and on horseback stretched in an unbroken line from the town to the hilltop cemetery, half a mile away.

Ranchers from the uttermost reaches of Palouse County and as far away as Walla Walla and Colfax wept unashamedly at the banker's grave, remembering how the genial Norwegian had tided them over drought years with uncalled loans.

If Cole Kerrigan had feared that Wheatville might turn against him as a result of Trondsen's murder, he was happily mistaken. The banker's untimely death was a part of the rising tide of range war which threatened to engulf them all, and was recognized as such. Palouse County, by common accord, accepted the *Spectator* and its new editor as the standard-bearer of their cause and girded themselves for battle.

Rona Prescott was among the mourners at Torvald Trondsen's bier, but when Kerrigan sought her out after the funeral he found the girl strangely remote and reserved.

The solemnity of the occasion was sufficient reason for her attitude, but after her departure for Eureka Flat, Kerrigan found himself nagged by a vague worry that she had disapproved of his taking such a belligerent stand against Ogrum and the Snake River cabal this near to the critical harvest season.

Coroner Art Matthews presided at an inquest over Rip Hoffman's remains and a jury returned a verdict absolving Cole Kerrigan of any criminal guilt in connection with the Flying H rancher's demise.

When the inquest was over, a group of Flying H cowboys claimed Hoffman's body, loaded it aboard a hayrick, and hauled it back to the home spread for burial.

The month of July was ushered in with a series of red sunrises which presaged a period of heat so intense that it drove the hardy dwellers of Palouse County indoors during the middle portion of the day.

But the summer heat wave was part of the weather cycle in Washington Territory's wheat belt. It was a dry heat, not so enervating as the humid summers in other sections of the country. The wheat was higher than a man's armpits now, heading out in a luxurious abundance of ripening grain.

July saw the rimming hills throw off their green robes and attire themselves in a deepening yellow which would give way to a browning gold in August.

The roads were troughs of dust, and the summer fallow baked until its furrowed clods were like adobe bricks. But the heat that punished men was good for the wheat. Ranchers who visited town to take delivery on new farm wagons and supplies of brown burlap bags took occasion to drop in on Cole Kerrigan at the *Spectator* office, unanimous in their predictions of a bumper crop.

And the newspaper was taking on a new lease on life under the Texan's experienced hand. Circulation jumped to a record high, with ranchers dropping in to pay for subscriptions or writing from outlying districts.

The steady flow of subscription money, two dollars per year, meant little to the *Spectator's* financial structure, in itself. But as the paper expanded, until it was going to over 90 percent of the R.F.D. boxes in Palouse County, Cole reaped a corresponding harvest in the advertising department.

He was beginning to get heavy advertising schedules from manufacturers of harvesting machinery, from as far east as Moline, Illinois. Grain buyers and millers in Spokane, Portland, and Walla Walla began bidding for the Palouse County crop through the columns of the *Spectator.*

With the rising circulation came a proportionate upward scaling of rates Kerrigan could charge for advertising space. The paper jumped from the four-page, six-column job which Jay C. Ellison had been publishing — crammed largely with filler material cribbed from exchanges — to a six-page edition with an insert sheet well loaded with advertising and local news.

When Torvald Trondsen's will was probated, Cole Kerrigan was astonished and humbled to learn that the banker, on the very afternoon of his death, had drawn up a codicil which deeded his interest in the Palouse County *Spectator* to himself and Dixie Whipple. It was another hint that Trondsen had anticipated an attempt on his life.

"How about this, Dixie?" Kerrigan asked his partner. "We can't accept this legacy. Mrs. Trondsen's had to sell her home here in Wheatville and move over to Ocean Park."

Whipple tamped a wad of long green in his pipe and waggled his head thoughtfully.

"The way business is comin' in, we could pay off a mortgage on the *Spectator* inside of five years, boss."

"A tramp printer with a wanderlust," Kerrigan pointed out, "wouldn't stand pat for five years, Dixie. When winter hits the Territory, you'll be pulling out for a warmer climate. I know your breed."

Dixie scratched his polished scalp with his pipestem.

"I been driftin' for fifty year," the veteran said reminiscently. "Maybe it's time I sunk a few roots, boss. This Wheatville is a lonesome an' monopolous place, an' it's got saloons that are a temptation to my stomach an' an abomination unto the Lord. But it's home."

So mortgage papers were drafted, principal and interest payable to the banker's widow on a quarterly basis, and a painter removed Jay C. Ellison's name from the false front and substituted a tangible epitaph to old Dixie's migratory days:

KERRIGAN & WHIPPLE, PUBLISHERS

The wheat fields were a billowing yellow sea now. The reedy susurrus of their restless stalks and leaves filled the days and nights with a whispering undertone which became an unnoticed background to the people, as coastal dwellers become unaware of the incessant roar of the surf.

The ripening fields brought an ever-increasing fire hazard. Wheatville became an island, and outlying ranches were rocks protruding from a limitless ocean of dry, inflammable wheat.

Sunlight concentrated by a cast-off bottle — a carelessly discarded match or cigar butt — heat lightning — any one of a score of things could touch off the powder keg that was Palouse County and reduce it to a prairie of smoking ruin overnight.

But these hazards could be expected. Arson was another thing. And against the likelihood of such a move by Giff Ogrum's element, Sheriff Scotty McCaw combed the far reaches of the county, organizing and arming ranch hands into trained squads which patrolled the ripening grain fields night and day.

Giff Ogrum and his cattle-raising neighbors had seemingly withdrawn to their home ranges, busy with their own affairs. But in Cole Kerrigan's eyes, the peaceful days were sinister, a lull before the storm.

As a result, Kerrigan supported the sheriff's campaign of vigilance with repeated warnings in the *Spectator,* to keep the wheatmen alive to the possibility that their tinder-dry fields could easily be destroyed by fire before the crops could be harvested.

CHAPTER NINETEEN:
AMBUSH

On July tenth — the occasion of Cole Kerrigan's thirty-third birthday — a freight train switched a flatcar onto the Yakima & Eastern siding at Wheatville. It bore a gleaming new combine harvester consigned to Rona Prescott.

Invented only a year before, as yet untried in Washington Territory, the combine attracted as much attention among the wheatmen as had its predecessor, destroyed by dynamite several months previously.

Rona Prescott rode into town with her foreman, Veryl Lasater, trailing a string of thirty-two horses which would be harnessed to the new miracle machine for the haul back across the hills to Pleasant View Ranch.

Cole Kerrigan was on hand at the Wheatville siding to see the combine rolled off its ramp, with Veryl Lasater hitching the team, two abreast and sixteen horses deep, onto the ponderous machine.

"Reminds me of the day I first got here, Rona," commented the Texan, moving over to where the girl was overseeing operations. "Let's hope this contraption proves as practical as you think. It's a pretty bold experiment on your part."

The girl laughed, almost shyly, Kerrigan thought.

"It's what Dad would have done if he were alive," she said. "I think it will revolutionize harvesting methods in Washington. If it doesn't, I'll have to write off five thousand dollars to mistaken judgment this year."

An awkward silence fell between them.

"How does the wheat look out your way?" he asked banally, falling back on safe ground for conversation.

The girl's eyes widened with a new but impersonal interest. "Veryl and I think the yield will average thirty-five bushels to the acre, Editor. We've already contracted with mills down in Walla Walla to handle our whole crop at six bits a bushel. And there isn't a speck of smut anywhere on the Flat."

Cole Kerrigan viewed the girl with an interest that bordered on awe. Barely past her twenty-first year, standing only five feet three in her riding boots, Rona Prescott was handling a big business enterprise with an assurance and skill which would have given credit to a wheatman with many years of experience.

"I'll drop by the office after I pick up the mail, Editor," she said flashing him the same smile that had haunted his dreams ever since his visit to Pleasant View. "I've been too busy out at the ranch to tell you what a grand asset you are to Wheatville and Palouse County."

When Rona Prescott crossed the street from the post office later that afternoon, her arms were burdened down with newspapers from other cities in the Territory.

"Looks like the *Spectator* has plenty of competition in your bunkhouse." Kerrigan laughed.

The girl dropped her load on Kerrigan's desk and spread out several papers which she had opened in the post office.

"Did you know you were getting to be a celebrity in newspaper circles, Editor?" she asked coyly. "Your editorial about Palouse County being at the crossroads is being quoted far and wide. Listen to this: *County Editor Rallies Territorial Wheat Ranchers to Fend Off Blows of Rival Cattle Interests.* That's from the *Spokesman Review* up in Spokane. And here's your editorial reprinted in full in the Portland *Oregonian.* And the same in the Walla Walla *Union* and the Chinook *Observer.* Aren't you proud, Editor?"

Strange reactions played over Cole Kerrigan as he stared at the glowing tributes paid him by fellow editors in the metropolitan dailies. His crusading efforts in this obscure corner of the frontier Territory were being applauded throughout the Northwest, praising him by name.

Invariably Kerrigan's mind turned to Marshal Ford Fitzharvey, half-forgotten now in his new world and work. Would these newspapers fall into the hands of the Texas lawman? Would they lead the doughty old marshal to this isolated community where he had hoped to take refuge West of Texas law? Would his own writings, broadcast over the land as seed is flung from a sower's basket, be the cause of putting a hangnoose around his own neck? The ghost of Kiowa McCord was ever at his elbow, haunting his waking and sleeping hours.

In his zeal to protect the interests of Palouse County, Cole Kerrigan had not considered the fact that his writings in the humble weekly might be worthy of reprinting in big-city dailies throughout the Northwest. Yet here was the proof, brought to his desk by a proud and shining-eyed girl.

"You look upset, Editor!" chided Rona Prescott. "You needn't be modest. You're a courageous writer, a great editor. That's what these other editors are applauding — your courage, your greatness. I'm terribly proud, Cole Kerrigan."

He looked down at her radiant countenance, tried to crowd from his memory the very name of Ford Fitzharvey. It was on the tip of his tongue, in this moment, to pour out his secret to Rona Prescott, to seek relief in confiding the story that had beclouded his dreams.

But he checked the impulse. Vaguely, somewhere in the back of his mind, he acknowledged that he was falling in love with this impetuous, capable girl, herself far more worthy of the adjectives she had applied to him.

But would she be as cordial and sympathetic if she knew the shadow of the hangman's rope lay over him, a barrier between them? Could she accept his version of the slaying of Kiowa McCord, accept it as truth in her secret heart?

"This — this sort of bowls me over, Rona," he admitted, picking up a copy of the Walla Walla *Union* and staring at his quoted writings without seeing the type. "I reckon it's flattering as all get-out."

He accompanied her out on the porch to watch Veryl Lasater, perched high in the driver's seat at the end of a diagonal boom, drive the combine down the street in triumphal parade.

Lasater's hands were filled with converging leather ribbons as he tooled the 32-horse team toward the county road leading to Eureka Flat.

The Pleasant View foreman grinned proudly from his lofty perch as the combine rumbled past, its cleated bull wheels and 128 hoofs of his team stirring up a dust which was unpleasantly reminiscent of the June dust storm.

A ragtag procession of overalled, barefooted schoolboys trooped after the combine, yelling shrilly in their excitement, as jubilant as if they were following a circus parade.

Rona Prescott walked down to the hitchrack and swung aboard her pinto, cuffing her white Stetson back off a sunbrowned forehead.

"You've been pretty standoffish lately, Editor," she called down to him, curvetting the pony out into the dust of the lumbering combine. "The latchstring's always out to you over at Pleasant View."

Kerrigan waved in farewell, conscious of a

quickening tempo in his veins. "I'll take a *pasear* over your direction as soon as we put the paper to bed this week," he called after her. "Tell the cookee I'm expecting fried chicken and ice-cold watermelon."

A clamor of sound, coming from the opposite end of town, distracted Kerrigan's attention from Rona Prescott, who was cantering out to overtake Lasater and the rumbling combine.

He turned, sensing a sinister undertone in the shouts which wafted across the sultry afternoon. Men were ducking out of livery barns and mercantile stores along the street. All were drawn to a common meeting ground, up by the grain elevator.

Kerrigan headed toward the elevator at a run, a swift premonition of disaster coursing through him.

The crowd was gathering about a woman mounted on a Morgan saddler, its flanks lathered from a hard trek across the sun-drenched wheatlands. Trailing from her saddle horn at hackamore length was another horse, across the mane of which was slumped a dusty, overall-clad figure, ominously inert.

As Kerrigan elbowed through the hushed crowd he recognized the woman as Edwina

Bainter, daughter of old Joe-Ed, who had visited his office on several occasions in the past. She met his eye, her glance drawn by the flash of sunlight on the deputy sheriff's badge pinned to his hatband.

"It's Scotty McCaw, Mister Kerrigan," Edwina Bainter called across the crowd. "He's dead. Murdered."

Shock and grief clawed at Kerrigan's heart as he ducked between the horses and stared up at the sheriff's corpse. He reached out to touch McCaw's limp, dangling arm. It was already stiff.

Bluebottle flies were buzzing over a black, encrusted stain across the back of the Indian fighter's shirt. A bullet had struck the oldster where his suspenders crossed. A rawhide lariat bound the corpse to stirrup and saddle horn.

"Must have happened sometime yesterday, Mister Kerrigan," Edwina Bainter went on tragically. "Pa seen buzzards circlin' over his north quarter-section of barley around sunup this mornin'. We thought maybe it was Old Blue, our collie, maybe caught in a coyote trap."

The woman paused to dab at her eyes with a neckerchief. "I rode over to investigate, an' found pore old Scotty tied to his saddle this way, down in the corner of

Grumheller's summer foller. His tracks come from over Snake River way."

An angry muttering went through the crowd, quick to catch the implication of her words. Kerrigan lowered his head, sickened by the stark tragedy which had struck down the old Indian campaigner.

In the space of a month Kerrigan had lost his two closest friends and advisors. He realized with a shock of dismay that he was now the only lawman in Palouse County.

"Scotty was patrollin' Ogrum's east range, watchin' for firebugs, Mister Kerrigan," Edwina Bainter was saying. "You ask me, I think one of them cowhands plugged him from ambush, same as they did Gov'nor Prescott two year ago."

CHAPTER TWENTY:
CLUES

Cole Kerrigan saddled before daybreak next morning and left Wheatville, headed for the north section of the Joe-Ed Bainter ranch where Edwina had discovered turkey buzzards spiraling above the murdered sheriff.

McCaw's death had brought a profound change in Kerrigan's destiny. Until such time as the county commissioners appointed a successor to Scotty McCaw's office, or a regular election could be held, Kerrigan fell heir to the sheriff's responsibilities.

Tracking down the old lawman's killer would probably be a futile undertaking, the Texan realized. Coroner Art Matthews was of the opinion that McCaw had been ambushed sometime during the night before the discovery of his body, so that the trail of his killer would be cold indeed.

The coroner had made the disturbing discovery that the killer had gone through the sheriff's pockets, cleaning them out. Perhaps this was a ruse to give the idea that McCaw had been shot by a roving Indian, with robbery as the motive.

Kerrigan thought differently. He knew that Scotty McCaw had been patrolling Ogrum's range boundary, taking over Joe-Ed Bainter's shift in order for the wheatman to make a necessary trip to town for supplies.

The sun burst over the brown-and-yellow checkered land like a copper globe, and within ten minutes of its lifting, the first waves of shimmering heat smote Kerrigan's face with a debilitating pressure.

He rode with the carbine in its boot under his saddle fender, and his Texas six-shooter was buckled at his thigh. Kerrigan knew he would wear that gun now until the crucial harvest season was finished.

Following fence lines, Kerrigan guided himself to the barley field at the extreme corner of the Bainter place with the help of a plat he had borrowed from the county surveyor.

The sun was past its zenith when the Texan came upon the trampled hoofprints in the hard-baked clods of the Grumheller summer fallow, where Edwina Bainter had made her gruesome find.

The sheriff's horse had followed a barbed-wire fence separating Bainter's barley from Grumheller's plowed field, heading for Wheatville with the unerring homing instinct of its species. Kerrigan set out along the Grumheller fence, the wide brim of his Texas Stetson shielding his reddening face from the heat, his shirt sopping with the salty moisture steamed from his flesh.

McCaw's trail veered off from the fence through a stand of brisket-high Jenkins Club wheat. Kerrigan followed the trampled spoor, a tiny speck in a restless ocean of wheat, letting his horse pick its own gait and following the line of McCaw's last homecoming across the rolling hills and dipping valleys.

The sheriff's horse had zigzagged around patches of whitish alkali deposits where the wheat had barely sprouted, perversely trampling Bainter's best grain, no doubt grazing on the succulent bearded heads as it meandered homeward with the stiffening corpse of its master swaying in the saddle.

The field became stippled with lava boulders which the seeding drills had veered around, leaving oval patches of open ground in the stand of wheat. The rocks were the outermost sentinels of the rough cattle range beyond the southern rim of Bainter's property. Somewhere immediately ahead, Kerrigan believed, his old friend had met his doom.

Kerrigan lost the trail in the thinning wheat of a sidehill when his horse bolted, panicked by the buzz of a rattlesnake sunning in a patch of rocks.

He topped the rise, circling to cut the sheriff's sign, to find himself at the fence corner where Bainter's ranch abutted the Ogrum range.

Kerrigan was now at a point five miles due north of the Rafter O according to the surveyor's plat. Kerrigan loosened his rifle in its scabbard, looked to the load in his Colt .45. There was good reason to suspect that Ogrum might have line riders patrolling this range, alert to pick off a Bainter fireguard.

He picked up McCaw's trail again where the sheriff had ridden back and forth on his lonely beat flanking the boundary fence.

It led for a mile in the direction of Eureka Flat, taking Kerrigan to the highest ground in this section of Palouse County.

Far to the northeast he could make out the magenta mass of Steptoe Butte, scene of the historic Indian fight where Scotty McCaw had been crippled by a Coeur d'Alene arrow three decades before.

To the south was the twisting line of the Snake. Westward through the heat-haze stretched the undulating ribbon of golden wheat marking Rona Prescott's South Strip, scene of the fence-cutting episode weeks before.

Midway down the steep slope below him, Kerrigan was startled to see a dark blot which meant a patch of burned wheat. Charred fenceposts, three in number spaced a rod apart, revealed the limited extent of the burn. Who had put it out?

Kerrigan rode down the slope, dismounted, and hitched his lather-flecked horse to a sound post.

The odor of freshly burned straw was pungent in his nostrils as he strode downhill to investigate, his spurs kicking up little snakeheads of powdery black ashes.

Sunrays glinted off a blackened, heat-fractured beer bottle lying in the charred stubble a few feet inside the fence. Kerrigan picked it up, smashed it against his boot heel, and sniffed the tarry deposit on the bottom. The bottle had contained lubricating oil.

"Somebody fired Bainter's wheat the other night," Kerrigan surmised out loud. "And McCaw must have been Johnny on the spot to tromp it out before it gained any headway."

Over at the edge of the narrow burn he came across a soot-grimed gunnysack which the sheriff had probably soaked with water from the canvas bag he carried on his pommel. Only by superhuman effort had the old lawman been able to beat out the blaze at its inception.

Then Kerrigan spotted the deep imprint of spike-heeled cowboots in the disturbed ashes a few feet from where he had found the oil bottle. And he found something else. A sticky brown patch soaked deep into the sooty ground, with red ants swarming over it. Blood.

"This was where McCaw fell when he was drygulched," the Texan muttered grimly. "Must have been outlined by the fire. Probably kept swinging his wet sack after he'd been hit, until the last spark was out."

Poking around through the seared milkweed which clogged the fence line, Kerrigan found boot tracks gouging the dirt where a man had straddled over the barbwire.

Tracks led off into Ogrum's sage-dotted grazing land, but Kerrigan followed them only a few yards before he lost them on the flinty soil.

For an hour Kerrigan explored the surrounding slope, covering an arc which he figured lay in the range of a rifle. A dozen times in as many minutes, his ears caught the *whirrr* of diamondback rattlesnakes denned in the rocks. Snake River had taken its name from an Indian tribe, but it could have well been named for the venomous reptiles which infested its surrounding hills.

A wink of sunlight on a metal object led Kerrigan to an outcrop of granite 100 yards above the burned wheat. There, lying on top of a huge anthill, he found a .45-70 cartridge. He blew off the swarming black ants and sniffed the casing. The odor of burned powder still lingered there.

Quite by accident, he discovered a tobacco sack which had been tossed over into a litter of small lava boulders. Further investigation revealed an odd assortment of objects hidden there: a barlow knife, a few nails, a worn leather purse which he recognized as the sheriff's.

This tallied with the coroner's report that McCaw's pockets had been looted. The purse was empty.

It took little imagination to reconstruct the circumstances of Scotty McCaw's killing.

From this outcrop, the ambusher had drawn a bead with his .45-70, cutting down on the sheriff as McCaw was in the act of beating out the grain fire set by the blazing bottle of grease.

Then the killer had crossed over the fence, looted McCaw's pockets, and had loaded the dead man astride his horse and tied the corpse securely to stirrups and saddle horn.

Why the ambusher had not rekindled the wheat fire Kerrigan could only guess. Perhaps he feared that the sound of the gunshot might draw Joe-Ed Bainter's fireguards to the scene. Perhaps the wind had shifted, threatening the Rafter O range with fire which could easily sweep to the Snake and destroy Ogrum's own property.

Kerrigan gathered up McCaw's meager possessions and placed them in a handkerchief, along with the cartridge case.

The search had netted him no tangible clue to the identity of McCaw's slayer, but it had established the fact that McCaw had been murdered from a site on Giff Ogrum's range. It had revealed the fact that the Palouse County sheriff had died in the line of duty, halting a fire which, if the wind had been in the right direction, might have ravaged unchecked across unbroken leagues of grain.

Kerrigan returned to his horse and took a refreshing swig from the water bottle hanging from the pommel. He poured the remainder of the water in the crown of his Stetson and let the gaunted horse slake its thirst.

Then he headed west along the boundary fence which set the wheat country apart from the cattle range. He might as well enjoy the hospitality of the Prescott supper table before he returned to Wheatville.

CHAPTER
TWENTY-ONE:
SMOKE

Twice in the next five miles Kerrigan was challenged by sweating, dust-grimed ranch hands, carrying rifles. They were Prescott riders, patrolling Rona's South Strip.

Kerrigan crossed over to Eureka Flat, and his first view of the Pleasant View ranch, placid under the westering sun, was strangely different from its aspect a few weeks before.

Where verdant green fields had set off the summer fallow on the occasion of his first visit to Pleasant View, the picture was now done in shades of brown and tan and ocher, the goldening wheat contrasting sharply with the alternating section of mahogany-colored plowed fields.

Oblique sunrays winked off the bright tin of slowly-turning vanes on the Prescott windmill, idling over The Well. The white, cupolaed ranch house was gray now under months of accumulated dust.

Kerrigan followed the county road due north and veered off on a side road at the floor of the valley, to head for the Prescott ranch. The sun was flattening like a pink egg into a scarlet nest of cloud at the far end of Eureka Flat when the Texan reined up under the shade trees in front of the ranch house.

Rona Prescott, showing the signs of a hard day's work out in the machine sheds, emerged from the door to greet him, her eyes unusually sober.

"I heard — about Scotty McCaw," she said gravely. "Did you find out anything, Editor?"

Kerrigan dismounted, marveling at her tininess now that she had discarded her riding boots for soft-soled moccasins. More than ever she seemed like a schoolgirl, rather than the manager of a busy ranch.

"Nothing I can pin on a murderer," Kerrigan admitted. "I do know that McCaw maybe saved this whole country from going up in smoke before he died, though."

When he had finished his account of the day's search, a look of momentary despair crossed the girl's face.

"Our harvest is at Ogrum's mercy in this dry weather," she said dully. "There's hundreds of miles of fence to patrol. A single match could wipe out thousands of acres of standing grain. Sometimes I think I ought to surrender the Flat to Giff Ogrum — maybe that would appease his greedy appetite for land and power. It would be a small sacrifice if it spared my neighbors this — this eternal threat of destruction that hangs over them."

Kerrigan shook his head. "Ogrum isn't the only rancher we're bucking," he pointed out. "Rip Hoffman's bunch will probably try to avenge his death. Mizzou Howerton's cut out of the same piece of goods as Giff Ogrum. They wouldn't stop with seizing Eureka Flat. They're after the whole county."

Twilight was deepening over the valley in an indigo pool, tempering the furnacelike heat of the July day. The shimmering image of a distant group of barns, a ranch beyond the horizon, hung in mirage above the rim of the valley. A cool breeze was whisking through the trees, whirling the blades of the windmill. It was the time of day Kerrigan loved best.

"Veryl's got a spare cot for you in the bunkhouse, Editor," Rona Prescott said. "Stable your horse and spend the night here. You look tuckered out."

Kerrigan was aware of a throbbing fatigue

deep in his bones as he unsaddled and turned his mount into the Pleasant View corral. A roustabout brought spare bedding over from the big house and Kerrigan spread the quilts over an empty bed in the bunkhouse.

More than half of Rona's crew was absent on patrol duty. The strain of past weeks showed on the haggard faces of the hands. Nerves were rubbed raw by the menace which touched every man who had any connection with wheat. And harvest still lay ahead, the most grueling season of the year.

They finished supper by eight o'clock, but daylight was still mellow over the land. Kerrigan accepted the girl's invitation to stay in the ranch house and chat, after the rest of the hands had drifted out to the corrals to saddle up horses and ride out to relieve the day shift on fire patrol.

They went into the spacious living-room and seated themselves on a divan before the massive rock fireplace. The evening was too warm for a fire, but the soft glow of a Coleman lamp illuminated a big oil painting above the mantel, the portrait of a distinguished-looking man with white goatee and mustaches and keen, determined blue eyes.

Kerrigan, at ease on the divan, stared at

the painting with new interest as he saw the resemblance of the portrait to the girl beside him.

"A fine painting," he commented, breaking a long silence between them. "Your father?"

She nodded, her eyes brooding and remote.

"It will hang in the Governors' Gallery at the Capitol Building in Olympia," she explained. "I plan to present it when Washington becomes a state. Dad sat for it the summer before he died. It was to have been an anniversary gift to Mama."

She excused herself and went upstairs. Kerrigan rolled a quirly and lighted it. He stood up, leaning closer to inspect the portrait of the martyred territorial governor.

The artist's signature arrested his eye. In tiny, flowing script, he read the name: *Rona Prescott.*

Rona was an amateur artist! It was another facet of this girl's remarkable make-up which he had not known. The hands that guided the stormy destiny of Pleasant View had wielded the brush to produce this excellent picture.

He was half-finished with his cigarette when the sound of rustling fabric caught his ear. He turned to see Rona Prescott coming down the staircase toward him.

She had changed into a flowing gown of lustrous saffron crinoline. The skirts cascaded in gauzy terraces down the stair treads behind her.

Fading sunset glow through the big west windows put golden tints in her hair, which billowed in soft waves to the ivory whiteness of her shoulders. The bodice was tight fitting, deepening the cleft of her bosom, emphasizing the narrowness of waist.

"How you do stare, sir!" she chided him gaily, pirouetting before him. "I just wanted to show you I don't have to be a tomboy. I had this sent up from Gardner's in Walla Walla — just in case you invited me to a dance in the Odd Fellows' Hall."

Kerrigan flushed, realizing that his mouth was gaping like a yokel's.

"I — I'd be the envy of every young buck in the county," Kerrigan stammered out. "Why, you're — you're a sight to make a man's heart turn flops. I'm not much at expressing myself this way, Rona, but you're — plain beautiful."

"Plain?" She laughed, a soft and musical laugh that put a throb in the Texan's throat. The subtle fragrance of gardenia perfume, elusive and heady, wafted to his nostrils as she linked an arm through his. "Let's go outdoors where it's cooler. I love the twilight."

They moved out onto the porch, down the steps, and around to the cool lawn on the west side of the house, where the vista was unbroken across the wide, dusk-purpled valley. Sundown glow still burned, a cerise line along the folded ebony hills to westward, tinting filigreed clouds in the remote distance with gold and rose and pearl white.

A wild longing to take this alluring girl in his arms welled in Kerrigan's breast. He curbed the fierce desire that burned through him, remembering, as always, Kiowa McCord and a murder warrant bearing his name back in Texas.

"There'll be a gorgeous full moon tonight, Editor," Rona whispered, the breeze stirring her honey-blond hair tantalizingly along the hard line of his jaw. "I remember when we lived over in Nahcotta, before Dad went up to Olympia to be governor. I was a girl in pigtails. I used to watch for the first evening star to pop out and the moon ram its sharp little horn over the hills above Willapa Bay. But it's just as beautiful here in the dry country."

Her hand was in his, warm and strangely thrilling, as they turned to watch the faint rosy glow which suffused the northern rim of the Flat.

Its brilliance deepened, flared higher against the blue-black bowl of the night sky, reminding him of the splendor of moonrises in his boyhood along the Rio Grande.

He turned, fighting back again the urge which threatened to master his will. In the soft dusk, Rona Prescott's face was turned up to his, her eyes wide and warm and intimate, her lips parted slightly as he reached up to touch her chin with his finger tips.

"I've got to tell you something, Rona," he blurted out. "Something I should have told you long before this. I can't accept your friendship freely this way until —"

Suddenly Kerrigan broke off, stiffening. The girl drew back, startled by the swift change in the man.

"Rona!" whispered the Texan, his fingers tightening on her arm. *"The moon doesn't rise in the north!"*

She whirled then, realization chilling her. Even as they watched the spreading red glow behind the jet-black rampart of Sky-rocket Hill, they saw the first ugly flicker of light along the underbelly of a cloud which mushroomed above the whaleback of the horizon.

"It's come, Editor — just as I've prayed it

wouldn't." She lifted a clenched hand to her mouth. "It's a fire in Sieg Grumheller's wheat — and the wind's blowing our way!"

CHAPTER
TWENTY-TWO:
HOLOCAUST

Across the cooling wheatland, smoke spread with a cloying odor like baking bread, carrying swift terror far abroad in the young night. Like a beacon marking the heart of the rich harvest fields, the northern face of Skyrocket Hill became a seething scarlet wall under erupting smoke, striking horror in the souls of wheat growers within a 50-mile radius.

Fire, the most dreaded outlaw of the wheat country, drew a quick response from the threatened legions of hard-eyed men whose lands lay in its path. They converged from all points of the compass to meet the terror, like hunters drawing in on a cornered beast of prey.

The blaze had started on an unbroken, mile-wide front at the base of the Skyrocket in a lush stand of Turkey Red which belonged to Siegfried Grumheller, the wealthy Bavarian pioneer who had homesteaded in

Palouse County in the '70's.

Before the conflagration was twenty minutes old, Grumheller's fleet of big mowers was sweeping in tandem along the crest of the Skyrocket, each machine sickling a nine-foot swath through the nearly matured wheat. Behind the mowers, desperate ranch hands driving four-horse rakes began dragging the flattened straw up away from the downhill edge of the cut, raking it in windrows well back from the fire which was eating swiftly up the long, gentle rills of the declivity.

At a dozen neighboring ranches men worked frantically at cistern pumps, filling tank wagons with precious water and dispatching them at top speed along country roads and across summer fallow toward Grumheller's doomed valley.

On horseback and in shays and carts and buckboards, residents of Wheatville came speeding to the scene, bringing with them scythes and shovels, bales of gunny sacks and old blankets, barrels and buckets — anything that would be of use in curbing the red monster which threatened to ravage the very heart of the wheat empire.

By ten o'clock the fire had spread to a three-mile front, whipped along before a northeast breeze at a gait faster than a horse could gallop.

Mowers and big gang plows from Joe-Ed Bainter's place east of Grumheller's reached the valley at ten-thirty and laid a firebreak between the holocaust and Wheatville. Across the ever-widening band of furrowed stubble advanced an army of fire fighters, men and women and boys, fused into a democratic unit by their common peril.

Silhouetted against the raging, seething front of the blaze which roared like the furnace grates of Hades, the fire fighters toiled like puny ants, beating out sparks that rained down on the new stubble, swinging wetted sacks and bedding, shoveling sand and clods, defying the blistering heat as long as human endurance could stand and then retreating to take brief rests and plunge their sacks into the water barrels which were being replenished from the gushing spouts of tank wagons.

Beyond the leaping wall of flame, hidden by the curvature of the hillcrest and the vast, gouting pillars of yellow-white smoke, hands from Rona Prescott's ranch were racing against time to mow a wide swath on either side of the fence which separated the Grumheller and Pleasant View fields.

The fire was bearing westward, where a thin red line of a backfire was being established to prevent the main conflagration from leaping through the gap beyond Skyrocket Hill where the country road gave access to Eureka Flat.

Down that road from the south, Cole Kerrigan lashed and spurred the fresh mustang he had saddled in the Pleasant View corral. A mile from the fire, he felt its hot breath on his face as he cut over the flank of the Skyrocket and headed northward to join the assembling armies of fire fighters.

Rona Prescott's crop was doomed if the flames broke over the backbone of the Skyrocket and spilled down its south slope. But Veryl Lasater and the Pleasant View harvest crew were already strung out along the threatened boundary with mowers and plows and tank wagons.

Kerrigan knew he was not needed there. His place was at the point where the fire had first started.

He skidded his horse to a halt along the road as he caught sight of flickering flames in the shoulder-high wheat 100 yards away, ignited by wind-borne sparks. He lost precious seconds hitching his horse to a fence post. Then he scrambled over the barbed strands and plowed his way into the bearded wheat, flinging his arms ahead of him like a swimmer to part the tall grain, cursing the fact that he was without a shovel or gunny sack or other means of stamping out this incipient holocaust.

Kerrigan lashed into the crackling flames like a man berserk, stamping the reedy stems flat with his cowboots, beating at smoldering wheat heads with his sombrero, scooping up double handfuls of soft dirt and throwing it like an automaton.

By the time he had ground out the last malignant spark, his body was as wet as if he had plunged into a lake, and blood was tom-toming in his ears.

He staggered back to his horse and rode on down the grade to where a tank wagon was funneling its load into a row of water barrels spaced along the roadside.

A grim, bony-faced woman in her late fifties was passing out gunny sacks from a bale in the back of her surrey. Kerrigan recognized her as the wife of the Baptist minister in town.

Kerrigan seized four of the sacks, dunked them in a barrel until they were saturated, then slogged out through a break in the fence to join the silhouetted ranks of the fire fighters who were challenging the advancing line of fire fighters.

The blistering heat forced him to rip out a section of gunny sack and tie the wet burlap over his face. He charged onward, passing men who reeled and fell and dragged themselves back from the super-heated air.

In the hellish red light which had transformed the night into an inferno, Cole Kerrigan recognized fellow citizens of Wheatville in the weaving, retreating, advance line of fire fighters.

He saw bartenders and school children, housewives battling with a zeal far beyond their frail bodies, standing shoulder to shoulder against a mutual enemy which threatened their homes, their lives, the very earth they lived on. Horsey Flathers and Ed Chellis, the station agent, were there. Kerrigan wondered vaguely if Dixie Whipple had joined the fight.

Somewhere beyond the twenty-foot bulwark of ruddy flame, horses trapped with a three-bottom plow on a cut-off firebreak were squealing piteously above the sullen bass roar of the fire. Faint gunshots racketed through the night as a grieving rancher put the trapped animals mercifully out of their misery.

Kerrigan beat the forked tongues of fire until his gunny bags were steamed dry and had begun to smolder. He lurched back to the road, aware that he had narrowly escaped being penned in as advancing pincers of fire attacked wheat which had burst into flame from the sheer heat of the atmosphere.

He gradually passed into a numbed condition which made him oblivious to the heat, the ripping pain in his lungs, a stupefaction that overcame the ache of overtaxed muscles and heaving lungs. Smoke bit at his eyes, filtered through his burlap mask to parch his nostrils and throat and lips. He soaked the gunny sacks and stumbled back to the water line.

The moon and stars had long since been blacked out by opaque smoke clouds which palled over dozens of square miles of sky. It seemed that the very planet was a seething caldron of hellfire, against which the puny assault of mere men could be only a feeble and futile thing.

But couriers on horseback, skirting the lines of fire fighters, shouted encouraging news as midnight neared.

The main fire had jumped the Skyrocket, but Rona Prescott's men had taken full advantage of their precious time and believed their firebreak would hold.

The wind was shifting, which might or might not be a gift from Providence. If it reversed directions, the fire might double back on itself and expire for want of fuel.

Or it might head northward and level Wheatville to ashes by morning.

Cole Kerrigan, wielding a shovel to stamp out a blaze which threatened to break out of Grumheller's field if the wind freshened, suddenly became aware of the fact that he was working alone.

Other fire fighters who a few minutes ago had been slaving on either side were no longer there. Then Kerrigan saw the reason. Embracing arms of fire had spread around behind him, circling him with blazing doom, cutting him off in a surrounded pocket.

He had lost his sense of direction, but he headed in what he thought was a northerly angle.

Then, insidiously, the fire reached out to claim Kerrigan without flames actually touching him. The oxygen was being sucked toward the blaze.

A weary, almost comfortable feeling suffused the Texan. Without knowing it he fell unconscious across his shovel handle, the first stage toward asphyxiation.

. . . He came to as suddenly as he had passed out. Someone was pouring tepid water over his face. He was stretched out along a roadside, an anxious group of womenfolk around him.

Then he recognized Dixie Whipple. The

old printer was swabbing his face with a wet sack, his accordion-pleated silk hat thrust back on his bald head. Charlie Fitzpatrick, the Wheatville photographer, hovered in the background.

"Dixie saved your life, Kerrigan," Fitzpatrick was saying. "Somebody told him you were cut off in that pocket of wheat."

Kerrigan propped himself up on one elbow. "I'm — *bueno*," he panted. "Was — the fire put out?"

Dixie Whipple helped him to his feet, chuckling. "Sure the fire's put out. But I got a hunch that Prescott girl would rather see the whole county go up in smoke rather'n have seen you fry."

Kerrigan bent a quizzical eye down at the diminutive printer.

"Rona Prescott? Is she around?"

Dixie Whipple shook his head. He tiptoed up to whisper in Kerrigan's ear.

"No. But when you were comin' around, you babbled out somethin' about lovin' that *senorita,* boss. An' some of the womenfolks said as how the Prescott girl felt the same way about you."

Whipple's words put a schoolboyish thump in Kerrigan's heart. He grabbed the old man's arm.

"Come on," he said. "That fire isn't licked by a damn sight. We've got work to do."

CHAPTER
TWENTY-THREE:
TRIUMPH

Siegried Grumheller rattled up and down the valley in his one-horse cart, his familiar gray beard singed to the roots. He directed the fire fighters, shifting men to where they were most needed, ordering retreats where human life was imperiled by surrounded pockets.

Grumheller was already ruined. His entire crop was reduced to ashes. But the stocky German was fighting now to save his neighbors a like fate, to save Palouse County itself, filling the vital need of a field marshal to direct the over-all offensive.

Reinforcements arrived in a steady stream from north and east and west; hayricks crowded with harvest hands and sturdy boys in their teens. Their help had come in the nick of time, for the original fire fighters had reached the last stages of exhaustion and there was an ever-increasing number of men fainting as the oxygen supply thinned, necessitating other men to carry them to safety.

Kerrigan retreated to the county road which had been chosen as the last line of defense to the west. He was near exhaustion himself, calling his last reserve of strength to keep moving until he reached the road.

He flung himself down on the ground along with a score of soot-blackened fire fighters of all ages. It was barely past midnight. The fire had been raging for only three hours. It seemed more like an eternity.

But some semblance of order was coming out of the chaotic scene. The burn was confined to the vast rectangle in Grumheller's valley and had made no serious advance in over 40 minutes.

Townspeople from Wheatville were massed on the county road which faced the threat of fire on the west. The long south front beyond Skyrocket Hill was being defended by the Pleasant View crew, augmented by harvest hands from Joe-Ed Bainter's ranch.

The wind and vast reaches of summer fallow would protect the eastern end of the box. The greatest danger was now on the north, where Grumheller was marshaling the ever-growing flood of new help from the ranches north of Wheatville.

Cole Kerrigan, after a ten-minute rest, toiled back up the road in search of a barrel with water remaining in it. The tank wagons had sped back to Wheatville to refill. He felt a numb sense of amazement when he discovered that he had worked more than half a mile below the point where he had hitched his horse.

He mounted and headed back around the northwest corner of Grumheller's blazing fields, where the need for fighters seemed most acute at the moment.

A dim figure took shape through the smoke. It was Siegfried Grumheller himself, standing beside the canted cart which had smashed a wheel in a deep chuckhole. Grumheller was busy unharnessing a horse from the broken rig.

"Any idea how this fire started?" Kerrigan yelled.

Grumheller's beefy Teutonic face peered up at him like a mask in the dancing witch-glow of the conflagration which in a space of three hours had tumbled him from his throne as the richest wheatman in the county.

"*Ja,*" panted the rancher. "Dose *verdamdt* cowpoys from der Snake River did it, Kerrigan. Mine younkest poy Franz saw dese riders go like der blitz lightning alonk der north fence, draggink behind them mit der bick buntles uff burning sacks."

Kerrigan felt a keen sense of responsibility for tonight's disaster. As acting sheriff of the county, he was unofficially in charge of the fire patrol squads.

Giff Ogrum had outfoxed the county wheat growers tonight. They had expected fires to be set along the fields adjoining the cattle spreads to the south.

Instead, Ogrum had sent his firebugs deep into the hills, choosing this night when a strong wind would lend a hand to his fiendish designs.

"Mine Gott, Kerrigan," Grumheller said, swabbing his face with a charred sleeve. "Ven vill dis bloody feud ever end? Vill Giff Ogrum drive us all to ruin before ve lick him?"

Kerrigan had no answer to that one. This was the opening gun in the cattlemen's last all-out assault to wipe out the wheat harvest. This was what Giff Ogrum had in mind that fateful afternoon on the Rafter O when he had vowed to Sheriff McCaw that no rancher with a kernel of wheat in the ground would see his crop harvested.

But as the night dragged on, Kerrigan began to feel that the impossible had been accomplished, the miracle performed. By the time the east held its first pale promise of dawn, the legions of fire fighters, over a thousand strong, had ceased widening their mowed corridors through the adjoining fields.

The wind died as the sun came up over a black and smoking vista of wanton destruction. The baked-bread smell had given way to the odors of charred hay and fused earth.

Minor fires were gutting out the last remaining pockets of standing grain, but the fight, to all intents and purposes, was finished. The wheatmen had won, through sheer overpowering determination and refusal to admit defeat.

Cole Kerrigan viewed the blackened acres from the hill overlooking Grumheller's valley on the north. The roads back toward Wheatville were packed with wheeled traffic in the dawn's early light, as the ragged, exhausted, soot-covered fire fighters lurched homeward like refugees from a battle-ravaged land, their work done.

Anger and grief and an unspeakable sense of despair were mixed in Kerrigan's soul. This night of red horror might be repeated again tonight, tomorrow night, any night to come.

Grumheller could absorb the loss of a year's crop. But most of his neighbors faced bankruptcy if they shared a similar fate.

The one bright thing in Kerrigan's outlook was the fact that beyond the smoking black hillside of the Skyrocket, the lush golden acres of Pleasant View ranch still stood intact, their promise of a bumper harvest still unimpaired.

Kerrigan's clothes were charred and ripped to shreds. His face was black and his eyes red-rimmed like a burned-cork comedian's. But in his heart was the humming song of victory.

Cole Kerrigan reined his horse around and headed down to join the plodding mass of humanity streaming toward town. They deserved the accolade of heroes, every one of them.

CHAPTER
TWENTY-FOUR:
HARVEST

The last half of July dragged to a close. It was a period of tense waiting that aged men ahead of their time. Days and nights dragged endlessly, with armed guards patrolling the whispering wheat fields, anxious eyes strained over the land for sight of smoke or flame. A time when men ate, worked, and slept with their hands never far from gun triggers.

Cole Kerrigan gave up his work at the *Spectator,* devoting his full energies to carrying out the program of the late Sheriff McCaw. On Dixie Whipple's capable shoulders fell the responsibility for getting the paper out, assisted by Kerrigan's staff of back-country correspondents and volunteer reporters in the town itself.

Kerrigan fitted into his new role as Palouse County's only lawman without difficulty. Despite his brief residence in their midst, the lanky Texan commanded a personal popularity on a par with Scotty Mc-Caw's. Wheatmen co-operated willingly with Kerrigan's demands that their guard should not be relaxed for a moment.

But Kerrigan saw his tight rein of authority pay off. For the first time since Wheatville had taken root in the wheat belt, the cowboys from the Snake River cattle spreads stopped coming to town for their Saturday night sprees.

Cole Kerrigan had laid down a decree that every stranger, cowboys in particular, who crossed the wheat belt must surrender his guns to border-guards and submit to a careful search for the tools of arson — greasy rags, bottles of oil, chunks of phosphorus. Only by such stringent measures could the harvest be saved.

Kerrigan had expected Giff Ogrum's crew, at least, to resist the search order with gunplay. But instead, the cattle faction began seeking their weekly diversion in Starbuck or other small settlements across the river.

Either Giff Ogrum was biding his time to make a surprise attack on the unharvested wheat, following his failure to destroy more than Grumheller's acreage by fire, or else there was discord in the ranks of lesser cowmen in his faction, an unwillingness to press the feud to its conclusion.

Whatever the cause of the truce, Kerrigan was taking no chances. He personally scouted the surrounding ranches, making sure they did not relax their vigilance or draw off their 24-hour-a-day guard.

Giff Ogrum stopped coming to Wheatville completely. Every few days Big Yoom would ride into town on a buckboard to pick up the mail and buy provisions. Occasionally she was accompanied by Dave Beechey, the Rafter O foreman. But Giff Ogrum and his chief lieutenant, Mizzou Howerton of the Slash M-H Connected outfit, remained conspicuous by their absence.

As August brought the full heat of summer upon Washington Territory — days on end with the mercury pushing above 112 in the shade — a new spirit stirred and quickened the hearts of men through the wheat belt. Already, ran the grapevine rumors, ranchers in the Palouse and down in Walla Walla County were harvesting.

Cole Kerrigan, gaunt and haggard now from the strain of recent weeks, his deputy sheriff's star pinned to his shirt and his six-gun never off his hip from dawn to dark, caught the dramatic tension which was sweeping in crescendo over the golden hills. In times when he had a chance to relax and think, he recalled Rona Prescott's words: "There's nothing on earth quite like a Washington harvest."

There was a critically precise moment for harvesting to begin; when the last moisture had ebbed from the stems and leaves, and before the cooking summer sun could burn and shrivel the full-blown heads.

Daily, watchful wheatmen in a thousand fields broke a ripening head from the stalks, ground out the fat yellow kernels with thumbs rotating like pestles in the leathery cups of their palms; blew out the chaff and sampled the plump ripe wheat expertly between their teeth.

And then it came.

Cole Kerrigan awoke on the morning of August ninth without knowing this day climaxed the year's work. The sky was cloudless, enamel-blue, the sun like a copper rivet. The land was alive to the dry rustle of fully ripened, head-high wheat. It was a spectacle to enrapture the most indifferent onlooker.

Case threshing engines, like locomotives magically divorced from their confining tracks, puffed out to harvest sites where headers and binders were whirring through the standing bulwark of gold, their wheeling blades bending the headed stalks against sickling cutter bars, fat sheaves thumping at ordered intervals onto the bristling stubble in their wakes.

Then followed pick-up wagons, with sweating harvest hands loading the sheaves and taking them to the shiny separators, connected to the shuddering steam engines by long, wide canvas belts crisscrossed in figure-eight fashion.

Dust and chaff belched from the long galvanized spouts, starting haystacks which quickly grew to house-sized proportions. Brown two-bushel bags of wheat disgorged from the separators to be stacked on sturdy wagons.

Fifty sacks to a load, the ponderous vehicles began their creaking exodus toward the lodestone of Wheatville. Sixteen-horse teams drew their heavy burdens over the crisscrossing roads which converged like spokes of a wheel to the common hub of warehouses and elevator which spanned the railroad yards of the wheat town.

Wheatville bustled with unaccustomed activity. Lines of loaded wagons were drawn up a half mile in length, awaiting their turn to reach the unloading platforms.

Each team's lead horses wore inverted U-shaped straps across their hames, with three-inch brass bells riveted thereto. The melodic jingling warned returning trains of empty wagons of approaching traffic through the blinding dust.

Soon the spreading leagues of Palouse County became stippled with the mammoth beehives of haystacks as the threshing rigs moved on to follow the binders, pausing two or three days at a site.

The harvest crews ate in shifts, in the open air near ugly square cookhouses mounted on wagon beds. Cooks toiled over hot ranges, inside screened windows with lifted wooden or canvas awnings which bore no resemblance whatever to the chuck wagons of the Texas ranges that Cole Kerrigan knew.

Each threshing outfit was a separate area of bustling confusion. Smoke drifted from the screened stacks of Case engines, their hungry grates fed by stokers who forked dry straw into the fireboxes.

When threshing occurred near home ranches, zealous housewives vied with each other in seeing who could set the most tempting tables.

For Kerrigan, the big thrill came when harvesting moved into Eureka Flat ten days later.

His job gave him a mobility which was denied to ranchers preoccupied with their own work, so he was one of the few outsiders to see the new combine harvester whir its way back and forth across the level acres of Pleasant View, cutting and threshing and sacking the golden grain in a single operation.

A novice though he was to the intricacies of threshing, Cole Kerrigan saw that the combine would revolutionize harvesting methods in Washington, as it was doing in the Dakotas.

Wagons followed the miracle machine, catching each sack as it was deftly bound with twine by the skilled needle of the sack-sewer, seated on his platform under the elevator spout.

High on his perch at the end of the front boom, Veryl Lasater — and even Rona Prescott on occasion — managed the 32-horse team, guiding the complicated mechanical monster expertly along the edge of the standing grain, its great mower cutting a 20-foot swath and conveying the cut stems on an endless canvas belt into the innards of the thresher.

On the steep hillsides rimming Eureka Flat, especially the dimpled area on the north face of Skyrocket Hill, known as the "hole in the wall," the combine met the threat of capsizement and surrendered the harvesting task to binders and steam-driven separators, following the conventional methods of the neighboring ranchers.

In general, however, Rona Prescott had won her gamble. The combine had more than paid for itself.

Then, in the space of two brief, exciting weeks of noise and industry, the harvest was finished.

Wheatville's warehouses were bursting with grain. Ranchers had vast piles of sacked wheat spotted at strategic points across the county, awaiting haulage to railhead.

The land itself had a ludicrous, naked appearance; the golden fields close-shaven now, with ordered rows of stubble browning under the sun, and everywhere the mountainous stacks of straw which would be used as winter fodder for the stock.

Gone was the soporific whispering of the standing grain, missed now in its absence. A deep, vast, contented silence settled over the fertile hills.

The tang of fall would soon crisp the air. Ranchers were already turning their thoughts to fall plowing and disking and harrowing, new seeding on ground which had lain fallow during the past year.

There was activity springing up on the cattle ranches bordering the Snake, and out in the vast Columbia Basin also. Autumn beef gathers were in the offing; the loading chutes at Wheatville and other railroad towns would soon be busy.

Wheatmen began to relax after the long strain of the summer, believing that Giff Ogrum and his ilk were too busy with their own interests to continue their feud.

A growing belief spread through Palouse County that the feud had burned itself out; that the bumper harvest, averaging 33 bushels to the acre, marked a smashing victory over the lawless element that had so long threatened them.

But Cole Kerrigan, without a financial stake in the wheat harvest, was not lulled into a false sense of security by the continued absence of the cowboys from Wheatville.

Kerrigan believed that the showdown still faced the wheatmen.

Advertisements in the *Spectator* and circulars dispatched to rural mail boxes summoned members of the Wheat Growers' Association to a mass meeting in the Grange Hall at Wheatville, to be held the last Saturday night in August.

Wheatville was a busy place when the appointed day arrived, with a heavy turnout of farmers.

Rona Prescott's crew was busy in the warehouses loading sacked wheat into a long string of boxcars drawn up on the Y & E siding, with a locomotive standing by to haul the first of the season's crop to flouring mills in Walla Walla.

Rona Prescott was in the audience at the Grange Hall, with Cole Kerrigan seated with her and Joe-Ed Bainter. The meeting was called to order by Sieg Grumheller, who called Kerrigan to the platform.

The hall resounded to an ovation as Kerrigan mounted the steps. He could count every man and woman in the hall as a friend and neighbor. Most of them he knew by their first names; all of them by their faces.

"Men," the deputy sheriff said when the applause had died down, "it appears that your long fight has been won. Your harvest, with the single exception of Mr. Grumheller's, is safely garnered in. But we must not underestimate the caliber of our enemy. Giff Ogrum can yet fulfill his vow to ruin each and every one of you in this hall tonight."

A hum of voices filled the room, subsided, anxious faces waiting.

"You've got all your eggs in one basket," Kerrigan went on. "I refer to the granaries and elevator here in town. Thousands of tons of wheat, sacked and waiting for shipment to the mills, would burn like ricked cordwood."

The expressions on the faces before him told Kerrigan that his warning had struck home, that the potentiality of disaster at this stage of the game had not occurred to most of his listeners.

"As acting sheriff of Palouse County," Kerrigan went on, "I am calling upon each one of you to furnish a guard according to the size of your crews, to be stationed here in Wheatville to protect the warehouses until the last sack of wheat is on its way to market."

Bluff old Joe-Ed Bainter rose from his seat. Next to Sieg Grumheller, he was the senior wheatman present, and his opinions carried weight.

"Kerrigan's talking horse sense, men," the rancher said gravely. "This afternoon I seen a big string of buckaroos ridin' down the Skyrocket Road, a good share of 'em forkin' Rafter O hosses. Maybe they're comin' to town to cut the dust out of their craws at the Last Chance bar. Or maybe they got other things on their mind. I'm in favor —"

Across the night came a sudden clamor of yells, a spate of gunfire. Men leaped to their feet, faces bonewhite in the glare of lamps.

And then the rear doors of the Grange Hall, propped open for ventilation, megaphoned to their ears a swift drumroll of footsteps crossing the street and mounting the hall steps.

Old Dixie Whipple burst down the aisle, clad in his work apron, his hands grimy with printer's ink.

"The elevator's been set afire!" yelled the printer. "An' Ogrum's cowboys are shootin' at the Prescott crew over at the loading yards. It looks like they're fixin' to fire the warehouses!"

CHAPTER
TWENTY-FIVE:
BETRAYAL

The audience froze in paralyzed tableau for a dozen seconds after Dixie Whipple made his announcement. Then there was a stampede for the doors.

Cole Kerrigan followed Grumheller out a side door leading off the speakers' platform. A cold sense of despair numbed the Texan as he headed out into the night, six-gun in hand.

The lofty roof of the Association's grain elevator was erupting smoke like a gigantic chimney. And along the warehouses flanking the Yakima & Eastern siding, catastrophe was in the making.

Judging from the roar of gunfire beyond the warehouses, Giff Ogrum's longriders had descended on Wheatville for a final, climactic showdown in the range feud.

Red banners of flame were spouting from the 50-foot tower of the grain elevator now. The malevolent red glare guided Kerrigan through the night.

He reached the railroad to see that Rona Prescott's ranch hands, who had been trundling hand-trucks laden with sacked wheat from the warehouse into the waiting boxcars, had been driven inside the buildings by a concentrated fire coming from the open fields across the tracks.

Kerrigan halted in front of the panting locomotive which was coupled to the freight train, in readiness to haul the first wheat of the season to Walla Walla flour mills.

As he moved down past the big drive wheels, Kerrigan saw that the engine cab was deserted. The fireman and hoghead had taken refuge inside the warehouses.

Kerrigan groaned. His intention had been to order the partially loaded wheat train to pull out of town, thus saving its cargo if Ogrum's night raiders succeeded in firing the warehouses. With the locomotive deserted, the long string of open boxcars would be at the mercy of the attackers.

Rona Prescott had wheat worth around $80,000 at stake, and other ranchers in proportion. Ogrum stood to win his victory and bankrupt Palouse County inside the next few minutes.

The gunfire had died off. Indistinct in the night, vaguely illuminated by the glare of flames which were gutting the Association elevator a block away, riders were dismounting alongside the freight train, ducking between couplings or crawling under the cars.

Kerrigan knew their purpose. The warehouse floors were four feet off the ground, supported by a forest of foundation timbers. Fires set in the weeds and rubbish under the warehouse could gain headway quickly and threaten the entire length of the railroad granaries with destruction.

A clamor of sound behind him reminded Kerrigan of the embattled farmers who were rushing toward the freight yards from the Association meeting.

He ran back down the tracks, waving his arms to hold back the advancing crowd as he saw Siegfried Grumheller leading them into the white glare of the locomotive head lamp.

The mob of overalled ranchmen and townspeople halted as the deputy sheriff met them at the Main Street crossing.

"We've got to work fast," Kerrigan yelled. "The main job will be to fight fire under the warehouses. Every man who's carrying a gun will come with me."

Only a dozen men in the group of a hundred-odd stepped forward with revolvers or rifles. The others milled restlessly in the background, their eyes on the smoke-vomiting elevator.

"Ve can't safe der elewator!" Grumheller yelled, reading the cause of their indecision. "Ve got to concentrate on der warehouses, *ja*. Bring vasser barrels und shoffels und sack —"

The crowd broke, scattering in a dozen directions to carry out the German's orders.

Kerrigan and his pitiful handful of armed ranchers headed back to the warehouses. Flames were already guttering at a dozen points under the elevated floor of the granaries.

The attackers had laid their plans well. Riding down from the south hill under cover of darkness, their first job had been to fire the interior of the elevator, as a diversion to draw the town's attention away from the warehouses. Then their fusillade of shots had forced the Pleasant View crew to leave the boxcars and seek the shelter of the warehouses.

Now, equipped with oil-soaked sacks, cans of kerosene, and other inflammable materials, Giff Ogrum's firebugs were igniting their incendiary substances along the entire length of the warehouses.

As Kerrigan ducked between the warehouse and the standing train, he saw the night raiders scuttling out from under the warehouses and crawling lizardlike across the cinder-ballasted roadbed under the boxcars, making for their horses.

The Texan triggered his six-gun down the line of boxcar wheels, then shouted for the armed ranchers behind him to circle in front of the locomotive and open fire on the riders as they made their getaway.

He crawled under the first boxcar behind the engine tender in time to see the raiders vault into saddles and spur toward the stubble fields which sloped above the town to the south.

Covering their retreat with a sprinkle of shots, the riders were moving fast in get-away, already beyond the range of most of the wild-shooting wheatmen who were running past the locomotive in pursuit.

Kerrigan saw one horse go down, hit by a lucky shot at extreme range. The rider somersaulted from saddle and crashed into the dirt, firelight playing on the cloud of dust flung out by his skidding form.

Holding his fire, Cole Kerrigan sprinted toward the unhorsed outlaw, saw the man struggle to his feet, then sag to the ground as a broken leg gave way under his weight. Kerrigan thumbed a warning shot into the weeds near the crippled man as he ran up.

The fallen outlaw drew a gun as Kerrigan approached, the guttering firelight flashing off drawn steel. He was attempting to drag himself toward a near-by section gang shack, pulling his fractured leg behind him like a wounded animal in a trap.

Seeing that resistance was useless, the outlaw tossed his six-gun aside as Kerrigan slogged up, his .45 ready. As the Texas deputy came to a halt, he saw that the rider was wearing a bandanna mask.

"Don't shoot — Kerrigan," panted the injured man. "I got a bellyful of this business nohow. I don't aim to stop a slug while I'm — doin' Giff Ogrum's dirty work."

The pain-racked voice was familiar. Kerrigan reached down to jerk off the mask. He revealed the harsh, sweat-slick face of Mizzou Howerton, owner of the Slash M-H Connected spread which adjoined the Rafter O.

Howerton writhed in pain as Kerrigan stooped to pull a second Colt from the cattleman's holster. He was clutching a chap-encased leg, which had suffered a compound fracture below the knee as a result of his spill from the slain horse.

"Was Ogrum with your bunch tonight, Howerton?"

Howerton shook his head, gritting his teeth in agony.

"Ogrum's over at his ranch, waitin' to see how this raid turns out. He's got another ace up his sleeve, Kerrigan. He — he always sends his tilikums out on jobs — where we might run into — gunplay. Ambush — is Ogrum's game —"

Kerrigan twisted his head to see how things were going over at the warehouse. Wheatville had turned out in force to battle the flames which threatened the wheat harvest, and from this distance Kerrigan believed they had better than an even chance to save the granaries.

"Ambush is Ogrum's game?" Kerrigan echoed Howerton's remark. "Such as what?"

"Such as murderin' Gov'nor Prescott two year ago," blurted Howerton. "So far as I'm concerned, from here on out Ogrum can go to hell by hisself. I'm through."

Kerrigan leaned forward, studying Howerton's sweat-polished face for some hint of treachery. If Howerton was ready to betray his chief, then the thing had happened which Sheriff Scotty McCaw had not lived to see — a witness with proof which could hold in a court of law, proof that would put a hangrope around Giff Ogrum's neck.

"Listen, Howerton. I've caught you red-handed. You're under arrest, you know that. But you could cut years off your sentence if you decided to talk. Would you swear before a jury that Ogrum bushwhacked Governor Prescott?"

Pain caused Howerton to retch. When the spell of nausea had passed, Howerton whispered hoarsely, "You're gawd-damn right I'd swear to it," he panted. "Me an' my oldest boy Norman was with Ogrum when he done it. I — I been after Ogrum all summer to call off this feud. Look where it got me. It was Ogrum who shot Scotty McCaw, too."

Kerrigan got to his feet.

"I'll send Doc Strang over here to splint your busted shin," he said.

"Listen, Kerrigan," the rancher wheezed. "I'm li'ble to pass out any minute, an' you got to listen to what I got to say. You ride over to the Rafter O an' dab your loop on Giff Ogrum before he leaves for the Snake River railroad bridge. That'll be around midnight. He aims to blow up that bridge, Kerrigan. You know what that'll mean to the wheat growers."

The Texan stared at Mizzou Howerton, struck aghast by his words. The bridge which carried the railroad across the Snake into Walla Walla County was the weak link in Palouse County's armor. It was a vital artery, carrying the very lifeblood of the wheat business; for if the Yakima & Eastern lifeline were severed, it would mean Palouse County farmers would be unable to ship their grain to market until the bridge was repaired, which might be a matter of months. The unballasted tracks which led to Spokane would never stand up under the burden of wheat-loaded freight trains.

"What do you mean, Howerton?" Kerrigan asked sharply.

"It's like this," he panted hoarsely. "Ogrum had Dave Beechey plant a couple barrels o' blastin' powder in the stringers under the railroad bridge yesterday afternoon. He figgered if tonight's raid didn't burn down the warehouses an' elevator, then he'd play his ace in the hole an' wreck the railroad bridge. He — he knows Rona Prescott's train is due to pull out sometime after midnight. Ogrum aims to dump that train — into the river."

Kerrigan turned to leave again, but Howerton gasped out, "You get Ogrum in jail, Kerrigan, an' you've busted the back of the cattle combine. He's the only man who was holdin' us together. The rest of us have been ready to bury the hatchet ever since Rip

Hoffman got killed."

Kerrigan hitched his gun belt grimly.

"I'll send a medico over to take care of you," he said. "I won't forget what you told me, Howerton."

But the injured rancher had sagged back in a cold faint.

Kerrigan headed back toward the warehouses. An army of fire fighters — Wheatville citizens and visiting ranchers — were swarming under the warehouses, sloshing water on charred timbers, shoveling dirt on burning weeds.

He saw Rona Prescott heading for the warehouse with two buckets of water, silhouetted against the raging flames which had transformed the Association elevator into a geyser of fire. The girl set her buckets down as Kerrigan approached.

"Mizzou Howerton's lying over by the shack where the section gang keeps its handcar, Rona," Kerrigan said. "Send Doc Strang over there, will you? And you might get Grumheller or somebody to ride herd on Howerton till I get back. He's my prisoner."

The girl gripped his arm, eyes wide with alarm.

"Get back?" she repeated. "Where are you going, Editor?"

"Over to the Rafter O to arrest Giff Ogrum. Howerton's in a mood to spill all he knows about Ogrum's crimes. We've finally got what it takes to send Ogrum to the gallows, Rona."

He checked an impulse to tell her that Howerton had cleared up the two-year-old mystery of her father's murder. There would be time enough for that later.

"You'll be careful, Editor?" She moved closer to him. "I — I couldn't bear it if anything happened to you —"

The Texan's face softened in the glare of firelight.

"The same goes for me, Rona. I — I reckon I've been in love with you for a long time."

He left her then, heading for the Black Stallion stable at a run. His was a race against time, if he were to reach the Rafter O before Ogrum's raiders returned with their report on what appeared to be the utter failure to destroy the Wheatville warehouses.

A few minutes later Kerrigan was riding out of Wheatville, headed along the Skyrocket road which led to the Rafter O and a long-delayed showdown with its owner.

CHAPTER
TWENTY-SIX:
JAILED

The windows of Giff Ogrum's ranch house were yellow squares in the midnight blackness when Cole Kerrigan reined up on the timbered knoll overlooking the Snake River ranch.

He wet a thumb and verified the direction of the night wind. Ogrum's watch dogs would betray his approach if they caught his scent. A dank, muddy smell was coming from the river bed.

The deputy sheriff hitched his mount to a scrub willow and headed down the slope past Ogrum's hog pens and chicken yard, mentally reconstructing the lay of the land from the memory of his past visit with the ill-fated Scotty McCaw.

He had reached the Rafter O in time. Horsemen were even now climbing into stirrups at Ogrum's front gate, heading for the bunkhouse and corrals.

Those riders, Kerrigan knew, were the fire

raiders who had attacked the Wheatville warehouses. Their delay in returning to the home ranch had probably been due to having halted on the hills overlooking the town, to watch the progress of the fires they had set under the warehouses.

By now, then, Ogrum knew that his attempt to destroy the harvested grain had met with failure, except for the 100,000 bushels belonging to Joe-Ed Bainter which had been stored in the Association elevator.

Dave Beechey's voice wafted across the night as Kerrigan reached the back yard of the ranch house.

"I don't reckon the Prescott train will pull out much before daylight, Giff. You got plenty of time."

Kerrigan scowled, fingers tightening on the cedar stock of his Peacemaker.

If Mizzou Howerton's tip-off was true — and Kerrigan had every reason to believe that the rancher was thirsting for revenge against the outlaw chief who had dragged him to ruin — then Beechey was referring to the barrels of explosive planted under the Snake River bridge.

Kerrigan moved up to the back door of the ranch house as the Rafter O foreman closed the front gate and mounted, ready to head for the horse corral.

He heard the screen door slam as Ogrum went back into the house. Ogrum had a saddle horse waiting at the front gate. He was making ready, then, to ride over to the Snake River bridge and wait for the arrival of the Prescott wheat train.

Kerrigan tried the latch of the rear door, found it open. He slipped into a room which, judging from its mingled smells of garlic and stale grease and wood smoke, was Big Yoom's kitchen.

Voices in the front of the house guided Kerrigan through a darkened hallway toward a door, ajar to admit a shaft of lampshine into the corridor.

Giff Ogrum was speaking in the Umatilla tongue to his squaw. Kerrigan reached for the doorknob with his left hand, jerked the door wide, then stalked across the threshold with his six-gun jutting from hip level.

He had surprised Ogrum in the act of hauling on a brush-popper jumper. His portly squaw was stoking a barrel stove with a chunk of locust wood.

"Hold it as you are, Ogrum. You're under arrest."

Kerrigan moved out into the room as he spoke, his gun swinging to cover Big Yoom, who had whirled her great bulk of flesh like a mastodon about to charge.

Ogrum remained frozen, his arms caught halfway through his sleeves, his green eyes flecked with the same yellow glints Kerrigan remembered seeing when they had been matched in a street brawl months ago.

"Under arrest?" Ogrum found his voice with an effort. He fell back a step as Kerrigan rounded the table in the center of the room and reached out to lift the cowman's big six-shooter from its holster. "You got nothing on me, Kerrigan."

The Texan thrust Ogrum's gun into the waistband of his Levis and sidled over to where Big Yoom stood, a great shapeless mountain of fat in her loose-fitting flour-sack dress.

He removed a butcher knife from a sheath hanging from a rawhide thong about her neck, then turned back to Giff Ogrum.

"Pull on that jumper and hold your arms out, wrists together," ordered Kerrigan, reaching in a hip pocket for the shiny handcuffs which had belonged to Scotty McCaw. "You're coming back to Wheatville with me."

Big Yoom looked on, her coppery face inscrutable, beady eyes half-buried in greasy folds of skin as she saw Ogrum shrug his fists through the sleeves of the denim jumper and hold out his arms.

McCaw's fetters clicked around the rancher's hairy wrists, and it seemed to Kerrigan in that moment that the old Indian fighter's spirit stood by his elbow. He had heard Scotty McCaw voice the dream on many an occasion that his handcuffs would one day bring Gifford Ogrum to justice.

Ogrum's face had gone gray, muscles twitching in his cheeks as the first reaction of fear dawned in his gooseberry eyes.

"Big Yoom," Kerrigan said, turning to the Indian woman, "I'm not tying you up. But I'm warning you not to unlimber that deer rifle of yours as we're leaving. Don't attempt to follow us. If you send anybody on our trail you're as good as putting a bullet into your husband's brisket. Understand?"

The Umatilla squaw stared at him stolidly, her flinty eyes registering no sign of comprehension.

"She don't speak English," Ogrum grunted. "I'll tell her."

The cowman spoke swiftly to the squaw in the guttural jargon of her tribe. She acknowledged her man's words with a porcine grunt.

"Your horse is waiting outside," Kerrigan said briskly. "Let's get started."

Kerrigan kept his eye on Big Yoom as Giff Ogrum stalked to the front door. But the

Umatilla woman had not moved from her tracks.

Five minutes later Kerrigan and his prisoner were northbound over the sage flats, with the hackamore of Ogrum's horse dallied to Kerrigan's saddle horn.

Playing it safe, Kerrigan had looped a *reata* around the cattleman's neck.

At the edge of the wheat fields, Kerrigan reined to a halt to let their horses blow. Twisting in saddle, he thought he saw a movement on the sky line behind them, a blot crossing the stars and dipping below the rocky teeth of a ridge.

Big Yoom, most likely, trailing her mate. She was probably carrying a rifle. But no horse could hope to overtake them now, burdened with the squaw's 300 pounds.

They slanted off across the starlit stubble fields, steering for the crimson glow across the hills which marked the blazing ruins of the Wheatville elevator.

CHAPTER
TWENTY-SEVEN:
DISASTER

The courthouse clock was striking four when Kerrigan arrived in Wheatville with his prisoner. Ogrum had made the trip in stolid silence, stunned by the turn of events.

Kerrigan noted, with relief, that the fires were out under the warehouses, their black outlines still intact against the red glow of the smoldering wreckage which had been the elevator.

They dismounted in front of the jail, which formed a rear addition to the court-house. Kerrigan removed the lass'-rope from Ogrum's neck and ushered him into Scotty McCaw's office.

Kerrigan lighted the desk lamp, keeping his gun trained on the cattleman, alert for treachery. From a desk drawer he took out McCaw's key ring, unlocked the iron door leading to the cell block, and motioned his prisoner inside.

Once more Kerrigan felt the presence of Scotty McCaw in the jail room as he locked the iron-barred door of a cell cage on Giff Ogrum. McCaw had dreamed for two years of this moment.

Ogrum thrust his wrists between the bars and Kerrigan removed the handcuffs. Then, for the first time, he sprung his bad news on the Rafter O boss.

"I'm bringing Mizzou Howerton over to have a chat with you, Ogrum. Mizzou was with you the day you ambushed Governor Prescott, remember?"

Ogrum's knuckles whitened on the iron bars. Raw fear replaced the defiance in his eyes. The news of his confederate's betrayal seemed to drain the fight from the big rancher.

"Howerton's a liar!" gruffed the Rafter O outlaw. "You won't get anywhere tryin' to prove that."

Kerrigan turned on his heel, locked the cell block door behind him, and thrust the keys into his pocket.

He left the two saddle horses ground-hitched in front of the jail and headed across the courthouse yard toward the main street.

A row of lanterns illuminated the platform of the grain warehouses, and Rona Prescott's workmen were busy finishing their job of loading the boxcars with sacked wheat.

Kerrigan headed over to the locomotive, relieved to find the engineer busy with an oil can, lubricating his drive rods. "When's this train going to pull out?" the deputy asked.

The engineer squinted down the row of boxcars.

"Around daylight, I reckon."

"Well, hold everything," he ordered the hoghead. "We've got to remove some explosives that have been planted somewhere along the Snake River bridge before it'll be safe for you to cross. I'll ride out with you when the time comes."

The engineer stared at Kerrigan.

"Just as you say, Sheriff. But I think somebody's already gone over to the bridge to inspect it."

Kerrigan crossed the main street and knocked on the door of Doctor Strang's house, next to the bank building.

The grizzled frontier physician admitted him into a room where Mizzou Howerton was reclining on a cot, his leg splinted and bandaged from crotch to ankle. The doctor returned to a workbench where he was mixing up a batch of plaster of Paris.

"I've got Ogrum locked up over in the jailhouse," Kerrigan informed the rancher. "Do you feel ready for a showdown with him?"

Howerton took a drag on a wheatstraw cigarette. His face was deep-lined with suffering, but raw hate still burned fiercely in his eyes.

"Bring on that squawman!" he said harshly. "If Giff had listened to me back in July, we wouldn't be in this mess now."

Doctor Strang looked up from his work.

"You'll have to fetch Ogrum over here, Kerrigan. Howerton is in no shape to move. He suffered a compound comminuted fracture of both the fibula and tibia. He'll have to wear a cast for weeks. Couldn't you postpone this interview?"

Kerrigan frowned. He felt that the situation called for quick action, before Mizzou Howerton's pain subsided and he had a chance to change his mind about bearing witness against his former chieftain.

"I'll bring Ogrum over here," Kerrigan decided. "I'll want you to witness what goes on, Doc. Okay?"

The medical man shrugged.

"It won't hurt my patient to talk," he said. "I understand your position, Kerrigan."

On his way back to the courthouse square, the Texan was startled to see a cattle train drawing into town from the east. The train

298

halted 50 yards from the smoldering wreckage of the grain elevator, while a brakeman went ahead to make sure the train could safely pass the smoking tower.

Kerrigan headed for the station at a run. He met the agent, Ed Chellis, returning from a conference with the engineer of the cattle train. Even as Kerrigan confronted Chellis, a bell clanged and the train, loaded with bawling cattle, started moving past the elevator.

"Stop that train, Ed!" the deputy shouted. "No traffic can cross the Snake until I've had a chance to —"

Chellis waved him off.

"We heard what Howerton said about dynamite bein' planted under the trestle," the stationmaster said. "But this cow train is headed for Pasco. It turns off at the junction this side of the bridge."

Kerrigan relaxed, cheeks ballooning with relief as he saw the red and green lights on the end of the caboose glide off down the tracks.

As he was turning to head for the jail, Chellis called him. "Dixie Whipple was lookin' all over for you, Kerrigan. Seems a stranger got off the seven-forty from Spokane tonight, and he wanted to see you."

Kerrigan shrugged.

"I'll see him later," the Texan responded. "If you see Dixie, tell him I'll be at Doc Strang's office."

Arriving back at the courthouse, Kerrigan was startled to observe that the door of the sheriff's office was standing open, sending a bar of lamplight out onto the yard. He had a vague recollection of having closed the door when he left.

Then the Texan halted stockstill on the threshold, staring at the wide-open door of the cell block. He was positive he had locked that door —

A premonition of disaster gripped Kerrigan as he snatched the lamp off McCaw's desk and leaped into the cell block. Ogrum's cell was empty, its iron-latticed door yawning wide. And a ring heavy with jail keys hung from the massive lock.

Kerrigan slapped a hand instinctively to his pocket. His ring of keys was still there.

Kerrigan whirled, carrying the lamp to the front door of the office. Its pale circle of light picked out two sets of fresh footprints leading away down the sandy path, trampled by the deep-heeled imprints of his own arrival a moment before.

Both tracks had been made by cowboots, with the telltale scratch of dragging spur rowels making little furrows in the dust.

Kerrigan knew the answer then, the appalling truth behind Giff Ogrum's jailbreak.

Big Yoom had sent a Rafter O cowboy on their trail tonight. And that cowboy had carried with him a ring of keys taken from the pocket of Sheriff Scotty McCaw when the sheriff had been dry-gulched weeks ago.

Kerrigan had not considered the existence of a duplicate set of jail keys when he had taken over McCaw's duties. He knew now what Giff Ogrum had said to Big Yoom in the Umatilla jargon over at the Rafter O tonight. He had told the squaw to get the keys to the Wheatville county jail.

Dawn was breaking as Kerrigan headed down the path, the red light revealing where Ogrum and his rescuer had cut across the courthouse yard in the direction of the railroad tracks. He followed the trail between two warehouses, saw it end beyond the wheat train, at the edge of the main line.

"Ogrum hopped that cattle train when it stopped in town — he's heading for Pasco —"

CHAPTER
TWENTY-EIGHT:
PURSUIT

Moving like a man in a nightmare, Cole Kerrigan climbed up onto the warehouse platform. Someone called his name and he turned to see Veryl Lasater, gaunt from a hard night's work, emerging from a wheat car.

"You heard about Rona's latest, Editor?"

Kerrigan shook his head. "I've been busy all night," he grunted. "What's she up to now?"

Lasater handed his manifest sheets to a helper who had just finished sealing the boxcar door. The Pleasant View foreman looked grave as he walked over to the Texan. "Howerton told you about Ogrum's scheme to wreck the bridge when this train showed up?"

"Yes."

"Well, Rona got the news from Howerton too. She said you would keep Ogrum from touching off his fuses, but that Dave

Beechey or somebody might do the job."

"I've thought of that. We'll stop this train short of the bridge and make sure it's safe. What has Rona done?"

Lasater regarded him quizzically. "Rona's gone out to the river. Her and Grumheller and Joe-Ed Bainter and old Dixie Whipple and another feller."

The locomotive engineer came up behind Lasater, tugging on a pair of buckskin gauntlets. He found Cole Kerrigan staring at Lasater in dismay.

A stunning thought had just occurred to Kerrigan. Giff Ogrum and one of his gunmen were heading westward on the cattle train, even now. What if the train halted at the junction switch this side of the bridge leading to Walla Walla? In that event, Ogrum might surprise Rona Prescott and her party searching the trestlework for the barrels of explosive Mizzou Howerton claimed had been secreted there.

"We're loaded and ready to roll," the engineer broke into Kerrigan's thoughts. "You said you wanted to go with us —"

The Texan stared at Veryl Lasater.

"Why did you let her go?" he demanded.

Lasater shrugged. "Who am I to give Rona Prescott orders? I had to see that this train got loaded. Rona knew what it would mean to the wheat growers if Ogrum managed to knock out that bridge. It's the only way we'd have of shipping our wheat out of the county, outside of wagons. By the time the bridge was repaired, wheat would be down to two bits a bushel."

Kerrigan turned to the jumper-clad engineer.

"How long will it take that cattle train to reach the Pasco junction?"

"It's prob'ly there by now."

"Will it have to make a stop this side of the bridge?"

"Most likely," the engineer said. "The main line runs to Walla Walla. The Pasco switch would most likely be red."

Kerrigan seized the engineer's arm.

"Giff Ogrum is riding that cattle train," he said. "He's liable to catch Rona and the others flat-footed. You've got to run me out there on your engine."

The hoghead started to protest about regulations, but Kerrigan was propelling him bodily down the platform.

"You can tell your division superintendent that a deputy sheriff commandeered your engine," he said.

A brakeman uncoupled the locomotive from the wheat train as Kerrigan and the engineer swung into the cab. The fireman dozed at his seat.

"It'll take around thirty-five minutes to make the run over to the bridge," the engineer panted, throwing his Johnson bar out of neutral. "No matter how we pour on the steam, I can't catch that cattle train."

Drivers shed sparks from protesting rails. The engineer had the old six-wheeler at wide-open throttle by the time they passed the smoldering elevator.

Kerrigan leaned from the grab rails between cab and tender, saw Wheatville rush from view around a wide curve of track. Stubble fields were a blur in the morning sunlight as the locomotive hurtled down the arrow-straight tracks at better than a mile a minute, black smoke pouring from its funnel stack as the fireman stoked his grates.

This was a grim race against time. More than the marketing of Palouse County's harvest depended on the outcome of it. If Ogrum trapped Rona Prescott and the men with her somewhere out on the long trestle —

Kerrigan grabbed up a scoop to help the fireman shovel coal onto the grates. A white plume tore from the whistle as they sighted a grade crossing a half mile down the tracks, blocked by a plodding line of grain wagons bound for Wheatville.

Teamsters had the track cleared by the time the locomotive hurtled past, giving Kerrigan a brief glimpse of cursing drivers whipsawing their lines to keep boogered teams from breaking out of the harness.

Ten, twenty, twenty-five minutes dragged by, with an equal number of miles flung back by the rocketing locomotive.

The cattle train for Pasco was nowhere to be seen up the line, but a feather of smoke smudged the western horizon, proving that the westbound freight had reached the junction and was now highballing down the river toward Pasco.

Then, far in the distance at the end of the converging V of steel, Kerrigan sighted the green line of the Snake River and the sheen of metal where a cantilever span crossed the main channel, sandwiched between long wooden trestles.

Kerrigan stopped his coal shoveling and yelled an order to the engineer. The hoghead eased off the throttle and laid a gloved hand on the brass lever controlling his brakes. For three miles the engine coasted, wheeling at dizzy speed over the rail joints.

Leaning from the cab door, Cole Kerrigan spotted the red disk of the Pasco junction switch at the mouth of a cut which hid the Snake River bridge from view at this angle.

His yell was a soundless lip movement to the engineer, but the trainman savvied the Texan's gestures.

Brake shoes bit into spinning drivers. The Iron Horse lurched, checked speed, was finally curbed to a panting halt a dozen yards after it rattled over the switch frogs.

The boiler was gasping like an exhausted animal as Cole Kerrigan swung down to the ground, six-gun palmed. He was moving up between the outbanks when his ear caught the whicker of a horse, off to the north.

Then he saw a trampled line of hoof-marks, where horses had been led off the right of way toward a motte of brush which screened the mouth of a coulee.

Kerrigan paused, breathing like a grounded fish. Then he left the roadbed and followed the line of hoofprints over to the fringe of dwarf cottonwoods. Through the jungle of foliage he sighted a group of horses hitched out of sight of the railroad.

He recognized Rona's calico pony, the dun which Dixie Whipple rented from the Wheatville livery, Sieg Grumheller's leggy Arabian, and Joe-Ed Bainter's lineback dun. There was a fifth saddler, bearing the livery barn's iron. That mount belonged to the stranger who had arrived on the seven-forty last night, probably —

Kerrigan pushed on by the horses, following a line of boot tracks which led into the brush-choked draw. Colt .45 ready, Kerrigan stalked along the fresh tracks, topped a rise and found himself looking down into a coulee which led to the riverbank.

A disconsolate group was huddled in the pit of the gully, their backs to Kerrigan. He recognized Dixie Whipple's onion-bald head, Rona Prescott by her white Stetson. His eyes flicked over to the right.

Dave Beechey, the hawk-nosed ramrod of the Rafter O, was squatted on a ledge of hard clay, covering the group with a .30-30.

Beechey, then, had been the rider Big Yoom had sent to Wheatville to spring Giff Ogrum from the county jail. From the spot where he stood on guard, Beechey could not see Kerrigan's head and shoulders topping the rim of the draw. The Texan faded back, crouched, and crawled on all fours toward the outbank immediately over the spot where Beechey squatted.

He inched his way toward the brink with infinite caution, opening his mouth so his breathing would not reach Beechey's ears. The slightest sound would betray him to the Rafter O foreman, might imperil the lives of Rona Prescott and the men with her.

He was thankful that the prisoners had their backs to him. If Beechey caught a telltale recognition crossing their faces —

Kerrigan drew up his knees, peered over the edge of the draw. Beechey was directly below him, the Winchester balanced across his knees while he shook tobacco into a thin husk, preparing to twist a cigarette.

Kerrigan jumped, his bunched heels crashing into the foreman's shoulder.

The .30-30 flew to one side as both men rolled down the short slope in an avalanche of rubble and dust.

Kerrigan regained his feet at the bottom of the coulee, even as Beechey pawed for the fallen rifle. The Colt in Kerrigan's fist whizzed down in a chopping arc, thudded hard across Beechey's temple. The Rafter O straw-boss sprawled, knocked out by the blow.

Dust blotted out the confused scene then. Dixie Whipple cackled out an oath and pounced to snatch up the Winchester. Hands gripped Kerrigan's elbow, and he turned to see Rona standing beside him.

"Thank God — you're safe, Editor —"

Relief and thanksgiving welled through Kerrigan as he slid an arm around the girl's waist. Siegfried Grumheller came up to them, his Bavarian features flushed and beaming.

"What happened here?" Kerrigan demanded. "How come Beechey got the deadwood on you?"

"It's like this, boss," Dixie Whipple explained. "We headed out here just after midnight to make sure the Rafter O bunch didn't beat us and blow up the bridge —"

"I know about that," cut in the Texan. "What —"

"We got here before daylight," Rona explained. "We didn't see anyone on the bridge so we hid our horses and decided to wait, in case any of Ogrum's men showed up. We were expecting trouble from the east, men on horseback. First thing we knew, Giff Ogrum and Beechey had us covered. Seems they jumped off that cattle train when it stopped at the switch."

Grumheller spread his hands sheepishly. "So our liddle scheme was *kaput* before it started," the rancher said. "They take away our guns, they make us come ofer into dis coulee to vait for the vheat train to show up, *ja.*"

Kerrigan scowled impatiently. "Where's Ogrum now?"

Joe-Ed Bainter, busy trussing Dave

Beechey's arms with a hank of binder twine, jerked his head toward the river.

"Out on the bridge, Kerrigan. Waitin' until the wheat train shows up before he lights his fuses."

Kerrigan started forward.

"You folks wait here," he ordered. "I'll attend to Ogrum."

And then another voice spoke up behind the Texan. A voice that had haunted Kerrigan's dreams for months past. "I'll go with you, Cole."

Kerrigan whirled, staring through the eddying dust at the black-coated man who had stood at his back.

He was U. S. Marshal Ford Fitzharvey.

CHAPTER
TWENTY-NINE:
BARGAIN

So Nemesis had overtaken him at last — Ford Fitzharvey had made good his vow to trail Kerrigan to the ends of the earth, if need be, just as he had sworn to do back in the jail at Longhorn, eons ago. O'Neil's warning had been true.

It was incredible, but Fitzharvey was here, come to reap his hangman's harvest. Kerrigan realized numbly that Fitzharvey was the stranger who had arrived on the seven-forty last night, looking for him.

Kerrigan finally broke the gelid silence. His voice was a hoarse caw in his own ears.

"Stand back, Ford. We can settle our business later." He felt suddenly resigned and old and without hope. "Don't try to stop me now. I've got a score to settle with Giff Ogrum first. Nothing can deny me that —"

He was aware of Rona Prescott's puzzled stare as he backed away, his gun swinging to cover Fitzharvey at point-blank range.

"I just want to help," the marshal said. A quizzical twist crossed his mouth under the sandy waterfall mustache. "If Dixie will let me have the rifle —"

"Ride herd on the marshal, Dixie!" Kerrigan ordered, turning to scramble up the steep end of the coulee. "I'll be back."

"Hold on, boss!" Whipple shouted, starting forward. "You can't tackle Ogrum alone. He's got a rifle —"

Fitzharvey stood glued to his tracks, menaced by the gun in Kerrigan's fist as the Texas editor backed up out of the coulee. He read the desperation in Kerrigan's eyes —

But Kerrigan was gone, running through the cottonwoods and down into the cut where the locomotive stood, its exhaust cocks hissing steam. He paused there, checking his six-gun cylinder.

He broke into a run, down the sweeping curve of the tracks and out of the cut, the Snake River trestle looming ahead.

Stalking out on the narrow plank catwalk between the rails, the sun at his back sent his shadow waggling over the rocky dry bed of the river twenty feet below.

A hundred yards down the trestle, at the near end of the cantilever span which rested on masonry piers on either side of the main channel, he saw a man squatting alongside the tracks, half-hidden against the background of metal bridgework.

It was Giff Ogrum.

The Rafter O boss was waiting for the wheat train to arrive from Wheatville, waiting for the proper moment to fire his fuses and escape to the opposite bank to witness his last desperate blow at the Palouse County wheatmen.

Ogrum caught sight of Cole Kerrigan then. He leaped to his feet, stepping out onto the crossties. Sunlight glinted on the blued barrel of the deer rifle in his hands.

The catwalk planks amplified the beat of Cole Kerrigan's boots. He knew he was beyond six-gun range of Giff Ogrum. The sun was against Ogrum, but even so Kerrigan knew he was a prime target for the outlaw's .45-70.

But something quite outside Kerrigan's will had taken possession of the Texan now. His every nerve and muscle and thought was concentrated on one thing: to force Giff Ogrum into a showdown, to kill or be killed.

Kerrigan broke into a crouched run as he saw Ogrum whip gunstock to cheek, squinting against the morning sunlight.

Kerrigan flung a glance over his shoulder to see Marshal Ford Fitzharvey emerging from the cut. The lawman was carrying the rifle Dixie Whipple had handed over to him —

Ogrum was kneeling now, elbow braced on a knee, lining up the sights of his rifle.

The Texan flung himself headlong to the catwalk as he saw the rifle buck against Ogrum's shoulder. A steel-jacketed bullet droned spitefully over Kerrigan's body, through space where his chest had been a shaved instant before. He picked himself up and charged forward, breath gusting across locked teeth. His idea now was to get within Colt range of his adversary, before Ogrum could cut him down.

A shot blasted behind Kerrigan and a slug screamed past his head. Was Fitzharvey opening fire on him, trapping him in a crisscross of lead?

Ogrum levered another shell into the breech of the .45-70 and took careful aim at his zigzagging target.

It was suicidal, bucking a rifle at such close range. Kerrigan side-stepped, flung himself down alongside a rail as Ogrum squeezed off a second shot. The bullet caromed off a rail behind Kerrigan, leaving a gray streak along the flange.

From a prone position, Kerrigan triggered his Colt in a test shot. He heard the slug ring like a gong off bridge beams behind Ogrum. That meant he had his enemy within range now —

A third lance of flame spat from Ogrum's gun muzzle. Something like a hot knife grazed the egg of muscle on Kerrigan's right shoulder, brought a warm gush of blood down his arm. The pain of the bullet burn went unnoticed as Kerrigan scuttled forward on hands and knees to cut down the range still further.

Fitzharvey's .30-30 was hammering incessantly now. Kerrigan knew now that the marshal was shooting past him, toward Ogrum.

A taut smile creased the Texan's face. At least the marshal was backing his play. The grim irony of it flashed across Kerrigan's mind. Fitzharvey, having trailed him this far, was determined to take a live captive back to stretch a Texas hangrope.

Ogrum retreated to the shelter of a rack of water barrels on a platform inside the cantilever span. Aiming around the edge of the barrel, safe now from Fitzharvey's fire, Ogrum triggered another shot at Cole Kerrigan.

The bullet thudded into a crosstie inches from Kerrigan's jaw and sprayed his face with slivers. Flat on his belly between the rails, Kerrigan made a difficult target to draw a bead on. The sun in Ogrum's eyes was Kerrigan's best ally.

Kerrigan thrust out an arm, steadied his elbow on a tie. He notched his gun sights on what little he could see of Giff Ogrum between the bridge beams and the water barrels.

He tripped gunhammer, saw Ogrum duck out of sight instinctively as the bullet punctured the barrel staves, a bright little stream of water fountaining forth like a rivulet of quicksilver in the morning sun-rays.

Leaping to his feet, intending to get back into the shelter of the slanting I-beams, Ogrum's left spur caught on a protruding spike and tripped him.

The Winchester clattered from Ogrum's grasp as he fell. In an instant Ogrum had regained his feet, but the rifle teetered off a rail, up-ended, and dropped into the river below.

Kerrigan got to his feet with an exultant yell. Ogrum was wearing a six-gun, but he faced Kerrigan on equal terms.

Ogrum stood at bay now. He paused, spread-legged in the center of the tracks, as if debating whether to take flight for the far bank of the river and seek safety in the breaks beyond the Snake.

But that would make him a prime target for Fitzharvey's .30-30. And the marshal was stalking up the trestle.

Kerrigan saw the outlaw clamber down off the tracks, swinging gorilla-fashion below the level of the rails and out of sight in the maze of heavy timbers supporting one corner of the cantilever span.

A 200-pound keg of blasting powder was wedged between the timbers which forked upward from the masonry pier, placed there yesterday by Ogrum's henchmen.

A match flared in Ogrum's fist. Clinging to an iron brace rod, he leaned far out and down, to ignite the fuse which ran to the explosive.

The acrid fumes spewed off by the sizzling fuse met Cole Kerrigan's nostrils as he reached the cantilever span and peered cautiously over the edge.

He had caught Giff Ogrum before the rancher could swing back onto a supporting beam. With both hands gripping the iron guyrod, he would have to buck a cold drop to reach his own holster.

Ogrum's face was lobster-red from exertion. Cords stood out on his bull neck. But there was only a taunting challenge in his yellow-flecked eyeballs as he stared up at the round black bore of Kerrigan's .45.

"I'll make a bargain with you, Kerrigan. Chuck your gun into the river. Give me a fightin' chance to make it to the other bank."

"No dice, Ogrum. I'm making no bargains."

The outlaw's face went livid. "Then I don't rip out this fuse. There's enough powder here to blow us an' the bridge sky-high. Take your choice."

Kerrigan's thumb eared the knurled gun-hammer to full cock. His eyes were drawn in spite of him to the sputtering fuse as it neared the powder barrel.

"Yank out that fuse while you can still reach it, Ogrum!"

Ogrum took a firmer grasp on the iron brace rod. His feet were resting on the concrete pierhead, the gliding yellow waters of the Snake dizzying Cole Kerrigan as he knelt on the edge of the ties.

"You won't shoot me, Kerrigan." Ogrum's voice held a gloating, hysterical note, the keening shriek of a man beyond the reach of fear. "You toss that gun down. If you think I'm bluffing, you'll be blowed to hash-meat."

Cold beads of sweat broke out on Kerrigan's face. The fuse was within inches of the oaken barrel now. Doom was a matter of clock-ticks away.

"I won't blow any higher than you will, Ogrum."

The outlaw's face went ash gray. He knew a bluff when he saw one. Cole Kerrigan wasn't bluffing. He would die in the face of the blast rather than relinquish his Colt. Ogrum was bucking a man who didn't give a damn if he lived or died.

"You win, Kerrigan."

As he spoke, Ogrum let go of the iron rod with one hand. He swung down, spread-eagled from the face of the bridge pier. And then, his finger tips brushing the fuming end of the fuse, Ogrum let go the brace rod and hurtled downward in a clumsy dive.

Chapter Thirty: Explosion

A cry of desperation left Cole Kerrigan's lips as he saw the cowman hit the muddy water with a geysering splash.

Holstering his gun, Kerrigan swung down over the edge of the ties. He saw Ford Fitzharvey running up the track, but there was no time to wave the marshal back out of danger.

Kerrigan scrambled recklessly down the latticed timbers toward the powder barrel. The fuse was out of reach now, dangerously close to the explosive.

Clinging to brace rods, Kerrigan launched both feet at the metal rim of the barrel. It slipped slightly. Again and again Kerrigan swung his boot heels at the barrel. Finally it joggled off balance, teetered. Then it plummeted down, hit the pyramidal face of the pier, and bounced into space.

Giff Ogrum's head broke surface in a smother of foam at the same instant that the powder barrel struck the water. Both were caught in a tight eddy below the pier.

A yell of terror gargled from the ranchman's lips. He was a poor swimmer, a common failing of his kind. The weight of boots and bullhide chaps and gun harness was bogging him down. Ogrum made a frantic grab for the nearest object — the powder barrel. It spun under his clawing hands, bobbed away.

Then Ogrum saw that the fuse was still spitting sparks, unextinguished inside its insulated casing.

From his precarious perch twenty feet overhead, Cole Kerrigan stared in fascinated horror as he watched the drowning cattleman flog the barrel as if fighting away an attacker.

Only by diving could Ogrum save his life now. The surge of the current had swept them both downstream, less than a yard apart.

Then the powder exploded. A pink flash blinded Kerrigan. A roar of sound smote his eardrums.

Smoke and debris and river water sprayed Kerrigan's body. A concussion wave tore at him like a giant hand, nearly breaking his grip on the iron guyrod. His ears ached under the numbing blast.

Opening tight-squeezed eyes, Kerrigan stared down through the boiling smoke. A rift opened to expose the surface of the river. He caught a whisked-off glimpse of a gory carcass floating down the crest of the current, a mass of splintered bone and mangled flesh that rolled over and sank in red-tinctured spume.

Kerrigan was remembering what Mizzou Howerton had told him back in Wheatville last night. With Giff Ogrum would die the range feud he had engineered in the last hell-bent years of a misbegotten life.

Blood was trickling warmly down Kerrigan's elbow, staining his sleeve, dripping from wrist and fingers.

He pulled himself wearily up the bridge work. Ford Fitzharvey, panting heavily and drenched by flying spray, reached down to help him up onto the bridge.

Kerrigan felt suddenly sick and beaten and overwhelmed by a rush of hopelessness and frustration. He had not been too late to save the bridge. That was all that mattered now.

"I'm ready, Marshal," the Texan said dully. "I reckon my job's finished now."

Fitzharvey mopped his streaming face with a bandanna.

"Your friend Jimmy O'Neil tipped me off

where you were, when I happened to be in Dodge City a couple weeks back, Cole. I looked him up when I remembered you said your dad knew O'Neil in the old days. I was heading for Seattle on a business trip anyhow, so I dropped off at Wheatville last night —"

Kerrigan closed his eyes. So Fitzharvey hadn't traced him by running across his name in the Washington newspapers after all. Funny, he felt no resentment at Jimmy O'Neil for turning traitor, betraying his hideout west of Texas law. That didn't amount to much now. Nothing mattered any more.

"I'm your prisoner, Ford," he said heavily. "Here's my gun."

Fitzharvey shoved back the Colt which Kerrigan extended to him, butt first.

"Prisoner, hell!" laughed the U. S. Marshal. "You were cleared of that murder charge within twenty-four hours after you and Dixie high-tailed out of Texas, man!"

Kerrigan could only stare. The words didn't make sense.

"You see, the county coroner dug that slug out of Kiowa McCord's brain at the inquest next day, Cole." Fitzharvey's voice seemed to come from a distant void. "It turned out to be a copper-jacketed thirty-thirty bullet.

Since you were packing a forty-five six-gun at the time of McCord's death, Sheriff Palmquist didn't have any excuse for wanting you arrested."

Kerrigan knew he was expected to say something, but his brain was foggy, bewildered. Back down the bridge, he saw Rona coming at a run, with Dixie Whipple and the two wheatmen at her heels.

"Palmquist," he said slowly. "I — I'd almost forgotten that four-flusher ever existed."

Fitzharvey leaned on his rifle, his eyes twinkling.

"Palmquist *don't* exist — any more," he said. "After McCord was killed, Palmquist got the idea of running that Red River toll bridge himself. The first trail boss he tangled with went for his gun instead of his pocketbook."

"And Palmquist backed down?"

"With enough lead in his guts to start a foundry, yes. Palmquist is nothin' but a name on a boot-hill tombstone now."

"How about the toll bridge?"

"She's been open to free traffic ever since, Cole. Your *Crusader* won its fight after all."

Kerrigan dragged a shaking hand over his eyes.

"But if Jimmy O'Neil knew all this — why didn't he let me know?"

"O'Neil didn't know the truth, Cole. He played dumb when I first went to see him, askin' about you. But after I told him your name was cleared —"

Rona Prescott brushed past the marshal then, and flung herself into Cole Kerrigan's arms. There was nothing of the tomboy about the thoroughly feminine tears she was weeping on the Texan's shirt now.

"Oh, Cole — my darling —"

Dixie Whipple came limping up, out of breath with exhaustion. The old marshal waved him and Bainter and Grumheller back.

"We'd better sashay out of earshot, boys," chuckled Ford Fitzharvey. "I think Cole's got business to attend to — private."

Twenty yards down the track, Dixie Whipple turned to call back to Rona Prescott and Cole Kerrigan, "Don't forget, boss — our shop ain't got a single font o' Script or Old English type. Nothin' that'd do for printin' up a batch of weddin' announcements!"

If Kerrigan heard, he gave no sign. He held Rona Prescott at arm's length, drinking in the love that shone through her tear-brimming eyes.

"You always hankered to write," Kerrigan whispered. "How about a job on the *Spectator*? Couldn't Lasater run the ranch?"

She moved closer to him then, her head tight against his shoulder, her throat too choked for speech.

"I forgot," the Texan went on. "You told me you didn't have room in your life for marriage and kids — And Ellison said the man doesn't live who could tame a tomboy like you —"

Her eyes met his as she drew back, smiling through the tears. The warm sunlight which hit their faces seemed an omen, the promise of a glorious future that was just beginning, a future they would both share.

"The right man," she whispered, "wouldn't find it hard to tame me, Editor."

Kerrigan's lips crushed against hers demandingly in their first kiss. And Cole Kerrigan discovered, as Rona yielded herself to him in unrestrained surrender, that she was absolutely right. It was the easiest thing in God's bright world.

We hope you have enjoyed this Large Print book. Other Thorndike, Wheeler, and Chivers Press Large Print books are available at your library or directly from the publishers.

For information about current and upcoming titles, please call or write, without obligation, to:

Publisher
Thorndike Press
295 Kennedy Memorial Drive
Waterville, ME 04901
Tel. (800) 223-1244

or visit our Web site at:

www.gale.com/thorndike
www.gale.com/wheeler

OR

Chivers Large Print
published by BBC Audiobooks Ltd
St James House, The Square
Lower Bristol Road
Bath BA2 3SB
England
Tel. +44(0) 800 136919
email: bbcaudiobooks@bbc.co.uk
www.bbcaudiobooks.co.uk

All our Large Print titles are designed for easy reading, and all our books are made to last.

QUARTZ CREEK RANCH

AT TOP
SPEED

QUARTZ CREEK RANCH

AT TOP SPEED

Kiersi Burkhart and
Amber J. Keyser

SCHOLASTIC INC.

ISBN 978-1-338-28455-3

Text copyright © 2017 by Kiersi Burkhart and Amber J. Keyser. All rights reserved.
Published by Scholastic Inc., 557 Broadway, New York, NY 10012, by arrangement
with Darby Creek, a division of Lerner Publishing Group, Inc. SCHOLASTIC and
associated logos are trademarks and/or registered trademarks of Scholastic Inc.

12 11 10 9 8 7 6 5 4 3 2   18 19 20 21 22 23

Printed in the U.S.A.   40

First Scholastic printing, March 2018

The images in this book are used with the permission of:
© iStockphoto.com/Piotr Krzeslak (wood background).

Front cover: © Barbara O'Brien Photography
Back cover: © iStockphoto.com/ImagineGolf

Main body text set in Bembo Std regular
Typeface provided by Monotype Typography

For every boy and girl who can't believe in themselves . . . I believe in you.

—**KB**

For my Steamboat family, the real cowboys.

—**AK**

CHAPTER ONE

Ella glanced once again at the map, then at the upcoming intersection. The green street sign read: BRIDLEMILE RD.

"Dad!" she cried. "You're supposed to turn here!"

Ella's dad yanked the steering wheel to the right, and the car's tires growled over the gravel.

"Could have said something sooner," he said.

"You're driving so fast I didn't even see the turn coming."

"Don't critique my driving. You're eleven."

Ella felt a wave of hot anger, starting in her chest and working its way up her neck. This always happened when they argued. It made all her limbs tense, and her mouth said things she regretted later.

"I get to critique your driving when you get lost and make me two hours late for camp," said Ella as they roared up the gravel road. The car passed under a giant iron archway reading QUARTZ CREEK RANCH, but she barely noticed it—she was glaring at her dad, who sat crouched over the steering wheel, equally furious.

"It wouldn't have been a problem if you hadn't taken so long to get ready at Uncle Nate's house," Dad said as they rolled through the gate, which someone had left open for them.

Ella wanted to throw something. This was supposed to be her trip, but now Dad was ruining it, like he ruined everything when his temper got hold of him. They'd driven out from California and stayed with her uncle in Boulder just so her dad could see the ranch himself, in person, before he left her there for six weeks. He wanted to make sure it was safe and vermin-free, or something like that. Then they'd say good-bye—there were no letters or phone calls allowed until she flew home at the end of camp.

"It's your fault it took me so long to get ready," Ella said as a big ranch-style house sailed by on their right. "You were the one who made me take out and repack my entire suitcase!"

When the driveway appeared, her dad took another sharp turn, jerking Ella against her seatbelt. Then he stomped on the brakes, and when the car had come to an abrupt stop in the parking lot, he ripped the keys out of the ignition.

"I made you repack because you don't even know how to pack your own things properly." Her dad threw open the car door and got out. Ella unsnapped her seatbelt, leaped out, and slammed her door behind her.

"I packed just fine the first time, Dad!"

"You brought way too much stuff." The volume of his voice was steadily rising. "Who needs all that junk at a six-week camp?"

"You don't get it at all!" Ella found herself starting to shout, too, to match him. "Just because I don't wear the exact same thing every day, like you—"

"It's practical, Ell," her dad said, yanking open the trunk of the car. Behind them, the front door of the ranch house opened. A short, wrinkly woman in an oversized T-shirt and curly hair came out first, followed by a pine tree of a man with skin as dark as Ella's, wearing a ten-gallon cowboy hat. A few kids Ella's own age peeked out the door, and another one gazed out the window at them.

"Practical for you," said Ella, starting to sweat in the hot afternoon air as her voice grew louder. "But you can't expect me to wear a suit every day, too! At least what I wear shows I have a personality."

Dad rounded on her. "What do you know? It's about looking professional so I can afford to put a roof over your head and food on the table."

"You go to work every day to pay for all the stupid stuff you buy online!" Each time her dad raised his voice, Ella raised hers more.

"You're such a brat!" shouted her dad, so caught up in the argument that he'd forgotten all about pulling her suitcase out of the trunk.

"And you're a workaholic!" Ella shouted back, starting to spiral with fury. Then she said the thing she knew would really make him mad.

"At least when Mom was around, you came home sometimes."

Her dad's face was turning a dangerous sort of red when the short, leathered woman hopped down the steps and jogged toward them, her expression stunned.

"Hello there," she said, interrupting. "Are you Ella?"

Ella opened her mouth to speak, but her dad glared at her, then at the older woman. "I'm

Jonathan Pierson," he said, then pointed at Ella. "That's my daughter. Ella." He probably thought Ella's skin color had confused the old lady, Ella figured. Since she was half Indonesian from her mother's side, white people sometimes didn't believe Ella was her dad's kid, even though they had the exact same nose and mouth.

"Yes . . ." the woman said, trailing off. "I know." She turned to Ella and smiled. "Welcome to the ranch, Ella. I'm Ma Etty."

Ella smiled back. The old lady wasn't confused—she had just been addressing Ella directly. Ella liked her already. She opened her mouth to respond, but Dad butted in again.

"'Ma Etty'?" he asked, crossing his arms. "Your first name is 'Ma'?"

"It's a nickname."

"Hmm," he said, unimpressed. He gazed around them at the parking lot—the beat-up old pickup, the horse trailers, the tractors. "I was expecting something a little different, for a . . . a rehabilitation camp. So, you're going to work with Ella on her . . . temper issues. Right?"

Ma Etty blanched. "Everyone gets a fresh start here at Quartz Creek Ranch," she said. "We try not to dwell on what brought our kids here, but focus on helping them grow once they've arrived."

"With horseback riding therapy?"

"We don't call it 'therapy,'" she said. "It's just horseback riding."

Dad opened his mouth to say something else, but a low, rumbling voice interrupted them.

"Mr. Pierson," said the ten-gallon-hat man, who had been on the porch a moment ago. He leaned over them. "Let me help you get your daughter's things so she can join us for dinner—get your money's worth, am I right?"

"That's a good point," her dad said, backing away from the car to give the big man access to the trunk.

"This is my husband, Will," said Ma Etty. "Willard Bridle."

"Bridle?" Dad asked. "And that's your real last name, too, I take it."

Ella wished he would just close his mouth and leave already. All the kids had come outside to watch her dad make a spectacle—four kids who looked about Ella's age and two much older teenagers stood on the porch.

Why did her dad have to be so angry all the time?

A month and a half away from him was starting to sound like the best vacation of Ella's life.

"Yes, Bridle is our real last name," said Mr. Bridle. He took Ella's bags out of the car and set them down.

"We'll take it from here, Mr. Pierson," said Ma Etty. "Dinner's almost on the table, and the kids were doing introductions."

"Actually," said a boy on the porch with a blond bowl cut, "we just finished 'em."

For once, Ella's dad looked relieved. Ella was not. She knew first impressions were important—and now she'd made hers by showing up late.

"Great. Thanks, Dad," said Ella.

Her dad wiped his forehead and stood back, not bothering to respond to her jab. He gave Ella a quick hug, and said, "Remember to keep your fists in your pockets. No hitting."

Why did he have to talk to her like she was seven? Ella jammed her hands in her front pockets and pulled away from the hug. Then she took her hands back out again and dropped them by her sides, shooting her dad a spiteful look.

But Dad hadn't noticed, and was already walking back to his car as he said, "I'll leave her in your capable hands, Mr. Bridle, Mrs. Bridle." He opened the door and climbed in. *So much for taking a look around*, Ella thought. "See you in six weeks, Ell," he called out the open window.

Then he peeled out of the driveway with a roar of the engine. The tires kicked up so much dust that everyone in front of the house burst into a coughing fit.

One of the two older teenagers standing on the porch—a girl with long brown hair and a kind face—approached Ella.

"Hey, Ella," she said, extending a hand. "I'm Madison, one of your riding instructors." Ella shook her hand and glanced at the other teenager, a tall black guy now suddenly occupied with breaking up the boy campers, who were prodding and poking one another. He looked like he was probably the other instructor.

"Come on," said Madison, heading past Ella. "Let's drop off your stuff real fast at the girls' bunkhouse, and then we can eat."

\\

As Ella followed Madison across a patchy yard of grass toward two weathered old bunkhouses, she sized up the ranch.

Chickens clucked and croaked in the nearby coop, and the whole place smelled like grass and sky and earth. The faint odor of cow manure reminded her that this place was chock-full of living things.

Impressive. Now that she was here in person, it really lived up to the brochure.

When her dad had laid out all the options for summer "rehab" camp, this feeling was what had endeared Ella to Quartz Creek Ranch—ranch life was supposed to be simple and beautiful, even if a little dirty.

"Remember that camp isn't for fun," he'd said, trying hard to play the role of Dad by using his stern voice. "It's punishment. You're supposed to learn something."

Maybe to him it was punishment, but to Ella, it was a six-week vacation. Horses—check. Ella adored horses. Beautiful, graceful, fast.

And no Dad? Check. She could start fresh here without his oppressive presence weighing her down.

But more importantly, this place was the real deal. The original article. An authentic, working cattle ranch out in Somewhereville, Colorado. Big sky. Gigantic mountains.

Check, Ella thought, looking around. This was

just the place for escaping Petaluma for a while—and the strange, distant way her friends treated her.

After Bianca.

But so what if they were afraid of her now? Nobody should get away with talking to Ella like that—especially about her pigtail braids. Mom had showed Ella how to make them connect in the back like that when she was little. It was hard to do by herself, holding up a hand mirror while she braided so she could see what she was doing, but she'd managed.

So of course Ella popped that trash-talking brat Bianca in the mouth when she insulted Ella's braids. Friend or not, Bianca got what she deserved, as Dad would say. He didn't tolerate insults either.

Madison didn't chatter as she led Ella to the girls' bunkhouse. They ascended a short, creaky set of stairs and ducked inside. The place was clearly built to house more than just two girls—there was room for at least five, probably more if the table were scooted aside for another cot. Ella wondered if, by chance, the Bridles ever ended up with all girls and zero boys.

That would be a big mess, Ella thought.

Top bunks were always the most fun, so Ella headed for the one nearest the window. "I've got to grab something," said Madison, pointing to the door of a separate room. "Just so you know, I sleep in there. Bathroom's over there." She gestured to the next door over. "Drop your stuff on whichever bunk you want, and let's head back."

"Aye, aye, cap'n," said Ella. She walked down the short row of bunks and stopped at the middle one, by the window. Perfect. The light came in just right so if she slept on the top bunk, she'd feel it on her face as the sun came up.

If there was one silly phrase her dad always said that Ella actually took to heart, it was, *Early to bed, early to rise, makes a man happy, healthy, wealthy, and wise.* He said it often, with emphasis on the "wealthy" part.

While Ella didn't really believe in the proverb, the early morning was quiet and calm—if she could get up for it. Having the morning light pour in on her face would help immensely, she thought.

Yes. This bunk would do great.

But when she got up to the top of the ladder and set her suitcase down on the bed, she found another girl's duffel bag already sitting at the foot.

Ella picked up the duffel. This girl, whoever she was, would just have to be happy with the other top bunk by the door. Ella tossed the ratty duffel over to the next bunk, then set her own by the pillow and dropped back down the ladder.

She met Madison at the door.

"Burgers," was all the trainer said, and they headed back to the ranch house.

CHAPTER TWO

When Ella and Madison walked inside, everyone was already sitting at the table in the dining room, assembling hamburgers. Paintings of galloping horses hung everywhere, and the house felt welcoming and rustic.

Ella took the one open seat left, between a brown-haired girl and a tall, wiry boy. The girl didn't even look up as Ella sat down. She was too busy eating. The boy, who looked vaguely mixed-race—probably the way she looked to others, Ella thought—turned toward her instantly.

"Hey!" he said, his mouth full of food. Ella leaned away a little as he kept talking, faster than she could keep up. "Bummer you got here late! We had homemade churros earlier, before dinner. It was great. I mean, dessert before dinner? Who gets to do that?"

"Yeah," Ella said, ignoring him as she forked the last hamburger onto her plate. She asked for the buns, which had to get passed from the opposite end of the table.

"Everyone," said Ma Etty from the head of the table, "let's do another round of introductions real quick for our newcomer, okay?"

"Aw," said the short kid with the awful blond bowl cut. "You can't recapture improvised genius or it just feels recycled. My bit about hamsters and basketball wouldn't be the same." He spoke with a thick Texan accent.

The tall boy next to Ella laughed. "How would they be able to hold it with those tiny, tiny hands?"

Great. They already had inside jokes. By being late, Ella was even farther outside the circle than she'd thought.

"Awright now," said Mr. Bridle. "Let's tell Ella your name and where you're from. I'll start." He cleared his throat. "I'm Will Bridle, and I live on this ranch with my lovely wife, Henrietta." He leaned over and kissed her cheek. One of the boys covered his face so he wouldn't have to watch.

Madison waved to Ella. "We already met," she said. "I'm Madison, I'm a trainer here, and I'm gearing up for tryouts again for my college swim team."

The teenaged guy next to her just dipped his head. "Fletch," he said. "Horse trainer, bronc rider, human being. Nice to meet you." Then he nodded to the Texan next to him, who sat across from Ella.

"I'm Ash," he said around a mouthful of hamburger, then swallowed it down with orange juice. "Ash Feezle. I'm from Dallas, home of the Cowboys. America's Team." He tapped the logo on the front of his Cowboys T-shirt. "Kind of ironic, now that I think about it . . . Sent away for the summer to become a real cowboy."

Introductions moved around the table to the boy sitting next to Ella.

"I'm Drew," he said, smoothing back some of his curly, dense hair. It was cut tall on top of his head and shaped kind of like a boat. "Drew King. Not like Martin Luther King. Everybody asks that because my mom's black, but you know, that's a stereotype of black people to just assume I'm related to MLK because my last name is King."

Ella had not assumed that, but she nodded any-way. Motor-mouth went on.

"And I think everyone assumes that stuff about MLK because I'm from Atlanta, but it's a great city. Everyone should make a point of visiting Atlanta, especially during peach season. We have every variety. Except maybe don't come next year, because I accidentally rode my BMX bike through all those experimental saplings and kinda ruined them—"

"That's plenty," said Ma Etty, interrupting him. "Thank you, Drew. Now, Ella? Will you tell us a little about yourself?"

Ella had thought about this on the drive up, so she was prepared.

"My name is Ella Pierson," she said smoothly. "I'm going into sixth grade at my new school in Petaluma, California. My favorite activities are drawing, riding my bike, and hanging out with friends. I'm excited to be here and meet everyone." She glanced around the table, smiling at each of the other kids in turn. They looked back at her like she'd descended from a UFO.

Ma Etty blinked. "We're glad you could make it, too, Ella."

Ella nodded back gracefully. If the other kids wanted to act like they'd been sentenced to six weeks in prison, that was their problem. She was excited about this place, even if they weren't.

Introductions continued with the girl sitting next to Ella, who so far had not spoken. Now, Ella had a chance to size her up. She looked almost like a young version of Madison: hazel-brown eyes, with long brown hair tied back in a ponytail and a pretty face.

"I'm Jordan McAdam." The girl didn't even look at Ella. "I'm from California, too, actually. Pretty close to you. Near Clearlake."

Ella hadn't been near Clearlake much. *Only rednecks live out there*, Dad would say. But it explained something about how Jordan was dressed. Ella might not have noticed her clothes except in comparison to Drew, who sported a fresh, striped T-shirt from American Eagle and new-looking dark jeans. Jordan wore a thin flannel shirt that looked a century old and a pair of holey, stained jeans.

"Clearlake," said Ella, trying to think of something nice to say. "Not much out there."

Jordan shrugged and went back to her dinner.

Ma Etty coughed.

"Okay, thank you, Jordan. Next?"

It was the last boy's turn. He sullenly looked up from eating.

"My name is Kim," he said. "Kim Do Yung. I'm from New Hampshire. I traveled an exceptionally long way just to get dirty and clean stalls." He made a face. "My dad teaches Korean at Dartmouth College, and my mom teaches Communications."

Both Drew and Ash chuckled.

Kim glanced at each of them. "What?"

"Nothing," said Ash, laughing harder. "It's just . . . is your name short for Kimberly?"

Kim gave him a flat look. "No. It's Korean. And in Korea, Kim is a boy's name."

Ella saw her chance to redeem herself in front of the Bridles after her dad's fit in the parking lot—but Jordan spoke first.

"Some names are both," she said, still not looking up from her food. "Like mine. I've met tons of boy Jordans, and a few girl Jordans, and that's just in California."

"It's a great point," said Ma Etty. "A lot of names can go either way. And around the country—sometimes you'll meet people with names that seem strange to you. Your name, Drew, is probably strange to a lot of people."

"Uh . . ." He looked momentarily perplexed. "Because it's not a nickname for Andrew, like most people named Drew?"

"Exactly."

Ash rolled his eyes. "Not really that strange," he muttered.

"I like it," said Ella, not wanting to miss her chance to chime in. "Kim is a nice name for a boy."

But Kim glared at her. "My name isn't 'nice,'" he said. "It's fierce."

Ella returned the look and bristled. She'd just been trying to help.

"Ooh," said Ash. "*Fearsome* Kim. He's short. He's scary. He'll suffocate you with kimchee."

In an ESPN voice, Drew said, "Our next wrestler is Fe-e-e-earsome Kim!"

Kim looked like he wouldn't mind putting his fork through Drew's eye.

"All right, all right," said Ma Etty, holding up both hands. "No making fun of anyone at my dinner table."

"We weren't making fun," said Ash. "We were imagining Kim's pro wrestling secret identity."

Ma Etty exhaled sharply. "None of that, either."

"Who ate all the hamburgers?" asked Drew, picking up the empty plate. Ella wondered if this guy would ever shut up.

"New girl did," said Kim, pointing at Ella as she took a bite of her hamburger.

"But I'm still hungry!" moaned Drew.

"Right," said Ella, trying her hardest not to get mad. "Sorry for taking one whole hamburger so I don't starve."

"Can't let her starve," said Ash.

"But what about me?" said Drew. "What if I starve?"

Ella started steaming. What was wrong with these kids? And was she really stuck with them for the next six weeks?

"Have more potatoes instead," said Fletch, passing the bowl of home fries.

"Potatoes do not equal meat," said Ash, and the table devolved into another argument.

Under her breath, Jordan said, "I guess introductions are over."

Ella took a big bite of her hamburger to occupy her hands. She was already hankering to sock one of these idiots right in the mouth, but she stopped herself. She couldn't mess this up already—not after promising herself a fresh start, away from Dad and his temper.

It was going to be a long summer.

\\

Even though it was dark, finding the way back to the girls' bunkhouse was easy with the boys galloping ahead of them across the chicken yard.

"Fe-e-e-earsome Kim!" Drew shouted, sending the chickens squawking back to their coop.

"Shut up, dude!" hissed Ash.

"Don't boss me around, Dallas."

"I'm going to put earwigs in both your ears if you don't be quiet," said Kim. "While you're sleeping."

Fletch had tried for a little while to corral them into some semblance of order, but it looked like he'd already given up as the boys ran up the stairs of their bunkhouse and vanished inside, hooting and hollering and sulking respectively.

The girls' bunk was stone silent in comparison. Madison went into her room to start getting ready for bed. As Ella took off her shoes at the door, Jordan climbed up the ladder to the bunk near the window.

"Oh," she said. "My duffel bag is gone."

Here come the water works, Ella thought.

Madison peered out of her room. "Your bag is gone?" she asked, eyebrows drawing together. "I hope one of the boys didn't come in here and swipe it, thinking they'd play a practical joke."

"It wasn't the boys," Ella said, neatly stashing her new white and pink sneakers next to Jordan's scuffed, dirty ones. "I moved it. I wanted that bunk for the light to help me wake up in the morning, or else I'm all groggy and grouchy. And you don't want to see me grouchy in the morning."

A frown crossed Madison's face. "Ella, it's first-come, first-served," she said. "And Jordan called that bunk first—"

"It's fine," said Jordan, hopping back down the ladder, then going up the one nearest the door. There, she found her duffel bag waiting and nodded to herself. "I don't care which bunk I have."

"Are you sure?" asked Madison, still watching Ella, though she was speaking to Jordan. "Because—"

"Really. It's fine, if she likes that one."

Ella knew fake when she heard it, and it didn't sound like Jordan was putting it on. She seemed unperturbed.

Madison's eyes narrowed.

"I'll sleep here just as well as there," Jordan said again. With that, she climbed up onto her bunk and started digging through her duffel bag for her toiletries, like nothing had happened.

Shrugging, Madison ducked back into her room, but not before shooting Ella a meaningful look. But Jordan obviously didn't care, so why should Madison?

By bedtime, Jordan still hadn't said another word. Madison suggested they give their cabin a fun, cheery name before bed, a camp custom. Ella thought it was lame, but after the duffel bag incident, she wanted to get back in Madison's good graces.

"What about—the Cowgirl Cabin?" said Ella. She imagined herself in a big Western saddle with a rope hanging from the horn, dressed in her best chaps.

Madison turned to Jordan for her opinion. Jordan just shrugged.

"Is that a yes?" Ella said impatiently.

"Sure," said Jordan.

"Cowgirl Cabin it is," said Madison. But *sure* was a pretty lackluster recommendation, and it annoyed Ella that she'd had to pick the name alone.

When Madison said good night and closed her door, she promised tomorrow would be a day of meeting horses and learning their way around the ranch. Ella couldn't wait.

As the lights clicked off, Ella lay in bed expectantly, waiting for Jordan to say something in the dark. Ella loved to talk after the lights went out at sleepovers, when you could no longer see one another's faces, but could still make out voices whispering, just out of the adults' earshot.

Except that Jordan said nothing. At some point, her breathing evened out, and Ella realized she'd gone to sleep.

She didn't quite know what to make of Jordan. Tomorrow would be interesting for more reasons than just horses.

CHAPTER THREE

Ella woke to warm sunshine drifting across her eyes. She opened them, rubbing the sleep from their corners, and let out a creaky yawn.

This was just how she wanted it. Dinner last night hadn't gone perfectly, but today would. She was Ella Pierson: thick, silky black hair like her mom's; a small, round face; and big dark eyes that could melt the hearts of most adults. And she was going to ace this horseback riding thing, like she had aced drawing, and math, and bicycling. That's what Dad had said.

It was early, so Madison's door still sat closed. Sitting up in bed, Ella expected to look over and see Jordan passed out on the next bunk.

But her bed was empty, the blankets strewn around. Strange. Ella shook her head and crawled down her ladder.

Going to put on her sneakers, she found Jordan's dirty ones were already missing. Where had she gone this early in the morning?

As she laced up her shoes, Ella spotted a new addition to the shoe rack: a small pair of worn riding boots, so dirty and well-used she couldn't tell if they'd originally been brown or black.

Ella's boots still sat, brand-new in their box, in her suitcase. She'd kept the box so the boots wouldn't get her clothes all dirty when she flew home, and had to repack twice to make it fit.

But Jordan had riding boots already—ones that looked thoroughly broken in. Ella wondered if Jordan had ridden horses before.

Couldn't be. This place was for kids who wanted to learn how to ride, not for kids who already did. That had been Ella's impression after reading the brochure that said, verbatim: *Learn to ride at Quartz Creek Ranch.*

When she chose horse camp, Ella had done it knowing she was going to be a natural on horseback. Today was the first day of lessons—her day to shine.

So why had Jordan come here, if she already knew how to ride?

\\\\\\\\\\\\\\\\\\\\\\\\\\\\\\\\\\\\\\

Jordan returned just as Madison started shuffling around in her room, and she mumbled something to Ella about taking a walk. When Madison stumbled out into the main room, she found both of her charges already awake, washed, dressed, and ready for the day.

Ella didn't ask Jordan about where she'd gone that morning, and Jordan didn't offer an explanation. Like last night, she stayed silent through breakfast, focusing on her eggs, bacon, and toast like it was the highlight of her Saturday morning.

But it wasn't even nine in the morning and the boys were already arguing. Drew claimed that Kim had spit on his toothbrush so he wasn't going to use it, and Ash—horrified and disbelieving that someone would refuse to brush his teeth for the next six weeks—begged Kim to intervene on behalf of everyone who would have to smell Drew's breath. Kim just glared at both of them and said, "If I was going to mess with someone's toothbrush, merely spitting on it would be at the bottom of my list of nefarious toothbrush deeds."

And then Ash didn't know what "nefarious" meant, and he accused Kim of intentionally talking in a way that he couldn't understand to hide his guilt. In the meantime, Fletch looked like his spirit had left his body and gone on a peaceful, astral hike.

"So what if he spat on your toothbrush?" Ella finally asked, working to stay calm. Their nonstop arguing grated her nerves. "Just wash it off."

"It's not like a hair brush," Drew said, rising into falsetto on the last words. "It goes on your teeth. In your mouth."

"So?" said Ella. Her voice rose. "You know what else goes in your mouth? Forks. And forks get washed and reused every day. That fork in your hand was probably in three different mouths yesterday."

Recoiling, Drew said, "Gross!" and dropped his fork. Ella rolled her eyes. Maybe the fact she'd shown up to camp late didn't matter. These kids were completely lost in their own stupid world.

Maybe she understood why Jordan stayed silent and out of the way.

The day was already hot, so the air inside the dark horse barn hit Ella like a splash of cool water. She stood among the rows of stalls, listening to horses snorting and eating inside. It renewed Ella's faith that this camp had been the right choice. Even Drew, who had come to the barn with Fletch, went silent as they stepped inside the cool quiet, and the heavy wood door closed firmly behind them.

As Ma Etty had outlined for them at breakfast, the trainers had hand-picked a horse for each of their students based on the short questionnaire they'd filled out. Behind one of these stall doors was a horse chosen just for Ella—a horse that she, and only she, would ride for the next six weeks.

"Ella?" Ella glanced up as Madison said her name. "Come with me. It's time to meet Figure Eight."

Figure Eight? Ella's heart leapt. What a fantastic name for a horse—for *her* horse.

Madison led her to the very end of the hall, where the last stall on the left had a gold plate on it that read *FIGURE EIGHT*.

Peering into the stall, Ella was surprised to find, well . . . nothing. No horse—just some scattered hay and manure. She turned around to ask Madison where the horse had gone and saw the trainer holding out a treat through the bars of the stall. There was a sudden, loud thump inside.

Knobby knees rose up from the floor. The horse had been lying down against the wall, making itself partially invisible. Now it straightened its front legs, stretching as it got up, and lapped the treat out of Madison's hand before it was even standing up straight.

"Figure Eight's kind of a weirdo," said Madison, as Figure Eight walked into the light. "She likes to rest lying down."

Figure Eight was also gorgeous—mostly white, but splattered with big splotches of light doe-brown, like an abstract painting. The brown covered both of her eyes, and the spots made her mane different colors as it ran down her neck. Ella knew right away Figure Eight was the perfect horse. You could see it in her lean, muscular body; in her graceful movements as she got to her feet; and in the shape of her square, strong head.

"Ella," said Madison, "please meet Figure Eight. She's one of Ma Etty's favorite horses—very beloved by everyone at QCR."

"I can see why," said Ella, as Figure Eight's soft, curious white nose pressed between the bars.

"We call her Eight for short," Madison said, taking a halter off the hook. She showed Ella how to safely open the stall door, step inside, and put on the halter. Once Ella got Figure Eight out of the stall, she could see all of her.

Yes, Ella would look fantastic riding Figure Eight.

Madison walked Ella through the process of brushing her coat, then picking the tiny stones and caked-in manure out of Eight's strong hooves. When they were done, Figure Eight simply gleamed. Ella's pulse thrummed with anticipation.

Madison led Ella and Eight to the arena out behind the barn, where Drew was leading his own horse—a light brown gelding with stocky legs and a blaze down his face—around the perimeter. There, Fletch was waiting, and he gave Ella basic handling instructions.

"Walk around the arena; get used to each other. Keep Eight walking next to you with her head at your shoulder, listening to your movements. She should respect your personal space and not get distracted eating grass."

Madison left to get Jordan, leaving Ella and Drew with Fletch as they led their horses around the arena.

Drew talked nonstop while they walked, but Ella

wasn't listening. She was thinking about Jordan's worn, dirty riding boots.

Drew persisted, and Ella had started to grow annoyed when suddenly the barn door opened and Jordan emerged. She led a big, tan buckskin horse with charcoal-gray feet, mane, and tail. That hadn't taken long, Ella thought.

"Where's Madison?" asked Ella as Jordan took up leading her horse behind Ella and Drew.

"She sent me into the barn to get Loco Roco," Jordan said, gesturing to the buckskin horse, "but then had to go get Ma Etty's help with Ash and Kim. They were having some . . . difficulties."

Madison seemed to trust Jordan a lot. Ella's heart beat more quickly.

Soon the other kids joined them, and the lesson started. Fletch and Madison walked them through basic handling procedures: turning, stopping, backing up. Eight executed each task with precision and, it seemed to Ella, a bit of boredom. This baby stuff was below Figure Eight.

Good. They were the perfect match she'd imagined.

Ella wanted to get on to the riding part, but the handling wasn't so easy for Kim, Ash, and Drew.

"You're messing up my mojo," Ash told Drew, huffing as his horse once again resisted backing up. "You're too close."

"Maybe you're the one who's too close, Dallas," Drew shot back. Hooting with exhilaration, he said, "I'll show you how this backing up thing is done!" and flung his lead rope around, trying to get his horse to take a step back.

But Drew swung the rope too hard, making a wide, threatening arc. The horse threw his head up, afraid of getting hit by the blunt end of the rope, and jerked away. He bumped into Jordan's horse, surprising him. Loco Roco instinctively threw his ears back and shot out a warning kick. The kick barely missed Drew's horse, but it left a dent in the arena fence.

"Drew!" said Fletch, jogging over to take the lead rope from him. "I said swing it lightly—not try to lasso him."

"She was in my way," said Drew, pointing at Jordan, who had been minding her own business. Jordan said nothing, but put more space between Loco Roco and Drew's brown bay horse. He was such a jerk, Ella thought.

"Regardless of where everyone else is, it's your

job to keep an eye on yourself and your horse," said Fletch. "But I don't think that's the problem here. Remember, horses are flight animals. They need a calm, collected rider to be constant and trustworthy, not shouting and flailing around. That will only frighten him and make him want to run away from you."

"I wasn't flailing," said Drew.

"You were totally flailing," said Kim with a laugh. Ella wanted both of them to shut up so they could get back to the lesson.

Fletch turned. "Thank you for the input, Kim, but it's unnecessary."

"Whatever," said Kim. He tried to get his own horse to back up, obviously trying to show off, but his motions were erratic, and the horse flattened his ears and stamped. When Kim saw he was only humiliating himself, he grew annoyed and swung the lead rope faster.

"Controlled, confident motions," called Fletch. "You don't need to make yourself louder for your horse to hear you."

"I wasn't saying anything," said Kim, scowling.

"But you were," said Fletch. "When you fling your lead rope around like that, it's like you're yelling at your horse, 'Back up!' But you don't need to yell. You can whisper, and he will still hear you. He's listening." Fletch took the lead rope and, gazing directly at Kim's horse with a gentle, patient look on his face, he said, "Back."

He only had to give a tiny flick of the lead rope for the horse to take one polite step back. How was Fletch so patient? Ella would have screamed at Kim by now. She already wanted to knock him flat on his back.

Kim snatched the lead rope back. "I can do that." He tried to mimic what Fletch had done, but his energy was anything but gentle and patient. Instead of backing up as Kim threw the lead rope around, the horse let out a nervous whinny and tossed his head. Kim snarled, "What's wrong with you, horse?" He flung the lead rope on the ground and crossed his arms. "I shouldn't be sentenced to this just for cussing a little on paper. Horses suck!"

Ella turned to Jordan.

"I don't think your horse is the one who's loco around here," she said, as Fletch retrieved the lead rope and tried to talk Kim down.

But Jordan just shrugged.

So much for girl kinship.

CHAPTER FOUR

They didn't get to ride at all their first day of lessons, which Ella felt was gravely unfair for a place calling itself a riding camp.

At lunch, Ash started to tease Kim about his outburst in the arena. "So you got sent away to camp for writing cuss words?" asked Ash. Kim gave him the stink-eye.

"It was a letter."

"To who?"

"Some girl. She dumped me."

"Hoo!" said Ash, slapping his thigh. "You wrote a girl a mean letter because she dumped you?"

Kim looked like he was about to snap back when Fletch let out a weary sigh. "Let it go, Dallas." In his impatience, Fletch had even adopted Drew's silly nickname. "You'll all have another chance at horses again tomorrow."

"And you'll get to ride then, too," Madison said brightly.

"Why didn't we ride today?" said Ella. "All that stuff we did seemed pretty useless. I want my money back." But she smiled.

Ash and Kim chuckled at her joke.

"Learning proper handling is anything but useless," said Mr. Bridle gruffly from the other end of the table. "You need to be able to completely control your animal, even when you're not riding. You won't always be on a horse's back. How can you get on a horse you don't even have a relationship with yet, and expect him to trust you?"

Ella fell silent. No one at the table had a smart-aleck response for Mr. Bridle.

After lunch, Fletch and Madison handed out chores. Ella ended up walking the whole pasture fence with Ash, checking for breaks and weaknesses. He talked incessantly about football and his beloved Cowboys.

"I already told you that I have zero interest in talking about football," Ella said, turning on him. "So shut it, Dallas!"

After that he sulked, which was fine with Ella, because it meant he was quiet.

But by afternoon free time, all that walking had made her calves ache. Dinner was a mess of food and noise as the boys argued about football teams, whose horse was cooler, and the proper amount of condiments to go on the Polish sausages that Ma Etty had served. It escalated to shouting, until Ma Etty let out a loud whistle.

Everyone stopped talking.

"I know it was a big day," she said, "but around the dinner table, I expect better. If you have a lot of leftover energy, there's always more work to do around the ranch that I can assign to you during your free time tomorrow."

The kids around the table stayed quiet. At this rate, the three boys would lose all their privileges, probably for the rest of camp.

Ella couldn't believe she was stuck with these people for the next month and a half.

When Ella got up the next morning, Jordan was gone again.

Putting on her sneakers as quietly as she could to avoid waking Madison, Ella slipped out of the bunkhouse into the cool morning air. Sunrise hadn't been that long ago. What was Jordan getting up to do at dawn every morning?

After half an hour scouring the ranch, birds singing their morning songs in the rustling trees, Ella still hadn't found Jordan. It was almost time for breakfast. In a last effort, Ella went inside the barn and wondered why she hadn't checked here first.

Loco Roco's stall door stood slightly ajar, just enough for a slender girl to slip through. Inside the dark stall Jordan stood by Loco's side, stroking his neck as he ate some hay.

Ella felt like an intruder in the cool morning silence. She kept out of sight, and it didn't appear that Jordan had heard her come in. The quiet girl was engrossed in her own thoughts, sliding her hand from Loco Roco's forehead down to his wither, ruffling his mane as he worked through his meal.

Backing away, Ella treaded silently out the way she'd come in, not feeling any more enlightened about the mystery that was Jordan McAdam.

\\

Even breakfast couldn't be a peaceful affair. Kim refused to eat his waffles on the notion that the holes made them inedible (though pancakes were apparently acceptable), and when Ma Etty suggested he fill the gap in his stomach with more sausages and fruit instead, Ash pinched the bridge of his nose.

"Kim was already farting all night," he said, "and now you're giving him fruit? Do you hate us?"

"That was Drew," said Kim, not even looking up from his plate.

"Nice try!" Drew barked out a laugh. "Passing the blame on to me—really, a solid attempt."

"Oh my god." Ella set her fork down on the table with a resounding noise. "Do you guys ever stop? Ever?"

"Someone got up on the wrong side of the bed," said Ash. He was probably still bitter at how she had shut him down yesterday.

"I got up on the perfectly right side of the bed until I came in here and had to be around you idiots!"

"No one at my table is an idiot," Ma Etty said. "And I don't appreciate name-calling." Ma Etty was chastising her, not them?

"It's not name-calling when it's true," Ella snapped, getting to her feet. The burning thing under her skin grew hotter. "I'm just defending myself!"

"Okay, okay," said Fletch, raising his hands. "Ella, sit back down and finish your breakfast." He turned to the boys. "What you said to Ella was pretty rude, too."

"She told me to shut up yesterday," said Ash. Ella clenched her hands under the table.

"Doesn't matter," said Fletch, and even his endless patience seemed to be running thin. "Eat. Then we're going to go ride some horses."

\\\

But breakfast couldn't ruin the excitement Ella felt as she found Figure Eight in her stall again, all fifteen hands of muscle and beauty just waiting to carry Ella off into the sunset.

She remembered Jordan in that stall with Loco Roco this morning, silently stroking his powerful neck. They'd looked so peaceful, so lost in their own shared universe. Ella paused long enough to give Eight a few pats of greeting before putting on the halter and leading her out of her stall.

"Eight is such a pretty paint horse," Jordan said, approaching with Loco Roco.

"Yeah," said Ella, nodding vaguely. "A pretty paint horse, all right." She didn't know what a paint horse was, of course, but she had an idea there was one standing right in front of her, covered in brown splatters.

Out in the arena, Madison did a small demonstration on saddling and bridling with her horse, Snow White, a beautiful little white Appaloosa with black spots all over her rear end. Then the kids saddled their own horses, and it was time to ride.

Fletch walked them through the basics—getting the horses walking, good saddle posture, neck reining. "Pull the reins in the direction you want to go," Fletch instructed. "Right across the neck." Ella didn't understand how this could tell a horse where to go, but it seemed to work if she tugged hard enough.

Remarkably, everyone appeared to be on good behavior. Ella was grateful; she didn't want any distractions keeping her from paying attention and cataloguing all the advice Fletch gave them so she could master this riding thing as fast as possible.

"Okay," said Madison, raising a hand for attention. "I want everyone to start into a walk. Keep your horses along the rail—that means, as close to the fence as possible. Don't let them cut corners."

The first few laps around the arena, Figure Eight kept close to the rail, staying at an even walk. Ella let the reins hang loose, as Fletch had instructed.

This was a breeze. Elation raced through Ella's nerves. She could do this, no problem! Eight's even, smooth gait felt like a dream.

On the third lap, Madison called out to them. "When you reach the far end of the arena—see the letter 'A' hanging from the post?—I want you to turn your horses to the left at the 'A,' toward the inside of the arena. Make a figure eight, please."

Ella grinned at the request. She'd make a figure eight on Figure Eight, all right!

Up ahead, Drew, who walked at the front of the line on his bay horse, reached the "A." He pulled his reins across his horse's neck and the horse turned, albeit slowly and stiffly, toward the middle of the arena.

Ash, who also struggled a little, went next, and then Jordan. She and Loco Roco moved through the turn flawlessly. This was obviously child's play for Jordan. Then Ella reached the "A."

Before she could even move the reins, Eight turned, following the path of the other horses, and headed across the arena. Ella frowned. She hadn't given Eight a signal of any kind—the horse seemed to be mimicking the others.

Ella let it go. It looked like she had done something, anyway, now that Eight was heading successfully through the figure-eight pattern. Neither Fletch nor Madison seemed to have noticed, because neither said anything to her.

"Hey!" Drew hollered from the other end of the arena. "Watch it!"

Ash, who'd been behind Ella, had cut completely across the arena and reversed. He passed Drew going the wrong way, bumping their legs together.

"You watch it," said Ash as he passed.

"You're going the wrong way, Ash," called Madison. "Turn around!"

Ash jerked his reins across his horse's neck, executing a sloppy turn.

When things were moving smoothly again, Fletch asked them for another figure eight at the opposite end of the arena. Again, before Ella and Eight had even reached the "C" sign on the far fencepost and Ella could tell her what to do, Eight was already turning. She headed smoothly across the arena and curved around the opposite end, making a perfect figure eight.

"Don't do that," Ella told her horse, quietly enough that nobody could hear. "Wait for me to tell you what to do."

Eight snorted as if she'd heard and didn't particularly care about Ella's preferences. Up ahead, Jordan rounded the curve and started to turn, gently pulling on the reins. She received an immediate response from Loco Roco, who coasted through the figure eight. Jordan said something to him, leaned forward, and patted his neck in praise.

A stone settled in Ella's stomach.

"Let's talk about using your body to help you turn," said Fletch. "Reins are only part of the bigger picture. The direction of your gaze, the angle of your body, and pressure from your legs all tell your horse what you want."

How could a horse tell where Ella was looking, when the horse was down there and she was up on its back?

"Everyone reverse at the 'A' again," Fletch continued. "But use your reins as little as possible. Look with your eyes where you want to go, angle your body, and apply a small amount of pressure with your outside leg."

It was a lot to keep in mind. Ella tried to remember

it all as Eight reached the "A" sign. Before Ella could give any commands, Eight did a flawless reverse.

"No!" cried Ella.

Madison glanced over. "What's wrong, Ella?"

"She's not listening to me."

"It looks like she reversed just fine," said Madison.

"But I didn't tell her to do it!" Ella's voice cracked with frustration, but she breathed deeply to calm herself. "Figure Eight did it on her own."

Madison considered that and then raised her hands. "Everyone, please stop for a moment. Remember, sit back in your seat, say 'Whoa,' and pull back on the reins."

The second Madison said "stop," Eight ground to a halt—before Ella could put any pressure on the reins at all.

Ella frowned. Sure enough, Eight was listening to the trainers, not to her. Not in the least.

CHAPTER FIVE

"**E**veryone stay stopped for a moment," said Madison in the center of the ring. She gestured to Ella. "Ella, tell Eight to go forward."

Before Ella could kick, Eight started to walk forward.

"Stop it," said Ella, yanking back on her reins. Eight kept walking. "Whoa! Whoa!"

Eight did finally stop, three steps later.

"Ask her to back up," said Madison. "Those same three steps."

But Eight was already backing up before Ella could ask for it.

"Agh!" cried Ella. "She keeps doing it!"

"It's okay, Ella," said Madison. "I won't speak

this time. Wait a moment, then ask again for the three steps."

After Madison had been quiet for a while, Ella pulled the reins tightly, sat back in her saddle, and shouted, "Back!"

Eight jerked her head, trying to free herself from Ella's iron grip on the reins. But Ella wasn't going to let her get her way that easily. "Back!" she said again, tightening her hold and pulling even more against Eight's mouth, and following it up with a firm kick.

"Not so forcefully," said Madison.

"But she won't do it otherwise," said Ella. The frustration grew and blossomed, turning her chest hot.

"Your arms are too high," said Madison. "Keep your elbows level with your hips. Pull straight back with the reins, not up by your shoulders." She turned to Jordan. "Could you demonstrate for us, Jordan?"

Jordan nodded. She dropped her elbows down by her sides, holding the reins in her fingers the way Ella's dad held the brakes when he took out his road bike. She gave a tiny tug, saying, "Back."

Loco Roco immediately took a step back.

"See the way she gives the command?" asked Madison. "Gentle tug with the fingers, elbows down."

"Sure," said Ella, but she had only half been

paying attention—too mad at Figure Eight to focus. Ella was going to make this horse listen to her.

Squaring up her shoulders, Ella yanked back on the reins, saying louder, "Back up!" Figure Eight resisted again.

"Back up!" Ella cried.

"Take it easy," said Fletch, approaching. "No need to yell."

"She's not listening!" Tears of frustration filled Ella's eyes. She couldn't cry. Just thinking about crying in front of everyone, on the first day of riding lessons, made anger boil up again.

"Let's let it go, then," said Fletch gently, and even the calm patience in his voice made Ella angrier, like he was condescending to her. "Everyone, resume a walk. Remember to stay on the rail."

Again, before Ella could even give the command to start again, Eight began walking.

"NO!" Ella shouted, yanking hard on the reins. "STOP!"

Then the angry tears broke loose.

"Ella, calm down," said Fletch again, then immediately looked like he regretted saying it.

"You calm down!" Ella roared at him. Then she turned back to Eight's reins in her hands and started yelling, "Back!" Now that she understood this was a remedial tactic for a horse that overstepped, she was going to use it. "Back!"

"Ella!" Fletch was at her side before she could blink and grabbed the reins away from her. "Stop right now. I will not allow you to treat your horse this way."

"She's the one who won't do what I tell her!" Tears rolled down Ella's face. The humiliation made her vision red. Even Jordan looked horrified, perhaps even ashamed for her.

Ella hated her for that look.

"Get off," said Fletch, his voice hard and stern. "Right now."

Ella climbed haphazardly out of the saddle, turned, and raced out of the arena, back to the bunkhouse.

\\

No one came after her, which made the fury bubble up even higher. Shouldn't someone care that she'd stormed off in a huff?

But no one followed her to the bunkhouse, where she crawled up onto her bunk and cried angry tears into her pillow. The one time she thought she heard somebody coming to check on her, she raised her head—but realized it was only chickens scuffling outside. When she looked down, she saw she'd left wet splotches on the fabric in the exact shape of her face.

When she was all cried out, Ella simply lay there, staring up at the ceiling with crusty, reddened eyes. What a disaster this day had been. What a disaster this whole camp was.

Outside, she heard the other kids pass by her window—arguing about something or other, Madison trying to quiet them down.

When they were gone, Ella crept to the bunk- house door and peeked out. Her stomach grumbled. Everyone was probably heading in to help fix lunch.

Ella slipped out the door and followed behind them, staying out of sight. The three boys blundered inside the mudroom at the back of the house, and Jordan followed in their wake. Ella stood outside, trying to decide whether she should go in and eat lunch with everyone like nothing was wrong, or mope for a while longer.

Voices—different ones, older ones—floated out an open window on the side of the house. Right away she recognized Mr. Bridle's deep rumble.

Creeping up to the window, Ella scanned inside. There was a little office with a desk, a computer, and a spinning chair. The door sat closed, but the window was cracked to let in fresh air. Fletch, Madison, Ma Etty, and Mr. Bridle stood in a circle, heads bent together.

"This is the toughest group I've ever worked with," said Ma Etty. "In the twenty years we've been running this program, I've never had kids who had so much difficulty . . . settling in."

"It's only the second day," said Mr. Bridle. But he shook his head anyway. "Sure has been a tough two days, though, I'll give ya that, Etty."

Ma Etty sighed. "I don't know what we were thinking, putting them all in the same group. So many strong personalities—we should have known they would clash."

"Can't know anything like that in advance," said Fletch. "We did the best we could. We are doing our best, still. And we will for the next six weeks." He said it with no question in his voice, as if once camp had begun, he'd see it through to the last minute.

Ma Etty nodded. "Somehow, they need to see

that they're in this together." She rubbed her chin. "That they're on a team, not opposing forces. It's not a competition. It's a cooperation."

Madison sounded defeated as she said, "But, Ma Etty, it doesn't even seem like they like horses all that much." Ella sank lower under the windowsill, guilt turning her stomach sour. "Except Jordan."

Ella had really messed up—and now Jordan looked even more glittery and perfect.

As the group stood in morose silence, Ma Etty's head popped up like a gopher coming out of a hole. Her eyes glittered.

"That's it!"

The other three stared at her like she'd grown an extra arm. "What's it?" asked Madison.

"The horses are the reason we're all here," Ma Etty said proudly. "We just need to remind these kids of that fact. They came because they wanted to ride, because they felt a connection with horses. And that connection will bring those kids together."

Even Mr. Bridle sounded baffled by Ma Etty's train of thought. "They already had a lesson today," he said.

"It didn't go well," added Madison.

"I know, I know. Just listen. Fletch—what inspired you to pursue horsemanship seriously?"

Fletch scratched his head at the obvious question. "Well, George Fletcher. Bronc riding. As soon as I saw those old photographs, I knew what I wanted to be."

"Exactly." Ma Etty's entire face lit up. "Let's take them to a rodeo."

Madison still looked like she wasn't following, but the delight had spread to Fletch, too.

"The rodeo!"

"Yep. The Steamboat County Fair is happening right now. We'll have to make some phone calls to get permission, but we can do it. Those kids take one look at true horsemanship, and things will change. You'll see. If it could turn your life around, Fletch, it can do the same for others. Everyone can see themselves in the rodeo."

Ella backed away from the window. Ma Etty thought she'd be surprising them with this great news. Ella couldn't afford to miss acting excited, and hopefully fix what she'd messed up with Fletch and Madison.

She scurried around the side of the house and went in the front door, where the other kids had already taken seats around the table and were now bickering over when lunch was going to come out. All except Jordan, of course, who sat picking dirt out from under her fingernails, unperturbed by the disorder.

When Ella sat down, everyone went silent. She knew this silence. It was the same silence that had greeted Ella at the lunch table after she hit Bianca square in the mouth for that snide comment about her hair. It was the silence of people who would now tread more carefully, afraid of what they might do or say to set her off next.

Ella liked and hated this feeling equally. Now they'd never be her real friends—but they'd also avoid pushing her buttons. It was a tenuous compromise.

Soon Madison and Fletch returned, followed by Ma Etty with steaming cast-iron pans full of fajita fixings. No one remarked on Ella's reappearance.

When lunch was over, Ma Etty called for everyone's attention.

"I have a surprise for you!" she said gleefully.

"A surprise?" Kim's lips puckered. "I don't like surprises."

But no one could bring Ma Etty's mood down. "We're going to the rodeo," she said, smiling more to herself than to them. At the word *rodeo*, Jordan's chin snapped up.

"A rodeo?" said Ash. "Sweet." Then he added, "Wait, what happens at a rodeo?"

Drew laughed. "And Dallas calls himself a Cowboys fan!"

CHAPTER SIX

Ma Etty set a dress code for her ranch kids heading to the rodeo, so after Ella and Jordan finished packing up their day packs, Madison gave them button-up shirts that were a little too big but served fine with the sleeves rolled up.

"Oh!" Madison said. "One more thing!" Diving back into her room, she rummaged around before returning with two big cowboy hats, which she gleefully stuck on their heads. She grinned at Ella and Jordan with pride, then put on her own hat just as they were readying to leave.

"Let's get along, dogies," she said in a low cowboy voice, swaggering as she walked, and both Ella and Jordan cracked up as she led them out of the bunkhouse to the waiting van.

It was a junky old thing, but with Fletch at the wheel, it got them safely to the fairgrounds. Ella had never seen so many cowboy hats in a single place. Drew gave a running commentary of every new thing he saw. "Those cows have huge horns!" "Whoa, that horse is as big as an elephant." "What kind of saddle is that?" "Those guys are riding without bridles or halters or anything! How do they do it?"

No one bothered shushing him anymore. Eventually the van pulled into a parking spot and stopped. They unloaded from the van, and the loud, bustling rodeo unfolded around them.

There was an event at every building in the county fair, and at every moment, some audience was hooting and hollering. Right at the entrance, in a long, oval-shaped arena, a woman stood in front of a horse, the two of them staring at each other like rivals before a duel. The woman dropped to one knee, and to the kids' amazement, so did the horse. Then she dropped to both knees, and the horse followed so it was bowing before her. Then, they both shot up to their feet again, and spun in matching circles, to roaring applause.

"Wow," said Drew, and that seemed to be all he could say. For a moment, none of the kids spoke. Then Ash clapped his hands together.

"I didn't know horses could do that! This rodeo thing is going to kill my friends back home. I gotta remember to take pictures."

In her peripheral vision, Ella glimpsed Ma Etty's mischievous grin.

After the show, the kids split up, allowed to wander in pairs ("Use the buddy system!" Ma Etty said) as long as they were all back at the meeting point by one for lunch.

Unable to stand any of his fellow campers for a moment longer, Kim left with quiet old Mr. Bridle to watch calf roping. Ash and Drew, always hungry for thrills, went to see the bronc riding that Fletch had talked so much about on the ride over. Fletch and Madison left to check out the livestock, leaving Jordan and Ella to pair up.

What luck. Ella wanted a partner like Madison, who'd at least speak to her. But Jordan didn't seem to care either way where she ended up, and when Ella prompted her about what she wanted to do, Jordan shrugged, pointed, and said, "Let's go that way, I guess."

So they took off toward the covered arena, where shouts echoed under the aluminum roof.

People had packed the bleachers to popping. Ella and Jordan found seats way down in the middle. They had a lame view, stuck behind a guy who was at least seven feet tall. At Ella's grouching Jordan said, "Let's stay for a little bit, and if it's boring, we'll go find something else to do."

This was the most words they'd exchanged since arriving at the ranch, so Ella took it. She still wanted to know about those worn-out riding boots, to assess her competition.

Then Jordan said, "Look—over there, in the starting pen."

On the other end of the arena, a woman in a red shirt and cowboy hat rode a big brown horse through the gate.

"What a gorgeous quarter horse," Jordan murmured. The horse looked a lot like Figure Eight in shape, Ella thought, even though the color was different. Its neck was thick at the base, the chest full and shaped like a barrel, and the hindquarters so muscular they appeared almost square. When the excited horse moved, raring to gallop forward into the ring, all its honed muscles rippled.

Then, suddenly, the horse and its rider were off. Hooves roared into the arena. The rider's hat flew off immediately, letting her black braid swing behind her, and the crowd around Ella and Jordan burst into laughter.

Three tall barrels, arranged in a triangular pattern, waited for the competitors in the back center of the arena. She blazed straight toward them.

The woman and her horse turned so fast and so tight around the first barrel that Ella stood up quickly, thinking they might fall over, wanting to make sure she didn't miss it. They ran around the second, then to the third in the back, and galloped toward home at a speed Ella had never seen an animal go in real life.

"Seventeen point seven three seconds!" an announcer's voice boomed over the PA. "A fantastic showing from Missy Elwood and her stallion, Achilles!"

Applause rattled the metal bleachers, and Ella covered her ears as she waited for it to die down.

Then the next contestant entered the ring.

\\\

Ella's eyes never once left the arena as another woman came out on a beautiful yellow horse with a white mane and tail, the yellow splotched a little like watercolor.

"Ooh," said Jordan. "Definitely a full quarter horse. Must be. And that beautiful palomino coloring."

Ella could see what she meant now by 'quarter horse.' This animal was built long and thick and sturdy like the last one, with the same pretty, square jaw and full nose as Figure Eight.

"Do most people ride quarter horses in this event?" Ella said, hating the ignorance in her voice. But even her dad had to take classes on new subjects sometimes, had to ask his colleagues questions.

Jordan nodded. "Quarter horses are the best breed for barrel racing. They're good at the quick turn because of those huge haunches, and those super-fast starts."

Barrel racing. That's what this event was. Ella returned her attention to the woman and her yellow horse.

After a brief wait, they shot into the arena just like the first competitor had, straight toward the first barrel. They wrapped around it like a snake, tilting toward the ground in order to make the sharp turn.

Once the woman and her horse had gone most of the way around the first barrel, they galloped on to the second, speeding around it at an even more ridiculous cut than they had the previous one. Sweat coursed down the palomino's thick chest.

A timer was counting up, approaching ten seconds. Horse and rider got so close to the last barrel that her boot tapped the side. It tipped precariously. The crowd, Ella included, took in a collective breath.

The rider galloped on, speeding toward the exit—all while the barrel continued to tip. But as the competitor raced out of the ring, it became clear the toe-tap had been minor and the barrel righted itself.

A cheer burst from the audience.

"Narrow escape," said Jordan.

Ella couldn't help asking, "Escape from what?"

"Knocking over a barrel is a five-second penalty."

"That's harsh," Ella said. That was basically an automatic loss.

How did Jordan know something like that?

\\\

Ella and Jordan didn't agree on it out loud, but it was clear after they'd watched four competitors that they were staying to watch the rest. Ella wanted to know who would secure the fastest time.

Each rider seemed better than the last—quicker, more daring, making even tighter turns. One was penalized for knocking over a barrel, another for missing a barrel and going around it the wrong way.

"How do they turn like that?" Ella whispered to no one in particular. The riders hardly used their reins, it seemed. How did the horse know what to do?

"See their thighs and knees?" Jordan pointed at a rider heading out into the arena. "All the cues come through the legs. They're really bending their horses around the barrels—putting pressure on the front inside with the knee, to make the body curve in toward the barrel on the approach."

Jordan sounded so smart as she talked about this. Ella was impressed.

"As you get close to the barrel, you apply pressure with your leg on the outside, and pull the reins the way you want to go." Jordan gestured to illustrate. "That forces the horse to curve away from the pressure but keep moving in the same direction as the reins. It wraps the whole horse around the barrel."

As Ella watched the next rider, she saw in action what Jordan had explained: the rider's hands gently urged the neck around the barrel, while the outside leg pressed the horse into the optimal curve, then the inside leg straightened them out again as they pushed off to the next barrel.

It was mastery of horsemanship, pure elegance in the saddle.

Ella had to say what she kept wondering. "How do you know all this, Jordan?"

Jordan shrugged. "Somebody told me. A smart woman I know."

Ella gave her a skeptical side-glance, but when Jordan offered no other explanation, Ella decided to take her word for it.

"They're so fast—I didn't expect that." Another rider came out and tore around the cloverleaf pattern. Ella found herself grinning hugely. "I love it."

Jordan smiled. "Yeah," she said. "Me too."

They both stood in awe of the performance, sharing silence amid the tinny clang of feet on the bleachers and cheers from the audience.

Barrel racing.

Ella wondered if this was something that she could do. It was a perfect balance of skill and speed, technique and thrill.

"How hard is it to learn barrel racing?" Ella asked.

Jordan gazed into the arena. "Not hard. The pattern's simple. It's the technique that's difficult to master." They watched the final competitor take the barrels at a speed that looked almost dangerous. The horse snorted with each labored breath as they galloped home. "Like anything, I guess, it takes time and dedication to be really good at it."

Ella nodded, but she was already picturing herself atop one of those big horses, hat flying off her head as they cornered a barrel at a risky, heart-pumping speed.

"You know," said Jordan, surprising Ella by continuing on unprompted, "I heard Figure Eight has a long quarter horse lineage. Her build is perfect for barrel racing. If you wanted to learn, I think you'd be all set on a horse like that."

Her words went straight to Ella's heart.

"You think?" Ella asked. "Figure Eight?"

"Absolutely. Maybe she's been trained to do it already. Who knows?" Jordan smiled again.

Two smiles in one day? Ella wondered if something was wrong.

CHAPTER SEVEN

Ella couldn't contain her excitement the rest of the rodeo. They had funnel cakes and threw darts at balloons, but as they stood eating ice cream by a game Ash was spending all of his money on, she said, "The barrels were the coolest thing at this rodeo." She glanced at Jordan. "Wasn't it, Jordan?"

Jordan stared back at her, like a deer caught in oncoming headlights. "Uh, sure."

"Don't say that yet, Ella," said Fletch, breaking into a grin, like he knew a big secret that she didn't. "You haven't seen the team roping yet."

In the afternoon competition, quarter horses again headlined the show. Fletch and Madison pointed out the colors and breeds they could recognize as the teams lined up to rope their steer.

Drew let out a hoot as the event started and the steer was let free. The front rider got ahold of him by the horns with a huge lasso, and he and his horse together pulled the steer in a half-circle so its hind legs were exposed. The second rider raced up behind him, lassoing the steer's legs. His horse planted its feet firmly, pulling the rope taut, and the creature was immobilized.

It all happened in a matter of seconds. Everyone cheered.

But all Ella could think about was racing around those barrels, pinning her turns as tightly as physics would allow, and tearing up dirt as she and Figure Eight sprinted back to home base. The crowd roared in adulation, stamping the bleachers.

Now that they were reunited with the group, Jordan sank quietly into the background. But talk spilled out of everyone else on the ride home.

"Fletch," said Ash, "is it hard to be a bronc rider?"

"Sort of," said Fletch. "At least, being a good bronc rider is hard. You have to have guts."

"I want to try it!"

"When you get a little older, why not?"

"Bronc riding looks like a good way to break

your neck," said Kim. "I'm going to teach my horse to do tricks, like that bowing horse we saw. Things that don't involve getting thrown down and stomped by a bucking bronc."

"Me too," said Drew. "I want my horse to bow like that. But I want to ride the broncs, too. I'd hang on real well. I'm great at hanging on. And I want to split up the cows! That looked like so much fun. Is it hard? I want to try before camp is over."

Ella couldn't wait for lessons tomorrow, either. She was going to ask Madison about learning to barrel race. Like Jordan said, Figure Eight was built to run the cloverleaf pattern. Ella imagined the crowd again, roaring, whooping, cheering for her and her beautiful horse. It was up to Ella to fulfill both of their destinies.

That night, Ella was asleep before she was all the way under the covers, and she dreamed of hooves kicking up clouds of dust.

\\\

The next morning, Jordan beat Ella awake again, and was gone before anyone else got out of bed. Jordan left her bunk a mess of blankets and sheets—as it always was, no matter how many times Madison told them to make their beds.

So Ella decided against going looking for Jordan, already knowing where she'd find her. If Jordan wanted to get up early and spend time with her horse, why not get special permission to ride solo? She'd easily get it. The trainers trusted her.

Instead, Ella put on her shoes and got down to the pasture so she could watch the sun come up. Even though the mantra was her dad's—*early to bed, early to rise*—Ella's mom had been the one to actually live it. When Ella was younger and her mom still lived with them, Mom was the one who'd get up at the crack of dawn just to watch the sun rise. When Ella climbed out of bed early to watch cartoons, she'd find her mom already awake, a mug of coffee in her hand, gazing out the kitchen window at the orange horizon.

Ella wondered what Mom would think of this ranch. She'd probably never find out, though, because Ella made a point of not calling her mom anymore. She hated when Mom popped into her thoughts like this, and she didn't want to encourage it. It was just like Mom to barge in and dump a bunch of feelings on Ella, without even being there in person.

Because thoughts like that—those wistful, pointless longings like *Mom would think this place is amazing*—were a distraction. They were the kind of thing Ella's dad warned her to avoid.

Have a couple school friends, he said, *but don't spend too much time with them and neglect your homework. Friends can be distractions.* Distractions from the big picture, from getting what you want.

Mom hadn't been the kind of person who was the best at anything, the way Ella and her dad were. Mom was mostly just okay at a lot of things. Maybe that was why she left. Maybe being around someone like Dad all the time was too hard. She'd sure had a lot more friends than he did, though.

A noise startled Ella. Someone else was hanging around the pasture, too. Ella scanned up and down the fence until she spotted Jordan, sitting on the top of the pasture fence, hidden from casual observation by the shadow of some stacked hay bales. She must have seen Ella long ago, Ella thought, and not said anything. How did Jordan blend in like that?

Neither of them greeted the other. At first, the silence made Ella itch with discomfort. She wanted to ask Jordan a million questions about why she was so strange, and how she was so good at horseback riding.

But Ella was unwilling to shatter the crystalline quiet that radiated from Jordan like a shield.

After a few minutes, Ella forgot what she'd wanted to say anyway, and got lost in the way the shifting light broke over the trees. She wasn't sure how much time had passed when they heard Madison calling their names. But Jordan climbed down from the fence, still not speaking, and Ella clambered down after her. Then the two girls silently headed inside for breakfast.

\\

On the way out to the barn for lessons, Ella was bouncing on the balls of her feet, thinking all over again about the riders roaring past at the rodeo, hats flying off, tearing turns around the barrels. The kids took turns tacking up as usual, until it came time for Ella to get Eight out of her stall.

"Actually," said Madison, stopping her. She pointed to a closer stall door, "you're riding Lacey today."

"What?" asked Ella, voice breaking.

Madison opened the stall and started buckling a halter onto the little brown pony inside.

"I've got you on a new horse," Madison said.

"Lacey may be small, but she's willing and fun to ride. You'll like her a lot, I think."

Ella felt like she'd been kicked. No—kicked and then punched. Then stabbed right through the chest.

"What about Figure Eight?" Ella asked, her voice rising an octave as Madison put Lacey into cross-ties. "I'm supposed to ride Figure Eight."

"I figured with Eight giving you so much trouble last time, we'd get you up to speed on the basics with Lacey, since she's a little more forgiving. Then, when you've gotten the hang of riding, we'll put you back on Figure Eight."

The image in Ella's mind—of tearing around a barrel at maximum velocity with Figure Eight—burst into flames.

"No." Ella glared at the little bay pony patiently waiting to be brushed. "No way. You can't do this to me."

A crease appeared on Madison's forehead. "Do what to you? Lacey is a fantastic pony. She'll teach you a lot."

"I don't want that horse!" cried Ella. "I want Figure Eight. I want my horse back."

"Well," said Madison, turning her back to Ella, "that's too bad. You've proven you can't keep your temper in check with Figure Eight, so I had to pair you with a different horse. If you show that you can be patient—"

"NO!" Ella roared, slamming one fist into the stall door. It rattled the metal bars up and down the barn, startling the horses.

"Hey now," said Madison, stepping toward Ella. "None of that in here."

"You can't!" Ella wailed, angry tears slipping down her face. How could Madison do this to her? Figure Eight was hers! They had a destiny to fulfill. "No! It's not fair!"

With a sob of anger, Ella kicked a plastic barrel full of horse biscuits. It went spinning across the floor, surprising Lacey.

"Ella Pierson." Ma Etty's stern voice sliced the air. "Get out of my barn. *Now.*"

CHAPTER EIGHT

The deep laugh-lines on Ma Etty's face were, for the first time that Ella had seen, completely devoid of laughter. The old lady's bright eyes had turned to ice as she regarded Ella.

Ella's temper flared, like a bonfire with new tinder. Who did she think she was, kicking Ella out of the barn? She was about to object to the humiliation, but Madison said, "I'll put Lacey back."

With no horse to ride, there was no point in Ella still standing there, so she crossed her arms and stomped outside. Ma Etty followed her and slowly, calmly, closed the barn doors behind them.

"How dare you?" demanded Ella. The old lady had actually kicked her out!

Ma Etty's lips were a thin line. "Luckily, Lacey is such a good pony she didn't spook when you kicked over those biscuits—but what if your carelessness had frightened her, and she hurt herself? Or hurt Madison? What about all of my horses who are now distressed because some young lady, who should know better, threw a toddler's temper tantrum in my barn?" The old lady stared Ella down. "I'm the one who should be saying 'How dare you.'"

Ella wanted to scream, to punch that retort right out of Ma Etty's mouth. At the thought, she jammed her hands into her jean pockets and bit her lip as hard as she could.

But Ma Etty didn't look afraid, the way everyone else did when Ella started thinking about socking someone in the mug. Ella had deduced that it showed on her face when she was about to punch, because most people got fear in their eyes and backed away.

Ma Etty only raised her eyebrows at Ella— almost, Ella thought, like a taunt.

That poured cold water over her fire. She would never hit an old lady, not ever. Ella glared bitterly at the ground as the rage melted off into tears.

"There now," said Ma Etty, leading Ella over to the bench next to the barn, where observers could watch activity out in the arena. "Feel better?"

Ella wiped at her face, wishing she was not crying in front of Ma Etty. The embarrassment made her angry all over again.

"No," said Ella crossly. "I don't feel better. You took away my horse. I want to ride Figure Eight. I want to barrel race."

That made Ma Etty sit up a little straighter. "Barrel race?" Her mouth curved up on one side. "Oh, I see. Did you and Jordan see the barrel racing at the rodeo?"

Ella nodded silently, sniffling.

"Interesting." Ma Etty *hmm*ed, looking out over the other kids and their horses as they did warm-up laps. "Well, I see why you threw a little fit over Madison pairing you up with Lacey. Figure Eight is the perfect horse for running barrels." She *hmm*ed again, and Ella felt her temper erupt once more at Ma Etty's calmness. It annoyed Ella how the old lady always seemed totally in control of herself, in a way Ella never was.

"If she's so perfect for it, then why can't I ride her?" demanded Ella.

"Good question," said Ma Etty. "Why can't you?"

Ella glared at her for tossing the question back. But Ma Etty sat patiently, awaiting an answer.

"Because you won't let me," Ella finally said.

"Even if I did let you, you'd still have trouble riding her. You might even throw a tantrum again, like at your last lesson. What's different now that you can suddenly ride a horse you couldn't ride before?"

"I want to barrel race now," said Ella. "I have to." Figure Eight would sense this immense shift in Ella's priorities, she was sure. And Eight would respond to her determination. They had a destiny to run those barrels together.

"I ask again," said Ma Etty, "what's different now? Just because you want to do something far off in the future doesn't change the fact that, as of this second, at your current skill level, you cannot ride Figure Eight without losing your temper."

This roundabout discussion made Ella want to scream. "Far off in the future?" she said. "I could start learning to barrel race today, this second, if you let me ride Eight!"

"No, you couldn't."

There was no room in that cool tone for argument. Ella felt like a bug squashed under a very large shoe.

"What do you mean, I can't?" Ella croaked. Her fantasy of Eight's hooves eating the dirt, of the cheering crowd in the stands, was dying.

"From what you saw at the rodeo, did barrel racing look easy?"

Ella was about to respond with an instant *yes, obviously*, when she thought about those steep, knee-to-the-ground turns. She remembered what Jordan had said about using knees and thighs together to wrap the horse's body so tightly around the barrel. "Well, no . . ."

"Let's say Figure Eight already knows how to run a cloverleaf pattern," Ma Etty said, though her tone carefully didn't give away whether or not this was the case. "Do you think that right now, you could barrel race and not hurt yourself? That you'd have even a chance of telling Eight what to do, and of her listening to you, after your last lesson?"

Ella didn't speak, but she shut her eyes and rubbed her palms against them, attempting to stave off more tears.

"I'm not trying to make you feel bad, but expert-level barrel racing takes years of hard work and training," Ma Etty went on. "But most of all, it requires an incredible degree of trust between horse and rider. And at the skill level you are now, what reason does Figure Eight have to trust you?"

"I can work hard," said Ella, with all the force she had inside her small body. That was the one thing she knew she could do: put herself to a task and work at it until she'd won, until she'd figured it out, until she'd hammered and clawed her way through every obstacle in her path. "I can work hard enough to do anything I want."

As she heard herself saying it, Ella thought, *That's what Dad always says, too.* That made her mad again.

"With horses," said Ma Etty, "just working harder isn't enough."

Ella couldn't imagine a problem that couldn't be solved by working a few more hours, trying a new tack.

"It takes patience," Ma Etty went on. "Kindness. Compassion. Thoughtfulness."

Not Ella's usual tools for success. But like anything, she figured, if she worked at it, Ella would bet money she could get good at them. She'd be the most patient, the most kind, the most compassionate—if that meant getting Figure Eight back.

"And when I have those things?" Ella asked. "When I'm thoughtful and compassionate and whatever, can I ride Figure Eight again? Learn to barrel race?"

Ma Etty raised both eyebrows.

"Ride Lacey," she said. "Stick with her for a while. Prove to me you're not just a good rider—that's required, too—but that you're a patient rider. A kind and sensitive rider."

"How do I prove that?" Ella asked, annoyed.

"I get regular progress reports from Fletch and Madison," said Ma Etty. "When you've got that temper under control, we'll talk again." She stood up. "Then you should ask Jordan for help with the barrel racing part."

"Jordan?" Ella frowned.

"She won first place at the California Junior Rodeo last year. She's an expert barrel racer—plus, she has a fantastic knack for horses. There's a lot you could learn from her, Ella."

This information stunned Ella so completely, she couldn't say anything for almost a minute. Her thoughts raced as she looked out into the arena, where the other kids were working on their posture. Jordan, with her little brown ponytail waving behind her, checked her heels along with everyone else.

How do you know all this, Jordan?
Somebody told me. A smart woman I know.
Jordan had lied to her.

\\\

Even after her talk with Ma Etty, Ella was still banned from the barn for the rest of the day, so she hung around outside kicking rocks and thinking.

First place at the California Junior Rodeo. What a whopper to keep secret. Why? If Ella had won something like that, it would have been the first thing she said at introductions.

When Madison handed out their chores, Ella found she'd been paired up with Jordan in the chicken coop. What luck. Now Ella had a chance to interrogate her.

Why had Jordan said someone told her about the finer points of racing, when really, she was an expert in her own right?

Ella wanted to expose Jordan, make a chip in her perfect image, and call her out on such a bald-faced lie.

But Ella remembered she already had one strike against her, so as angry as she was, she decided not to speak to Jordan . . . yet. She might say something that would get herself in trouble again.

In the chicken yard, Ma Etty gave the girls a rundown of their duties, and finished by saying, "Now, these chickens are my babies. Treat them like you would treat, well, someone's babies." She stooped, patted a chicken on the head, and said, "Sesame Seed here is my favorite, but don't tell Dumpling." Then she left them to it.

They gathered the eggs in silence, startling a few chickens still sitting on them. After off-loading the basket in the kitchen, they returned to refill the chicken feeder and check the water level.

Finally, as they started sweeping out the chicken coop, Ella couldn't hold it in any longer.

"What's your deal?" she said, halting her broom.

Jordan looked up. "What?"

"You lied to me, Jordan."

Her eyebrows knitted together. "Did I? I don't remember—"

"About knowing how to barrel race." Ella gave a short, bitter laugh. "Ma Etty told me that you won a barrel racing championship. Why didn't you tell me?"

The color drained from Jordan's high cheekbones.

"O-oh," she said. "That."

"'Oh that'?" Ella mocked. "That's all you have to say?"

"It . . . it was just a fluke." Jordan clutched her broom handle. "It wasn't me at all. It was Mrs. Rose's horse, Antonio."

Ella crossed her arms. "Who's Mrs. Rose?"

"A real nice lady who lives down the road from me," said Jordan, looking anywhere but at Ella. "She lets me ride Antonio sometimes. He's . . . he's a really fantastic animal." Jordan's hands trembled as she started sweeping again, avoiding meeting Ella's gaze by staring hard at the broom handle. "Antonio knows the barrels by heart. Just runs them on his own. I don't even have to do anything, besides hold onto the reins and lean forward."

"You're trying to tell me a horse won a championship for you?"

Jordan nodded rapidly. She got the broom stuck in a cranny and pulled on it, but her movements were sloppy and distracted.

"Like I said, I don't know a lot about barrel racing. But Antonio is the whole package. He loves the barrels, you know? He'd run them even if I wasn't on his back. Loves the thrill—eats it up. Especially once people start yelling and cheering, he's a big ham."

Ella let this wash over her, because as unlikely as it sounded, she could imagine a smart horse like Figure Eight acting like that, too. But Ella couldn't believe Jordan had nothing at all to do with winning a regional championship.

"You knew all that stuff about barrel racing at the rodeo," said Ella. "You must be kind of good at it."

Jordan gave her trademark shrug. "Mrs. Rose taught me a little, and lets me exercise her horses for her after school. When she suggested I compete on Antonio because he loves the spotlight, I agreed. That's all. It was just good luck, and Antonio."

"Then why did you come here?" asked Ella, her tone accusatory, feeling she still had something to be mad at Jordan about, that there was still some inherent deceit. "I thought this place was for kids who wanted to learn how to ride, not for people who are already good at it."

"I . . ." Jordan swallowed, her eyes never leaving the floor. "Ma Etty said it was fine. My parents thought that since, you know, I've had one good thing happen to me on a horse, that coming here would be good for me. That it would teach me focus, or determination, or something." She sucked in a big breath, and she gave Ella the impression of a vase, perched precariously on the edge of a shelf, about to tip over and smash on the ground. "I only came here because my parents sent me. It wasn't my choice, you know."

She said this last part almost angrily, and turned her head away, cradling the broom handle to her chest.

That made it a little better to Ella, that Jordan had been sent here against her will. She felt sympathetic to that, also having a strong-willed parent.

"How long have you been riding?" asked Ella, incredibly curious now about how this shy, quiet girl had won a championship. "How did you hook up with this lady, Mrs. Rose?"

But Jordan stared at the floor, sweeping the same spot she'd swept five times already. "Not long," was all she said.

After that, Ella couldn't wiggle even one more word out of Jordan—only grunts and shrugs and head shakes. Ella regretted calling her a liar, because now Jordan wouldn't even look Ella in the eye.

They spent the rest of the afternoon cleaning the chicken coop in total silence. If only she hadn't slammed the door to Jordan McAdam, just as it was starting to open.

CHAPTER NINE

Ella had her dad's persistence, so she didn't let what had happened with Jordan trouble her. The next day during the morning riding lesson, she threw herself into becoming the best horsewoman she could, even though she had to ride snooze-fest Lacey.

And as Ma Etty had suggested, Lacey did listen to Ella. Whenever Ella asked, Lacey walked or turned or backed up around the orange cones Fletch had arranged. The rodeo seemed to have worked a bit of magic on the other kids too, because all their attention was focused on speeding up to a trot. Ella watched Fletch and Madison's faces, wondering if this step was enough, and when they'd report back to Ma Etty that she was ready to ride Figure Eight again.

Probably not, though. Ella had a feeling that impressing Ma Etty wouldn't be easy.

Ella and Lacey were walking directly behind Jordan and Loco Roco. Ella hated watching them, the way they seemed to work in perfect tandem, like two halves of the same whole. He anticipated her commands, often sliding to a smooth stop before she could say "Whoa." Jordan barely looked like she was doing anything to get sharp turns and careful, snakelike bends around orange cones.

As Ella watched Jordan silently sway in her saddle, moving in perfect rhythm with Loco's walk, she wondered if Ma Etty's prescription could actually work—if Ella could ever become the kind of horsewoman that Jordan was.

\\

Ella got paired up with Kim that afternoon for chores, and though she'd dreaded it during lunch, it turned out that Kim was good company. He kept to himself unless he had a sarcastic remark to make, like, "You'd think this fly would get the hint after the fifth time I've almost smacked him." There wasn't much glory in gardening—just a lot of dirt. Ella wanted to complain, but she didn't.

Patience. Kindness. Compassion. Thoughtfulness. She kept repeating the words in her head.

She tried the thoughtfulness part out while they worked, but it was deadly boring. She couldn't think about anything except how badly she wanted to be racing around those barrels on Figure Eight's back.

Saturday was supposed to be blazing hot, so Fletch and Madison planned a ride out into the wilderness that bordered the ranch, where the trees and the mountains would keep them cool.

Ella wanted to ask about taking Eight, because they'd just be plodding along at a walk the whole time, but she remembered: *patience.* Ugh.

As the kids gathered with their horses in the gravel parking lot for the ride, baking under the hot sun, a man rode a huge horse down Bridlemile Road from the northern end of the ranch. Ella had heard from Drew that the Bridles grazed cattle up there.

The man had windswept blond hair and a bushy mustache. His enormous horse, colored the strangest deep brownish-red, stopped in front of them. Three handsome, black-and-white dogs trailed along behind.

"Paul, glad you could make it," said Madison,

waving from the ground. "Think you can handle this group?"

Paul emitted a bellyful of laughter. "Handle?" he said. "Who needs handlin', Maddie? We're just gonna go walk through some woods and enjoy the scenery together."

At this, Madison stifled a laugh. "All right then," she said, and then waved to the kids. "Paul here is the ranch manager at Quartz Creek Ranch, and he offered to lead your trail ride today. Fletch and I are staying here to catch up on exercising our own horses. So please listen to Paul as if he were us." She paused, then said, "Scratch that. Don't listen to him as if he were us. Listen to him as if he were a two-hundred-pound man who knows how to fire a rifle through a coyote's heart at three hundred yards. That's more accurate."

Paul gave her a perplexed look, but Madison just winked and sauntered off.

"Okay then," said Paul, pointing off toward the green mountains lying to the west of them. "Let's go!"

"This all is White River National Forest," said Paul, gesturing grandly at the blue-green trees sprouting up all around them as they wound uphill, into the woods. "One of the prettiest darn places in the whole wide world, if you ask me."

"I don't remember asking," said Kim near the back, so only Ella, Drew, and Jordan could hear. Ella and Drew both chuckled.

"What's that back there?" called Paul.

"Nothing," said Kim. "Just agreeing with you."

"Hmm," said Paul.

That made Drew and Ella giggle even harder. Jordan, who followed behind Kim at the very back, stayed silent. It reminded Ella about her pledge to Ma Etty, and her own laughter tapered off.

How was she going to master any of the traits that old lady wanted? Kind people were like Jordan, like Mom. They went quiet and looked away when the conversation turned against them. They didn't fight for themselves. They were doormats.

And people like Ella, people like Dad, who were willing to step on and over those doormats—those were the people who made it ahead in this world. Who got what they wanted.

There had to be another way of becoming the

type of horsewoman who was allowed to ride the beautiful, graceful, powerful Figure Eight.

Then, as Ella turned her head to take in the trees passing by, she spotted Jordan and Loco Roco in her peripheral vision.

A thought struck. Ella needed a teacher, like Ma Etty had suggested—someone who had what she was missing. Someone who had the trust of Fletch, Madison, and most importantly, Ma Etty.

Ella leaned back in her saddle and whispered to Kim, "Hey, trade places with me?"

He arched an eyebrow at her, but then he shrugged. "Whatever," he said and passed her in line, putting Ella just in front of Jordan. Ella could practically feel the other girl tense up behind her.

This was one benefit of Lacey, Ella thought, as she turned all the way around in her saddle so she could face Jordan. Lacey kept moving just behind Kim's horse, taking no notice of her rider's misbehavior—or if she did notice, she didn't care at all.

"What's up?" Ella asked. She realized as soon as she said it how lame it was.

Jordan just looked at her posture with wide eyes, and then looked away.

With a sigh, Ella sat normally in her seat again

and pulled back on Lacey's reins. Confused, but ever willing, Lacey slowed down so Loco Roco could catch up to her. Then they continued on, side by side, a few paces behind the rest of the group, as Paul began telling a long-winded story.

"Good work in the arena the other day," said Ella. "You know, when we . . . walked around."

Man. Ella could not seem to stop with the lameness.

"Uh," said Jordan, "thanks."

"How long have you been riding horses?" Ella asked, trying out this question for the second time now.

"Um . . . two years, maybe three?" Jordan shrugged.

That's what she always did, it seemed like—shrug as if she didn't know a single thing in the world, as if she had no authority on anything, including how long she'd been riding horses.

"How could you not know?" Ella asked with a chuckle, before she could think better of it.

Jordan's lips pressed together and she answered with silence, and another shrug.

This was going about as poorly as Ella's original plan to get Eight back. She didn't know how to talk to someone like Jordan. She could volley easily with someone like Dad—someone who believed completely in his abilities, sometimes beyond them. Nothing Ella said could chip his armor or make him think less of himself. Sometimes Ella hated that.

But then, she also could never hurt him by accident. So they made an okay team.

Or they did after Mom left. She could never take that stuff—too delicate, Dad said. Sometimes, during the divorce proceedings, he had called her a wimp. Thin-skinned. Fragile. Even though Ella had decided to stay with her dad when they went to court, she'd never been able to decide if she agreed with that assessment of Mom or not.

Maybe Mom just didn't like having her confidence and patience tested every moment of every day.

"Sorry," said Ella after a long while had passed. Jordan had kept pace with her and Lacey.

Jordan gave her a strange look. "For what?"

"For what I said. For being sarcastic."

Jordan shrugged. Again.

"Jeez," said Ella. "Don't you feel things besides 'I don't know' or 'I don't care'? Like, didn't that annoy you, that I said that?"

Another shrug. Jordan started slowing her horse down, falling behind again.

"What are you gals doing back there?" called

Paul from the front. "I don't want you to fall behind and get lost."

Ella sighed. This wasn't going to work. "Okay," Ella called back. "On my way, Captain." She gave Lacey a little kick to catch up with the others, leaving Jordan alone in the back. Probably the way she wanted it.

Up at the front, Paul regaled the kids with a tale of the time a cow escaped onto the neighbors' property. Neighbors who—from what Ella could tell this far into it—were pretty mean, grouchy people. Worried what might befall one of his prize heifers, Paul had bemoaned the pickle his cow found herself in to a previous group of ranch kids. They heroically marched in after her, rescuing her, and barely escaped with their lives. At least, that was how Paul told it.

"That's a dumb story," said Ash. "Something like that would never happen at this ranch."

Paul frowned. "Well, that's rude. It did happen— I saw it. I was there."

"Uh huh," said Ash, rolling his eyes. He always had to take somebody down with him.

"Shut up, Ash," Ella said. "I liked Paul's story. Well told. Very dramatic." She even clapped a little.

Paul frowned. "I'm pleased to hear that, Ella. But no telling people to shut up on my watch either, okay?"

Ella sighed. "Okay."

The dogs had found a bone as they ran circles around the slow-moving horses, and they were taking turns carrying it around. Soon, Paul slowed down and said, "Here we go."

The forest opened up before them. Hills rolled out below, the edges tinged blue-green. The immense, snow-capped Rockies took over the skyline.

Paul turned away from them to focus on the path as he began talking. "This part of White River is known for its natural spring water," he started saying.

Ash and Drew were whispering and giggling. In the two seconds Ella had been gazing out at the scenery, Drew climbed up in his saddle so he was half-standing on top of his horse, like one of the trick riders at the rodeo. Ash was on his way to the same position. When he saw she was watching, Ash gave Ella a challenging look.

"What? Gonna throw a fit about it?" he said quietly. The dare to join them went unspoken.

If there was any horse you could pull a stunt like this on, it was little Lacey. Ella felt enormous pride in her boring, constant pony as she got onto her knees first, grabbing the horn with one hand for balance. It would be a shame if Paul turned around, she thought briefly. Lacey didn't bother with whatever Ella was doing and kept walking.

Drew had gotten all the way up on his feet, looking back at Ella, when Ella saw a low-hanging branch just ahead of him. She pointed, mouthing, "Duck!"

But instead of doing as she instructed, Drew turned to see. The branch hit him across the side of the face. He started sliding off his horse with comical slowness as both the branch he'd run into and the steady, slow pace of his horse radically delayed his fall.

Paul decided right then to turn and ask them a question.

"What on God's green Earth?" he cried. He flipped his horse around and jogged back down the line. Ella slid back properly into her saddle. Drew's horse, sensing he was losing his rider, abruptly halted.

This motion sent Drew sliding all the way off, still desperately clutching the tree branch, and he dropped unceremoniously onto the ground. The dogs ran up to Drew, yapping and licking, and he laughed as he pushed them away. He didn't look hurt in the least, maybe a bit dirty.

"That was the dumbest thing I have ever seen," Paul said, his expression somewhere between astounded and furious. "Who tries to stand up on their saddle? Were you raised in a barn?"

"Obviously not," piped up Kim. "If he had been, he might know better."

Drew stood up and dusted himself off, sheepishly taking his horse by the reins. "Hey," he said. "Worked out better than that joyride I took on my bike, at least."

"And you two," Paul said to Ash and Ella. "Motor-mouth is one thing, but the two of you!" He couldn't even seem to find words for how angry he was.

Ella opened her mouth to say something, to explain herself somehow, but Paul raised his hand to stop her. "No," he said. "Don't say anything. We're going back. Now."

A gasp rose up from the very back of the train of kids, and Ella was sure it had been Jordan.

"But we've only been out here—" said Ash.

"Back!" Paul hollered. "Now!"

No one spoke as they turned around and headed back down the hill toward Quartz Creek. Paul rode at the head of the line, no longer full of stories. Even his horse walked more stiffly, and his dogs took up what seemed like guard positions all along the line of kids, no longer playing or arguing over bones.

Ella fell in line behind Jordan this time. The other girl looked absolutely miserable as they stalked back down the mountain and onto the ranch land. It really was hot out, Ella thought, so heading back down to the ranch was a bummer. But it wasn't like Jordan had done anything wrong up there. What was eating her?

CHAPTER TEN

"**W**e're back!" Paul hollered gruffly as they rode back into the parking lot.

Fletch poked his head out the office window. "So soon?"

"So soon," Paul confirmed. "I don't want injured campers on my watch, you know what I mean?"

"Injured campers?" Fletch sighed and ducked back into the office. After some scuffling, Madison and Fletch both came out the front door and helped the kids off their horses. They didn't bother to ask what had happened, and Paul didn't tell them.

He stuck two fingers in his mouth, let out a sharp whistle to call his dogs to him, and galloped off on his big blood bay, back the way he'd come earlier that morning.

Why did Ash and Drew have to ruin everything? That stupid trick-riding idea had obviously been Drew's, and Ash shouldn't have challenged her.

Where Ella had missed the heat up in the forest, down on the ranch it was dry and suffocating. Even the grass seemed wilted and brown. They sat on it as they ate their lunches, because they hadn't been gone long enough to eat them on the trail ride.

"Man," said Jordan. Everyone turned to look at her when she spoke. It was the first time she'd ever done so freely. "We could have been swimming right now."

"Swimming?" asked Ella. "Where?"

"Fletch mentioned a glacial lake up there, on the trail."

"Glacial lake?" Drew asked with his mouth full of food, then swallowed it. "Like the kind that's so clear you can see to the bottom?"

"Yeah," Jordan said.

"Whatever," said Ash. "It probably wasn't that cool. All lakes look the same."

Ella felt so outraged at this that she couldn't even bring herself to speak at first. There had been a gorgeous glacial lake waiting as their final destination, and they'd missed it?

"Wow," said Ella sarcastically. "Thanks a lot, Drew."

"Hey," said Ash. "You got up there too. Wasn't just Drew."

Ella wanted to argue with him, but there was no point. So the kids fell quiet and ate the rest of their food in silence, baking in the afternoon sun.

\\\

After the morning's events, and an afternoon sweating and toiling in the heat, everyone came to dinner grumpy and tired. As plates were handed around, they bickered over who had taken more than their fair share of Ma Etty's stew, and the tension in the room swelled.

The hot food was exactly the opposite of what Ella wanted to be eating right now, but she spooned more into her bowl anyway. She was famished. Her clothes stuck to every square inch of her because she'd been sweating so much. Why didn't the Bridles have A/C if the summers here got this bad?

"Hmm," said Kim, stirring his food with a pinched look on his face. "Totally overcooked."

Ma Etty didn't even look offended. "Happens," she said.

"You shouldn't cook meat for so long," Kim went on. "Makes it carcinogenic. Can give you cancer. When my mom makes Korean food, she cooks the meat real fast, in boiling water. It tastes a lot better."

"I'll try to remember that," said Ma Etty, even giving Kim a little smile that annoyed Ella.

"Nobody asked you, Kimberly," said Ella. The talk of boiling water in this heat made her feel sick. Or maybe she just wanted Kim to shut up. "Stop bragging."

"Ella," said Madison. "Respect."

"What?" Ella demanded. "He's insulting Ma Etty's cooking and going on about how Korean food is better, and you're telling *me* to show respect?"

"It's true that it's not healthy to overcook things," said Ma Etty, as if just to show she wasn't injured and didn't need Ella to defend her. "You lose good nutrients."

"My dad's Irish," said Ash. "They overcook everything! It's so gross. I hate family reunions."

Ella directed her annoyance into cutting a big piece of gristly meat. She wanted Ash and Kim to stop talking because Ella had nothing to contribute. Mom had left before Ella was old enough to learn about Indonesian cooking. All she knew was that it used a lot of hot peppers.

"You guys are lucky," said Jordan, who watched her bowl while she spoke. "There's no traditional food in my family. Well, besides sloppy joes and hot dogs. And my mom puts mayonnaise on everything."

"All-American, huh?" said Drew. "My mom's family are all from South Carolina, and they take their barbecue sauce seriously there. At least we have some heirloom barbecue sauce recipes."

"'At least'?" said Ella, bristling. Drew, of all people, making fun of Jordan? "Who cares about barbecue sauce?"

Fletch put down his knife. "Come on, now, guys. Everyone can be proud of where they came from and the food their families make. Jordan, I ate the same kind of stuff as you growing up. It's definitely All-American."

"Broke American, you mean," said Kim under his breath.

"Kim!" said Ma Etty, the patience in her voice evaporating. "What is with you all tonight?"

Ella glanced at Jordan as she went back to eating. Her face was red.

Kim was probably right. Jordan didn't seem to have much money, but she had made it work. She'd even managed to get a regular gig riding horses—and probably not by taking expensive riding lessons.

Ella glared down into her food and stirred.

\\

Sunday was supposed to be another group activity, but before the day had even begun, Ash and Kim were already yelling at each other over the last pancake. Ash picked up a tin cup full of maple syrup and hurled it at Kim, hitting him in the head and spilling sticky, slippery syrup all over his hair, the wall behind him, the table, and the floor.

Mr. Bridle got to his feet and slammed his utensils down on the table with a resounding clang.

"That's it!" he said, huge voice filling the dining room. The boys ducked back into their seats. "I've had enough. That incident yesterday with Paul, then the insults at dinner last night, and now this?" He took a long, calming breath. Ella felt dread curl up in her stomach. Even Mr. Bridle's tolerance appeared stretched to its limit.

"Everyone is going to be separated this afternoon," he said finally, wiping his lips with his napkin. "All chores, all day. No partners."

"What?" cried Drew.

"And," Mr. Bridle continued, as if nobody had spoken, "I'll be teaching lessons tomorrow. You're off, Fletch and Maddie. Feel free to take a trail ride, or go help Paul's boys with the new calves, or whatever you want to do with your free time."

Neither of the trainers actually looked pleased about this, but they nodded and said nothing.

Had this happened before, that Mr. Bridle took over teaching? It seemed unlikely. Ella saw him as the sort of guy who sat quietly and did paperwork, or fielded phone calls and marketed the ranch to parents. Not the sort to get in front of kids and teach.

A spike of fear ran through her. And, looking at the other kids' faces, she wasn't the only one.

They'd really, truly messed up.

\\

Sunday was another sweaty, hot day, and this time, Ella had to suffer through it alone.

First, Ma Etty showed her how to milk the goats and then left her to do every single nanny goat alone—all nine of them. By the end, her wrists and hands felt like lead weights, and one of the nannies, whose teat she'd pulled on too hard, had kicked her in the thigh.

Then, after lunch, Ella mucked stalls. All. Afternoon.

"This should be illegal," Ella said to herself, since there was no one else around to complain to. "This is indentured child labor. This is illegal, I know it."

But nobody cared, because nobody could hear her.

For the first hour, Ella repeated her complaints to herself, until even her own voice annoyed her. So she stopped talking at all.

When the complaining ceased, she seemed to find a rhythm: stick the fork-rake-thing under the poop, tilt it back up to keep as much poop on the rake as possible while lifting it, then toss the poop into the wheelbarrow. Occasionally, as she went to dump each wheelbarrow of manure onto the manure pile behind the barn, she caught sight of the horses out in the pasture.

They couldn't look more pleased with the sunny weather, or the day off. They chased one another, flinging their manes around, running back and forth like puppies playing in a yard—even sweet Lacey, who she'd said such mean things about, was romping with the others.

What a jerk Ella had been.

Happy, at least, that the horses were having fun when she couldn't, Ella went back inside with the wheelbarrow to fill it again. Her sore arms cried out, *No more poop! Not another wheelbarrow!*

And yet, there was more poop. There was always more poop.

By late afternoon, Ella had reached a meditative state. Stick the poop, lift the poop, toss the poop. She even stopped swiping at the bugs, because she felt bad for killing them. They were just trying to live too.

Ella lost track of time, no longer caring whether her punishment ever ended. She was starting to think she deserved it.

She deserved it for yelling at Figure Eight.

Ella wheeled out another load of poop and dumped it, stopping for a moment to wipe sweat from her forehead and gaze up at the fiery sun.

No wonder Jordan avoided her. Ella had mistreated her own horse. Ella would avoid somebody like that herself.

Ugh. And then Ella had gone and called Jordan a liar, too.

Once she got thinking about it, Ella found her list of sins was long: She'd egged Kim on at dinner. She'd punched Bianca at school.

Ella looked down at the wheelbarrow, and shame crept up in her chest.

She'd chosen Dad over Mom.

And she'd let Mom leave. Her kind, loving mother . . . Ella had let Mom go without even telling her she loved her.

As Ella headed back into the barn, tears starting to work their silent way down her cheeks, a blaze of white and fawn-brown shot across the pasture.

Ella blinked, rubbing her eyes.

Figure Eight galloped from one fence to the other, bucking and swinging her head. She looked utterly magnificent, that painted horse, frolicking in the green grass under the sunshine. As Ella watched, she couldn't even feel angry at Madison and Ma Etty anymore for taking Figure Eight away. She just felt joy watching her.

"Ella!" She turned at the sound of Ma Etty's voice. "Come on inside! It's time for dinner."

Ella had a vaguely disappointed feeling. She'd miss the predictability of the stick-lift-dump, because who knew what trouble might erupt at the dinner table?

Ella sighed, put down her rake and wheelbarrow, and followed Ma Etty inside.

\\\

But she had nothing to fear. The others were all just as tired as she was, and hardly anyone said a word during dinner. Afterward, the kids stumbled back to their bunkhouses like zombies.

As the girls went inside to change out of their dirty, sweaty clothes, Jordan held up a hand with her palm facing Ella. At first, Ella was so tired that she didn't understand what was happening. Eventually she raised her own hand and met Jordan's high-five, smiling.

"You're alive," Jordan said, grinning in that unguarded way only total exhaustion can bring.

"So are you!" Ella laughed, suddenly giddy. Jordan had chosen to approach her. Jordan had talked to her. Even high-fived her!

The girls high-fived again at the fact they had both survived the day, and that was the last thing that Ella remembered before she dragged her numb body into bed.

CHAPTER ELEVEN

Everyone was slow to breakfast in the morning, and there wasn't much talking.

Ella figured their penance wasn't over yet.

She knew about penance. When Mom still lived with them, she made Ella attend mass with her every Sunday. Keeping still and silent for that long was hard even for some of the adults, but Ella had learned how to daydream while still looking attentive as the priest droned on.

She'd learned how to confess, too. How to say her rosaries to make up for each mistake she'd made during the week.

It seemed all the kids at the table knew they were finally saying their rosaries today.

When breakfast was over, Mr. Bridle got up, hat so low it partially covered his eyes. He folded his napkin and set it on the table.

"Let's go."

Quietly, the kids got up out of their seats and followed Mr. Bridle out to the barn. He dragged out five wooden saddle stands, each with a student's saddle already on it.

"Get on up," he said. Ella saw Kim bite back a sarcastic remark, and he climbed up on his saddle on the wooden horse with everyone else.

Mr. Bridle meticulously corrected their feet, their knees, their legs, their seats—even their shoulders. He never raised his voice, never needing to. And when they were done, he put them on their real horses and made them walk around the arena for what felt like hours, doing the same thing. He nitpicked everything about their posture, their seat, their feet, their attitude.

"Your horse feels what you feel," he said in his deep, mahogany voice. Ash chuckled and Mr. Bridle said, "What about a thousand pounds of lean muscle and the power to read your mind is laughable to you, Ash?"

Ash's smile fell away. "Uh," he managed.

"You get on there thinking this is a joke," said

Mr. Bridle, "and what's your horse to think? That this is just a game for him, too? That's a horse that doesn't back up when you ask, because he thinks you're a clown for his amusement."

Ash flushed red.

Next, Mr. Bridle picked on their hands, making them do figure eights around the arena, one after another, never changing speed. If a horse slowed down or sped up, Mr. Bridle jumped on the rider.

"Why is your horse moving faster right now?" he'd say. "Bring it back down." The horses were just as bored with the endless walking around the arena as the kids were, and would sometimes try to start jogging.

Ella started to feel when Lacey was about to speed up, usually when she sensed the horse in front of her start to trot. Ella would adjust her posture to match, sending her weight back in the saddle and giving Lacey a tug on her mouth with the reins.

"Don't pull so hard, Ella," called Mr. Bridle, and Ella hated how he seemed to see every single thing she did. "Small motions. Whispering, not yelling, not unless Lacey ignores you and you need to yell."

Obediently, Ella tried out using smaller, precise

motions. When she did, Lacey paid closer attention and would listen to Ella's quiet requests right away.

Ella focused on getting better at this, keeping in constant contact with Lacey about what speed she wanted, about how close to the rail they should be.

"Tell them with your eyes where you want them to go," Mr. Bridle would say, over and over, as they cut across the arena one way, then the other, then back again. "You should be twenty-five feet ahead of your horse at any time. Look at the top of the fence posts. Pick the one twenty-five feet ahead of you and stare at it. Then the next one. Then the next one."

He was right. Ella found if she looked where she wanted Lacey to go before she signaled her to turn, it didn't take much pressure on the corresponding rein to make her turn. It was as if Lacey got the sense, long in advance, of what Ella wanted, what she was going to ask—then prepared herself to do it.

Ella thought of Jordan's Antonio, Mrs. Rose's horse.

Mr. Bridle stopped them for lunch, and the kids fed and cared for their horses before eating. Ma Etty brought out burritos so they wouldn't have to leave for too long. As they stood in the cool, dim barn, silent except for the rustling of paper burrito wrappers, Kim pointed at Jordan and started laughing.

"You got some sour cream on your pants," he said. "And it looks exactly like Mr. Bridle's head."

Everyone stopped to peer down at the sour cream stain.

"You're right," Ella said. "It looks just like Mr. Bridle's head. The big hat, the square chin—it's even got his ears."

As they all stood gaping, Jordan wiped it off, leaving a wet splotch on her jeans. Ash laughed. "Still looks like Mr. Bridle's head."

"You should go inside and have Ma Etty wash that off for you," said Ella, "so they don't stain."

Jordan shrugged. "No biggie. These old jeans are so beat-up, you won't notice later. They were already pretty ratty when I inherited them from Olly. Anyway, I'm up to get a new pair next month." She smiled at this.

Kim turned away at this information about Jordan. His cheeks flushed pink, while Jordan just picked at the stain thoughtfully. So even Kim could regret being so mean to her the other day.

Ella finally broke the silence. "I really like your jeans, Jordan," she said. "I thought you got them from a thrift store back home. I love thrifting. I mean, why buy new stuff when there's plenty of great used stuff out there?"

Jordan shrugged. "I guess."

"I buy almost all my stuff thrift," said Kim suddenly. His face was still red as he pulled the collar of his GI Joe shirt out to show them. "This is my favorite find ever. Vintage. Very rare."

This was probably the closest to an apology Jordan would get from Kim.

"What do you know about T-shirts?" asked Ash, snickering.

"A lot. I collect them." Kim grinned. "What about you, Dallas? You do anything interesting besides rabid fanboying over your favorite football team?"

Ash wiped his mouth and balled up his empty wrapper. "Yeah. Art. I do art."

"Art?" asked Drew, leaning in. "Like what?"

Ash lowered his voice as he said, "Street art. That's why I'm here."

"You got caught tagging something?"

Ash barked a laugh. "Tagging is for noobs. My buddy Cruiser and I were at my house one night and made this amazing wheat-paste piece."

Ella stared at him. "Where was your mom?"

"She's a waitress. She works late. So Cruiser and I take it a couple blocks down and start putting it up—"

"You did it near your house?" said Drew, covering his mouth.

"Sure. There's a lot of art where I live. Anyway, we'd just gotten most of the Cowboy up when the cops caught us."

"You were putting up *Cowboys* graffiti?" asked Jordan. Even she looked aghast.

"Yeah, of course. Why?"

Jordan just shook her head, and Drew laughed so hard he had to sit down.

"It was a work of genius," Ash said wistfully. "And nobody but us ever saw it."

\\\

After lunch, Mr. Bridle drilled them about pieces of tack, care and grooming, even horse anatomy. Once they'd parroted back to him all the facts and techniques he wanted, they got back on their horses and worked in the pasture. It was harder to control the horses out here, at least for Ash, Drew, and Kim. Lacey was too compliant to be much trouble, and Jordan had a perfect handle on Loco Roco.

"Keep your legs back, Ella," Mr. Bridle said as they made circles in the grass around him. "Heels down—no, that's too much. Let them fall naturally; don't shove them down. Press the balls of your feet into the stirrup, and the rest follows."

Why couldn't Ella do it right? There were too many things to track and control: your hip, your leg, your heel and your toes, and that was before you'd gotten to just holding onto your reins right.

"I'm trying," said Ella.

"Your elbows are sticking out," said Mr. Bridle. "Elbows down by your hips. Reins right in front of you, not out over the horn."

"I'm trying!" It was too much to focus on at once. She couldn't manage it all in her brain.

In Ella's frustration, a quiet thought occurred to her. Nobody was arguing. Nobody was mocking one another. Mr. Bridle had forced all of them to focus so much on their horses, on their seats, on their hands and their feet, that they had nothing left for squabbling. And slowly, they were starting to improve.

Unfortunately, still always at a walk.

Yet it had stopped being boring. Now Ella could see what she was doing wrong—why sitting incorrectly in her saddle, even just a fraction, could make a big difference. She saw it in the two laps she did sitting stiffly in her saddle, then the following two, where she sat down and back, like Mr. Bridle kept telling her.

So she worked on correcting the tiny imperfections that showed themselves as Lacey walked and walked and walked. She could feel Lacey's mouth now through the rein, and kept it just taut enough that a small movement of her finger brought an instant response.

"See, Ella?" called Mr. Bridle. "It's all in the whisper, not the yell."

Ella knew what he meant now. The more quietly she "whispered" to Lacey what she wanted, the more Lacey was willing to give it to her. By the end, Ella hardly had to move to request a turn or to hug the rail closer. She and Lacey shared the same goal.

When the day was up, Ella was reluctant to get off Lacey's back, as much as her thighs hurt. She'd gotten so used to riding that she felt like the pony's four legs belonged to her more than her own two did.

Now, in addition to her arms aching from mucking the day before, Ella's legs burned from thigh to ankle. All the kids walked like they were made of Jell-O.

"This is abuse," Kim muttered as they headed to the ranch house for dinner, tripping over chickens in the yard that they were too tired to step over. "I know it is. It has to be."

"We signed up for this," Ella said.

"Not me," said Ash. "My mom was the one who picked cowboy camp. She has a weird sense of humor."

"I think Ella means us acting like idiots," said Drew. Ella had to give him credit—even he was acting a little more perceptive after their lesson.

"Oh, yeah." Ash sighed. "That's annoying, isn't it."

No one had a response to that, because before that lesson with Mr. Bridle, it was hard to say that any of them except Jordan had been taking horse camp all that seriously.

"Sorry you had to go through that with us," Ella said to Jordan. "You haven't really caused any trouble at all."

Jordan gave her usual shrug, but this time, Ella thought that was nice of her not to say anything. She could have gotten mad at them for dragging her into this, and she'd have had every right to.

But she didn't.

That night around the dinner table, Madison and Fletch were in a chatty, boisterous mood after their day off. Mr. Bridle seemed to have decided that, with penance over and the day's grueling lesson at a close, he could return to his usual jovial, quiet self. He offered the kids rolls with butter slathered on them, baked potatoes, turkey and gravy, and even cranberry sauce.

"Thanksgiving in August?" asked Kim, pouring gravy over every single thing on his plate until it was swimming.

"That's a lot of food, Kim," said Madison. "I hope it doesn't all go to the compost."

"Oh," he said, "don't worry. I'm going to eat all of it."

"Thanksgiving in August," agreed Ma Etty. "Why not? You kids need the protein after the last two days."

At least she acknowledged how much work they'd done, Ella thought, and followed Kim's example with the gravy. The boy did understand food. Gravy on a crescent roll, with butter also, was the best thing ever.

Then, after dinner, it was strawberry rhubarb pie with vanilla ice cream, and the kids all thought they'd died and gone to heaven.

Even though it was Monday night, they didn't go back to their bunkhouses after dinner. "Everybody follow me," Fletch said, getting up from the table and looking a bit mischievous.

He led them out of the house and around to the side, where they found Paul already standing by the fire pit, warm flames billowing up from the tinder pile in front of him. Ella squealed in joy. Goofy Paul was back, and he didn't look the least bit mad at them as they took seats around the fire.

"Before you get too comfortable, let's take care of the important things," said Paul, and distributed two bottles of bug spray. The kids covered themselves in it from head to toe, at his urging. "Don't want you to wake up itching all over tomorrow! You don't see 'em now, but they're nasty little buggers after dark."

Madison, Ma Etty, and Mr. Bridle joined them with s'mores, passing out long sticks, chocolate, graham crackers, and two bags of giant marshmallows.

"Didn't we just have dessert?" Ella whispered to Jordan, hoping all the activity had put her in a conversational mood.

"You know what they say," whispered Jordan. "Don't look a gift horse in the mouth."

"Who says that?" asked Ella. "And why?"

Jordan laughed. "It's about being grateful for gifts. Someone gives you a horse, you don't look at its teeth right there to see if it's old. It's free. Be happy."

"I've always wondered what that meant." Ella grinned. "Thanks. You're pretty smart."

Jordan cracked half a smile, but stayed looking at the ground.

As they overlooked the few glimmering lights of the town of Quartz Creek, Paul pulled out a banjo that looked as old as Mr. Bridle. "This is an antique," he was eager to point out. "Real deerskin drum." He tapped the wide, round base of the instrument.

Ella expected some dreary old folk music, but the first song Paul played was a loud, fast, bluegrass song that made her feet tap. Ma Etty and Mr. Bridle must have felt the itch, too, because soon they were up on their feet dancing. They swung around, hands intertwined, like they were thirty years younger. Then Fletch and Madison joined them, and one of Paul's ranch hands who worked with the cows even pulled out a tiny drum to keep some rhythm.

Then Jordan got up, swinging a long imaginary

skirt around, twisting and twirling with the music in a country way Ella could only describe as highly experienced. Mr. Bridle whistled and the trainers started clapping. Soon Drew was up too, tossing himself all around like a puppet on a string. The ranch hand whooped. Then Ella was up and spinning in circles around the fire, unable to fight the music anymore, and Ash and Kim joined her.

After the dancing, Mr. Bridle told a surprisingly scary story that involved howling wolves that weren't really wolves—they were moon people, from an old legend about people that could turn into wolves and hunt at night. But then came strange foreigners who didn't understand. As Ella predicted, the foreigners tried to kill the moon people.

"And then," said Mr. Bridle, as a coyote with flawless timing yipped off in the distance, "the wolf came at him, and nearly bit off his face!"

Jordan and Kim both yelped as Mr. Bridle abruptly raised his voice and threw his hand out at them.

Later, Paul played some slow, soulful banjo songs that Ella liked even better than the fast ones. Within minutes Drew was half-asleep on Ash's shoulder, which made all the kids crack up. Ma Etty finally roused him and sent everyone off to bed.

"Easy day tomorrow," she promised.

"Oh good," said Kim as he waddled off to the boys' bunkhouse. "Only three hours of poop-scooping instead of five." Ella and Jordan both laughed as they made their way to their own bunk.

CHAPTER TWELVE

Ma Etty kept her promise.

"Free time," she said at breakfast. "All day." She held up a finger. "But any bickering, any at all, and the day resumes as normal. Horse lessons and chores and you-name-it."

The five of them nodded furiously.

"All right. Go forth, then, and have fun. There's a list of things you can do posted on the wall over there."

Ella scanned the list with the others—bean bag toss, Frisbee, music, and more. But the thing she was looking for wasn't there.

Learn barrel racing on Figure Eight.

Even the television was teasing her. Fletch and.

Madison had put on the stock show in the living room, although they were sticking to the strict no–screen-time rule for campers. But the trainers kept dashing there and back to see riders they liked or livestock events that were interesting. From the dining room Ella could hear the announcer reeling off winning times in barrel racing.

As Ella stood in front of the list of activities, she wondered why even horseback riding wasn't on it. That was all she thought about doing these days. Wasn't it the same for everyone else?

She jumped when Madison tapped her shoulder.

"I want to talk to you."

Uh-oh. It sounded so ominous—but what had she done? Ella followed Madison outside, wondering what this was about.

Then they started heading to the barn in silence, and Ella's heart skipped a joyful beat.

Inside the barn, Madison stopped in front of Figure Eight's stall. Ella took a breath. She could only hope.

"Mr. Bridle spoke with me after your lesson yesterday," Madison said, leaning against the stall door.

"What . . . what did he say?" Ella asked, trying to keep her voice cool.

Finally, Madison grinned. "He said you were a natural. Working with Lacey has been good for you—but she's too easy. He told me to bump you back up to the big leagues." With that, she grabbed Figure Eight's halter off the hook and opened the stall door.

"Think you can handle working with Eight again?" Madison asked.

Ella's mouth fell open.

"Yes! Yes, please!" Ella wanted to bounce up and down, but she wasn't going to pull a Drew and scare Eight, just as they were getting paired up again. "I mean," Ella corrected herself, straightening up, "thanks, Madison."

"Thank Mr. Bridle," she said, handing Ella the halter. "Now show me what you can do."

\\\

"I wasn't sure if a lesson was what you'd want to do with your day off, after the day you had yesterday," Madison said as Ella led Figure Eight out of her stall and put her in cross-ties.

"Ha!" Ella had to laugh at that. Throwing a Frisbee around didn't hold a candle to the possibility of riding Eight again—not to mention one-on-one instruction from Madison.

Out in the arena, climbing up on Eight was a completely different experience from getting on little Lacey. Ella could see everything with Eight's extra two hands of height. And Figure Eight felt different underneath her. Maybe it was her imagination, but Ella thought she could feel the horse's taut muscle through the seat of her saddle, could sense the power in her huge lungs.

Sitting on Eight's back felt, to Ella's immense satisfaction, like being inside an overfull hot air balloon, just waiting for someone to twist the valve and start the fire.

"Very good seat," Madison called. "Heels are perfect, your legs are back, and your shoulders are relaxed. Memorize that feeling, Ella. That's your go-to point. Now take her into a walk."

Eight tried to move forward at Madison's utterance of the word *walk*, but Ella said "Whoa" and tugged her backward. Eight reluctantly stopped.

Ella tried to remember everything she'd learned in Mr. Bridle's lesson. She drew her hands up to the spot in the reins where she had contact with Eight's mouth, but wasn't applying any actual pressure. Satisfied, Ella gave a single click of her tongue to start into a walk.

And Figure Eight listened.

At first, she refused to stay on the rail, pulling her head back toward the middle of the arena—and toward Madison.

"Correct her each time she tries that," said Madison, and Ella pulled Eight back to the rail.

On the other end of the arena, Eight cut the corner dramatically, and Ella corrected with another tug on the rein, toward the railing where she should have been walking. Eight straightened, but only a little.

"Use your inside leg to reinforce your request, if you need to," Madison called.

But Eight was wise to what Madison was saying, and she didn't cut any more corners. Now that Ella could see how shrewd Figure Eight was, she felt intimidated. This wasn't little Lacey anymore.

After a few laps Madison said, "She's done warming up. Take her to a trot."

At Ella's first small kick, Figure Eight hurtled into a lopsided canter. It tossed Ella to and fro, and she lost her gentle hold on the reins. One of her feet slipped out of its stirrup.

"Slow her back down," Madison called. "And don't let your legs go rogue like that. You're throwing her away just when she needs you to be firm. Show Eight she can put her trust in you."

That feeling returned of there being too many moving parts to control all at once. How could Ella keep her foot in the stirrup while flopping all over Eight's back?

Ella finally got Figure Eight back to a walk again, and they did another lap before attempting the trot a second time. She gave the signal—pressure on both of Eight's sides—and again, Eight leapt into a fast, bouncy, nervous canter.

"You're too tense," said Madison. "That's why Eight keeps trying to go fast. She thinks you want her to go fast."

Ella tried to relax, to soften her shoulders, but she was annoyed now. Not at Madison, though. She was irritated at herself. Why was this so hard?

She kicked for a trot again, but Eight wanted to run, and the loose reins whipped about like an attacking snake as Eight sped up again.

"Don't let go of your reins," said Madison. "Pull her back, Ella."

She was trying, but Eight wasn't listening to

her—again! Ella tried to breathe, but Eight was still lunging ahead.

Ella remembered Mr. Bridle's lesson: lower your elbows. Sit deep in the saddle. She focused on one aspect of her posture at a time. Suddenly, Eight's pace slowed. Ella applied a little more pressure to the reins, pulling them directly into her torso instead of up toward her neck, and Eight slowed down more— until she ambled along at a nice, even trot.

"There you go!" called Madison, giving her a thumbs-up from the middle of the arena. "Keep her at a trot. Relax more, Ella. You're trying too hard to match her gait, and that's why you're bouncing all over the place. Let your body match up to hers naturally."

Naturally? There was nothing natural about this motion. It hurt less at this speed, but Ella still couldn't stop bouncing. At this rate, she'd never get to a gallop, and she needed to gallop in order to run barrels.

"Relax!" Madison called to her. "You're so stiff."

"I'm trying!" But the bouncing only got worse. Why was she so bad at this? Relaxing should be the simplest thing in the world.

"You're even stiffer now." Madison went quiet

for a while as Ella and Eight bounced around the arena. Then Eight started speeding up again, her trot getting faster and rowdier. "Slow her down."

Ella jerked too hard and Eight slowed all the way down to a walk. At least now Ella could breathe again. Her whole body hurt. Why couldn't she do a simple trot right? Her annoyance at her own inexplicable lack of skill rose to full-blown anger.

"You've got to relax," said Madison as Eight continued at a walk, and Ella tried her hardest not to snap back with a retort. "You're bouncing because your hips and legs are fighting Eight's. You have to let your body synchronize with hers."

"Easier than it sounds!" Ella couldn't understand why riding Figure Eight was so hard for her. She'd been good at this yesterday.

She supposed she was actually a terrible horse-woman. Lacey was a beginner pony who had made Ella feel too comfortable.

"Here," Madison said, gesturing for Ella to return to the center of the ring and climb out of the saddle. Once Ella was off, Madison took her place on Eight's back in a quick jump.

Madison easily guided Eight back out to the fence. She gave a light kick. Eight, sensing she had a much more experienced person riding her who wouldn't put up with that jump-into-a-canter business, glided into a smooth, slow trot.

"This is what you're doing," Madison said. She went rigid, like a human iceberg, and immediately Eight's bouncy gait tossed her into the air. They bounced like that for a few steps and it made Ella's legs ache to watch. Eight's gait immediately changed and she lifted her head, looking unsettled.

"This is what you should be doing," Madison said. "See, I'm not stiff. I'm not forcing myself to move. I've just freed up my hips to move however Eight moves."

Something in her posture went slack, and Madison settled into the saddle like she was out in the car for a cruise. Her shoulders dropped forward, not so much that she was slouching, but enough that she looked at home—comfortable, even.

"Don't try to force a straight posture," Madison said as she and Eight sailed around the arena, her legs moving with the horse, her hips and stomach and shoulders all rising and falling at the same speed, in time with Eight's own motion. "No need to be nervous."

Pfft, Ella thought. *Don't be nervous.* How was

Ella supposed to feel, doing so badly in front of Madison?

"I'm not judging you," Madison went on, as if she could read Ella's mind. "I'll keep helping you until you figure it out."

"What if I never figure it out?" Ella asked sourly as Madison came back to the center of the arena.

"Don't worry," she said. "You will. Just give yourself the same leeway you gave Eight today."

"Leeway?"

"You were so patient with her!" Madison smiled as she hopped off Eight's back and handed the reins back over to Ella. "You corrected all her mistakes without getting mad. I was really proud of you."

"But I did so badly!" Ella's eyes burned. Madison had given her this great opportunity, offered to teach her on her off-time, and Ella had disappointed her.

"You did great," Madison said. "I don't know what you're talking about."

But the torrent came anyway. "I suck at this." Now that Ella had seen Madison in the saddle, so perfectly relaxed and comfortable and not bouncing around at all, she felt like even more of an epic failure. "I was supposed to be good at this, but I just really, really suck."

"Ella," Madison said, "you are learning. Everyone has to start somewhere. Cut yourself some slack."

But how could she? Yesterday, Ella had finally felt that connection to her horse, finally got a handle on all of the parts and pieces and they'd fit together so wonderfully. How come today, on the horse she'd dreamed about riding again, it had been so different?

"Eight is just so difficult to ride," said Ella, her eyes feeling wet and glassy.

Madison nodded, and did not suggest otherwise. "Every horse is different," she said. "You have to learn your way around each one individually. Just like with humans."

Ella had never thought about it like that. She glanced down at Eight's long, elegant, spotted neck, and ran a hand along it. Figure Eight dipped her head and leaned into Ella's arm.

If the two of them were ever going to race, Ella thought, she would have to figure out what made Eight tick.

CHAPTER THIRTEEN

Madison introduced them to the "gymkhana" events that week—which, to Ella's great pleasure, included barrel racing. They were events designed around obstacles like barrels and poles to help them develop handling. "And it's always fun to race," said Madison.

Everyone was excited to try them out after the rodeo. Madison asked Jordan to demonstrate each event at a trotting speed—pole-bending, where Jordan weaved Loco through a row of poles and back again. Then keyhole, where Jordan ran Loco inside a small square of poles, performed a loop, and sprinted home. And last but not least, they performed the cloverleaf barrel pattern—flawlessly.

Ella was so excited to try the barrels that by their turn, Figure Eight was dancing in place, sensing her impatience. Ella wanted to run the pattern, to take those sharp turns at a hard gallop like the racers at the rodeo. But she knew she hadn't reached that level with Eight yet, and without that connection to each other, Eight might just gallop off, out of control.

Ella couldn't afford to mess up again and have Eight taken away.

They were supposed to walk each pattern, but by the time they reached the barrels, Eight started off at a slow trot. Madison didn't object as they headed for the first barrel, but Ella was nervous after her last lesson.

Nevertheless, Eight seemed to be in a good mood out here. Her ears perked forward, toward the first barrel. Keeping that close contact with her through the reins, Ella focused on relaxing. She sank into the saddle and kept her eyes on the spot just to the left of the barrel—where she wanted Eight to go.

As the barrel came up on their right, Eight's neck bent underneath her, around the barrel. Still moving at a slow trot, they cleared it and headed to the second one.

Ella's gaze stayed twenty-five feet ahead of Eight.

She was thinking about going around the obstacle when Eight anticipated her. They cruised around the barrel, so close to the side Ella could have reached out and tapped it with her foot. She cheered inside her head.

Then, the last one. Another left turn. The other two had gone so well, she worried this was when Eight would decide to act up. As if in response, Eight tossed her head and sped up her trot, tossing Ella into the air.

"Relax!" Madison called. "You're tensing up!"

Ella let out a long breath and focused again on where she wanted to go: around the barrel. She barely had to tug on the rein for Figure Eight to wrap around it.

And then, they were clear.

Eight, her neck low, sped up her trot. She was just as eager as Ella to finish out with a bang. Deciding Eight had done a good enough job to warrant it, Ella let her go at a fast trot back to the end of the line, where the other horses were waiting their turns.

"Wow!" said Ash, flicking his blond bowl-cut out of his face. "You two looked sweet out there."

Drew's head bobbed up and down. "Totally sweet."

Madison rushed out into the arena. "See how Eight's neck dropped like that?" She grinned at Ella. "That was her relaxing. When you're calm, she's calm. She feels safe with you. That's what I like to see."

Ella tingled from neck to ankle. They'd done the barrels! Even if it was just at a trot.

But even better, Eight had trusted Ella. In that moment they'd moved as one unit, with one mind. Ella had thought, and looked, and Eight had followed.

Ella just hoped they could do it again tomorrow.

\\\

But after that, they left the gymkhana events behind and returned to horsemanship. Ella's stomach dropped.

She'd wanted to gallop those barrels, and now she'd lost her chance. She wanted to scream, *Let me keep practicing them!* But Ella wanted to appear subdued, to show the old lady she had mastered those irritating virtues.

Anyway, when did she have time to practice? Ma Etty would never let her out of daily lessons with Fletch and Madison. Maybe she could use her free time. Ella would prefer riding anyway to Frisbee or bean bag toss or whatever else.

As soon as she had the idea, though, she knew she couldn't ask Figure Eight to work hard two times a day.

So Ella did something she never thought she'd do. As they were taking food scraps out to the compost after lunch, Ella asked Madison if she could be paired up with Lacey again.

"Really?" Madison upended her container of peels and eggshells over the fence. "But you and Eight are doing so well together. I don't understand."

"If I'm going to work Eight separately on the barrels, I can't be riding her all morning, too."

Madison frowned. "Work her separately on barrels?"

"Sure. I want to practice with her every day, for at least two hours. I'll spend half of it on the barrels and half of it on just horsemanship."

"Where will you find time for that?" Madison asked. "You still have to do your chores every day."

It was Ella's turn to look confused. "Free time, duh."

"So, let me get this straight. You're going to ride two hours a day on Lacey with Fletch and me, and then another two on your own time, with Eight?"

"Yeah, sure." Ella shrugged. "I'd rather do that

with my free time than play soccer. I'll do my chores, then go work with Eight."

"Who's supervising you?" Madison asked.

Ella hadn't considered that. She'd thought Mr. Bridle's recommendation would be enough. "No one," Ella said tentatively.

Madison bit her lip. "That won't work. And I can't be out there watching you myself because I have things I have to do around the ranch." She glanced at Fletch, who was at the table handing out chores. "Neither can Fletch. He's up to his ears in work helping Paul get ready for new yearlings to arrive next week." She thought for a moment. "Perhaps Mr. Bridle could help you. He has a little bit of barrel know-how. But you'd have to ask him—he's crunched for time, too."

The little lesson plan Ella had built in her head burned to the ground.

"But Madison . . . !" she said, as they headed back to the house. "Eight and I are doing so well together. We'll be fine alone."

This had always worked on her dad. All Ella had to say was, *I know I can do it. I'll make it happen, Dad.* And if she spoke in that confident tone of voice, he would smile at her and say, *Okay, Ell. Do it. Make it happen.* He liked her best when she acted like him.

Madison shook her head. "I'm sorry, I don't know what else to tell you."

"But—"

"Sorry," Madison said. "Not alone."

\\\

Ella wanted to break something.

She couldn't believe it—Madison turning her down like that. Ella tromped into the house with her boots still on. Ma Etty, who was sitting at the dining room table, raised her eyebrows.

"Ella, leave those boots in the mudroom."

Ella glanced down at her feet and practically snarled when she saw what she'd forgotten. She tore the boots off her feet and stalked back out again, dumping them in the mudroom. There she ran into Jordan, who was sliding hers off, too. Literally ran into her.

Their skulls knocked together and they both shouted, "Ow!" as they stumbled backward. Ella rubbed her head. Without thinking about it, Ella said, "Watch where you're going!"

Dang it. She always seemed to slip up around Jordan.

"Sorry," was all Jordan said, and she made sure

to right both of their pairs of boots by the door. "I'm sorry, I wasn't looking."

Ella wanted to roar something at her. *Stop apologizing! Have a backbone!* But getting mad at Jordan wouldn't accomplish anything. It might even set her back—though Ella wasn't sure how much farther back it was possible to go.

"It was my fault," Ella said. "I'm the one tromping around like a bull in a china shop."

Jordan glanced at her. "What's wrong?"

The question, and the eye contact, took Ella by surprise.

"Uh . . . I'm mad, I guess."

"About what?"

"Madison won't let me practice barrels during free time."

"Hmm." Jordan closed the door behind her and they walked together back toward the kitchen. "That's silly. You should get to do whatever you want with your free time. Though that is a lot of work in one day for Figure Eight."

"I know! So I told Madison I'd ride Lacey for lessons, and only work Eight in the afternoons."

Jordan's eyebrows knit together. "She shouldn't have a problem, then."

"She said nobody has time, except maybe Mr. Bridle." Then a thought occurred to Ella. "I think she doesn't trust me in the arena alone."

As soon as she said it, Ella realized it was true.

Jordan had an expression on her face like maybe she agreed with Madison on this assessment. If it had been anyone else, Ella would have socked them.

But Jordan was probably right. Ella hadn't exactly proven herself to be the most in-control around horses.

Then you should ask Jordan for help with the barrel racing part, Ma Etty had said.

Maybe that's what Ella needed: Jordan. The trainers trusted her. If Ella could get Jordan on her side, could get her to teach her the barrels, they would let her practice alone.

During free time, Ma Etty decided to take them on a trip to see the new frogs that were starting to appear down at the creek. On the way home for dinner, Jordan fell to the back of the group as she usually did—and Ella followed her.

Ella didn't speak first, and Jordan didn't start a

conversation, either. Ella wanted to demand that Jordan become her teacher. But she knew where that would get her.

Instead, Ella waited. Then, after a while she said, "How's it going with Loco Roco?"

Jordan gave her a surprised look.

"He's a good horse," she said. "Smart, eager. Funny, too."

"Funny?"

"Yeah. He likes to nibble on my pockets when I turn my back to him, or play with his lead rope while we're tacking up. He has a good sense of humor."

Ella had never considered that a horse could have a sense of humor. But if anyone would know something like that, it would be the girl who spent her mornings quietly sitting with her horse in the barn.

"That's so cool," said Ella. She wished she had that kind of relationship with Figure Eight. It would probably make the riding part a lot easier. "Hey, I want to ask you something."

"Like what?" Jordan asked, giving her a sideways look. Ella barreled on, sensing that she needed to assure Jordan she didn't have a nefarious purpose, as Kim would say.

"I just want to learn how to run the barrels

properly," Ella told Jordan. "And you know how, right?"

"Well, sure," said Jordan. "But so do you."

"Not as well as you. You won a championship."

"It was a—"

Ella held up one hand. "I know you're going to say it was a fluke," she said. "But I've seen how you ride Loco Roco, and you're obviously better at this than I am, by a long shot." It wrenched Ella's gut to say it out loud, but there was no more obvious truth.

"I couldn't teach anyone," said Jordan, and Ella saw her clamming up again.

"Yes, you can!" Ella said it forcefully, with complete confidence, hoping her faith would be contagious—that Jordan would sop up some of it and keep it for herself.

"I don't know," said Jordan, hesitant. "I've never taught anyone anything. I could mess you up."

"No, you couldn't."

Jordan shrugged. "Who knows what I'm capable of?"

Frustrated, Ella wanted to try harder to convince Jordan that what Ella had said was the truth—Jordan couldn't mess anyone up. But she'd seen what that had done last time, so Ella went quiet as well. She just kept pace with Jordan, as if agreeing to the silence.

Jordan's anxiety seemed to fade as they approached the house. As they started heading inside, Jordan stopped on the stairs. Even though she didn't look at Ella, Ella knew she was talking to her when she said, "I'll maybe think about it, okay?"

Ella nodded and said patiently, "Okay."

"It still doesn't guarantee we'll get permission to practice alone," said Jordan.

"I know," said Ella. "That's okay. I just want to try."

CHAPTER FOURTEEN

The next day, Ella and Jordan were assigned to deep-clean the kitchen with Mr. Bridle.

"Hey," Jordan said to Ella as they entered the kitchen, equipped with matching rubber gloves. "I've been thinking about your . . . practice issue. Maybe you can talk to Mr. Bridle about it, like Madison said."

"Talk to me about what?" Mr. Bridle said, getting up from the floor. He had a bucket of dirty, soapy water in one hand and a huge sponge in the other. The knees of his jeans were soaked through.

"Ella wants to spend her free time practicing barrels," said Jordan. "But Madison told her no."

"As well she should. You all haven't been riding

long enough to be left unsupervised, and we older folks have things we have to do in the afternoons. That's why we give you free time. It means 'off time' for us." He winked at them, then realized Ella wasn't in the best mood about getting turned down, and cleared his throat. "Well . . . what if you supervised her, Jordan?"

Jordan's face drained of all color.

"What?" she squeaked.

"What?" said Ella. But Jordan was the same age as Ella! What business did she have supervising another kid? Teacher, sure. Overseer? No way.

"Sure." Mr. Bridle squeezed out his sponge into the dirty bucket and dug two more out of the cupboard under the sink. He handed one to each of them. "Why not? Jordan's been riding for years. I've seen you out in the arena, little lady. You have what it takes to handle the situation if anything goes wrong."

"N-n-no, I don't," said Jordan, backing away from them both like they'd come down with a highly contagious disease.

"Sure, you do," said Mr. Bridle gently. Jordan was about to object again, so Mr. Bridle said, "How about this, Jordan? I'll let you out of your chores for the week if you can supervise Ella during her extra horse work."

Jordan frowned. "But I like doing my chores. Gathering the eggs and milking the goats, at least."

He rubbed his chin. "Hmm. I didn't anticipate that."

This was Ella's chance. Her only chance. "Please, Jordan? Pretty, pretty please? I'll make your bed every morning."

"Every single morning?" said Jordan hopefully. Ella nodded. "I don't know . . ."

"And I'll take your plate to the sink after every meal."

"Whoa," said Mr. Bridle. "The stakes get higher."

"Every meal?" asked Jordan.

"Every single meal," said Ella.

Jordan swallowed, looked between Mr. Bridle and Ella, and gave a slow, reluctant nod. "Okay, fine. I'll do it. But I still want to do my chores. The others will get mad if they see I get to play around while they're all working."

Mr. Bridle stared at her, then laughed. "Okay. Sure. If you want, you can still do your chores."

Ella just shook her head. Jordan was still beyond her understanding. But Ella offered a big smile and said, "Thanks, man."

"All right, enough talking. More scrubbing." Mr. Bridle let out a sigh that didn't sound all too thrilled about getting stuck with this job, either. He pushed the bucket of water toward them. "Ella, you're on that end of the kitchen. Jordan, you're taking the pantry. We get through this early and I'll sneak us each a piece of pie from the fridge."

"Pie!" said Ella and Jordan together.

As they got to work, a thrill ran down Ella's spine. She was going to learn the barrels!

\\

The moment they were in the arena the next afternoon, Figure Eight wanted to go, go, go—just like Ella did. Then she thought of the way her dad drove, always needing to get there *right now!* The way he blew through intersections, too impatient to stop, terrified her.

So Ella decided she was going to take it the way Mr. Bridle had forced her to with Lacey: slow and steady, to make sure she did it right this time.

Eight refused to walk along the rail as they warmed up, playing the same game—drifting toward the middle, cutting corners. Then, after the first two laps, she wouldn't stay at a walk and kept breaking into a trot. When Ella corrected her, Eight threw her ears back irritably, and sometimes simply ignored her.

What was Ella doing wrong? Each time Eight misbehaved, Ella jerked the reins back toward the rail and kicked harder, and harder, with her inside leg. But it seemed the harder she kicked, the less Eight listened.

Jordan didn't speak as Eight and Ella worked. At first, Ella liked it; this wasn't Madison, shouting instructions at her constantly from the center of the ring. But when Ella couldn't get Eight to listen, correction after correction, she grew irritated. She wanted Jordan to say something, to give her some kind of advice.

"What am I doing wrong?" Ella finally asked, yanking Eight to a stop near the railing where Jordan was standing.

"Um." Jordan scratched her head. "You're correcting only when she's totally out of sync—and you're pulling on her really hard. She's probably as frustrated as you are. Wouldn't it be annoying if you were screamed at for doing something wrong, but only long after you had started doing it?

Wouldn't you wish someone had told you sooner, more gently?"

Ella nodded slowly. Was that what she was doing to Figure Eight? She remembered what Fletch and Mr. Bridle had said about "yelling." Heat crept up Ella's neck. Had she been yelling at Eight this whole time without realizing it?

"You have to correct the moment you feel her start to come off the rail—like in that lesson we had with Mr. Bridle. Remember how when you felt Lacey start to speed up, you reminded her you were there and that you didn't approve of the gait change? She knew that you were paying attention and she immediately slowed down."

Jordan had been watching what Ella was doing?

"Yeah . . . I remember."

"Same thing. When you feel Eight start to come off the rail, just give her a gentle reminder that you're watching. And then if she continues to ignore you, correct her more severely."

Digesting this, Ella took Eight back at a trot. Within half a lap, Eight turned her head slightly toward the middle of the arena and began drifting.

"Correct now," called Jordan. "Just a whisper."

Ella gave a gentle tug on the rein, matching the

slight amount Eight was diverging from the path. She felt that connection again—that invisible line of tension between her hand and Figure Eight's mouth—and immediately, Eight answered, drifting back to the rail.

But there came no praise from Jordan, the way it would have come from Madison. Ella clenched the reins. She was going to have to do a lot better if she wanted applause.

"Remember to look where you want to go," said Jordan as they continued on around the arena, Eight still occasionally testing Ella, and Ella giving the same gentle corrective tug in response. "That will help her stay on the rail. Keep your eyes on the place you want to go, out toward the edge of the arena, and she'll follow. Look in the middle of the arena, and that's where she'll drift."

Soon Ella asked for a canter. Ella's eyes remained on the post just ahead of them, and Eight stuck to the outside of the arena like she had glue on her side.

"Awesome," Jordan called, giving a double thumbs-up. "But wrong lead."

"Lead?"

"She started cantering with the wrong front leg. Slow her to a trot and try again, and when you ask for the canter, do it just before the turn—that will help her take the right lead."

Ella restarted the canter a few times before Jordan said, "Yeah, that's it." And Ella could feel what she meant: the rhythm of the canter felt right, more balanced, on the correct lead. She'd never thought that much about the way a horse's legs moved.

After they were done warming up, Jordan ran out into the arena and set up the barrels without Ella saying a word. Once they were all arranged in a triangle shape, she scampered back out again. Ella trotted Eight through the pattern once, then twice.

"Looking good," Jordan said.

"That's all?" said Ella. She'd done at least three things wrong, she thought.

"Well . . ." Jordan climbed up onto the fence and sat on top of it. "You're just reining. But to get those really tight turns, you'll have to use your whole leg. Thigh, knee, heel."

"I don't know how to do that."

Jordan opened her mouth to speak, and then closed it again. She hopped down from the fence. "Here, stop real quick."

Ella slowed Eight to a halt and Jordan walked over, patting Eight's neck.

"When you're going around that first barrel—it's a right turn—you want to bend her around the barrel with your legs," Jordan said. "Why don't you start with your outside leg? Just move your knee forward." She took Ella's knee in one hand and set it forward on the horse. "Apply a little pressure just before you're ready to go around the barrel."

Jordan hopped out of the arena again as Ella took the barrel pattern a third time, still at a trot. Ella was so busy focusing on her knee that she didn't look where she was going. They were sailing past the barrel when she realized it was time to turn, and ended up jerking Eight's rein at the last moment. Figure Eight, surprised, flung her head toward the barrel and made an awkward loop.

Ella felt like there were just too many moving parts to track. But Jordan didn't say anything. Ella was the only one criticizing her own work.

On the second turn, Ella prepared. She looked where she wanted to go, and pressed in with her knee at the same time.

Eight bent perfectly around the barrel, and away from Ella's leg.

"Awesome," said Jordan. That was it. One word. Ella finished the barrels and waited for Jordan to say something else.

But she didn't. So Ella tried it again.

And again.

By the third try, her hands and her knee worked in perfect sync, and they cornered each of the barrels so closely that Ella even made one of them tip.

Jordan glanced at her watch. "I think we should go in," she said, and climbed down from the arena fence. "A few cool-down laps?"

She never gave orders, Ella realized—simply made requests, suggestions. It was nice. Ella always felt like she had a choice. Ella wondered if Jordan used that tactic with horses, too.

"Sure," said Ella. "And Jordan?"

Jordan paused before leaving the arena.

"Thank you."

She shrugged. "No problem," Jordan said. "Just doing what Mr. Bridle told me to do."

As Jordan walked away, Ella felt a twinge of disappointment. She wished Jordan *wanted* to be there, helping her, instead of simply doing it because Mr. Bridle told her to, or because Ella had bribed her.

But that was okay for now. Ella knew that the more she tried to force Jordan to be her friend, the more likely she'd push her away.

So she simply cooled down Figure Eight and then took her inside to brush her down.

\\-

Ma Etty was standing by the barn door when Ella approached with Eight.

"Looking really good out there," she said, and Ella wondered how long she'd been watching. "You're on your way to becoming the kind of horse-woman you'll need to be."

"For what?"

"For the amateur gymkhana show," Ma Etty said, grinning. "That's what."

"Gymkhana show . . . ?" asked Ella, not under-standing. And then, it hit her. "There's a show? Can I enter?" she asked, speaking so fast that the words almost didn't come out right. "Can I ride Figure Eight?"

"Sure," Ma Etty said, smiling smugly, as if she had anticipated this reaction. "If you work real hard, practice, and have lots of patience." She rubbed Figure Eight's big neck.

Ella couldn't believe this was happening.

"Yes!" she said. "Yes, I want to do it!"

"Great," Ma Etty said. "Willard will sign you up. It's in three weeks. And the first prize is a belt buckle! But you have to be on your best behavior, or you won't be going."

Ella nodded a dozen times. "Yes, yes! I will."

She put Eight away as quickly as she could and sprinted off to tell Jordan.

CHAPTER FIFTEEN

"**C**ool!" Jordan exclaimed when Ella told her about the show, during the tiny break they had before dinner to get cleaned up and changed. "So you get to be in a show." Jordan's eyes closed for a moment, like she was imagining the spectacle in her mind's eye. "And you get to show Figure Eight!"

"I know, right?" Ella sighed. "She's going to do so well out there." Ella hoped both of them would look awesome out in the arena, too, roaring around those barrels.

"It would be cool to go home with your own belt buckle," Jordan said.

"Heck yeah."

Ella was walking on clouds. Coasting on sunshine.

She wanted to hug Jordan, but didn't want to push her luck. So instead, as Ella took off her muddy riding boots and put on her sneakers, she said, "I'm going to have to learn how to go faster. Can't win barrels at a trot."

"Don't worry," Jordan said. "You're doing fine. I'm sure you won't have a problem getting to a gallop."

And sure enough, the next day Ella progressed from going at a fast trot around the barrels to taking them at a canter. She wanted to gallop so badly—to speed from barrel to barrel like those racers at the rodeo. But that was her instinct speaking. That was Dad, saying, *Go for it! Get what you want!*

For this, Ella needed to think like Jordan. If she wanted to do this right, she had to progress slowly, carefully. The understanding that Ella and Eight were forging only existed at the slower speeds so far. Ella could completely control Eight at a walk, a trot, and a canter around the barrels.

Galloping—that wild, speeding gait that she had only practiced along the rail—would require a different set of skills.

It was clear, though, that Eight wanted to run the

barrel pattern. She itched for it, jumping into faster gaits than Ella asked for as often as she could. Sometimes Ella let her sprint home from the last barrel, and Eight devoured it.

So, on their third lesson with Jordan, Ella decided to let her run.

"Any tips?" asked Ella, as she proposed her plan to Jordan.

"Don't fly off," she said, and climbed up to her usual spot on the arena fence to watch. "Hold onto your horn if you need to."

As Ella and Eight took off from one end of the arena toward the first barrel, Jordan shouted, "Woo hoo!" Then: "Remember to look!"

Ella's gaze locked onto a spot on the other side of the barrel. At first, her body flew up in the saddle, unused to the speed. But she adjusted her weight and settled deep in her seat, right on the pockets of her jeans, and flew right back down again.

As Eight approached the barrel, Ella pulled the reins to the side. With her legs she guided Eight around the barrel. Then they were clear of the first and it was on to the second, at full speed.

Ella dropped forward in the saddle, giving Eight

the reins, telling her she could finally go as fast as she wanted—as fast as she could.

Around the second barrel they flew. Ella guided Eight's big body around the turn, feeling the horse's muscles bunch up underneath her as she compressed her haunches and wrapped herself around the barrel—tight as a python strangling its prey.

Then, clear of the barrel, Eight extended again and exploded off the turn. They sprinted toward the last barrel.

Exhilaration filled Ella to the brim. The dirt sailed past beneath Eight's neck as the wind tossed Ella's braid. She hadn't known a horse could move this fast, hadn't imagined it even in her fantasies.

"Ella!" shouted Jordan. "Watch out!"

Ella snapped out of it to find that, rather than aiming for the spot just to the right of the third barrel, she'd guided Eight straight into it by staring at it.

Ella yanked the rein hard to one side. Eight veered, her head pulling against the sudden movement, but she didn't have enough time.

Eight's shoulder collided with the barrel. Then so did Ella's foot. Ella yelped in pain while Eight neighed in surprise, and they careened off to the side of the arena.

"Stop her!" called Jordan. "Ella! Whoa! Whoa!"

Jordan's urgent, steady voice drew Ella out of the panic. She pulled back hard on the reins as the far end of the arena loomed big and close—too close.

Eight slammed her hooves down into the dirt and came to an instant stop.

They both stood, breathing hard, for a tiny eternity. Jordan climbed down from the fence and jogged over to them. She patted Eight's sweaty neck, then Ella's sweaty leg.

"It's all right," she said, and Ella couldn't tell if she was speaking to her or the horse. Maybe to both of them. The panic that had overwhelmed her senses drained off, leaving Ella shaking and tearful.

Ella took a big gasp of air as the fear finally left her, leaving an aching chasm of disappointment.

"What did I do?" Ella asked, staring down at Eight's sweating neck. "What did I do wrong?"

"You didn't do anything wrong," Jordan said. She offered a hand up to Ella and Ella took it, letting Jordan help her down from the saddle. Jordan put an arm around her shoulders and squeezed.

Still holding onto Ella with one arm, Jordan checked the condition of Eight's shoulder where she had collided with the barrel.

"No harm done," Jordan said, showing the unmarred, doe-brown hair to Ella. "See?" Eight's velvety white nostrils flared with each deep breath, and her eyes were wide.

"I terrified her," said Ella, hiccuping with a sob that she held in. "I ruined her."

"You didn't ruin anything. You were both caught up in the moment." Jordan, one arm still wrapped around Ella's shoulders, took Eight's reins in her other hand and began walking the two of them around the arena to cool down. Silently they did one entire lap. Ella's breaths began to even out, and so did Eight's. The horse's great neck began to droop—stretching out, lowering to the ground.

"Look," said Jordan. "Everything's okay. Figure Eight's already relaxed again. She's not upset at you."

Ella glanced over. Eight looked so beautiful—her faded brown splotches, her white nose—and not injured at all. She probably had just been surprised by Ella's poor horsemanship.

"Jordan?" Ella asked.

"Yes?"

"Can . . . can you put Eight away for me?" Ella hated asking for the favor after causing this big mess, but she felt like an old statue slowly crumbling to bits. She couldn't bear to be around horses anymore today. She wanted to go sit down in the grass and cry alone for a while, until all the fear and frustration melted off her like a crust of ice in the sun.

"Of course," said Jordan. "No problem." Giving Ella one last squeeze, Jordan took Eight on another lap around the arena.

Ella jogged to the pasture, where she found a cool, grassy knoll overlooking the creek. She sat right at the top and watched the sun dip behind the mountains.

Why did Ella always screw up like this, right when things were starting to go right?

The tears that had been building up in the arena all tumbled out of her. She didn't even try to stop them.

Ella hadn't hurt Eight, and she hadn't been hurt herself. But if Ella got distracted again for even a second, the next time could be worse. What if it happened at the gymkhana show, in front of every-one? Jordan might not always be there.

If Eight got hurt, Ella would never, ever for-give herself.

\\

Awhile later, someone padded up the hill behind Ella. Jordan sat down in the grass. For a long time, she didn't speak, and for once, Ella was fine with it. She didn't want to hear her own miserable voice anyway.

"You know," Jordan said after a while, "Eight gets excited whenever you come into the barn."

Ella glanced up, her face a crackly mask from crying. When she thought about it, Jordan was usu-ally in the barn already when Ella showed up. Jor-dan observed things like that, things Ella didn't see. She was always paying attention.

"That horse loves to run," Jordan went on. "Don't think she ever got to run this much before you."

Sometimes the way Jordan talked about horses, it sounded like she was one. She seemed to understand them better than people.

"Why do you love horses so much?" Ella asked.

If the question surprised Jordan, she didn't show it.

She shrugged, her usual answer. Ella was going to leave it at that, but then Jordan said, "They're innocent. Pure. Like Eight—even though she seems a bit bratty, she's not. She just wants to run. Her desires are simple." She sighed. "I wish people were that simple."

"Huh." No one had ever spelled it out that way for Ella. People really were complicated. "How did you get into horseback riding?"

"It's the one thing that's mine," Jordan said. "And only mine."

That wasn't even close to an answer that Ella had expected. "You usually have to share?"

"I have five brothers and two sisters. I'm the third oldest."

Ella didn't know anyone who came from a family with eight kids.

"None of them ride?" she asked.

"We couldn't have a horse, even if my parents wanted one."

"Then how did you learn?"

"It found me. I was selling eggs to Mrs. Rose and I said something about her horses—she had three big, pretty quarter horses. I told her they were beautiful. She said, 'They are, aren't they? But I don't have time for them all.' Her husband had died and she had to take over his workload around the property. She didn't have enough time for the horses anymore and felt terrible about it.

"So after a while of me coming over and telling her how much I liked them, Mrs. Rose asked if I could help exercise them. She said she'd teach me how to ride in exchange for working them out a few times a week." It was the most Jordan had ever said at once. Ella wanted to keep her going.

"An initial investment for a long-term payoff," Ella said, repeating what her dad always said about why he worked so many long hours. This Mrs. Rose sounded like a clever lady. "That's really lucky for you. Free lessons!"

"Yep," said Jordan. "She taught me as much as she could and then she sent me out into the field. I ride three times a week and exercise all three horses. Mrs. Rose gives me a small lesson when she sees I need to learn something. For a while I had time to eat dinner with her before going home to do homework. But now, with Dad's gout, he can't walk much. Me and Olly had to pick up the slack—babysitting, helping with cooking, putting the kids to bed. So I just go over to Mrs. Rose's, ride them quick as I can, and run home."

The puzzle that was Jordan McAdam started to click together, forming a picture that Ella could finally make out. She was one girl out of eight kids, trying to help keep her family afloat.

"Is Olly your brother?" asked Ella.

"Older brother. My oldest sister's gone off to college, so Olly and I help out with the younger kids now while Mom works and takes care of Dad, since Dad can't work. Olly does even more around the house than I do so I can have my afternoons free for Mrs. Rose's horses." Jordan stared down at the open palms of her hands. "I try to do as much as I can to make up for it—make the kids breakfast, help them with their homework, wash Olly's clothes. But the best thing is to just be quiet, because noise upsets Dad."

Ella didn't know what to say. After a moment she asked Jordan, "Would you run the barrels tomorrow?"

"What?" asked Jordan.

"Ride Loco Roco through the barrel pattern so I can watch. I want to see how you do it."

"I don't know how I could show you anything helpful, Ella . . ."

Her enduring humility was almost annoying. "You know tons more than I do," said Ella. "You've already given me so many helpful tips. But now I want to see it in action. I want to observe you."

"Like I'm a science experiment?"

"Exactly! Just imagine I'm the mad scientist and you're the experiment. I want to watch you do your thing and take notes. Would you do that?"

Ella realized it was unfair of her to phrase it as a favor, after Jordan had spilled her guts. Jordan was the kind of person that wanted to help everyone, to fill all the gaps, and Ella already knew Jordan would agree.

"Yeah, I guess I can ride for you," Jordan said.

"Great. Tomorrow, then." Ella stood up, already feeling better, and stretched. "Thank you, by the way."

Jordan gave her a funny look. "For what?"

"For everything. For teaching me. For calming me down. For putting Eight away."

"I'm just doing what Mr. Bridle told me to do," Jordan said, as if gratitude was a foreign language she didn't understand.

This time, Ella smiled at that. The way Jordan had helped her back there—she wasn't doing this anymore just because Mr. Bridle told her. The barrels held the same power over her that they did over Ella.

"Thanks again," Ella said. And she meant it.

CHAPTER SIXTEEN

The next day, when they were done with their chores, Jordan and Ella met up at the barn. Jordan didn't speak as she tacked up Loco Roco. She did in five minutes what usually took Ella twenty. Tacking up, riding, and putting away two or three horses every afternoon? That would make Ella pretty fast at it, too.

Once on Loco's back, something in Jordan's demeanor shifted. She sat straight, but not stiff. Relaxed and poised at the same time, like she belonged there.

"It's all in here," Jordan told Ella, who was watching from Jordan's usual perch on top of the arena fence. Jordan patted her belly as she said it. "All good riding starts right here."

It was a mysterious way of putting it, but Ella knew what she meant. She'd felt that, too—how everything she did on her horse rotated around that center of gravity right in her abdomen.

Jordan started with a simple warm-up, walking Loco in patterns around the arena. Half the time, Ella couldn't even see the commands Jordan was giving—but after a while she could make out Jordan's thighs giving a squeeze, or her heel nudging his side, or her left elbow tucking just a little further in to put more pressure on the reins.

Jordan finished the warm-up with scientific precision. When she was done, Ella ran out to set up the barrels.

Without preamble, Jordan kicked Loco and they leapt into a gallop. Ella felt like she was at the rodeo again as Loco's legs flew, kicking up clouds of dust. Jordan had only been riding Loco for a few weeks, but already they seemed as close as Paul and his horse, Roy: speaking without words, listening to each other's thoughts. Loco turned so tightly around each barrel that the angle of his body tipped nearly parallel with the ground. Jordan's ponytail sailed behind her like a brown flag. Horse and girl moved in perfect synchronicity.

They came to the final barrel. Jordan sat forward in the saddle, lending her momentum to her horse. Her thighs and knees and heels all worked together as Loco whipped around the barrel so fast that Jordan had to hold onto the pommel of her saddle to avoid falling off. Loco's breath came in great gusts as he passed Ella and sprinted to the finish line.

Ella clapped as Loco slowed to a trot and made a loop on the opposite end of the arena. Jordan walked to where Ella sat on the fence. Loco was sweating.

"Was that helpful?" Jordan asked.

A mixture of feelings had overcome Ella. Why couldn't she ride like Jordan? She made it look so easy. But now, after the hours Ella had already put into it, she saw that it probably hadn't been.

Still—what an amazing thing to witness up close! Jordan and Loco were the real deal. And Ella was lucky.

"Yeah," she said. "It was incredibly helpful. Thank you, Jordan."

Jordan looked away. "I didn't do anything."

"You've done a ton. Look, you're spending your free time teaching me how to ride. That's a pretty big deal."

"Just paying forward what Mrs. Rose did for me. Anyway, I've already taught you everything I know. I told you it wasn't very much."

"You taught me so much already today," Ella said. Why couldn't Jordan give herself any credit? "Just watching you, I learned a ton."

"Oh." Jordan appeared stumped by this answer. "Well . . . okay. As long as it's helpful to you."

"Will you do it again?" asked Ella.

Jordan finally looked up. "Um, sure. Why not?" She turned back to the starting line. "Loco, let's go try that one more time. For Ella."

\\\

Half an hour before dinner, Jordan stopped her demonstration.

"Hey, Ell, want to tack up Eight and do a short ride for our cool-down? Even if she doesn't get a real big workout today, I bet she'd enjoy getting out."

"Oh yeah," said Ella, jumping off the fence. She went inside, tacked up Eight quickly, and mounted. She jogged out to meet Jordan at the gate leading out of the arena.

"Shoot," said Ella, shooting an accusing look at

the gate. "Should have stayed on the ground so I could open that."

"Got it," said Jordan.

She tapped Loco Roco's shoulder with her heel and tugged only his opposite rein toward the gate. He took a step sideways toward the fence, to avoid coming at it head-on, but Jordan was still too far away to reach the latch.

It was like watching the trick rider and her horse. Jordan clicked, repeated her request for a side step, and Loco sidled up to the gate. She reached over, plucked the latch open, and managed to hold onto the end of the gate while Loco walked through. With a subtle motion of her heel and her rein, Jordan pulled Loco around sideways so she could get out of the way and let Ella through. Once Eight had trotted out of the arena, Jordan pushed the gate closed behind them.

"Wow," said Ella. "That's a good trick."

"Not a trick, just closing a gate."

"But it looks hard!"

Jordan smiled. "It's not, I promise. Just use your legs the same way I've been showing you out in the ring." She patted Loco on the neck. "And think about what you want to accomplish. Remember what Mr.

Bridle said—your horse feels what you feel."

She made it sound like some kind of animal magic, but Ella didn't think it was quite that simple.

"Try it when we get back," said Jordan.

So after their short ride, Ella tried to position Eight by the gate, just so she could reach the latch. But Eight flung her head around, and kept turning side to side so Ella couldn't reach. Ella grew irritated that Eight wouldn't listen.

"It just takes time," said Jordan, climbing off Loco Roco and opening the gate by hand. "You're already almost there."

CHAPTER SEVENTEEN

Lessons during free time continued all that week, and the next. The show bore down on Ella like a squealing steam engine.

That Friday night, Ella took Jordan's dishes to the sink after dinner, as usual.

"Still at it, Jeeves?" Kim asked as Ella dumped her two piles into the sink. He poked fun at her for this every single night, but not in the poisonous way he used to. Ella liked having someone she could spar with.

"Still at it, until the day I wake up a barrel-racing prodigy," said Ella.

"Let me know when you figure that magic potion out."

When they re-entered the dining room, Ma

Etty was bringing out cinnamon rolls. They seemed full of meaning, or maybe it was the extra layer of frosting.

"You all have been so focused this week," said Ma Etty. "So we wanted to surprise you with something cool."

Ella perked up. What would the Bridles offer them that qualified for the word 'cool'? Whatever it was, Paul, who had joined them for dinner, was practically bouncing in his seat.

"Okay, tell them," Mr. Bridle said, giving a little eye roll.

"We're going on a trail ride!" Paul said, obviously thrilled.

Ella didn't know whether to be ecstatic or worried. The last trail ride had been disastrous. She and Jordan exchanged a look.

"What about practice?" Ella whispered.

"It's okay," said Jordan. "A day off would be good for Eight. Horses need them, just like people do."

"All three of us are taking you," Paul went on, managing to sling a single arm over both Madison and Fletch. He gave them a comrade's squeeze. "We'll stop at the lake and make a picnic out of it, maybe do some fishing?"

"Fishing!" Drew's hair seemed to stand up straighter. "If we catch something, can we cook it for dinner? Please?"

Ma Etty raised both eyebrows. "Sure. Why not?"

"Blech," Jordan whispered to Ella. "Fish!"

"Not a fan?"

"Not in your lifetime. Tastes like . . . fish."

Ella preferred this version of Jordan—the funny, sometimes downright talkative Jordan that had started making the occasional appearance. Ella didn't know if that Jordan had always been there, or if the two of them were rubbing off on each other. Maybe, Ella thought, it was Loco Roco's influence.

They feel what you feel. Could it go the other way around, too?

She had thoughts like this all the time now, thoughts that sounded like Jordan or Mr. Bridle—or even her mom—was speaking.

"Great," said Paul. "Tomorrow morning, nine o'clock sharp, meet me outside the barn with horses saddled and ready." He turned to his plate to start tearing into his cinnamon roll. Then he stopped and said, "But no risky business!"

"Aw," Ash said to Kim, with his lower lip protruding. "There go our nefarious business plans."

"But, Dallas," groaned Kim, "what about my secret lair? I was promised a secret lair."

"Don't worry. We'll build it out of the bones of our enemies if we have to."

"No bone lairs, either!" said Paul.

\\\

"So you're telling me the Falcons are going to not only beat the Cowboys this year," said Ash, turning halfway around in his saddle, "but will make it to the Super Bowl? You realize it's been years since the Falcs even got close, right?"

"Yeah, but we have this new guy this year." Drew raised two fingers to his chest. "Trust me. It's going to happen. Your beloved Cowboys are going down."

"The Falcons are losers."

Drew opened his mouth to say something, but their argument had agitated his horse. "Whatever, man," he said, slowing down so he fell in line next to Ella, instead of Ash.

"Wouldn't be unheard of for the Falcons to beat the Cowboys," said Fletch. "Those mid-list teams always make a comeback eventually."

Ash was about to reply, but Ella broke in. "Could

we please talk about something besides football? My eardrums are melting."

Jordan raised her hand. "I second that motion. Dogs, maybe? Like, how cute are these three goofballs?"

The dogs chased one another in circles in the woods, running back occasionally to make sure they hadn't lost their master, then taking off again.

"Actually," said Paul, "the big surprise is coming up." He pointed off in the direction of the distant tree line.

"Aren't we almost to Cougar Point?" asked Madison.

"Cougar . . . Point?" asked Kim, his voice faltering a bit at the end. "Why is it called that?"

Madison laughed. "Why do you think? This place used to be overrun with cougars." Kim's eyes widened and he wrapped one hand around the pommel of his saddle, like it would save him from a cougar attack. "But that was a hundred years ago. The sheriff put a bounty out on cougars decades ago because they were killing sheep, and the hunters went wild. Not many cougars left now."

"That's sad," said Jordan. "They're just trying to live. It's their role in the ecosystem to eat other animals."

Ella marveled that Jordan could feel so much sympathy for cat-shaped killing machines.

"I'd put a bounty on any animal that could end me with one paw swipe." Kim batted at the air with one hand. "Forget it."

Jordan pressed her lips together and didn't speak, but Ella could practically hear the diatribe she was biting back. The other night, Jordan had found a spider crawling on her pillow and screamed. Instead of killing it, she urged it onto a paper towel and sprinted outside, where she set it down in the grass.

"Why bother?" Ella had asked.

"They eat bugs," she said. "Mosquitos and stuff. Without them, the mosquitos would take over. Just trying to maintain the balance."

They crested a ridge and from the front Paul said, "Guess you're right, Maddie. We've reached Cougar Point. Look."

A valley swept out below them. A lake, clear and still as a mirror, had carved out a bowl in the valley basin. Their mouths hung open as they took in the view.

"And that is the glacial lake we missed last time," said Paul.

"I guess I'll be okay fishing there," Drew said.

As they headed down the mountainside, Fletch told them, "Lean back! Center of gravity!" Figure Eight's feet expertly picked a path down the steep slope. The drop-off on the other side made Ella's heart race, but the horses seemed to know exactly what they were doing.

Half an hour later, everyone arrived safely at the base of the hill. Paul tied the animals nearby while the kids helped Fletch and Madison unpack the food and the blankets. Then they stripped to their swimsuits and leapt in the lake.

"Hey!" hollered Drew, just sitting down with the fishing line he'd rigged up. "Stop scaring away my fish!"

But they got out quickly because the water was ice cold, and only Fletch seemed immune to it. Ella and Jordan dried off and pulled out their lunches, joining Madison on a blanket.

"How's barrel racing camp been going?" Madison asked Ella and Jordan. "You two missing your free time yet?"

"What free time?" asked Jordan. "I don't know what that is."

"Pfft," said Ella. "Not like you did anything cool with it before. You were always moping."

"Yeah, but now when will I get my moping in?" asked Jordan.

Ella laughed. "I carved out a slot for you in the schedule right after dinner."

"Great. Now you want me to mope and brush my teeth at the same time? What do you think I am, your trick pony?"

Madison rolled her eyes. "Okay, okay. So you're having fun, I take it. Think you'll be ready by next week?"

"Of course," Ella said, folding her arms. Wow. She sounded like her dad. Probably looked like him just then, too, arms crossed over his chest as he said, "Of course." Like you'd just asked him the most obvious question possible.

Madison laughed. "Okay. Good. Not that I had any doubt, of course. The two of you must make a killer team." She snorted a little. "Like Jekyll and Hyde."

"Hey!" Ella said. "Does that make me Hyde?"

"I'm too tall to be Ella's Jekyll," said Jordan. "And Jekyll and Hyde are the same guy, right? They couldn't exist at the same time."

"Well, uh, yeah," said Madison, caught off guard. "But one was the scientist, you know . . . The other one was the monster." She shook her head. "Okay, bad analogy."

"No, no." Ella snickered. "That's accurate. Jordan's the brain, I'm the maniac."

\\\

As Ella watched Ash, Fletch, and Madison throwing a Frisbee, and Paul showing Drew how to cast the fishing line, she had the unwelcome thought that days like this were limited.

"Only ten more days of camp," Ella said to Jordan, passing back the apple they were sharing. She sighed. "I don't want to go back to Petaluma."

Jordan raised both eyebrows as she bit into the apple. "Really?" she said, a little food in her mouth. "I can't wait. I've really missed Olly and Lola and the others."

"I guess I wouldn't know," said Ella. "No siblings."

"None? Not even step-siblings?"

Ella shook her head. "Maybe my dad will remarry," she said. She'd come to terms with this eventuality when Dad started dating again. That she might have a step-mom someday. Step-siblings. Half-siblings.

"What about your mom?" asked Jordan.

Ella shrugged. "Dunno. We don't talk."

"Oh."

Ella could tell Jordan wanted to ask why, but she probably didn't want to seem nosy.

"We don't really get along," Ella said, but as soon as it came out of her mouth, she wondered if what she really meant was, *She and my dad don't get along.* Ella hadn't seen her mom in almost two years, making up reasons why she couldn't visit. She had no idea if they'd see eye-to-eye at all anymore. During the divorce proceedings, the judge had determined both of Ella's parents fit for custody—but with her mom moving across the country, they had left it up to Ella to decide where to spend the majority of her time.

Of course she'd thrown her chips in with Dad. He was staying put in their old house; he understood her the way Mom couldn't.

Or, at least, she'd thought so.

"I'm sorry," Jordan said.

Ella batted a hand at her. "Whatever. I'm not hung up on it." But she had started thinking about Mom a lot more since she'd been at the ranch. Especially since she'd become friends with Jordan.

The sure way in which she thought about being

friends with Jordan took Ella by surprise. When had that happened?

Jordan didn't say anything else, and Ella supposed her flippancy hadn't been encouraging, either. So Ella said, "Jordan, can I ask you a personal question?"

Jordan turned her head away, and Ella was worried she was drawing into herself again—but she returned a second later with another apple.

"Ask away," Jordan said.

"Why are you even here?" asked Ella. "You're like . . . the least troublesome person I bet they've ever had at Quartz Creek Ranch."

Jordan laughed. "I doubt it. What did Ma Etty say, that they've been doing this for twenty years?"

"Come on, Jordan."

The smile fell off Jordan's lips. She searched Ella's face, as if she expected to find that Ella was joking—that she didn't actually expect an answer to her question. When Jordan seemed to realize that Ella was perfectly serious, she sighed.

"Grades."

Then she took another bite of her apple and stared at her feet.

"Like, you failed a class?" said Ella.

"*Like*," said Jordan, mocking Ella's tone, "I failed all my classes."

There was a long pause. Ella waited, thinking Jordan would give her more. But she didn't.

"Why?" Ella asked. "Did you get sick?"

Another long pause.

"Why not?" Jordan asked, surprisingly forceful and a little angry. "Why try? Trying is a waste of time when you know you're going to fail."

"Each year is a chance to start over," Ella said. "You don't know for sure you're going to fail."

"No," snapped Jordan. "I do know." She looked Ella right in the eyes as she said, "Every time I try, I fail. I've worked and worked in school but even my best isn't enough. So why bother?" She stood up and threw her apple core. Ella, perplexed, watched it roll away. Jordan had given her a hard time the other day just for tossing a strawberry head.

"You've succeeded at lots of things, Jordan," Ella said. "You're the best horseback rider I know."

"My folks thought that, too. They sent me here hoping it would magically make me good at everything." She narrowed her eyes. "As if spending half a summer riding horses would turn me into somebody like you—somebody who believes totally and blindly in themselves. But I'm not. And I'm not the rider you think I am."

Ella ignored the insult. "Yes, you are!" She wanted to yell it at Jordan but she knew it would only scare her. "I think you're great," Ella said, feeling heat work its way up into her throat. But it wasn't anger—not like usual. She was sad, frustrated, that Jordan was acting so obtuse. "Does what I think not matter at all to you?"

"You don't know anything about riding, Ella."

It hit Ella like a kick to the rib cage.

"So how would you know it if you saw it?" Jordan went on. "Psh, 'the best horseback rider.' What do you know?" Jordan turned away. "Nothing, that's what. So stop pretending you do. I'm going for a swim."

Sticking her hands in her pockets, Jordan walked away, leaving Ella alone on the picnic blanket.

Ella stood up.

"You're . . . you're . . ." Ella couldn't think of anything better to say, so she shouted after her, "You're a jerk for saying that, Jordan!"

But Jordan didn't answer from down the hill. Paul and Drew looked up, probably wondering what she was yelling about.

Ella sat back down, wanting to strangle someone.

She hastily wiped at tears forming in her eyes and steeled herself against them. She wasn't going to give Jordan the benefit of crying.

Ella hadn't thought that quiet, shy girl had it in her to be cruel like that. It hurt worse than being punched.

So maybe Jordan was right and Ella didn't know much about horsemanship. She could cop to that. But Ella had seen Jordan ride. She'd heard about the regional championship. The Bridles trusted her.

How could Jordan think so little of herself?

CHAPTER EIGHTEEN

Jordan didn't speak at all on the ride home, and when the other kids occasionally asked her things, she responded with *yes*, *no*, or a shrug. Ella hoped Jordan would be out of her funk by tomorrow, when they needed to resume training for the show the next weekend. They couldn't afford to lose even a single day.

Ella still had a lot to do before she was ready to perform in front of a judge.

\\\

But Jordan didn't speak to Ella at all during the daily lesson with Fletch and Madison. Then, after chores, it was time for practice.

Jordan wasn't in the barn waiting when Ella arrived, so she tacked up Eight and went out to warm up while she waited. But ten minutes later, Jordan still hadn't appeared.

Ella couldn't waste time waiting, so she decided to get on with her practice. She took Eight around the barrels at a canter, but felt nervous going whole hog without Jordan there.

And what if someone caught Ella working out here alone? She couldn't afford to mess up before the show and risk Mr. Bridle changing his mind about letting her go.

Ella walked Eight up to the gate leading out of the arena. She didn't want to waste time getting off and on the horse. She remembered Jordan and Loco Roco opening the gate together, and decided to ask Eight to sidle up to it.

Eight was coming in at a direct angle, though, and Ella was too far away.

She thought about it for a moment. Her lesson with Jordan returned to her.

Ella pressed in with the heel opposite the gate, keeping Eight's head positioned straight ahead. *I want to open the gate*, she thought, directing her gaze at the latch she wanted to reach. *Let's open the gate together and go on a nice long ride.*

Eight immediately stepped sideways, lining up with the gate. Ella reached over and lifted the latch, letting the gate swing open beside them. Then she walked Eight through the open doorway, using opposite leg and rein to spin her around. Ella had to get Eight even closer on the other side so she could reach the open gate and pull it closed again.

When she finished, Ella glanced up automatically to look for the approval on Jordan's face. But she wasn't there.

Ella wandered the ranch, looking for signs of her absent teacher. Kim and Drew were playing bean bag toss.

"Whoa, hey, Ella," said Drew, dropping the bean bags when he saw her ride up on Eight. "What are you doing out here?"

"Seen Jordan?" she asked.

"Not since lunch."

"I had chores with her," said Kim. "She left right after. What are you doing riding around on this side of the ranch alone? Won't you get in trouble?"

Shoot. Ella hadn't thought about that. She'd been on a mission to find Jordan and thought this was the fastest way to do it.

Ella dismounted and led Figure Eight back to the barn before any of the trainers saw her. Inside, she found Loco Roco's stall empty.

Silent and stealthy. Jordan must have come as soon as Ella left to go find her.

Ella exhaled and glanced at Figure Eight. The horse nudged her, hoping for a treat. Ella dug one out of her pocket and handed over the goods. Where had Jordan gone?

Trying is a waste of time when you know you're going to fail.

You don't know anything about riding, Ella.

Maybe Jordan looked at Ella as a venture. As something she had tried. Teach that loud, angry girl how to talk quietly to her horse.

Maybe Ella had failed, so Jordan had given up.

"Well," Ella said aloud to Eight, "I haven't failed *me* yet. I'm still signed up for the show."

She had to trust herself if she was going to take the barrels at full tilt. She had to be careful. Back out in the arena, Ella set up the barrels alone, then climbed on Eight's back.

Figure Eight knew what was coming as soon as they reached the starting line, and broke into a nervous trot. Ella took a deep breath and sat deep in her saddle.

She tested the reins, and felt Eight respond to them. Gentle reminders to slow down brought Eight back to a walk. Another deep, relaxing breath. The barrels didn't exist yet. Ella kept her eyes on the barn, away from the barrels.

Eight's neck drooped as she relaxed. She was ready.

Ella looped them around to face the three barrels, off on the other side of the arena. Then, she leaned forward, and kicked.

Eight leapt into motion.

She galloped toward the first barrel. Ella kept her eyes on the spot behind it, where she wanted Eight to go, and indicated with her heel and just a bit of rein. She wanted to turn soon. Eight leaned her head in.

She had heard.

Just before the barrel, Eight's body curved. They spun around the first barrel and whipped on to the second.

Nothing slipped through Ella's mind except: *Look. Heel. Rein. Body.* She helped Eight around each turn with her own weight, using her thighs to keep them in sync.

Then they were clear of the second barrel and cannonballing toward the third. Eight's breaths went *huf huf huf* in time with the beat of her hooves.

Ella gazed past the next barrel and Eight slowed, just enough for Ella to push her around it. Ella felt the barrel graze the tip of her boot.

Then they were clear of the last barrel.

Facing the final length of the race, wind hurling her braid all around her neck, Ella leaned forward and let Eight have the reins. Figure Eight leapt forward, toward home, hurling dust into the air as they raced to the finish line.

Reaching the other end of the arena, Ella slowed Eight to a trot. As they started a cool-down lap, someone clapped.

"Looking good," said Mr. Bridle. He leaned against the fence and glanced around. "But where's Jordan?"

Ella shrugged. "She didn't show up today."

He rubbed his chin. She hoped he wouldn't chew her out for being here alone.

"Should have told someone," he said.

"I'm sorry. I just have so little time left to prepare for the show, I didn't want to waste it."

Mr. Bridle nodded. "It's done," he said. "No use dwelling on it. But I wonder what happened. Did you two have a fight?"

"I guess. But it wasn't my fault. I didn't lose my temper."

"That's good. I'm sure she'll come back when she's ready."

"Everyone says that." Ella walked Eight away from the fence and did a figure eight. "But I need her now."

"I don't think so. You looked pretty good out there." Mr. Bridle stood up straight and tipped his hat. "I think all that needs is some spit and polish, and you're ready."

"Whoa," Ella said to Eight, just sitting up in her seat a little to earn a halt. "You think so, Mr. Bridle?"

"Of course I do. I wouldn't say it if I didn't. Jordan's been a great teacher."

"I know!" Ella urged Eight back into a walk to work off the sweat. "I tried to tell her that, too, but she wouldn't believe me. She said I didn't know enough about horses to know the difference."

Mr. Bridle's eyebrows went up. "Our Jordan said that?"

Ella nodded.

"Well, from what I saw, she's doing something," said Mr. Bridle. "Still has a lot to learn, but don't we all? I've been teaching people how to know and ride horses for half my life and I'm always learning new stuff."

"Jordan doesn't see it that way. I think I failed her."

"I'm sure that's not true."

But Mr. Bridle didn't know Jordan.

"Well," said Mr. Bridle, "I guess I better come out and watch you if Jordan's falling down in her duties. You still have a show to prepare for."

That's right—the show! An idea occurred to Ella.

Maybe she could prove to Jordan that she hadn't failed . . . by winning that first-prize belt buckle.

\\

On Thursday, they were all told they'd be going on a field trip to the gymkhana show to cheer Ella on. The other kids wanted to know how training was going.

"Minus a teacher," Ella said, looking at Jordan as she said it, "but just drilling exercises with Mr. Bridle. One day at a time." She'd stopped taking Jordan's plates to the sink and making her bed. Now Jordan took her plates herself, and the bed sat unmade all day, to Madison's annoyance.

"Hard core," said Kim. "Figure Eight's gonna be great."

"If anybody can kick butt at this, it's you, Ella," said Drew.

It was sweet of them to encourage her, but she wished Jordan would say something, instead of just pick at her food. Ella missed her friend—goofing around, talking about horses. This silent war sucked.

Before Ella knew it, Friday rolled around: her last day before the show. Madison came into the barn just as Ella was tacking up and said, "Take the day off."

Ella remembered what Jordan had told her about horses needing a day off, too.

"We will be working pretty hard tomorrow," Ella said, lowering the blanket she was about to put on. "Maybe we should just walk around today, huh, Eight?"

"Go take Figure Eight and see if Paul needs help with something," said Madison. "Spend some time with her meditating about your future victory."

Pleased that Madison was allowing her to ride alone, Ella finished tacking up and mounted outside. She headed north along Bridlemile Road, where Paul and his ranch hands did their work, secretly hoping she'd run into Jordan.

She wanted to be mad. Her teacher had abandoned her just a few days before the big event. But more than anything, she just wanted things to go back to the way they were.

As Ella and Eight padded through the pasture, following the creek, Ella spotted a dark shape sitting up in a tree. A tan horse stood underneath it, drinking out of the creek. It was Loco Roco.

Up in the tree, Jordan ignored Ella's approach and kept staring up at the sky.

"Jordan?" asked Ella, flabbergasted. So this was where she'd been. "This is what you're doing with your free time now?"

Jordan shrugged, not saying anything.

"Great," said Ella. "First you're mean to me. Then you abandon me at practice. Now you're going to pretend like I don't exist?" She reined Eight around. "Fine. I don't need any of your mopey self-loathing anyway."

"First, you're going to pretend like I don't exist," said Jordan, mocking Ella's tone again. "Then you're going to be mean to me. Now you're going to call me a liar and then expect me to be your friend?"

Okay, so maybe Ella did call her that one time. "I'm sorry I said that," she said. "But it was . . . before, you know?" Before what, Ella wasn't exactly sure. Before she decided to stop being a jerk to everyone?

"Whatever." Jordan leaned back in the tree. Ella waited for her to say something else, but Jordan just plucked leaves off a branch and tossed them to the ground.

"Urgh!" Ella said. "You're so irritating!"

Ella backed away from Jordan and Loco Roco, turned Figure Eight around, and urged her up out of the creek bed. She wanted to knock Jordan's lights out. Maybe that's what it would take to wake her up.

No, Ella thought. Jordan would come around on Saturday. With that first-place ribbon hanging off Figure Eight's saddle, and the buckle clipped onto her belt—then Jordan would see.

CHAPTER NINETEEN

Saturday morning, anticipation got Ella up earlier than Jordan or even the sun. She found Eight in the barn and took her outside, tying her up by the pasture with a bucket of grain and standing with her as she ate.

Paul pulled the trailer around and they loaded up. The two of them drove to the fairgrounds alone; Fletch, Madison, the Bridles, and the other kids would join them later.

First, they registered and parked among the assorted cars and trailers. This was much smaller than the rodeo, but even this early in the morning, the place buzzed with activity. It was a youth show, so she wouldn't race against adults. But some of the kids she saw warming up looked like they'd grown up in the saddle.

Paul offered Ella a cowboy hat. "Here. This will help you blend in, city kid."

They unloaded Figure Eight and gave her something to eat as they relaxed, getting accustomed together to a new environment. Then it was time to tack up and start warming up.

The morning was hot and full by the time the white Quartz Creek Ranch van appeared. The kids piled out and checked out the surroundings, but Ella was focused on what she had to do.

It was time to win.

\\

There were twenty-one contestants in Ella's group.

Ella glanced around at the other people waiting. Some her own age, some younger, most of them older. A serious-looking boy in a nice hat rode a big bay quarter horse. A tall girl sat on a small Arabian who obeyed her every command. They all warmed up with expert hands.

"Hey, tiger," Drew said to Ella, patting Figure

Eight on the neck as he, Kim, and Ash wandered over. "You're gonna do great."

"Never said I wouldn't," said Ella.

Ash barked a laugh. "That's Ella, always confident. Hey, have you seen Jordan at all?"

Ella slowly shook her head. She'd been looking, but Jordan had turned invisible. "No, I haven't."

"Hmm. She took off right when we got here. Haven't seen her since."

"Whatever," said Kim. "You've got to focus on winning that prize, Ell. What was it, a gift certificate or something?"

"A belt buckle," said Ella. "One of those big ones."

"Oooh," said Kim, laughing. "I'd prefer the gift certificate."

"I think belt buckles are sweet," said Drew. "It's something you can't just buy. It's special. Anyway, good luck! I hope you win."

"Thanks, Drew." Ella rolled her eyes at the other two. "Can't just root for me, can you?"

Kim made a *woo woo* noise. "I'll root for you to win a gift certificate."

Ella wasn't really listening to them. She was watching the other contestants. The guy with the nice hat was up. He led his massive quarter horse into the arena, and it pawed at the ground as they waited to start.

It was like being at the rodeo again, watching him tear around each barrel and hurtle through each curve at enviable velocity. The time had barely started counting down when he'd completed the pattern and was thundering home again.

The crowd roared.

"Twenty-two point one seconds!" said the announcer.

As the guy with the nice hat, now minus the hat, led his bay out of the arena, the announcer called, "In the hull is Ella Pierson!"

Two more people ahead of her. Ella's pulse leapt to full throttle and Eight threw her head up. Ella could tell the horse felt her excitement. Eight already wanted to head toward the arena.

"Not our turn yet," Ella told the horse.

"Come on, everyone," said Ma Etty, appearing with food and drinks, Mr. Bridle at her side. "Let's leave Ella and Eight alone to get ready."

"Good luck," said Ash, waving, and the kids left to get good seats.

"You'll do great out there," Ma Etty said, walking away. "Don't worry!"

But Ella wasn't worrying about out there—she was worrying about right here. Eight wouldn't stop dancing, yanking on the reins, wanting to be out in the arena and running already. No matter how much Ella tried, she couldn't calm Eight down.

Paul strode over, eating a hot dog. "It's your nerves," he said. "I bet she's responding to your anxiety."

"My anxiety? What anxiety?" Ella demanded, and her voice cracked. Eight tossed her head back. "Okay. Maybe I see what you mean."

She wished Jordan were here. Jordan always knew what to say to calm her down.

"Hey, hey," said Paul, rubbing Eight's neck with one hand as the horse hopped from one foot to the other. "Settle down, girl."

"On deck," said the loudspeaker, "is Ella Pierson!"

The contestant out in the ring galloped back to the finish line and the announcer called out, "And Juniper Crowley goes home with twenty-one point eight seconds!"

The next contestant, a round guy on a draft pony who had been standing patiently in the starting pen, entered the ring. Next was Ella's turn.

As she approached the gate to the starting pen,

Eight flung her head to the side, ready to jump into the arena and run the race. Ella had never seen her like this. The more Eight slipped out of her control, the more Ella grew afraid. She knew the basic rules: if your horse couldn't stay under your control on the way into the starting area, they wouldn't let you race.

Paul took Eight by the reins and led her to the gate.

"Ella Pierson?" asked the attendant.

"That's me." Figure Eight tried to pull away from Paul and danced sideways.

"Calm that horse down," the attendant said. "Or I can't let you in."

Ella couldn't get Eight to slow down to a walk, no matter how many times she gently corrected her. Her nerves wouldn't settle, and Eight knew it.

"Sorry," said the attendant, making a check on his sheet. "Too risky."

"Too risky?" asked Paul. "The horse is just a little excited to race, that's all."

The attendant eyed them. Time was ticking—the contestant currently in the ring was almost done. Ella was up next. She tried to relax, as Madison had once told her. While Paul tried unsuccessfully to calm down Figure Eight, Ella remembered opening the arena gate back at the ranch.

We're back at the ranch, Ella thought, closing her eyes. *It's just us and the barrels.*

Ella tried to recall that feeling—the gentle calm they shared before Ella gave the cue. She needed that focus now.

Gently, Ella tested the connection in the reins.

She sat deep in her saddle seat.

She thought only about the race. She looked where she wanted to go—inside the starting area. She thought only of her goal—to win. She let her shoulders relax.

Eight's breathing slowed and her neck dropped. While Paul debated with the attendant, Ella and Eight calmly walked past them, into the starting pen, just as the previous contestant exited.

"Guess they're ready," said Paul, closing the gate behind them.

"Next contestant is in," the attendant said into his walkie-talkie.

"And Jack Lipman walks away with twenty-two point one seconds!" roared the announcer.

Ella and Eight faced the starting gate.

Eight didn't paw. She didn't dance. Ella and Eight

stared ahead at the barrels and for a moment, Ella thought she could hear what Eight was thinking. How she was seeing the pattern ahead of them as a series of timings, of curves, of twists and sprints.

The gate opened.

Eight stepped into the arena. Around them, the sky and the people and the announcer's voice vanished, and all that was left were those three white metal barrels, arranged in a triangle.

The attendant gestured at her. "Go!" he mouthed. "Your turn!"

Ella stared straight ahead at the first barrel. Then she leaned forward in the saddle, let Eight have the reins, and kicked.

Eight sprang into a gallop. She roared toward the first barrel, perfectly following Ella's line of sight.

Look.

Ella let her gaze wrap around the barrel.

Feet.

She guided the front of Eight's body around the barrel with one knee, the back with her outside knee.

Reins.

Ella pulled the reins in, and Eight knew what came next. She turned at the barrel so steeply that Ella felt her knee bump it.

Ella focused on each of Eight's hooves clawing the dirt, grabbing traction, pushing off again; through Eight's reins, the corners of her sensitive mouth directly connected to Ella's hands.

Then they were clear of the first barrel and headed like a freight train toward the second.

Ella's feet moved automatically, pressing Eight's body around the barrel, harnessing their momentum. As they hurtled around the second barrel, Ella forgot where Eight's body started and hers ended. They took the turn together like a single creature: Eight's hooves were Ella's hooves. Ella's hands were Eight's.

Together they cleared the second barrel, and thundered on to the third.

This was the toughest turn. She had to go around the barrel almost a full revolution, and Eight had sprung off the second barrel with so much momentum that they were coming in too fast.

Ella panicked. If they overshot, they'd lose entire seconds.

She slowed down Eight as they approached the barrel. But they were going too slow now, Ella realized. Still, she'd rather her turn be careful and safe than end in disaster.

Eight was ready when the turn came.

Her whole body tilted into the barrel. Ella had to push her foot back and out of the way to avoid hitting the barrel with her stirrup. Knocking over a barrel would ruin their time.

The turn was long. Ella felt the seconds tick by until Eight had gone all 360 degrees around the barrel, and now faced toward home. It was time to put the pedal to the metal.

Ella crouched as far forward in the saddle as she could, gave Eight plenty of slack in the reins, and said, "Go!"

Eight put on a last burst of speed. Her breath came in huge gulps, in time with the beating of her hooves in the dirt.

The wind pummeled Ella's cheeks. It tossed Eight's mane into her face. But none of that mattered as Eight's powerful muscles tore up the dirt, and her huge, strong legs carried them flying toward the finish line.

They passed through the laser and the buzzer went off. The crowd, as she had hoped, roared.

"Twenty-one point four seconds!" came the announcer's voice, fueling the audience's furor. "Twenty-one point four seconds for the new competitor from Quartz Creek Ranch, and a new best time in today's competition!"

Ella sucked down air as Eight, lathered in sweat, trotted out of the arena. Paul was waiting, and he grabbed Eight by the reins while Mr. Bridle helped Ella out of her saddle. So much adrenaline raced through her that she felt like she was floating, and when Mr. Bridle set her down, she wavered a little on her own two feet.

"That was incredible!" said Paul.

"A really solid run," agreed Ma Etty.

"You did great," said someone behind Ella.

Ella spun at the sound of Jordan's voice. Jordan held Eight by the reins, patting the panting horse's velvety nose. "You should take her for a cool-down walk," Jordan said, handing the reins to Ella.

Ella stared at Jordan, then down at the offering in her hand. Ella was still in shock from the race.

"Yeah, okay," she managed at last, taking the reins.

Why was Jordan here now, after ignoring her all week? But Ella felt too elated by what she'd just done to care.

She'd done it. She'd really done it. And she was at the top of the leaderboard. That belt buckle was practically hers. And the cheering! It had been everything she'd hoped for.

But Ella wanted to see her competition, to be

there when she got that first-place ribbon. So she loosened Eight's saddle cinch and led her around the perimeter of the audience, as Jordan suggested, to cool her down.

Jordan walked with her, not speaking. Ella couldn't read her face, nor the set of her shoulders. But Ella had raced! Her entire body was warm with victory. She and Eight had done it together.

Out in the arena, it was the last competitor's turn.

The tall girl was on fire. Her small spotted horse easily folded its compact body around the turns at breakneck speed. It seemed like she was done as soon as she'd started.

But surely Ella and Eight had gone faster. Except for that slight speed loss before the third barrel . . .

"Twenty point nine seconds!" shouted the announcer. "Holy cow, a twenty-second run at the junior level? With that time, Delia Perez takes the top spot on the leaderboard!"

The crowd went wild. Ella clenched Eight's reins.

There went everything.

"Ella?" asked Jordan. "Are you crying?"

Ella stuffed her palms into her eyes, trying to stem the flow of tears, and dropped Eight's reins in the process. "No."

"Why are you crying?" Jordan stared at her, dumbfounded, as she picked up Eight's reins. The announcer was listing rankings.

"Third goes to Mike Rogers," the speaker boomed. "Second, to Ella Pierson!"

"You got second!" Jordan whispered, leaning in. "Second, dude!"

"Don't 'dude' me," Ella said, fresh tears sliding down her face. "I didn't win."

"Seriously?" asked Jordan. "You're crying because you got second instead of first?"

It did sound ridiculous when Jordan put it like that. But Jordan didn't understand what first place meant to Ella.

"I wanted to show you," Ella said. Eight pawed the ground at the distress in her voice. "I wanted to—" She shook her head. "Whatever. It's pointless." And Ella started to walk away, taking Figure Eight with her.

"Wait," said Jordan. "You wanted to show me what?"

"What do you care?" asked Ella, but she didn't have the energy to put any venom behind it. She was tired and sad and she wanted to be alone. "You ditched me."

Jordan met Ella's gaze for a moment, then she flushed and dropped it again, hunching her shoulders. "Yeah. Sorry about that."

That was all she had to say? But the fury Ella expected didn't come. She had been the one who failed Jordan, after all, just like the other girl had predicted.

Second place.

"I just . . ." Jordan bit her lip. "I got so attached to the two of you. To your success. I wanted so badly to help you win."

At this, Ella's mind went blank.

"What?" When she'd had a moment to think, she added, "Then it especially doesn't make sense why you abandoned me right at the end."

"I know!" Jordan was crying now, too, and tried as hard as Ella had to hide it. "But when you asked me about failing and I realized what I'd taken on by teaching you alone, I couldn't take it. It was too much pressure, Ella! Whether you won or lost would be a direct reflection of how good a job I'd done as a teacher. And because I don't have a clue what I'm doing, I didn't want to be the one to make you lose."

"First place," boomed the announcer, "and this handmade belt buckle, go to Delia Perez!"

Ella tried to understand what Jordan was telling

her. "That's . . ." She wanted to say *That's ridiculous*, but that wouldn't help. Ella sighed. "Well, I wish you hadn't left me. I needed you."

"I know," said Jordan miserably. "I'm sorry."

"I am, too." Ella glared at the announcer's box, like the second-place win was actually his fault. "I had meant to get first place. I wanted to win that belt buckle and show you what a great teacher you were."

"Why did you need first place for that?" asked Jordan. "You got second! In an event you only learned a few weeks ago. It's . . ." She searched for the right words. "It's amazing."

"The only reason I'm even here is because you trained me," said Ella. "But maybe you were right. I only got second."

"Only!" A small laugh burst out of Jordan, unexpected, through the tears. "Nothing's ever good enough for you, is it?"

"What about you?" said Ella, sniffling. "Even if I had gotten first place, you wouldn't have believed me. You would have called it a fluke, or—"

"You have natural talent, Ella."

Ella pointed a finger at Jordan. "See? That's exactly what I knew you'd say. I don't, Jordan. You saw me when I first got to Quartz Creek Ranch. Eight was way too much for me. I couldn't jog barrels, not to mention run them. I was a mess."

"You practiced."

"Only what you told me to practice."

Ella knew she wasn't getting anywhere, so before they could argue again, she said, "Whatever, Jordan. You're right. Second place isn't bad. And you helped me get it. I'm not a failure, and neither are you."

With that, she turned and led Figure Eight back to the Quartz Creek Ranch trailer that was parked on the other side of the arena. As she led Eight over, Paul came out and took Eight's reins.

"Go over there! They're giving out the ribbons."

Madison found her as she was walking back to the event area.

"Did Jordan find you? She was looking for you."

Ella just nodded.

Back at the main gate, the attendant was handing out ribbons and trophies. Ella got a huge red ribbon with *2nd* written across it, and a little gold plaque with the show's name.

CHAPTER TWENTY

On the final day of camp, the kids packed their things, and then it was time for one last riding lesson before they boarded the van for the airport.

"Why is this with my stuff?" Jordan held up the big ribbon that Ella had shoved into her duffel bag.

"I put it there." Ella didn't wait to hear Jordan's objection. She headed out to the barn to tack up Eight for the morning lesson. Figure Eight had been in great spirits since the show, and was eager and waiting to run when Ella took her out each morning, anticipating a day of practicing barrels.

But Ella had stopped practicing. Who knew when she'd get a chance to race again? She wanted her free time to play games with the other kids while they still had time, and to give Figure Eight treats.

When the kids showed up with their horses for lessons, Paul was waiting for them in the arena.

"Wanted to do something special for your last day on the ranch," he told them. "Thought I'd give you a tour of what I do around here."

Ash and Drew were almost electric in their saddles.

"Do you have to rope cows?" Drew asked.

"Yep," said Paul, patting the rope hanging from his saddle horn. "To deliver meds, or fix 'em up when they hurt themselves."

"What about calves?"

"Sure, when it's time to brand 'em."

They headed up north across the ranch lands. Paul talked to them about the cattle business and showed off the training a few of his ranch hands were doing with the dogs. Soon Paul fell behind, engaged in conversation with Drew about cattle work. The group approached a fence, the gate closed and latched.

"Can someone get that?" Paul called. Madison was a few horses back, with Ella, Kim, and Jordan at the front.

"I can," said Madison, working her way up.

But Ella was already walking Eight over to the

gate, using her heels to sidle up to the latch. She pulled the lever, let the gate swing open, and allowed the other horses to pass through.

Jordan stared at her, and waited next to her as the caravan passed.

"Nice work," Paul said to Ella as he passed.

"Go on," Ella told Jordan. "So I can close it."

Jordan opened her mouth to say something, then snapped it shut, nodded, and went through. Snatching up the end of the gate, Ella pulled it closed behind Eight and dropped the latch back into place.

As they continued their ride, Ella fell to the back of the line. Jordan, up ahead, slowed down Loco Roco so she fell into step beside her. Ella had a sense of déjà vu.

"When did you learn how to do that?" asked Jordan. "You handled it like a pro."

"I learned when you taught me."

The words hung thickly between them. After a long while, Jordan said, "I actually did something good here." She stared off into the distance as she said it, so Ella wasn't sure if she was talking to herself or to Ella. "I actually helped someone."

"Of course you did."

Jordan shook her head. "But you didn't back down, either. Every time you messed up, you just tried again."

"And again, and again, until it worked. Perseverance is my superpower."

"Or stubbornness," Jordan said, laughing.

\\

That evening, while the other kids ate churros and played cards at the dining room table, Ella snuck out. She walked to the dark barn, slipping through the creaky door and flipping on the light.

Stopping in front of Figure Eight's stall, Ella grabbed a handful of biscuits. Inside, she saw a familiar scene—the stall appeared empty.

"C'mon now," Ella said. "Get up, silly girl, or there's no treat!"

Hearing this, Figure Eight scrambled up to her feet, just like that first day, and poked her nose through the stall door. Ella opened it and stepped inside, giving Eight the promised reward.

While Eight chewed, Ella combed her fingers through the paint horse's beautiful, splotchy mane. Man. She had gotten so lucky, being assigned to

Figure Eight. Fast, smart, gorgeous—she was as perfect a horse as you could hope to get.

"Thank you," Ella said, leaning her head against Eight's soft, doe-brown neck. Eight stopped chewing and turned her head just a little so she could see Ella's face. "Thank you for putting up with me. For working so hard. For everything."

Eight let out a little nicker, like it had been no big deal for her. Ella had to laugh. Then the horse dipped her head, snuffling the ground nervously.

"Don't worry," said Ella. "Someone else will come along and want to run just as badly as you do." She ran her hand down Eight's forehead, and Eight seemed content with this answer.

It wasn't until Jordan came looking for her that Ella finally gave Eight the rest of the biscuits, and left the barn for the last time.

\\\

Ella and Jordan were on the same flight back to California. They called to each other over the seats until the woman sitting next to Ella insisted Jordan switch places with her. They drew pictures of Figure Eight and Loco Roco for Jordan to show to her siblings.

"Hey," said Jordan suddenly, as the plane started to descend. She tore a piece of paper out of her notebook and handed it to Ella. "My number. Since I don't live so far away . . ."

A grin took over Ella's face. "Yes! I would love to come visit you. I'm sure I can get my dad to drive me out there. Could we ride Mrs. Rose's horses?"

"I'm sure we can," said Jordan. "And I can keep teaching you barrels, if you want." She blushed at that. "And you can meet Antonio!"

That was all Ella needed to hear. If Jordan loved Antonio even a fraction of how much Ella loved Figure Eight, he was sure to be an amazing horse.

"I would love to meet him," Ella said.

"Maybe we can enter more shows," added Jordan, boldly.

Ella's eyes grew wide and eager. "More competitions?" She clapped her hands together. "Definitely yes!"

Jordan burst out laughing. "It's a deal, then."

At the airport, five small Jordan look-alikes and one tall one were waiting outside security. The kids swarmed their older sister the second they saw her, shouting, "Jordy! Jordy!" The tall boy, who must have been her brother Olly, stood off to one side as he waited for the youngsters to finish. Then he swooped in to welcome his sister home, picking her up as he hugged her. Ella rather liked looking at Olly, and definitely wouldn't mind driving out to Clearlake if he was there.

Then Ella recognized Jordan's mom as she stooped down to hug her daughter. What a big, loving family. Her face was lined with kindness; Ella liked her already.

Ella glanced around the waiting area, looking for her own dad. Then she remembered that he had said he was getting off work late, and would meet her outside.

As usual.

After she picked up her luggage and the McAdam family said good-bye, Ella went out the double doors to wait with her luggage. Eventually the BMW pulled up. Dad was on the phone when she climbed in, arguing with someone about contracts and signatures. He gave her a quick hug and tossed her bag into the trunk, and then they were off.

When he got off the phone, he asked, "How was camp?"

"Great," Ella said. "I got second place in a barrel race."

"Only second place?"

She showed him the plaque. "Yeah, Dad. Only second place."

"Well, good job."

"Hey, Dad?"

"Yeah?"

"Can I use your phone?"

"What for?"

"I want to call Mom and tell her."

Her dad took his eyes off the road long enough to turn his head and quirk one eyebrow.

"Your mom?" He handed her the phone and shrugged. "Be my guest."

She found the number quickly and dialed. It rang three times before her mom answered.

"What is it, Greg?" her mom asked brusquely as she answered.

"Hi, Mom."

"Oh, Ella! Honey! Hello!" Her mom exhaled a great sigh, and her voice softened. "So nice to hear from you. How was horse camp?"

"You knew?"

"Your dad told me."

"I won second place in the barrel race."

"Wow!" Mom laughed. "Amazing. You learned to barrel race in the short time you were there?"

"Yep. I had a good teacher."

"Ha. I bet you did. You're a good learner, something any teacher can appreciate. Congratulations, sweetie. I'm so glad you had a good time."

"I made a new friend, too."

"Did you?"

"I think you'd like her."

"I bet I would."

"Can I come visit you, Mom?"

There was a long pause on the other end of the line.

"I thought you weren't interested in visiting, Ella."

"I am now."

Her mom didn't answer for a while, as if perhaps expecting Ella to explain herself. She used to hate those pregnant silences. She never understood what Mom was waiting for.

"Mom," she repeated. "Can I?" She'd explain when she got there.

"Absolutely," her mom said, sounding like she'd been holding her breath. "Have your dad get you a ticket as soon as you get home, before summer break is over."

"Thanks, Mom."

"I can't wait," her mom said. "I love you."

"Love you too," said Ella, for the first time in who knew how long, and hung up the phone.

"Dad?" said Ella.

"Yeah, honey?"

"I need a ticket to go see Mom."

He gave her a sideways look as if he were saying, sarcastically, *So I gathered while I sat here listening.*

"Sure," he said. "Whenever you want."

They went quiet.

After a while, Ella said, "Dad?"

"Yep?"

"Can you drive me out to Clearlake next week? You can, y'know, watch me ride horses. I'm pretty good."

"I bet you are, Miss Prize Winner." He nodded, glancing at Ella and smiling. "Okay. Horseback riding in Clearlake, next Saturday. I'll block off the whole day. Will you put it in my calendar for me, Ell, sweetie?"

ABOUT THE AUTHORS

KIERSI BURKHART grew up riding horses on the Colorado Front Range. At sixteen, she attended Lewis & Clark College in Portland and spent her young adult years in beautiful Oregon—until she discovered her sense of adventure was calling her elsewhere. Now she travels around with her best friend, a mutt named Baby, writing fiction for children of all ages.

AMBER J. KEYSER is happiest when she is in the wilderness with her family. Lucky for her, the rivers and forests of Central Oregon let her paddle, hike, ski, and ride horses right outside her front door. When she isn't adventuring, Amber writes fiction and nonfiction for young readers and goes running with her dog, Gilda.

ACKNOWLEDGMENTS

Big thanks to our agent, Fiona Kenshole, for all the encouragement in the development of this novel; our editor Anna and the rest of the Darby Creek team; and huge thanks to Audra, the best horse teacher there is. Thank you for dropping everything to make sure we did this right, and for teaching Kiersi how to whisper. She needed it.

When she was Ella's age, Kiersi rode another horse that loved to run: an appaloosa pony named Frosty. Together, they took home many first, second, and third place ribbons in the barrel race. Thank you, Frosty, for being the calm in the storm.